CORENTYNE THUNDER

CORENTYNE THUNDER

EDGAR MITTELHOLZER

INTRODUCTION BY JUANITA COX

PEEPAL TREE

First published in Great Britain in 1941
by Eyre & Spottiswoode
This new edition published in 2009
Peepal Tree Press Ltd
17 King's Avenue
Leeds LS6 1QS
England

ISBN13: 978 1 84523 111 8

 Peepal Tree gratefully acknowledges Arts Council support

INTRODUCTION:
'A QUIET REVOLUTION'

JUANITA COX

If a would-be novelist ever wanted confirmation that he should look around him at the possibly-despised physical environment that lies to hand ('after all, we live in a colony, you know'), he can turn to Edgar's work and see how by skill in provocative narrative, a writer can make alien geography acceptable to the most sophisticated cosmopolitan reader.[1]

When the Guyanese novelist, Edgar Austin Mittelholzer (1909-1965) decided to become a writer in the late 1920s he did so at a time when the coloured middle class in New Amsterdam believed that creative writing was the preserve of Americans or Europeans; young colonials who thought otherwise were, apart from acting above their station, considered to be incapable of contributing anything new or noteworthy. Mittelholzer, like most of his middle-class counterparts, was expected to take up a respectable position in the civil service. He did, but not for long. According to one anecdote he was reprimanded by his Town Hall employers for failing to salute the visiting white Governor. After asking why it was his job to greet the man (he having been there first), he retorted that they could 'keep their blasted job'. Since jobs were hard to come by, this incident, combined with his unorthodox practice of selling his self-published collection of skits, *Creole Chips* (1938), from door to door, compounded the prevailing belief that he was 'mad'. Although Mittelholzer was inevitably embittered and alienated by the general hostility towards him, he remained determined to become a professional writer and in the absence of publishing houses in the Caribbean (and indeed of a reading audience) turned his attention to the British publishing industry. At this juncture, only three West Indians had had their novels published in the UK: C. L. R. James and Alfred Mendes (both Trinidadians), and H. G. De Lisser, a white Jamaican supporter of the colonial order.[2]

The publication of *Corentyne Thunder* by Eyre and Spottis-woode in 1941 by an unknown from Guyana[3] was thus an extraordinary accomplishment, particularly within the context of wartime shortages. It is unlikely that many copies made their way back to Guyana, whilst preliminary research indicates that the novel wasn't reviewed by the local press. However, according to the uncorroborated account of one Guyanese contemporary, Dr L. Bone, *Corentyne Thunder* appeared in serial form in 1938 and was sold by the author whilst working at Davson's Bookstore in New Amsterdam. It was during this period that Bone obtained an excerpt of the book and came across 'in black and white' the never discussed word, 'SEX'. His encounter with the text left him in a state of shock and typifies the way many in Guyana were to respond to his later work. *Corentyne Thunder*'s reception in Britain was, in contrast, positive though the following review in *The Observer* typifies the mix of praise and prejudice:

> ...*Corentyne Thunder*, by an author of mixed English, French, German and negro blood, is a brilliant and relentless study of primitives.[4]

Sadly for Mittelholzer, only a small number of copies were printed and perhaps because of wartime conditions, interest in the book was short-lived. *Corentyne Thunder* remained out of print for thirty years until its republication in the Heinemann Caribbean Writers Series in 1970. With the exception of seminal studies by A. J. Seymour, Michael Gilkes, Frank Birbalsingh and Louis James (who introduced the Heinemann edition), this novel has not received the serious critical attention it deserves. Comment has focused largely on Mittelholzer's pioneering treatment of the Indo-Guyanese peasant as a worthy subject for fiction and discussion has tended to see the novel in quasi-sociological rather than literary ways.

In my view, *Corentyne Thunder* is a remarkably rich and sophisticated first novel, not just in terms of its narrative but also in terms of the range of literary strategies Mittelholzer employed. One aim of this introduction is to show just how 'literary' Mittelholzer's approach to the writing of this novel was. This can be seen from the wide range of intertextual references employed in the novel, some of which are explored briefly below: Molière's *L'Avare,* Stapledon's *Last and First Men,* Beethoven's *Pastoral Symphony,* Francis Bacon's *The Vicissitude of Things,* and some of the more subtle passing references to Conrad and Shakespeare's *Hamlet.* Whilst some of the intertextuality reveals what books Mittelholzer admired, it is also evident he used it as a way of challenging the prejudices within Guyanese society, as well as the prejudice he expected his writing would attract as the work of an 'inferior' colonial.

Mittelholzer's insights into the lives of Indo-Guyanese peasants on the Corentyne coast, as revealed in his autobiography, *A Swarthy Boy* (1963), came directly from experience. Though a significant number of his 'coloured' class held their Indian counterparts in contempt,[5] viewing them as untrustworthy, cunning and secretive 'coolies', his mother had been inclined to allow the young Edgar unrestricted contact with their professionally successful neighbours, the East Indian Luckhoo family.[6] The importance of Mittelholzer's relationship with this family, as far as the writing of *Corentyne Thunder* is concerned, cannot be overestimated:

> We had no car, but the Luckhoos had one, and there were occasions – the most dazzling of all – when we were invited to spend a day on the Corentyne Coast at the home of some relative or friend of the Luckhoos. But for these trips to the flat, savannah lands of the Corentyne Coast, with their canals and smells and scattered sugar plantations and villages, I would probably never have been able to write my first published novel, *Corentyne Thunder.* It was on these outings that I absorbed the atmosphere of the district and even got to cultivate a deep affection for it. [7]

Prior to the writing of *Corentyne Thunder,* most of Mittelholzer's literary efforts had been handwritten in notebooks and only very occasionally typed when he had sufficient funds to hire the necessary equipment. Lionel Luckhoo, his close friend and one of the few supporters of his literary aspirations, gave him his first typewriter (circa 1938). Mittelholzer's relationship with the Luckhoo family more importantly led him to question the racial prejudices of the society he lived in and expose, in *Corentyne Thunder*, the hypocrisies and snobbery of the middle classes as well as the racial tensions between members of the Black and Indian community. Readers who are unaware of this background might conclude that the representation of Ramgolall, as a miserly peasant, was an ill-conceived reinforcement of the prevailing racial stereotypes about East Indians and a reflection of the author's own internalized prejudices. On the contrary, we should look for Ramgolall's origins in literature and see *Corentyne Thunder* overall as a tribute to the Luckhoo family (for their unfailing support of him) and by extension to the Indian community.

The very explicit reference to Molière's *L'Avare* in Chapter 17 (when Beena talks to Stymphy about Ramgolall's canister of hoarded savings) points to this literariness:

> 'Yes. 'E got dem tie up in bundle,' she smiled. 'Me an' Kattree used to spy on 'e plenty time when 'e open it to put in mo' money.' [Stymphy] grinned and muttered something about Molière's *L'Avare* [i.e., *The Miser*].[8]

Indeed deliberate similarities between the two pieces of literature are made evident with respect to elements of dialogue and plot. In *The Miser*, the key protagonist, Harpagon, becomes hysterical on discovering that his money-box has been stolen (by his son, Cléante) from its hiding place in the garden:

> 'Ahh! My poor, my dear money, my lovely money, my friend, they've taken you from me! And now you've gone, I've lost my prop, my comfort, my joy. I'm finished. There's nothing for me now. I can't live without you. It's the end, I can't go on, I'm good as dead and buried'.[9]

Sosee, (Ramgolall's daughter by his first marriage), mirrors Cléante's behaviour by stealing money from her father's hoard; in her case to buy a sexually alluring dress which she hopes will make her more attractive to James Weldon, the planter who later sets up home with her.[10] In Chapter 7 when Ramgolall reflects on the events of that day his response to the theft patently echoes Harpagon's hyperbole:

Sombre day! He thought he would have died from very sorrow. He had been ill and fevered for a week after, talking wild tales and fighting so that he had to be strapped down to the hospital bed. [11]

In Molière's play, Harpagon profits from the theft of his money: his son, Cléante, repays what he has stolen as soon as he secures his lover's hand in marriage, whilst his daughter-in-law's father generously shares his wealth. In Ramgolall's case, Weldon sends him a gift of fifty pounds which allows him to start a new independent life of cattle rearing and more than makes up for the stolen fifty shillings. Unfortunately for Ramgolall, the story does not end here. Towards the end of the novel, his money is stolen once again: this time by his daughter Beena who uses it to pay the legal fees of Jannee, a married rice farmer who, though guilty of murder, she secretly loves. This time there is no happy ending and Mittelholzer breaks through the literary archetype, making a genuinely imaginative response to the life sealed up in the canister.

Ramgolall is here portrayed as a character whose miserliness, when compared to Harpagon's (who is a member of the gentry), can be exonerated or at least understood. His was not a 'background of material solidity'[12] but rather a life rooted in hard struggle and suffering:

> He crouched…looking at the fat bundles [of money], looking at them and smiling a smile of memory, for he had had to work very hard for the money in these bundles. The rain had soaked him and the sun dried him. He had walked knee-deep in mud, surrounded by clouds of mosquitoes. The ague of malaria had shaken him and the fever scorched him so that his anguished brain dreamt weird visions. Angry shouts from the overseers he had borne without a murmured word, without a frown. He had nearly been beaten to death in a riot when the labourers went on strike. Many had been shot by the police, many had been wounded.[13]

By drawing upon Molière's play, Mittelholzer achieves various objectives. It firstly allows him to address the social perceptions of East Indian frugality, whilst demonstrating that miserliness was not the preserve of East Indians as stereotyped but rather an idiosyncrasy which can be found anywhere. Some critics have contended that Ramgolall's miserliness is 'too excessive'.[14] In my opinion Mittelholzer's treatment of Ramgolall needs to be seen in a wider perspective.

The injection of caricature arguably has the important effect of enforcing a degree of emotional detachment between Ramgolall and the reader. He represents an old way of life. Whilst his children adapt to the changing society, he is too old to embrace the wearing of shoes or of banking with the Post Office. He must therefore die, in accordance with the laws of nature, to make way for a modern generation. The 'failure' of Mittelholzer to develop Ramgolall's character thus enables the reader to respond to the news of his death in the same unperturbed way as does the environment:

> Surely the savannah must know that Ramgolall was dead and that there were pebbles and pieces of dried mud lying scattered on the floor of the mud-house. It all looked so untroubled, so flat and at peace as though nothing at all happened. And the sky, too, and the wind, the sunshine – all untroubled, the same as they had been yesterday and all the days before: the sky blue, the wind cool, the sun red because it was low in the west.[15]

The above passage which appears towards the end of the book links in neatly with one that appears at its beginning. On that occasion Ramgolall had ironically feared that his daughter Beena might die:

> And Ramgolall, weak in body and in mind, could only look about him at a loss. His dark eyes seemed to appeal to the savannah and then to the sky. But the savannah remained still and grey-green, quiet and immobile in its philosophy. And the sky, too, would do nothing to aid him. Pale purple in the failing light and streaked with feathery brown and yellow clouds, the sky watched like a statue of Buddha.[16]

The emotional detachment we feel towards Ramgolall, along with the representations of a detached environment, serve the added objective of reinforcing Mittelholzer's ideas about the aloneness of man within the larger scheme of the universe. It is a reflection of the author's early loss of faith in orthodox Christianity, combined with his attraction to oriental theologies (e.g., Hinduism and Buddhism), which remained with him for life. His semi-autobiographical character, Garvin, in *The Jilkington Drama* (1965) articulates what the author demonstrates through his representations of environment in *Corentyne Thunder:* '…It's the weather that acts as my link with God'[17]; but the author's God is one who doesn't intervene in the everyday affairs of man.

Mittelholzer uses other intertextual references to express his interest in 'laws' of the universe. In Chapter 23 of *Corentyne Thunder*, Dr Roy refers to Olaf Stapledon's *Last and First Men*, which Big Man Weldon tells us would appeal to his son, Geoffry – a key character who makes a prophecy of his future suicide that uncannily foreshadows the author's own. Stapledon's book, though a novel, reads much more like a scientific thesis on the evolutionary rise and fall of man over a future period of two thousand million years. His thesis expounds views on cycles of life, civilization, human development and the converse possibility of degeneration: views which appear to be echoed in microcosm in *Corentyne Thunder*. Thus, for example, while Ramgolall's death marks the end of an era (as experienced by the first generation of Indians in Guyana), the lives of his children highlight the gradual process of creolization: Baijan saves his money in the Post Office; Beena travels beyond plantation life to New Amsterdam where she learns how to exploit the legal system and Sosee sets up home outside her ethnic group. Although these events are intended to reflect generational changes, Mittelholzer also suggests some of the degenerative aspects of a so-called civilized society. It clearly does not benefit society, for instance, that a murderer (i.e., Jannee) escapes imprisonment, purely because his lawyer has the skills to manipulate the jury into finding him not guilty. Though accomplished in a controlled, well-balanced manner, Mittelholzer's intertextual references reveal that his later preoccupation with particular ideas – e.g., issues of civilization, human progression and degeneration – are present at the beginning of his literary career.

The reference to Stapledon's novel, evidently being a book the author wants others to read, moreover exemplifies his conscious attempt to educate his readership:

> '... I've just finished reading Olaf Stapledon's *Last and First Men*. If you want to read about civilisations read that. / ... / Oh, it's a wonderful book, man. You should read it....'[18]

Recommendations of this type run throughout all of Mittelholzer's published novels. In *The Weather Family*, for instance, the Princess offers the character, Eva, a book to read with the added assurance that it is the best translation in existence:

> 'This is the *Bhagavad Gita*. It is a good translation – the best. Do not bother with Isherwood's. This is the best. It is by Yogi Ramacharaka.'[19]

This inclination as an author to be didactic, was, according to a contemporary, mirrored in Mittelholzer's everyday life:

> In the early 1930s Edgar worked for a short time as a clerk in what was known as the 'Berbice Gazette Store'. During that time he tried to educate the mind of the people by suggesting books he considered better reading than those they asked for, but much to his disgust they insisted on purchasing what they wanted...[20]

Writing evidently meant more to Mittelholzer than just becoming 'rich and famous'. It offered him the opportunity to reach a wide audience and voice ideas that he hoped would provoke intellectual debate, in particular, on subjects that he thought would benefit Caribbean society.

Hence, not satisfied with merely recommending *First and Last Men*, Mittelholzer (speaking through Dr Roy) draws attention to specific passages he would like his readers to take note of:

> 'A particular chapter there towards the end – it's entitled "Cosmology", I think – the thing reads like a piece of music, the movement of a Brahms sonata or something.'[21]

Apart from highlighting Mittelholzer's interest in cosmology, the passage also draws attention to the possibilities of weaving musical accents and rhythms into prose. As this is a technique

Mittelholzer employs, the reference also serves the purpose of validating his own aesthetic innovations.

In Chapter 19, following heavy rains on the Corentyne, Geoffry observes that:

> There was something detached about them [i.e., the sound of the cockerels crowing], yet serene and yearning, like the shepherd's song of thanksgiving after the storm in… [Beethoven's] Pastoral Symphony. They soothed his soul.[22]

The reference to Beethoven's *Pastoral Symphony*[23] is significant since events that occur in *Corentyne Thunder* loosely reflect its five-movement structure. The first movement – '*Awakening of cheerful feelings upon arrival in the country*' – is recreated in Chapter 10 and opens with the excitement Big Man Weldon feels as he anticipates the arrival (from school in Georgetown) of his son, Geoffry:

> Today, when Geoffry was coming home for the Easter vacation, Big Man felt the magic of life quickening the beats of his heart…[24]

The second movement, '*Scene at the brook*', is briefly echoed in Chapter 17 when Geoffry and Kattree spend the day fishing along the canal, while Stymphy and Beena talk in Ramgolall's hut. The third movement, '*Happy gathering of country folk*', is played out in the scene where Beena and Stymphy join Kattree and Geoffry in the adventure of catching fish and similarly ends with the approach of rain:

> Looking towards the east and the north-east, they saw a hazy, grey-white curtain of rain approaching swiftly across the savannah. Full of power and menace it seemed. They could hear it in the breezeless silence coming with a hollow, far-off roar – an awing roar that came in waves, rising to a whoop and then falling to a soft swashing as though thousands of busy devils were groaning and hissing for all they were worth behind the thick misty sheet of drops. The savannah hazed and vanished at the edge as if it were crumbling off into a fog of space beyond the horizon and would never reappear. Flocks of white birds uttered thin, harsh cries of panic and flew waveringly towards the south and the west.[25]

As in Beethoven's symphony, the third movement is 'interrupted' by the fourth – '*Thunderstorm*' – with a sudden and dramatic change in atmosphere:

> In less than half a minute they were all huddled together within the frowsy gloom of Ramgollal's home. The rain hissed down in a fierce, slating drop of showers. It crashed and prattled on the dry-leaf roof…

The conceptual similarities between novel and symphony are reinforced by the unsettled feelings the storm appears to cause. In *Corentyne Thunder* these feelings, occurring in only two of the novel's characters are not, however, an inextricably linked side-effect of the weather as proposed by Beethoven:

> The crash of the rain troubled him [i.e., Ramgolall] and the thought of the future. Even the sight of Geoffry, for some strange reason, had within the past few minutes begun to raise dark phantoms in his mind.[26]

On returning home with Stymphy during a lull in the storm, Geoffry's thoughts are similarly troubled (in his case about the possible contents of his girlfriend Clara's letter). The scene in Chapter 19 where Geoffry feels calm following the end of the storm is, meanwhile, suggestive of the fifth and final movement in allegretto of Beethoven's symphony: '*Shepherd's song; cheerful and thankful feelings after the storm*'.

Mittelholzer's application of Beethoven's *Pastoral Symphony* serves various purposes. While both novel and symphony follow the same basic 'movements' and are about life in the countryside, Mittelholzer's objective is to counter Beethoven's notion about the inextricable link between environment and the various human emotions supposedly produced by it. Whilst the 'silent peace' that succeeds the storm soothes Geoffry, it is only able to do so 'in a cold and forlorn way': his personality and personal circumstances having a much more significant impact on his mood than anything else. It is furthermore legitimate to assume Mittelholzer hoped alert critics would recognize that he interpreted *his* world and *the* world in musical terms, following Stapledon, in *Last and First Men*:

Man himself, at the very least, is music, a brave theme that makes music also of its vast accompaniment, its matrix of storms and stars.[27]

It should be evident by now that the novel's title is not a just a reference to weather, but also to musical drama and the rhythm of life. The narrator in effect invites the reader to think about the sounds produced in nature as a form of music and to take artistic inspiration (as did Mittelholzer and Beethoven) from this. By reworking European classical music into a Caribbean context, Mittelholzer aimed to demonstrate that British Guiana was a legitimate territory for sophisticated fiction, and that Caribbean people were more than capable of creating literature that engaged with a venerable tradition and made something new and note-worthy out of it.

Relevant to Mittelholzer's counterargument to Beethoven is an intertextual reference to Francis Bacon's *The Vicissitude of Things*. While Geoffry ponders over a letter from Clara (containing news that she is pregnant), Stymphy states:

'Well look here, you'd better stay up here and read this fateful letter of dread. I'll go downstairs to the others and give you a chance to ponder in solitude on the vicissitudes of life.'

'Oh, don't make an ass of yourself.'

'That essay of Bacon's on the vicissitudes of things ought to be of some help. "Certain it is, that matter is in a perpetual flux, and never at a stay. The great winding-sheets that bury all things –"

'Oh, shut up! I don't want to hear any silly Bacon.'[28]

Bacon's short essay explores the changing fates of mankind across the ages and the differences between human groups across geographical regions of the world. He argues that regions such as the West Indies are prone to earthquakes, lightning, deluges, and conflagrations which 'bury all things in oblivion'. Survivors of these natural disasters are 'commonly ignorant' and can give: 'no account of time past; so that oblivion is all one, as if none had been left'.[29] Here Mittelholzer's tendency to question, challenge or reject colonial representations of British Guiana (and the West Indies in general) and specifically the prevalent belief that tropical climes had a degenerating effect on its inhabitants is embedded in a seemingly casual piece of dialogue.

We know that Mittelholzer had been required to study Bacon at school and evidently considered his essay nonsense.[30] Only five years after the publication of *Corentyne Thunder*, he sent a letter to the editor of the *Trinidad Guardian* refuting reports about a hurricane that had allegedly brought destruction to British Guiana, before going on to make general observations about the Western tendency to portray inhabitants of the tropics as both primitive and exotic.

> A country in the tropics, according to the best romantic fiction and journalism originating in England and America, is a place where the sun shines fiercely and 'natives' disport themselves nude or semi-nude in the vicinity of trash-huts, with occasional war-dances, ritualistic tribal orgies, hurricanes and volcanic eruptions thrown in for colour and excitement.[31]

The need to challenge these representations was thus one of the key stimuli behind Mittelholzer's early novels. In a letter to A. J. Seymour,[32] he wrote:

> I want to have the truth out, I want the English and Americans to realize that there are coloured 'natives' out here who can be just as educated and refined as they can be.../...[whilst depicting at the same time] all our failings and foibles...without bias.[33]

Thus whilst he satirizes how pathetically pretentious Geoffry's and Stymphy's speech frequently is, as in the excerpt below, he is on another level articulating his aforementioned objectives:

> Geoffry grunted. 'There's the rub, my dear chap, as our friend Hamlet said.'[34]

The passing reference to Hamlet also points intriguingly to similarities between Shakespeare's eponymous hero and Mittelholzer's Geoffry. For those who care to note them: both characters harbour incestuous feelings (Hamlet for his mother, and Geoffry for his half-Aunt, Kattree); both treat their 'loved' ones (Ophelia/Kattree) with cold detachment and then despondently reflect on what wretches they are for doing so; both have a dim view of human existence – Hamlet recommends that Ophelia goes to a nunnery rather than be 'a breeder of sinners', whilst Geoffry refers to Clara's unborn child as a 'contemptible little foetus'; both contemplate suicide and both believe in 'duppies'/ ghosts.

These literary resonances usefully warn against the temptation to interpret Mittelholzer's work as largely autobiographical and the pitfalls of attempting to match *events* in his characters' lives with those of the author's, though such connections may have more basis in reality in the literature he produced toward the end of his life. Whilst his 'Romantic' inclination towards self-portrayal is much more subtle in *Corentyne Thunder*, we can nevertheless see, through aspects of Geoffrey's characterization, how Mittelholzer finds by writing in relation to the literature of others, ways of unravelling and expressing his own complex personal traits:

> He had power, a deep, tight-locked power that, one felt, might make a terrible whirl of damage, like a cyclone, if unlocked without warning. Seeing him [Geoffry], one thought of a coppery sky and a dead smooth sea – the China Sea of Conrad – and a falling barometer.[35]

The reference to Conrad is worth noting here. It almost certainly relates to the short novel, *Typhoon* – a story about a sea captain who is tasked with delivering a steamer load of Chinese 'coolies' to Southern China. When he and his crew first set off on their journey, the sea is calm but a vague awareness of pending adversity is marked by the steady fall of the barometer.[36] Rather than circumvent the signs of trouble by altering his route, Captain MacWhirr decides to face the typhoon head on, leading him and his crew into a struggle for survival against the elements. In addition to possibly identifying with the lonely single-mindedness of Conrad's Captain MacWhirr, Mittelholzer might well have derived confidence concerning the viability of publishing a novel based upon the East Indian ('coolie') community – and 'thunder' – from his reading of Conrad's *Typhoon*. At the same time, in view of Mittelholzer's commitment to subvert marginalized representations of the 'Other', Conrad's novel might also have been another provocation to write a story in which 'coolies' were central figures, since in *Typhoon* they (the Chinese 'coolies') are notably dehumanized, faceless and voiceless.

The hard-working Ramgolall and his five children represent a broad and diverse range of Indian characters. Whilst Sosee is the plump, class-conscious, poorly treated submissive mistress of Big Man Weldon, her beautiful half-sister, Beena is portrayed as an independent, proud, strong-minded, intelligent and self-sacrificing young woman. Sosee's brother, Baijan has none of the snobbery of his sister. As a successful rice mill owner he returns to the Corentyne to get married and generously share his wealth, in stark contrast to his miserly father, Ramgolall. Kattree is meanwhile characterized as an enigmatic young woman who, in swimming nude, harbours none of the sexual repressions of the coloured middle classes. She chooses the path of a single mother, unlike her half-sister, Sosee, and appears to live the type of relatively uncomplicated life that Geoffry finds enviable. Apart from Ramgolall's immediate family, Mittelholzer creates a host of cameo Indo-Guyanese characters, from gate-porters, butlers, butchers, and grocers, to doctors and lawyers. Even the murderer, Jannee, invites a certain degree of sympathy since we, as readers, witness his distress at being constantly mocked by Boorharry. Mittelholzer's novel was thus quietly revolutionary; giving humanity and voice to those who, in literature, had been marginalized.

But *Corentyne Thunder* offers the reader much more than a simple tale about an East Indian peasant. Whilst European literature heavily inspired Mittelholzer, a careful reading of *Corentyne Thunder* reveals how thoroughly he filtered this material: rejecting, adapting and adopting ideas for his own purposes; never accepting as absolute truths concepts that emerged out of Europe simply on the grounds of their alleged superiority. By daring to experiment and incorporate musical motifs into *Corentyne Thunder* (as he was also to do in later work), Mittelholzer produced a novel that makes a bold commitment to the Caribbean reality and is an aesthetically rich work of fictive art.

Endnotes

1. Seymour, A .J., 'West Indian Pen Portrait: Edgar Mittelholzer', in *Kyk-Over-Al* (Vol.5, No.15, Year End 1952), p. 17.
2. The novels referred to here are: C.L.R. James's *Minty Alley* (1936), Mendes's *Pitch Lake* (1934) and *Black Fauns* (1935) and De Lisser's *White Witch of Rosehall* (1929), *Under the Sun* (1937) and *Susan Proudleigh* (1915).
3. Known during Mittelholzer's lifetime as British Guiana.
4. Swinnerton, F., 'A Review of *Corentyne Thunder*', in *The Observer* (1st June 1941).
5. Mittelholzer's autobiography covers his life from birth in 1909 through to 1928 when he would have been 19. It is thus limited in terms of the critical periods of his life when he was a published author.
6. The Luckhoos were one of the most prominent East Indian (this was the colonial term preceding the contemporary use of Indo-Guyanese or simply Indian) families in colonial British Guiana. Mittelholzer's friend Lionel (1914-1997) was one of three sons of E.A. Luckhoo, first Indian solicitor in Guyana and a founding member of the B.G. East Indian National Association. The Luckhoos were a Christian Indian family and this may well have been a significant factor in Edgar Mittelholzer's mother's positive attitude to them. All three sons became Q.C.s and Lionel later became an unsuccessful conservative politician, swept away by the nationalist movement of the 1950s.
7. Mittelholzer, E., *A Swarthy Boy* (Putnam: London, 1963), p. 70.
8. Mittelholzer, E., *Corentyne Thunder* (all page references are to this edition), p. 81.
9. Molière, 'The Miser', in *The Miser & Other Plays*, translated by John Woods (Penguin Books: London, 2004), p. 202.
10. Cléante requires the money to woo Mariane, the woman who he loves and later marries.
11. *Corentyne Thunder*, p. 43.
12. Ibid., p. 55.
13. Ibid., pp. 42-43.
14. Birbalsingh, F. 'Indians in the Novels of Edgar Mittelholzer', in *Passion and Exile: Essays in Caribbean Literature* (Hansib: London, 1988), p. 76. [Also published in *Caribbean Quarterly* (Vol. 32, Nos. 1 & 2, March-June 1986).]
15. *Corentyne Thunder*, p. 229. A similar concept to this is expressed in

Olaf Stapledon's book, *Last and First Men* (Gollancz: London, 1999 [1930]) when he states: 'Great are the stars, and man is of no account to them', p. 303.

16. *Corentyne Thunder*, p. 23.

17. Mittelholzer, E., *The Jilkington Drama* (Corgi Books: London, 1966), p. 30.

18. *Corentyne Thunder*, p. 116.

19. Mittelholzer, E. *The Weather Family* (Secker & Warburg: London, 1958), p. 315.

20. Hahnfeld, D. 'Tribute to Edgar Mittelholzer', in *Edgar Austin Mittelholzer 1909-1965 'Serve your Country': Guyana Week 1968* (The Government Printery: Georgetown, 1968).

21. *Corentyne Thunder*, p. 116.

22. Ibid., p. 92.

23. See Jones, D.W., *Beethoven: Pastoral Symphony* (Cambridge University Press: Cambridge, 1995).

24. *Corentyne Thunder*, p. 52.

25. Ibid., pp. 82-83.

26. Ibid., p. 84.

27. Stapledon, O., *Last and First Men*, (Gollancz: London, 1999 [1930]).

28. *Corentyne Thunder*, p. 87.

29. Bacon, F. 'Of Vicissitude of Things', on <http://www.westegg.com/bacon/vicissitude-of-things.cgi> [site visited 28/07/05].

30. See *A Swarthy Boy: A Childhood in British Guiana*, p. 141.

31. Mittelholzer, E., Letters to the Editor: '"Hurricane" in Guiana?' in *The Trinidad Guardian* (Port of Spain: 12th March 1943), p.4.

32. A.J. Seymour (1914-1989) was the other founding father of Guyanese writing. He was Guyana's first really significant modern poet and a tireless advocate of the country's literary culture as the editor of the magazine *Kyk-over-Al* and encourager of countless Guyanese writers, not least of Edgar Mittelholzer.

33. Seymour, A. J., *Edgar Mittelholzer: The Man and His Works* (The Edgar Mittelholzer Memorial Lectures: Georgetown, 1968), p. 13.

34. *Corentyne Thunder*, p. 96.

35. Ibid., p. 53.

36. A sense of impending disaster notably runs throughout *Corentyne Thunder*: Ramgolall worries about Geoffry and Beena about Jannee; and rightly so, since Geoffry gets Kattree pregnant and Jannee murders Boorharry.

1

A tale we are about to tell of Ramgolall, the cow-minder, who lived on the Corentyne coast of British Guiana, the only British colony on the mainland of South America. Ramgolall was small in body and rather short and very thin. He was an East Indian who had arrived in British Guiana in 1898 as an immigrant indentured to a sugar estate. He had worked very hard. He had faithfully served out the period of his indenture, and now at sixty-three years of age he minded cows on the savannah of the Corentyne coast, his own lord and guide.

He had married twice and begotten five children, two being sons and three daughters. His eldest son had died in a dray-cart accident at the age of five. The other children were still alive. Baijan lived far from his father, for he was the owner of a rice-mill in Essequibo, the largest of the three counties of British Guiana. Sosee, the eldest daughter, had become the mistress of Mr James Weldon (Big Man Weldon as he was known along the coast, for he was big in body). A rich cattle-owner, he was the proprietor of the estate called Little Benjamin. Sosee had borne him seven children. She possessed a car and many jewels. She had done well in life and Ramgolall was pleased with her. Beena and Kattree, who were eighteen and sixteen, respectively, were children of the second wife. They lived with Ramgolall on the savannah and helped their father to mind the cows and keep the home. Very good daughters they were and a great help to their parent. They loved their father and their father returned their love threefold.

Beena was thin and very brown, like Ramgolall. She had beauty like the beauty of the savannah before the sun rose in the morning.

Kattree was of a lighter brown and her eyes were like the dark lowing of the cows in the afterglow of sunset. She was not very pretty, but a dim mystery dwelt about her when she sat before the small mud furnace to watch the pots boil. This was her beauty.

It happened that under a quiet sky one afternoon Ramgolall and Beena were driving the cows home, forty-seven in all, including bulls and calves, when Beena complained of not feeling well.

Ramgolall's mind was fixed on the cows and he looked at her with eyes that were more curious than anxious, and asked her what was wrong.

'Me na feel good,' Beena replied. She walked with lagging steps, and her head was slightly bent. 'Me belly a-hurt me,' she said.

'We soon reach home, bettay. Drink lil' sugar-water. Hey! Hey! Go-'long deh! Hey!'

A loitering calf obeyed the voice of Ramgolall and continued its blithesome way homeward.

But the steps of Beena faltered more and more, and her face grew strained. She put a hand slowly to her stomach. 'Ramgolall, me feel bad-bad.'

And now her voice came low and ill, so that Ramgolall glanced at her in sudden anxiety. His thin, brown body was naked, save for a loincloth. He carried a shiny stick, thin and brown like his body. He forgot the cows and approached her, stick held as though he might be intent on attacking her.

'Beena bettay, wha' wrong?'

'Me belly a-hurt me bad.'

Beena stood still and kept her hand pressed tightly to her stomach. Her face had grown greyish like the savannah racked in the pain of drought.

The cows, ignoring them, plodded onward toward their pen which stood in the south about a hundred and eighty rods off. The calves frolicked and rubbed themselves against the pale brown bellies of their mothers. The light of day was fading, for the sun had fallen behind the hillocks of cloud painted in purple and grey low on the western sky. A tiny frog kept whistling.

'You' belly a-hurt you, bettay?'

Beena nodded her head limply. The pink and rather dirty folds of her long skirt began to crumple inward as her body sagged. She stumbled slightly… And then Ramgolall dropped his stick and tried to support her.

'Beena bettay, is wha' wrong, na?'

This was all Ramgolall could say, staggering to support her, for he was weak from age and want of good food. 'Bettay. Beena bettay, you sick? Eh? Is wha' wrong, na?' And he lowered her to the ground and kept looking at her face in a fixity of expression like slate clouds piling tensely in the east.

Beena moaned softly and her breathing came in heavy gusts as though her soul were fatigued with the things of this life and wished to leave her body in gasp after gasp of wind. And Ramgolall, weak in body and in mind, could only look about him at a loss. His dark eyes seemed to appeal to the savannah and then to the sky. But the savannah remained still and grey-green, quiet and immobile in its philosophy. And the sky, too, would do nothing to aid him. Pale purple in the failing light and streaked with feathery brown and yellow clouds, the sky watched like a statue of Buddha.

'Ow! Bettay, you na go dead. Eh? Bettay? Talk, na? Is wha' wrong, bettay?'

But Beena moaned in reply, doubled up.

'Talk, na, bettay? Try. You' belly a-hurt?'

The moan came again like a portent, like the echo of a horn sounded in the depth of the earth. 'The Dark gathers', it seemed to tell the soul of Ramgolall, 'and Death cometh with the Dark. Be resigned, my son.'

Ramgolall stood up in a panic, looking all around him. He saw the cows, a group of moving spots, headed for their pen and getting smaller as they went. He could smell their dung mingled with the iodine in the air. He could see the tiny mud-house, with its dry palm-leaf roof, where he and Beena and Kattree lived. It stood far off, a mere speck. Kattree must be boiling rice and salt-fish. In his mind he could see her squatting before the mud furnace, quiet and engrossed in her task. He could see her glance round as he and Beena came back with the cows. But tomorrow, he thought, she would see him alone because Beena would be dead. Beena would be lying stiff in a white coffin…

Ramgolall hailed out in a small, strained voice. 'Come, Kattree! Hey! Kattree! Hey!' he called, knowing that Kattree was too far to hear, but calling all the same, because he was in a panic. He would have called to the yellow clouds or to the fringe of courida trees low down in the north. He would have called to anything for help because his daughter Beena whom he loved greatly was dying.

'Hey! Kattree! Hey! Come, Kattree! Hey!'

And he groaned in his impotence and wagged his head and made little whinnying sounds, looking all about him for help. 'Savannah,' he seemed to say, 'help me. Beena bettay is dying. Help me to keep off Death. Help me, savannah. Help me, please.' But the savannah seemed only to smile dully in reply, passive as Destiny, still as Mystery.

Then Beena bettay sat up, and he saw that her eyes were open and alive and her face brown still and not grey with death. She was pretty still and not ugly with the blankness of death.

'Beena bettay, you na dead?'

Beena smiled and stood up slowly, and her eyes twinkled. 'Me feel lil' good now,' she said, touching her stomach lightly. 'Me belly na hurt so much. Me na eat nutting since morning. Me been aback help Jannee plant rice.'

'Ow, bettay! You frighten me. Me t'ink you dead. Why you na eat? You mus' eat. Jannee finish plant rice?'

''E got two mo' fiel' lef' plant.'

'Dis year crop na go pay good. Too much rain fall dis year. Me warn Jannee.'

'Me warn 'e, too. But 'e seh wha' fo' do? 'E mus' mek try radder dan lef' de fiel' waste.'

And so Ramgolall and Beena walked slowly home through the deepening twilight. Behind them the wind blew softly, laden with the cool damp of evening. Many tiny frogs were whistling, and one or two crickets made clicking noises or cheeped and stopped, cheeped and stopped.

2

That evening, squatting before the doorway of their small mud house, Ramgolall beat the goatskin tom-tom and Kattree and Beena sang. Tum, tum. Tum, tum, tum, went the tom-tom.

The earth on which they squatted was plastered smooth with clay and dung, this being the work of Kattree, for Kattree could plaster walls and earth with much skill. It was she who had done the walls and the floor of this small mud house, their home. Whenever the walls or the floor, inside or around the house, began to crack and flake it was Kattree who did the work of mending. She liked to work hard in cooking meals and doing things for the home, as Beena liked to work hard in planting and cutting rice for Jannee and helping Ramgolall to mind the cows.

In the still night the sound of Ramgolall's tom-tom went far across the savannah to Jannee's mud-house which stood in the south-west, near the public road where cars and buses ran to and fro by day. By night only a few cars ran. Even now, in the west, a white fan of light, like ghostly dust, wavered against the dark blue sky, and Ramgolall, beating his tom-tom, saw it and was faintly troubled far inside, though he knew not really why. Perhaps it was because years ago Big Man Weldon's car had thrown such a light when Big Man was coming to the sugar estate to take Sosee for a drive. How Ramgolall's heart would beat in fear lest Big Man did harm to Sosee! Ah! But those days were past and Sosee was happy now as the mistress of Big Man and the mother of his seven children. No need for Ramgolall to think darkly of it. Let him be cheerful with Beena and Kattree.

Tum, tum. Tum, tum, tum, went the tom-tom, and Beena bettay swayed her slim body and wailed a sweet tale to the stars up there. And then Kattree joined the tale and told her bit, and the stars answered in tiny twinkles. Tum, tum. Tum, tum, tum. Hear the hum of the car coming. The bright light daubed them swiftly and was gone. Ramgolall shivered, but so that only he could know that he had shivered. Beena bettay and Kattree bettay would never know of the worry and strain of that time when Big Man Weldon came almost every night to take Sosee driving. And Sosee with such a hot temper. One night when Ramgolall had tried to stop her going with Big Man she had taken up a cutlass to cut Ramgolall. Big Man had to hold her quickly and wrest the cutlass from her. Big Man slapped her face and that quietened her. He could manage her well, Big Man Weldon. A fine big fellow and so rich. But how could Ramgolall have known that he liked Sosee so much that he would take her home to live with him and give her jewels and a car? Ramgolall had feared that Sosee's children might have to live in his small house and be fed and minded by him, him a poor man – a poor cane-cutter.

But all that was gone years and years ago. Why think darkly of it? The years smoothed over everything. Sosee's eldest son was now as old as Beena, and he was fair-skinned like Big Man Weldon. One day he might go to England and become a doctor or a lawyer, because it was said that he was clever at school and always came top in lessons. He went to a big school in Georgetown and learnt big languages and read big books which taught him how to speak well like estate managers and overseers, and taught him how to work out big figures and sums on paper. Think of a grandson of Ramgolall being able to do all that! Yes, Ramgolall was well pleased with Sosee. Sosee had brought him honour in the world. No matter that she was ashamed to own him as her father and kept away his grandchildren from him. That was nothing. She was his daughter and no man or thing could make her otherwise. Geoffry, her eldest son, was his, Ramgolall's, grandson. He carried Ramgolall's blood in his veins, and Ramgolall was proud to have a grandson who was so learned that he might soon go to England and be a doctor or a lawyer. Nothing could change that. No one or nothing.

Tum, tum. Tum, tum, tum, went the tom-tom.

And a quiet wind, cool and dry like delicate china, came over the savannah from the north-east and carried the sounds far to the south and to the west. Perhaps Big Man Weldon, eight miles away though he was, heard them faintly. Perhaps he sat at this moment with Sosee on the back veranda of his large house. All was silent, the night and the house. He was smoking his pipe while Sosee was rocking silently in one of those chairs that swayed backward and forward. Each of them perhaps looked out separately at the night and thought of the many things which had happened in the

26

years gone by. And thinking in this way, the sound of Ramgolall's tom-tom, like black specks out of the dark-blue sky, padded softly on their hearing and made them fidget without knowing why they fidgeted.

Tum, tum… Tum, tum, tum. Faint and mysterious. Corentyne thunder perhaps from over the distant courida bush. It awakened the odour of fish and dry cow dung. Or it might merely be the humming of the trade wind through a crack in the wall of that decayed wooden house. If not, it could even be the gurgle of water in the broken koker. Or the soft whirr of wild duck wings. Who knew what varied magic might not stir in that far-away phantom sound? The dying groan of the overseer who shot himself last year. Or just the heavy clank of chains in the punts bringing canes from aback. The splash of an alligator in a pungent rice field. Tum, tum…Tum, tum, tum … A shower of rain approaching mistily from the east across the greying savannah. Watch the flight of a scarlet curri-curri.

A cow lowed dismally in the pen yonder, and Ramgolall stopped beating the goatskin tom-tom and Kattree and Beena brought the song to an end. Kattree yawned and said that she was feeling sleepy. But Beena wanted to sing another song, so Kattree remained and Ramgolall began to beat the tom-tom again.

The rhythm now was different, fast and lively, and Ramgolall joined in the singing, for he remembered happy days at a Pagwah festival when he was a young man on the sugar estate. His soul seemed to grow pink and white with the spirit of youth. He swayed his body to and fro, and though his voice was strained with age, it came forth with a livening vigour like wind from the sea when the sky was harrowed with shreds of hurrying clouds.

3

The night was very young when Ramgolall and his two daughters went to bed, the time being only ten minutes past eight, though Ramgolall and his two daughters were not aware of this, for they had no clock, and, in any case, did not know how to tell the time.

Ramgolall slept in a small hammock made of canvas – canvas

that was shiny from age and dirt. Beena and Kattree slept on a crude bed raised only a foot off the ground. It was made of broomsticks cut short (these for posts; six in all), a crab-wood frame and slats of loose boards placed crosswise and covered with rice-bag cloth. A very hard mattress this made, but Beena and Kattree did not find it hard, for they had been accustomed to it since babyhood. For pillows they had what they called 'bedding', this being a mass of dirty rags and two rice-bags, all of which gave off a strong, sour smell of coconut-oil and bred lice. There were many lice in the smooth black tresses of Beena and Kattree.

It was Kattree who put out the lamp – a two-ounce Capstan tobacco-tin with a hole in the cover and a wick drawn through the hole – and when she had done so the dark closed in around them like a quiet scarf soothing to the soul and tired body of Ramgolall. Doubled up in his hammock, Ramgolall felt himself dropping, dropping delightfully into the deep black hole of sleep.

Kattree bettay settled her head on her rag-bundle and thought dimly of a cow and of the mud-furnace, of both as one, of wind humming around the mud-house, and then – and then of nothing.

Beena bettay was already breathing in slow rhythm.

And while these three slept the wind trailed over the savannah like cool threads of silk, and the stars winked and wheeled in a pageant of slow fireworks. Then clouds came from the sea and the fireworks ended. Rain fell heavily for an hour, after which the clouds moved on and the stars winked again, but mistily, as though a wizard had changed them from fireworks sparks into serene fireflies trapped in the huge web of a celestial spider. The moon, a waning horn, rose two or three hours after midnight, and spread a light, silken sheet over the savannah.

At length, Ramgolall stirred, for the pale finger of dawn had touched his sleeping brain. He opened his eyes and looked around him, and though everything still lay cloaked in dark, he knew it was dawn. He knew that the east was fair like the bellies of the cows in the pen. He heard the lowing of the calves, who, separated from their mothers, hungered for the milk in the swollen udders.

Maw-aw-w-w, went the calves, and Ramgolall felt the blood

of life run afresh within his veins. This was a new day. Let him get up and go with Beena and Kattree to milk the cows. Ah-h-h! But the air felt damp. It must have rained during the night. Bad for the cane-cutting on the estates, but good for the pasture. The cows would have much green grass to eat.

Ramgolall shivered and got out of the hammock.

'Beena bettay-y-y! Kattree bettay-y-y! Mornin' come. Wake up, bettay!'

Kattree sighed and groaned, turning over slowly. Beena had already sat up. She yawned loudly in the dark. 'Rain fall a-night, na, Ramgolall?'

'Eh-heh, bettay. Rain fall.'

'Me feel lil' col'.' She yawned again.

'Me na feel like get up today,' groaned Kattree.

'You lazy, na, girl?' said Beena, chuckling sleepily.

Ramgolall parted the flour-bag curtain that hung in the doorway, and the dim light of dawn came in, making them all grey like clay-mud near the cow-pen gleaming dully after a shower of rain.

'Rain go fall plenty today,' said Kattree, bunking at the east. 'Grey cloud pile up high.'

''E might pass off,' said Beena who thought of going aback with Jannee and preferred to be hopeful. 'Wind go start blow soon as sun come up.'

And Beena's hope was not let down, for indeed, when the sun came up the wind began to blow strongly and steadily from the north-east. The grey clouds in the east broke up into filmy fragments that melted overhead, leaving a blue sky streaked faintly with feathery tendrils of cirrus. The savannah glistened wetly in the sunlight, and flocks of white birds settled on its surface, making faint, harsh cries that mingled with the lowing of the calves to form the strange dawn-music that freshened the spirits of Ramgolall.

The spirits of Beena, too, felt freshened as with Jannee and his wife and two small sons, she walked slowly along the narrow mud-dam towards the two unplanted rice-fields far aback. On every hand lay the square-cut lakes of still water with the newly-planted rice pushing up above the surface in straggly tufts, seeming weak and half-dead, but soon to sprout up, as Beena knew, in a vast carpet of bright green. In the south-east lay the nursery, a small, square patch of yellowish green, thick and soft like a Persian rug, and varying in tint as the wind gently ruffled it. Emerald now it looked in the bright sunlight and then pea-green at one corner. The pea-green spread, mingled with the emerald which retreated in a rapid wave and then moved back and reigned all over, though more pea-green and a flash of pure yellow were forming shiftily in a corner. And so it went on until the shadow of a cloud, like a hurrying chariot of gloom, romped darkly over the square and made the green deep and still as though a painter, in a sullen whim, had daubed it over to portray his mood.

Jannee, that day, sang fitfully as he worked and so did Sukra, his wife. He and Sukra planted one field, while Beena and the two boys planted another. Jannee was short, but thick in body. He was young and strong, with limp black hair which always lay plastered flat on his head and around his forehead. He wore khaki trousers and a khaki shirt, both very grey with dirt and torn in parts from rough wear. His trousers were rolled up now above his knees, and his legs gleamed with water.

Sukra's dirty blue skirt was rolled up, too, above her knees. She was a trifle taller than Jannee, but very thin, so thin that her small round belly, swollen with child, looked oddly prominent, as though it might be an inflated rubber bag strapped on closely in front of her, under her skirt. She wore a reddish head-cloth which kept her long, black hair from falling about her neck and face and thus hindering her in her task.

The two boys who worked with Beena wore nothing at all, not even a loincloth. They were eight and nine years of age, Chattee being eight and Boodoo nine. Boodoo had great likeness to his father, while Chattee had a face of his own.

'Boorharry' cow go drop nex' week dis time,' said Sukra. 'Me tell 'e seh if is a bull-calf 'e mus' mek me present wid am, an' 'e seh awright.'

'You mek too much fun wid Boorharry,' said Jannee, without looking up. ''E got too much air fo' put on. Me na like got too much talk wid 'e.'

'Ah, wha' mek you stan' suh? Me na see nutten wrong wid 'e. 'E does mek we laugh plenty.'

'Go live wid am, na?'

'When you dead, bury me go tek 'e,' laughed Sukra, and broke once more into song.

But Jannee did not join her, for he seemed a little put out at the way she had spoken of Boorharry. Jannee did not like Boorharry who could read and write English and worked as gate-porter at the hospital three miles away on Speyerfeld sugar estate. Boorharry thought much of himself and made plenty clever jokes so that everyone who heard laughed and called him a nice fellow. He made love to many women and would marry none, and he had nine cows and twelve sheep, nobody knowing where he had got them from, because he told lies and might even be a thief. Moreover, he was a Brahmin, and though Jannee had many friends who were Brahmins, he could not excuse Boorharry for being a Brahmin. Indeed, one may say, to sum it up, that Jannee had no love for Boorharry. He was envious of Boorharry because of Boorharry's cleverness in being able to read and write English and to make jokes so that people laughed and women loved him, and for his nine cows and twelve sheep.

'You na like me sing, Jannee?'

'Sing, na? Me got business?'

Sukra laughed. 'You vex' wid me, baaya?'

'Shut you' mout', go on wid you' wo'k.'

Sukra broke into song and Jannee, in a fit of impatience, shouted at her to shut her mouth and splashed her with water scooped up with a sudden sweep of his hand.

Sukra gave a nasal cry of protest, and after that, she worked in silence, her face sulky. Jannee, too, worked in silence after that, his face sulky.

4

Whenever Jannee and Sukra came aback to plant rice they brought food to eat at midday, for their home was many miles distant and it would have taken them over two hours to walk from here to there and back. They brought their food, boiled rice and salt-fish, in two saucepans (cooking-pots made of tin, with tight-fitting lids), these saucepans being tied up in cloth and left on the mud-dam until Jannee and Sukra were ready to eat.

Yesterday the rice and salt-fish had barely been enough to feed Jannee and Sukra and the two boys, and even though Jannee and Sukra had insisted on sharing their portions with Beena, Beena had refused, saying that she had drunk plenty milk before setting out (this being an untruth) and so could do without food until evening.

Today, however, Jannee and Sukra had taken care to bring enough rice and salt-fish for them all, and so Beena ate with them, and a very friendly meal it was, Jannee and Sukra forgetting their slight row and making much fun and many jokes. Sukra even sang a song, and then Jannee sang part of one, then Beena joined in with him and finished it off. She sang some words wrong and Jannee and Sukra laughed at her, and she laughed, too, the while Boodoo and Chattee wrangled over a brown snail-shell, a creketteh shell, which Boodoo had found. Chattee said that he had seen it first, but Boodoo claimed that he had picked it up. They began to wrestle and Jannee gave them a shout, so they stopped fighting, Boodoo still holding the shell tightly. Chattee began to cry nasally, then Boodoo opened his hand and saw that the thin shell had broken, so he began to cry, too. His mother said: 'A-you shut you' mout'! Is wha' you cryin' fo'?' But Beena tried to soothe them. 'Na cry, bettay. Boodoo baaya, na cry. Me going look fo' mo' shell fo' you.' She stretched out and stroked his head, while Jannee frowned and said: ''E wan' somet'ing mek 'e cry in trut'. Shut you' mout'!'

The sun glared very brightly upon them, a trembling fire-ball right overhead. It dried the tears on Chattee's cheek when Chattee stopped crying. It dried the hem of Beena's skirt. Two hawks were making spirals in the air over the nursery, looking for the creketteh snails on which they fed. Harsh, screeching cries came from their throats, cries going round in spirals. One dived abruptly. It had found a snail. The other dived after it, giving a screech. Their wings made a whirring flutter amidst the thick green blades sprouting in the nursery. Up darted the one that had dived first, and a dark shell was in its bill. The second bird curved up after it. Swift spiral mingled with swift spiral, up and up they went and still farther up, harsh screech curving, too, through the hot air, across the fire-ball, past white cobwebs of cloud, down, up again. Then the shell dropped, a black pip, down into the grey water of a newly-planted field, the field Beena and the boys had planted. Little jagged blobs of water sprang up, settled, made ripples, and the screeches overhead broke out in fresh spirals. Screech after screech going round and round, upward and then downward, and the sun glared very brightly, blindingly, trembling, a hot fire-ball that dried the tears on Chattee's cheek, on Boodoo's now, and the hem of Beena's skirt.

5

Big Man Weldon was ill with malaria and Sosee had sent for the doctor. The doctor came in a small green car that bumped a great deal on the rough grass track leading from the public road to the house where Big Man lived. The doctor came up the stairs slowly, taking his time, for he seemed that kind of man. He was short, not tall like Big Man. He had grey-green eyes, was light brown, the hair on his head being black and slightly wavy. He was a Eurasian called Roy Matthias (Matthias being his white mother's name), though everybody along the coast knew him as Doctor Roy. He practised privately, unlike most other doctors in the colony, who were in the Government Service. His father, a rich East Indian rice-man, had died and left him much money so he did not need to earn his living from the Government. Moreover, he had built up a good practice along the coast because he was very clever at his job and was famed for having cured many sick people.

Sosee greeted him at the top of the stairs. She gave a wide smile, showing many gold teeth, and said: 'Doctah Roy! How you do, na? We ain' see you dis long, long time!'

And the doctor smiled, shaking a plump hand she extended (the fingers wore several gold rings). 'Oh, I'm all right, Sosee,' he replied in a casual voice. 'My not coming to see you for a long time is a good sign, I should say. Shows you've been keeping good health.'

'Ow! But naw! Is only when we sick you going come see we? You mus' look we up, Doctah Roy. We glad to see you *any* time.'

He chuckled and patted her shoulder. 'You're all right, Sosee. I'm a busy man, don't forget. Can hardly call my soul my own. Where's Big Man? Fever worrying him again, eh? Let's go up.'

'Yes, man, 'e roas' all las' night. We ain' know *what* to say to dis fever.'

She led him from the veranda (which went right round the house) into the sitting room which was cluttered up with shiny furniture: chairs, rockers, tables, settees, what-nots and a piano that nobody could play, except Geoffry when he was home on holiday. There were many brass *jardinières* and pots and pans of Indian workmanship and silver cups won years ago by Big Man Weldon's racehorses. The walls had hung on them abundant pictures in gold frames and in brown frames, pictures of English scenes and people, many of them from almanacs, for they were very brightly coloured. The floor was very dusty, and the younger children (gone to school for the day) had left crumpled scraps of exercise-book leaves lying untidily under chairs and tables. The whole room smelt of dust, furniture and coconut-oil.

After Sosee had led him through the maze of furniture, they entered the dining room where two dinner-wagons, packed with glass and electroplated ware, stood in opposite corners, while the big dining table in the middle of the room was covered with a cloth stained brown in patches with cocoa, and green and yellow with curry – a very dirty tablecloth. Bottles of pepper and chutney and used crockery stood here and there, and one or two flies buzzed swiftly in the spaces between them, making the cloth their playground.

Sosee, all the while, kept making comments on Big Man Weldon's health and telling of her treatment. 'Every mornin' ah used to give 'e a five-grain quinine. You know? De Gub-ment quinine. But it ain' mek no difference. De fever come on las' night hot-hot, jus' like de time before, couple mont' back.'

'I remember,' nodded the doctor, to indulge her.

'De *whole* night 'e roas'. Ah ain' get a wink o' sleep las' night. Ah set up watching 'e, you know, an' rubbing 'e down wid bay rum. 'E groan an' groan de whole night.' She sighed. 'Ah tell you, we ain' know *what* to say to dis fever, Doctah Roy.'

From the dining room stairs led up to the upper storey, and

up these stairs Sosee led him, plodding with a breathing sound of effort, for she was very plump (being well fed) and seemed quite plainly not used to much hard work.

'Me ain' like go up dese stairs,' she panted. 'Ow! Me getting ol' nowadays, Doctah,' she smiled. 'Wha' wid one t'ing an' de odder. You hear Geoffry pass 'e exam, na?'

'Oh, yes, I did read of it in the papers some time ago. I forgot to congratulate you. That boy is clever. He ought to get somewhere.'

'Big Man wan' to sen' 'e to England to study fo' doctah.'

'Good idea. He should get through easily.'

She took him into the large bedroom that was Big Man's. It was a tidy room, but the walls were like the walls of the sitting room, full of bright pictures. When the windows were open it was a very cool room, because it was in the north-east of the house. But the windows were all closed at the moment and the air was very stuffy, smelling faintly of bay rum.

Dr Roy frowned at once and told Sosee to open the windows. 'You can't expect him to get better in a room locked up like this. You ought to know better than that, Sosee. Open all of them.'

'Ah t'ought 'e might ha' tek chill, you know,' she smiled, flushing, abashed, and set about to open them.

Dr Roy moved over to the Simmons bed where Big Man lay covered with a red blanket. 'Well, Big Man!'

Big Man Weldon grunted deeply and stirred, making new folds appear in the blanket. His grey-brown eyes were watery and a little bloodshot. He looked worn out and pale as though last night the malaria had wrapped itself around him like a huge leech and sucked his energy while he wrestled in vain to shake it off. When Dr Roy put his hand on his forehead he found that Big Man was sweating coldly. The fever had broken for the time being.

Under the blanket though he was, it could be seen that he was a big man of great length and of great width and depth of chest with great arms and calves. He had a high, bony Roman nose, and he was handsome, even though now at fifty-four one or two deep wrinkles had tried to make him look old. His lips were rather wide (though not thick) like the lips of his mulatto mother. His hair was straight and yellow-brown like the hair of his English father.

'How're you, Roy?' he smiled, and his voice came as though from out of a well, for when in good health he had a voice of much power and sound.

Dr Roy chuckled. 'Asking how I am, Big Man? I'm pretty all right. It's you we've got to ask after, man. Fever giving you old Harry again, eh?'

Big Man grunted assent, smiling and nodding weakly.

Dr Roy took his temperature and his pulse and sounded him with a stethoscope all over his body, doing all this not because it was really necessary, but because it impressed the minds of both Sosee and the patient. When he had finished he wrote out a new prescription full of Latin words, but which was merely the same old prescription for a quinine mixture, for with malaria the only remedy is quinine.

In going away, he said to Sosee: 'He'll be up in a day or two. But see and keep those windows open. A sickroom *must* be properly ventilated. He can't get well without fresh air.'

'Eh-heh. Na fear,' she reassured him, smiling. 'Ah going keep dem open, Doctah Roy. As long as you say ah mus' keep dem open ah going keep dem open.' She continued to smile, regarding him with admiring eyes. 'And don' forget. You mus' come look we up often when you get time. Drop in *any* time you like. We always glad to see you.'

'All right, Sosee. All right. But I'm a busy man, you know. Can hardly ever call my soul my own.'

6

Ramgolall had driven the cows into pasture for the day, and he was returning now to his home to see after the milk. Every day he sent three gallons of milk to Speyerfeld for the overseers' mess-room. The milk was put into two tin containers, one of which held two gallons and the other one gallon. These were taken to the public road, Ramgolall lifting the smaller one, being weaker than either of his daughters, and Beena or Kattree the larger. They waited by the public road, with the wide parallel canal on its north, until the yellow bus called *Clark Gable* (No. H 5691), driven by a black young man named Joseph McLeod, came up and stopped, when the milk-cans were handed over to Joseph for delivery.

This morning, like yester morning and one or two other mornings in the past few weeks, the milk had fallen short by a little over a pint, so Ramgolall made Kattree fetch some water from the canal which ran past to the sea, not many rods off, and poured the water into the larger milk-can to make up for the shortage, for it was the larger milk-can that wanted the pint to complete its two gallons. The smaller was full. It was always full, because, reasoned Ramgolall, if the larger can was short and water was added the difference would not be so easily seen because the larger can contained much milk and much milk was not readily thinned by water.

The water Kattree fetched was fresh water, but not clean. It looked cloudy, for there was mud in it, mud and vegetable matter; perhaps, too, even some of the germs that gave one the sickness called dysentery, or the worse one, typhoid fever. But Ramgolall did not think of these things, hardly ever having heard of disease germs and not being naturally clean in his habits.

Thus he and Kattree, a full can on shoulder, made their way leisurely south towards the public road, Kattree silent and dull-faced as if reflecting the mood of the rigid pile of clouds showing like distant mountains behind the courida bush.

The sun shone hotly on the brown, bare body of Ramgolall, but Ramgolall, being used to its heat, felt in no way ill at ease.

They had only to wait about ten minutes by the roadside, which was already dry and dusty in the fierce sunlight, then the bus called *Clark Gable*, a bright yellow in colour, approached in a cloud of dust, going east. It droned to a standstill as it droned every morning, and Ramgolall squinted in rapid little blinks, for the gleaming bonnet and mudguards always hurt his eyes when the sun shone brightly like this.

Joseph, the driver, alighted, fumbling in his trousers pocket for the money from Jairamsingh, the butler of the overseers' mess-room, in payment for yesterday's milk supply, for Ramgolall was paid daily, and not weekly or monthly. Jairamsingh, the butler, had from the outset insisted on this way of payment. 'We prefer it so,' he had said, and would give no other reason, nor would he explain himself in any other way. Ramgolall had made no objection, but he had decided to himself that Jairamsingh was a clever man, possessing many secrets, even secrets that concerned the overseers and the manager. Perhaps he even dealt in Black Arts or in obeah. He was, therefore, a man to be treated with caution and great respect.

'Heh,' said Joseph, handing over the money. 'Count it an' see if it right,' he added as he always did, and stood gazing in his sulky way at Ramgolall as Ramgolall counted the money.

One, two, three, four, five shilling pieces and a sixpence. Three gallons at two shillings a gallon made six shillings. Less a sixpence for Joseph left five shillings and sixpence. Right.

'Eh-heh,' said Ramgolall, nodding and smiling humbly. ''E right, Joseph. Five shillings, sixpence. 'E right.'

Ramgolall was about to bend down to lift up the one-gallon can to give Joseph when Joseph tapped him on the shoulder in a way that was not usual. 'Ah got a word to seh to you, Ramgolall,' said Joseph in a lowered voice, and he looked more sulky than ever standing there, sulky like a sombre afternoon deepening into a sombre evening after the sun has sunk with purple and orange. Joseph said: 'Ramgolall, Jairamsingh seh as mus' warn you. If you go on putting water in de milk 'e going stop tekin' milk from you.'

Ramgolall's eyes opened wide. He lifted his face and his arms to the sky. 'Oh, me Gaad!' he exclaimed fervently. 'Joseph! Me na put water milk! Ow! *Ow!* Me na put water milk. Kattree! Kattree bettay!'

'Eh-h-h-h?' said Kattree in a sudden manner as if she had not been paying attention to the argument.

'Me put water milk, bettay?'

Kattree shook her head, her face growing dismayed. 'Na,' she said, looking at Joseph and shaking her head. ''E na put na water milk. Me help am milk all dem' cow. 'E na put na water. Never na time.'

'Me swear to Gaad!' said Ramgolall, lifting his right arm to heaven. 'Me na put na water milk! Never na time!'

All the while Joseph was smiling in a slow, sickly way. He said: 'Ramgolall, you t'ink me fool, na? Well, me na fool, so na worry tell lie – '

'Ow, Joseph! Me swear to Gaad!'

'Me na care *wha'* you swear to in dis heaven an' eart'. Me know you lie! An' me only telling you wha' Jairamsingh seh. An' wha' is mo', de police testing milk now. One o' dese days, when you leas' expec', deh going hol' you up, an' den is a hundred-dollar fine you going got to pay de magistrate or go to gaol. Gimme de milk.' He took up the two cans, one in each hand, as though they were no heavier than eggs, and put them in the bus while Ramgolall still swore to God that he had never put water in the milk. He groaned and wagged his head and swayed his body from side to side, clasping his hands together and making a very pitiful picture of aggrievement. So much so that several of the passengers in the bus gazed at him with a little compassion. One black woman even said to Joseph: 'Is why you mus' say de pore man put water in de milk? You caan' prove it.'

Joseph only sucked his teeth.

'Judge nat dat ye be nat judged,' quoted the black woman, and Joseph sucked his teeth again. He glanced sulkily at her and said: 'You ain' know coolie yet, is day's why you can talk so.' He engaged his gears and the bus droned off on its way east, leaving Ramgolall behind to moan and wag his head.

But no sooner had the bus departed in its cloud of reddish dust when Ramgolall stopped moaning and wagging his head and looked very thoughtful.

'Ha! Me tell you Jairam clever man, bettay?' he said. He grunted deeply. 'Clever, clever man. 'E does wo'k Black Arts. Eh-heh.' With another deep grunt, he began to count the money again as though to make sure that it was still five shillings and sixpence. For who knew? Jairamsingh, far away as he was, might by some dark magic have caused a shilling or two to vanish into the air. Clever, clever man. He worked with Black Arts. Ah! He had many deep secrets.

Finding that the money still reckoned up to five shillings and sixpence, Ramgolall tied it up in a very grey and dirty rag which he stuffed away safely amidst the folds of his loincloth.

'Jairamsingh magic-man, Kattree bettay,' he said, wagging his head wisely. ' 'E go bring bad story if we na watch out. 'E clever, clever man, bettay.'

Kattree nodded in silence, her face as immobile as the paler blue of the sky low in the north-west.

'Clever, clever man, bettay,' repeated Ramgolall, wagging his head over and over and smiling. He groaned nasally and scratched his thigh in a slow, thoughtful way, his wrinkled old eyes fixed on the savannah as he and Kattree returned home through the growing heat. ' 'E does wo'k wid Black Arts, bettay. Eh-heh. Me feel so long time.'

And still Kattree would not break the mystery of her calm silence. Her thoughts seemed rigid like dream-incidents in time past. Her soul seemed poised at the middle point between the past and the future and troubled by the dark thunder of neither. Walking with grace in her dirty clothes, she looked like a figure created by the magic of the savannah and the sunlight. She looked aloof from the good and the evil of the earth, and yet a chattel of both. She looked serene like the far-reaching plain of stunted grass and earth. If Ramgolall had suddenly been attacked by some fearful wild creature and mauled to death, the savannah would have smiled on in passive secrecy, moving not a finger to aid him. And looking at her now, so one felt Kattree would have behaved if such a thing had happened, though one knew that she would never in reality have behaved so, for her love for Ramgolall was too great. One could see it lingering far down in the sombre depth of her eyes.

7

On reaching their mud-house, Kattree went to the fireplace to light a fire to cook the midday meal, while her father entered the mud-house, and, drawing the flour-bag curtain, moved into a corner where lay an old dented canister. Stooping before this canister, Ramgolall scratched away a little lump of earth near its base and brought to light what looked like a grey rag of cloth rolled up in a loose ball. He unrolled this rag and revealed a small key. Taking this key, he fitted it into the brass padlock that secured the canister. He unlocked and took off the padlock, then, as though by instinct, he grew rigid and gazed all round the gloomy inside of the mud-house. After a while, feeling satisfied that no thief or evil person lurked near, he lifted the lid of the canister. Inside it lay several dirty grey bundles. Each bundle contained money, money in coins. One bundle had two hundred shillings, another had two hundred florins, another five hundred pennies and another five hundred half-pennies: money saved during the long years of his labour as a cane-cutter.

But the bundle which Ramgolall took out contained one hundred and fifty-eight shillings. This was the bundle to which he added every day. He made Joseph pay him every day in loose shillings, for not being learned in big money matters, he was always fearful of mixing coins in various values lest he grew confused in counting them. Joseph, whose one fear was that Ramgolall some day might say that he had not paid him correctly, was only too eager to comply with Ramgolall's wishes, so he always paid Ramgolall in loose shillings.

Untying the dirty rags, Ramgolall saw with delight the one hundred and fifty-eight shillings. This was his moment of supreme pleasure. Singing with Kattree and Beena in the early evening gave him delight. The curry-feed twice a month gave him delight, too, especially if the mutton was fatty and the roti well stuffed with dholl. But no pleasure was equal to this daily pleasure of untying his growing bundle of shillings and seeing the silvery glint of them and hearing the sweet tinkle they made. It was like nectar oozing from the savannah on a dewy night.

Taking from his loincloth the rag in which he had tied up the five shillings and sixpence received from Joseph, he unloosed it. Then, reckoning the coins to make certain for the last time that they did amount to five shillings and sixpence, he dropped the five shillings, one by one, slowly into the big pile, counting as he did so.

'One hundred, fifty-nine, one hundred, sixty, one hundred, sixty-one, one hundred, sixty-two, one hundred, sixty-t'ree.'

He gave a grunt of satisfaction. 'One hundred, sixty-t'ree.' That number would remain fixed in his mind until tomorrow when he came to add another five shillings to the pile. The sixpences he always put aside. With this daily sixpence Beena and Kattree had to buy food to feed them all, besides saving a little daily until they had enough to buy them cloth to make clothes. A little had to be saved, too, to go towards the curry-feed every new moon and full moon. Kattree it was who worked this miracle of economy, and she never failed to bring it off.

As Ramgolall tied up the bundle he thought of the morning soon to come when he would put in the shillings that would bring the total to two hundred. When that morning came he would tie up the bundle for good and begin another. It was a pleasant thought – a thought only darkened a little by the memory of Joseph's warning a short while ago, for if Jairamsingh stopped taking the milk it would mean that Ramgolall would have to go from house to house in Speyerfeld Village and sell the milk by the pint – a slow process, and he an old man; though, of course, he could send Beena or Kattree sometimes. There would be a great deal of trouble, too, in collecting the money, for many people would want credit, and apart from that, they would not want to pay him more than five cents a pint, wherefore Jairamsingh paid six cents (three pence). If only Jairamsingh were not so clever and did not work with Black Arts... And what was that Joseph had said about the police testing milk? That was a deep warning. In what way could they test the milk? Was it possible that they had clever instruments that could find out if he had put water in the milk? Ah! But then the police had dark ways of finding out things. They were men who worked like ants, probing and probing into shady corners. And the questions they asked! The police were dangerous men. He would have to take care not to fall into their talons.

He kept grunting deeply the while he tied up the bundle. When he put it back in the canister he did not close the lid at once. He crouched there for a time, looking at the fat bundles, looking at them and smiling a smile of memory, for he had had to work very hard for the money in these bundles. The rain had soaked him and the sun had dried him. He had walked knee-deep in mud, surrounded by clouds of mosquitoes. The ague of malaria had shaken him and the fever had scorched him so that his anguished brain dreamt weird visions. Angry shouts from the overseers he had borne without a murmured word, without a frown. He had nearly been beaten to death in a riot when the labourers went on strike. Many had been shot by the police, many had been wounded. He could see, too, the blue sky of that Saturday when he had discovered that fifty shillings of his savings had been stolen. Sosee had robbed him to buy herself pretty clothes! Sombre day! He thought he would have died from very sorrow. He had been ill and fevered for a week after, talking wild tales and fighting so that he had to be strapped down to the hospital bed. They had thought he had gone awry in his mind and nearly sent him to the home for mad men miles away in New Amsterdam. Yes, a black week, that, though brighter days had come when Big Man Weldon had taken off Sosee to live with him and sent Ramgolall a gift of fifty dollars. Fifty dollars! Over two hundred shillings. He had spent a hundred shillings out of it on two cows that were being sold cheap by an overseer who was going back to England on holiday. It was from those two cows that he had by hard struggling built up the number to forty-seven – the number he now owned. A hard, hard struggle, indeed. Brine for the body and gall for the soul.

Crouching there, he looked at the bundles, and he kept smiling and wagging his head faintly while the events of the time gone rumbled through his memory like drums in the fantasy of a drowning man.

8

A few days later Big Man Weldon was out of bed, but not downstairs and about, for the fever had left him pale and low in energy.

It was raining outside – it had been raining since early morning – and all the bedroom windows were closed. Clothed in pyjamas and a dull yellow dressing-gown, Big Man sat in a rocking chair near the bed, smoking his pipe and reading a letter which he had just received by post.

When he had come to the end of the last page, he stamped heavily on the floor and then sat waiting for Sosee to come, his grey-brown eyes staring stolidly at the streaming panes of the window opposite him.

Pale and weakened as at present he was from the fever, the

power in him could still be seen and the determination and dominance. Had he lived years and years ago in England he might have been a great general like the Duke of Wellington or Lord Clive of India, or a great sea-adventurer sailing to foreign lands and capturing much booty, like Drake or Frobisher or Raleigh. He looked the sort of man who, one felt certain, always got what he set out to get, caring nothing for the dangers and difficulties that might come in his way. One could see him hacking with a big sword from right to left and trampling down whatever came in his path.

And this, indeed, was the sort of way in which Big Man Weldon had reached the position of wealth he now held. He had worked very hard, he had toiled honestly, but he had hacked right and left and cut down all who had tried to deter him. Yet there ran in him a kindly vein, kindly like the golden vein of light that one can sometimes see running along the horizon when all the sky is heavy grey.

The footsteps and panting breath of Sosee sounded after a little while, and Sosee came in, a look of inquiry on her face. She was bare-footed. Her hair hung greasily behind her in a loosely plaited pigtail and she was not as tidily dressed as the day on which Dr Roy had paid his call. She wore no corsets and her fleshy belly protruded in a rather ungainly way. She was wiping her wet hands in the front of her dress and smelt of curry and Sunlight Soap. 'Ah been washing you' kerchiefs, man,' she said, with a heavy sigh of fatigue. 'You wan' lil' somet'ing to drink, na?'

'No,' said Big Man. He rested his pipe on the floor and jerked his thumb towards the bed. 'Sit down. I want to talk to you.'

'Oh!' she said, her manner becoming subdued at once, because she knew that whenever Big Man told her to sit down it meant that he was going to take her to task about something, and his way of taking her to task was not gentle. He used harsh words, and often handled her.

Even though he was still weak, she feared him.

She sank down clumsily on the edge of the bed and looked at him a little coweringly, as though waiting for the moment when his wrath would break over her like thunder from out the lowering sky.

44

As he continued to be silent for a long while, the suspense got too much for her and she asked: 'Is wha' wrong, Big Man?'

'Did I say anything was wrong?' He snapped the words out in a cold, rough tone, without looking at her, his eyes still fixed on the streaming windowpanes.

She was silent, hearing only the rain, and that deepened her fear.

After an interval, Big Man said: 'I've heard from Geoffry.'

'Oh! Yes. Ah did t'ink de handwriting did look like he-own when Ah tek de letter from de pos'-boy. 'E gettin' on good wid 'e school-work, Big Man?' She leaned forward as she asked the question, showing her gold teeth in a hesitant smile and trying to sound very amiable.

Big Man ignored the question. 'He says he's coming home for the Easter holidays day after tomorrow.'

'De Easter holidays? Oh-h-h! Yes. Holiday start, na?'

'He has written asking my permission to let him bring one of his school-friends to spend the holidays here. He asks me to wire him as soon as I receive his letter and say whether it will be convenient.'

'Oh-h-h-h!' said Sosee, staring at him foolishly.

'Bring me my writing-pad and fountain-pen.'

She rose as clumsily as she had sat down, making the springs creak loudly. She went to a small table in a corner of the room and from it brought his writing-pad and fountain-pen. He scribbled a few words on the pad, thrust both pad and pen back at her.

'Go at once and give that message to Joshua to take to the post office. It must go at once. I shall listen to hear the car start up.'

'Yes, Big Man.'

'And come back here within two minutes.'

'Yes, Big Man.'

She hurried out, her plump hips rotating ungracefully, and was back within a very short time.

'Sit down,' Big Man ordered her, and she sat down, breathing hard still from her exertions up and down the stairs. The bedsprings squealed so loudly under her that they might have been feeling the pain of hurt pigs.

'I haven't heard the car start up yet.'

But he had hardly spoken the words when a throbbing drone came up from under the house, making him grunt deeply, while the fierce frown on his face faded off slowly, though not completely. He stared at the window, while Sosee stared at him, waiting in anxiety for what more was to come.

At length, Big Man spoke. 'Sosee, you're keeping my house in a filthy condition. I've spoken to you about it before and I'm not going to continue speaking. The next thing I'm going to do is to kick you out of the bloody house and get someone who can keep the place clean and not like a damned pigsty.'

His words sounded very terrible, especially as he kept staring at the window as he spoke them. It always seemed more terrifying to Sosee when he spoke to her without looking at her. She would have preferred him to glare angrily at her. Even though his eyes would have burnt holes into her, she would have found this less frightening. There was something unearthly about the way he avoided looking at her in his wrath, something of the dark Unknown. It doubled her fear. She could say nothing.

'Geoffry and his friend are coming here day after tomorrow, and between now and then you're to have Geoffry's room as well as the spare room cobwebbed, dusted, scoured and thoroughly cleaned and tidied. I shall come in and inspect them myself, and God help you if it isn't properly done.'

'Yes, Big Man. Ah going do it good.'

'And the sitting room also is to be scoured, the furniture dusted and some of the chairs and tables neatly arranged on the front, back and side verandas. If I come down and find that room cluttered up as it generally is I'm going to kick you as you haven't been kicked before. And the dining table must have a clean cloth and all the glassware on the dinner-wagons washed and neatly put back.'

'Yes, Big Man.'

There followed an interval of silence, then Big Man barked: 'What are you waiting for? Get downstairs and begin at once! Send one of the servants for Bijoolie and Reynolds to give assistance, and make them understand that they are to come today – at once. I want to hear no excuses about the rain. Do you understand?'

'Yes, Big Man. Ah going sen' tell dem now.'

She went hurrying out, her bare feet making plump, slapping thumps on the floor; unpretty sounds.

9

Jannee's rice-fields had now been all planted up, so Beena did not have to go back any more with Jannee and his family. Instead, she assisted her father in driving the cows into pasture and in taking the milk-cans to the highway, as she had done before the rice-planting.

One morning, not many days after the rice-planting, the bus had just departed with the milk and Ramgolall was tucking away the five shillings and sixpence into his loincloth when Beena, happening to glance up the road, saw a donkey-cart coming towards them, moving east along the road, in the same direction as the bus.

'Jannee a-come!' she exclaimed.

'Eh-heh?' said Ramgolall, in an absent voice, for he was reckoning shillings in his mind to the beat of bony fingers against bony chest.

' 'E mus' be going a-Speyerfeld.'

'Eh-heh?'

'Me go wait ask 'e wha' 'e going a-Speyerfeld fo' dis time o' day.'

'Eh-heh. Awright, bettay,' nodded Ramgolall. And, moving off, he began to make his way slowly back along the mud-dam, the absent look still on his face, for he had not yet finished reckoning shillings in his mind.

Jannee came jogging leisurely up while Beena advanced a little way along the road to meet him.

'You a-go Speyerfeld, Jannee?'

'Eh-heh,' smiled Jannee, bringing the cart to a stop. 'You wan' go dah side, too?'

'Na. Me go tek walk deh af'noon time.'

'Oh-h-h! Me can gi' you drop now if you want.'

'Wha' me got do deh now?'

47

'Come wid me keep me company.'

Beena hesitated for a moment, then said: 'Awright. Me na got nutting partic'lar do now. Kattree a-ketch fish in Long Canal. Mullet plenty now rain a-fall.'

'Eh-heh. Sukra ketch nuff-nuff yesterday.'

As Beena drew herself up beside him in the cart, she felt the warmth of living quicken her blood. Whenever she found herself with Jannee she knew that life was good to live. Bright sunlight with blue sky, or dim sunlight and thick white clouds as now, or if it drizzled thinly or rained from a hanging sky of grey, if there were pale moonlight like the moonlight to come next week, it made naught to Beena, so long as Jannee was there. But this love-secret none knew but herself. Deep in his instinct Jannee heard it as an unquiet murmuring, but his mind was blank to it, for Beena took every care not to reveal it – even by a look. Whenever with him, she talked casually and treated him as a planter of rice and the husband of Sukra, the father of Boodoo and Chattee. If Sukra and the two boys were also present she gave nearly all her attention to the two boys or to Sukra, making fun and talking lightly or seriously about the practical things in their everyday lives.

She said to Jannee now: 'Tomorrow dis time we a-mek big prepare fo' de feed-up.'

Jannee grunted nasally in assent. 'Me hope rain na fall plenty. Me wan' borrow Bijoolie' drum, but if rain fall plenty 'e na go wan' len' me am.'

'Ow! Bijoolie so partic'lar wid 'e drum, na!'

'So he stan'. 'E frighten rain go spoil de drum-skin. 'E t'ink nobody na got drum like he-own.'

Tomorrow night, the moon being new, was the time of the fortnightly curry-feed. At full moon the feed had been held at Ramgolall's home, so now at new moon it would be held at Jannee's, this being always the way of arrangement, for Ramgolall was full in years while Jannee was new in years. The glow of life in Ramgolall, as the days went by, would wane and wane, but the gleam of life in Jannee would wax until the fullness of the glow.

The cart jogged slowly onward along the red road, the wheels crunched on the burnt earth. Through a gap in the sky of ragged woollen clouds the sun shone palely on them, while the wind blew in long, faint puffs, warm and damp and a little stifling. On the northern side of the road the wide canal of muddy water was waved like the back of an alligator, and one could smell the Corentyne rankness of it, the odour of fish and sherriga crabs, of mud and dead wild plants.

But slow as was their progress, Beena did not find the three miles to Speyerfeld tedious, nor did Jannee, for Jannee and Beena always found much of which to speak; little things but great in worth; for though the light of the moon is brighter than the light of a star, how many times bigger is not a star than the moon?

Beena spoke of the songs she would sing tomorrow night and those Kattree would sing, and Jannee said that he was learning a new one from Bijoolie. Bijoolie knew many songs and had great love for music. He was the best drum beater on the Corentyne, being also a good player of the sitar and the serangee.

Jannee spoke, too, of the mutton for tomorrow night's feed and said that he would order it from the Speyerfeld Estate Butchery and not from Balgobin, because the last time Balgobin had not sold them a good piece. Balgobin's trade was widening and so he thought he could sell poor people any sort of meat, while for the rich people he reserved all the best cuts.

Beena agreed, and said that she would not buy meat from him again. She would tell Kattree, too, not to buy from him, though Kattree often liked to have her own way in spite of what anyone told her.

The two tall brick chimneys of Speyerfeld sugar-factory grew gradually taller in the lessening distance. Through the jolting of the cart they seemed to waver faintly against the heap of grey-white clouds in the low south-east, as though they might be huge guns of unreckoned age trained upon Eternity. Thin black smoke drifted from their tops like a thunder-cloud gathering to be born but dying in a sad brume. Far away, in the south and the south-east, the pale green cane-fields could be seen, befogged by distance and the remnants of a blue morning mist, and looking very aloof and elusive like a rug in Fairyland made of rain and the broken fragments of clear green bottles.

The urgent tooting of a car's horn sounded far behind them,

and Jannee guided the cart to the left side of the road, close to the edge of the canal, for the road was very narrow. The car turned out to be a green bus, and it passed them with a tin-like rattle and a rough grating drone, leaving dust and the stink of petrol behind it. They could see the lettering of its name painted on the back and coated now with red dust. The name was *Claudette Colbert*, though Beena and Jannee could not tell this from the lettering, not being able to read. They recognized it by its colour and shape, however, and Beena smiled and said: 'You' frien' deh inside *Claudette Colbert*.'

'*Me* frien'? Wha' frien' dah?' asked Jannee.

'Boorharry,' chuckled Beena. 'Me see 'e in de front row. 'E mus' be bin to town.'

Jannee frowned and sucked his teeth, uttering a deep ominous sound. 'One o' dese days me an' he going come to grip. Yesterday me pass hospital gate an' 'e shout out provoke me. Me na say nutten. Me waitin' good. One o' dese day 'e go provoke me bad an' me go bus' 'e tail.'

Beena laughed. 'Is wha' you bodder wid 'e fo'? Boorharry na right in 'e head. You musn' bodder wid 'e.'

Jannee grunted again – ominously. 'If 'e head na right 'e mus' keep am to 'eself. Na bring am to me. He's a fool. Me go put 'e in 'e place good-good one o' dese days. You wait, see.'

'Is wha' 'e provoke you say yesterday?'

'Some stupid talk. 'E call me Jannee – pannee – chimpanzee. Leh 'e go on wid me. 'E na know me in true. Me don' mek too much sport.'

Beena laughed. 'Is wha' is chimpanzee?'

Jannee shrugged. 'Me know? Some stupidness.' He grunted. 'Leh 'e go on wid me.' And he grunted yet again, frowning ahead at the brick chimneys of Speyerfeld that wavered against the clouds like guns trained upon Eternity. He saw the thin black smoke drifting from their tops and looking like a thunder-cloud gathering to be born.

10

After Big Man Weldon had lumbered slowly round on his tour of inspection, he grunted to himself, feeling satisfied that Sosee had had the place tidied and rearranged in keeping with his instructions. He did not tell her so, however. He never complimented her on anything because he considered compliments bad in their effect upon her. Praise of any kind made her grow slack, and Big Man deemed her slack enough as things stood.

On the day when Geoffry and his school friend were expected, Big Man attired himself in clean khaki shorts and shirt, in grey stockings and heavy brown shoes, this being his outdoor garb. But he did not go out. He only came down from his room in order that he might direct, in person, the preparations for Geoffry's arrival.

On the day before, he had given orders to Sosee what to cook for breakfast (the midday meal), because the boys were expected at one o'clock and would need breakfast, and Big Man was determined that they should have the best of good things to eat. He had ordered Sosee to kill three chickens and a sheep – the chickens for breakfast and the sheep for dinner – and he had himself written out and sent off an order to the grocers for tinned fruit, ham, cheese, butter, aerated drinks and cider, cabbage and jams, toffees, nuts and milk chocolate.

He had arranged for double the quantity of ice usually supplied to him by the ice-dealers in New Amsterdam and he had ordered a new ice-cream churner, a larger one than the one already in the house.

Indeed, Big Man felt great love and pride for his son Geoffry. Pondering the things of his life, as he sometimes did when smoking his pipe on the back veranda of an evening, Big Man Weldon felt that Geoffry was the only magic symbol that the world contained for him. The yellow glamour of money, the pink glamour of Sosee, had years ago faded into the grey of commonplace reality. Money, to him now, meant only the crude power to obtain things – food, clothes and comforts. The thought of it no more made his heart throb. It was a background of material solidity – something taken for granted, and, thus, unsatisfying, unexciting. And Sosee, Sosee was only the plump, lazy mother of his children. For her he felt apathy, or disgust, or anger. But Geoffry, Geoffry glowed with a green young glamour. He was the symbol of hope, of a new Big Man, of a mightier Big Man, perhaps. When Big Man thought of him a glow formed around his heart, as though warm nectar were oozing from out the core of his soul; he felt the interest and excitement that years ago he had felt when engaged in amassing money and in making love to Sosee.

The rest of the children did not interest him very much. David, who came after Geoffry and was sixteen, gave no promise at all. He lacked brain-power and still attended the elementary school in the village with the younger children. Moreover, he was thin and sickly, being often ill with a cold or a cough. The twins, Dora and Belle, though pretty at fifteen, resembled their mother too much to please Big Man. Even in their ways and habits they seemed to be growing like their mother. John, thirteen, might develop like Geoffry – he took an interest in lessons – but Big Man deemed him too young and sportive to be thought of yet as a future Big Man. The two younger children, Elsie and James, ten and nine, Big Man dismissed as makers of noise and disorder, nuisances to be scolded, whipped or petted.

Today, when Geoffry was coming home for the Easter vacation, Big Man felt the magic of life quickening the beats of his heart, even while it flooded his veins with the lethargic fluid of content.

The large maroon Vauxhall car, driven by Joshua, the chauffeur, left for New Amsterdam at eleven o'clock to meet the small steamer that conveyed passengers over from the train terminus on the western bank of the Berbice River, and the time was five minutes past one by the clock in the dining room when Big Man stood on the front veranda and watched the car, on its return trip, approach along the grass track. He had to squint his eyes, for the glare of the day was white and trembling, painful to the head as well as to the eyes.

The car, however, soon droned to a standstill near the foot of the enclosed stairway (enclosed with latticework), and Geoffry and his friend came up to the veranda with muffled thumps made by their rubber-soled shoes on the treaders.

Even though only eighteen, Geoffry was already as tall as Big Man, though slimmer in build. He had Sosee's dark eyes and dark eyebrows, but Big Man's Roman nose and square jaw. His mouth, however, had a humorous curve at the corner (and his eyes an ironic twinkle) that neither Big Man nor Sosee had. He had power, a deep, tight-locked power that, one felt, might make a terrible whirl of damage, like a cyclone, if unlocked without warning. Seeing him, one thought of a coppery sky and a dead, smooth sea – the China Sea of Conrad – and a falling barometer.

His friend was swarthy-skinned: deep olive. He was coloured; that is, of mixed bloods: white, black and perhaps even Indian. His hair was curly and rather closely cut. He was shorter than Geoffry by half a head, with thin and rather gawky limbs. He had a very learned head: broad, domed forehead, heavy eyebrows, bat ears, and he wore American horn-rimmed spectacles that made him look even more learned than he might have done without them. He had a shy, boy-like smile, and, on the whole, a very taking manner.

'Hallo, Dad!' said Geoffry, and he and Big Man gripped hands very tightly. A strong young hand and a strong old hand. 'This is Baxter Menges. We call him Stymphy – short for Stymphalian.'

'How do you do?' smiled Stymphy shyly, and Big Man shook hands with him, welcoming him in a deep, hearty manner like the sound of his voice.

Then, all at once, Sosee came out in a gush from the sitting room, wearing a pink dress of silk, many gold necklaces and bangles, her face white with powder and her whole plump body reeking of a pungent perfume. 'Eh-eh! Geoffry! How you do, na, boy?'

'Hallo, Mother!' smiled Geoffry, and a carmine colour came to his cheeks as he kissed her. 'This is Baxter Menges, my good pal.'

'Pleased to meet you,' said Sosee, taking Stymphy's hand and continuing to show her gold teeth, and Stymphy smiled and said: 'How do you do?' very boy-like, but very refined. He shook Sosee's fat hand heartily.

'All-you wan' wash-up now, eh? Ah got de bat'room ready. Come up straight away. You mus' mek you'self home, boy,' she smiled at Stymphy. 'We ain' got too much fuss-fuss here, you know.'

'Oh, thank you,' smiled Stymphy.

'Geoffry, you must show him to his room,' said Big Man. 'I've had the spare room prepared.'

'You prepared the spare room!' said Geoffry in some dismay. 'Why, you shouldn't have bothered. We could have lumped it together in my room. That old bed is big enough to hold six of us.'

'I hadn't thought of that,' rumbled Big Man, frowning heavily and shifting about with slight discomfort. But Geoffry hurried on to say: 'Oh, but it doesn't matter, Dad. No harm if we each have a room. When I get fed up with mine I can go into Stymphy's, and vice versa. How say, Stymphy?'

'Oh, I don't mind a bit.'

Big Man suddenly guffawed, his eyes twinkling at them. He clapped them both on the back and said: 'All right. Run upstairs and take a quick shower and come down and have something to eat. You ought to be starving by now.'

'I can eat a rhinoceros, two pterodactyls and a – and a – what's that other thing, Stymphy?'

'A plesiosaurus.'

'And a plesiosaurus. That's the beast. Slipped me for the mo.'

When they were passing through the sitting room Stymphy looked around very critically. 'Not so dusty,' he murmured. 'If there'd only been one or two ancestral portraits instead of those pictures it would almost have had a stately old manorish look.'

'This barn a stately old manor? Not in my wildest, Stymphs. Not even if the walls were lined with Vandyke and Rembrandts. I can't somehow see this place in a romantic light. I like it because I grew up in it, but...' He made a wry face and shook his head.

'I could weave heaps and heaps of romantic things around it. All these doors. And the veranda going right round. The wind rushing through, and the smell of the savannah. Oh, heaps!'

'Yes, but you're poetical. All that sort of thing would appeal to you. But I...' He made a wry face, looking baffled, and shook his head.

'You're a materialist, I suppose you want to say. You only think you are. At heart, you've got plenty of imagination and poetry in you – only you like to go stifling it like a silly jackanapes.'

Big Man, following them far behind, overheard the vital part of their conversation, and he smiled to himself, but to his heart there came an uneven little throbbing fear, a fear that might have come with the droning wind through the northern door, borne from the rippled canal near the public road, or from the far seashore fringe…or even from the black chimneys of Speyerfeld which he could see, like tiny prongs pointing upward on the brink of the east. He turned off with a faint grunt.

11

Save for a brief, drifting shower at about four in the afternoon, the weather turned out fine and dry for the curry-feed. At six o'clock, when Ramgolall and Beena were driving home the cows, the sky had taken on a soft, mauve tint patterned with a curtain of cirri that trailed over the dome-like phantom fronds of a dead palm. Low breeze came weakly across the savannah, seeming as though it were breathed from an organ playing a dirge in the dank twilight of the far-off courida trees.

As soon as the cows had been safely penned for the night, Ramgolall and his two daughters set out for Jannee's home, all three of them in very good spirits, Beena intoning a tune and Kattree nodding her head in time. Kattree carried the goatskin tom-tom. Ramgolall carried his thin, shiny cowstick, for it was of help to him in walking over those parts of the savannah made rough and uneven by the hoofs of the cows. When rain fell and the earth was soft, the cows made deep holes with their hoofs, and then the sun dried the earth and left the holes hard and treacherous: half-dried holes, some, and slippery, with caked cow-dung, pungent in smell, and short, sharp-bladed grass to tickle the feet… And if it were morning, perhaps far off in the blue mist, the cooing moan of a conch-shell, the fisherman's horn, would come soothingly to the hearing, making the rough savannah at once seem filled with a friendly magic, so that even the cow-holes and the tickling grass became tinted with Corentyne glamour…

Beena wore her one clean dress, and so did Kattree. Beena's dress was of pink-striped cloth and Kattree's of green. Kattree had put up her hair in piled knots, but Beena allowed hers to hang behind her back in two long plaits. (Jannee, Beena felt, would prefer to see her hair in smooth, shiny plaits.)

They walked south to the public road and then turned west, for Jannee lived in that direction. And now the afterglow of sunset fell full upon their faces, a dull orange light, the glare of many woollen clouds piled low down along the dark, ragged horizon. It made Kattree's face more dreaming, dreaming like the clouds themselves which seemed like minarets of tarnished gold wafted into being by a genie. Beena had stopped intoning and was talking of trivial things with her father, for her spirit grew lighter and lighter as they drew nearer to Jannee's home. Kattree, therefore, walked in the silence of herself, dreaming like the clouds that now had changed in hue from orange to brown.

To the right of them the canal flowed with calm, telling nothing of what it knew of the rainstorms and the high winds, and the droughts of years gone by, of the stench of dead cows and the thunder of purple clouds. Only now and then a sherriga would scramble to the surface and claw redly at the air, so that two bubbles made a tinkling gurgle and sent ripples hooping wider and wider into the nothing of the mirrored sky.

They must have reached within a hundred yards of Jannee's cottage when a loud hail came behind them. 'Hup, hup!' went the hail, and Beena laughed and Kattree smiled, and they all looked round, knowing well that only one person could have uttered that hail – the one person who came towards them on a bicycle, pedalling with ease, attired in his white dhoti and turban, his handsome, full-bearded face all alight with good cheer, his eyes crackling youthfully despite his patriarchal beard. 'Hup, hup!' he hailed again. 'Harry Lall Boorharry ahoy! Wait for Harry Lall Boorharry!'

His voice rang on the air and compelled them to stop and wait for him. As he approached he released both handles and waved his arms in wide arcs around his head, keeping perfect balance the while and shouting 'Hup, hup!' in his loud, cheerful way that made everyone who heard him laugh and like him.

He dismounted with an elaborate swing and hop, and shot out his arm in a Roman salute. Then he said: 'Bettay, bettay,' and at each 'Bettay' he chucked Beena and Kattree, in turn, under their chins and then tapped Ramgolall on top of his white head, doing it all so quickly that if even they had wanted to avoid it they could not. 'Taking walk by evening? Beena bettay, Kattree bettay. Where all-you going dis time evening?'

'We got curry-feed a-Jannee,' smiled Beena.

'Hey! Curry-feed a-Jannee! Jannee – pannee – chimpanzee. Hoy! Come, Beena bettay. Get on de bar lemme tek you de rest o' de way!'

'Na-a-a-a,' laughed Beena, retreating a pace. 'Me go walk. Me prefer walk.'

'Hoy! Walk! No! Beena bettay! Come, bettay! Harry Lall Boorharry tek you to Jannee! Hup, hup!' And he gripped her arm while she protested: 'But is wha' wrong wid you, Boorharry? Me wan' walk – '

'Hup, hup Beena bettay! Up she come. Lil' coolie woollie gal!' And he helped her up to the crossbar in spite of her giggling protests and her half-hearted efforts to resist him.

'But, Boorharry, me tell you – '

'Hup! Hoy! Beena bettay gone! Hup, hup!'

And with a running jump, he was on the saddle and pedalling away fast along the road towards Jannee's home, Beena laughing and resigning herself to the trip. 'Hup, hup!' went Boorharry. 'Beena bettay! Teena bettay! Hoy-poloy!' Boorharry hunched his shoulders up and down in rhythm with his words, ringing the bicycle-bell, too, a large bell that made a rich, tinkling jangle.

Beena gurgled and giggled in great mirth, liking Boorharry more than ever, but feeling dimly afraid in the back of her mind, because she knew that Jannee did not like Boorharry. Jannee would frown when he saw her being towed by Boorharry.

Ah! Her heart started within her. There stood Jannee at the side of the road awaiting their coming. Perhaps he would not want to speak to her for the whole evening. 'Boorharry, wha' wrong wid you? Why you na put me down? Put me down here, na?'

But instead of putting her down, he stroked her head playfully and broke into a wild song at the top of his voice, a song partly in

English and partly in Hindi and without any meaning whatever. 'Bee-eena! Beena-a-a-a bettay-y-y-y!' So one part of the song went, and then it plunged into Hindi, with a word or two of English in between. Then again: 'Beena-a-a! Beena-a-a-a bettay-y-y-y! Beena bettay riding wid Harry-y-y-y! Harry Lall Boorharry-y-y-y! Hup, hup, holoy! Beena, teena! Jannee – pannee – chimpanzee! Hup, hup, holoy! Hup, hup, holoy!'

Then he dismounted with a great hop right before Jannee and gave Jannee the Roman salute. 'Harry Lall Boorharry bring Beena bettay to Jannee' curry-feed!' And Beena, giggling and gurgling in mirth, lowered herself to the road, looking the while, however, in anxiety at Jannee who was smiling faintly, in silence, the queer smile he always smiled when Boorharry was present with his foolery.

'Boorharry, is why you so stupid, na?' laughed Beena. She looked quickly from Boorharry to Jannee and added: ' 'E say 'e mus' bring me here, Jannee. 'E meet we coming yonder. Wheh Sukra?'

'She deh behin' de house mekin' roti,' said Jannee, still smiling his queer smile.

'Sukra making roti!' exclaimed Boorharry, loosing hold of his bicycle, raising his arms aloft and then dropping them quickly to hold the bicycle again before it fell. 'Hip-hurrah! Sukra making roti! Boorharry want some o' Sukra roti! Sukra!' bawled Boorharry. 'Sukra gal! Wheh you deh?'

'Ay-y-y!' came the answering voice of Sukra near Jannee's mud-house. 'Boorharry! Me making roti, man! Me busy too!'

'Hup, holoy! Sukra making roti! You go keep piece roti fo' me, Sukra gal?'

'Yes! Eh-heh! Me go keep piece fo' you, Boorharry!' laughed Sukra. 'Tomorrow me go sen' am gi' you! Two big-big piece!'

'Hup, hup! Sukra good gal! Hup, holoy! Tomorrow morning Boorharry look out for Sukra' roti!' He waved at Jannee and Beena in wide, windmill sweeps of his arms, then bowed swiftly, sprang on his bicycle with a great comical hop and went pedalling off along the road, making queer, wriggling motions with his shoulders the while and shouting 'Hup, hup!' all the time. 'Hup, hup, holoy!'

12

Kattree and Ramgolall came up not half a minute after Boorharry had ridden off. Kattree was smiling. 'Boorharry a-mek noise again, eh? Me never see big joke-man like he in all me life. Eh-h-h-h!'

Jannee grunted. 'One o' dese days 'e go mek too much noise,' he said, and his voice sounded low and deep like the anvil of slate-grey cloud in the west, for the dreaming brown had changed to slate-grey and overhead a star or two had begun to wink palely through the cirri fronds. Beena gave a brief laugh, fidgeting, Kattree was silent and Ramgolall smiled, wagged his head and remarked that Boorharry had nothing but play in his head. 'From lil' boy so high, Boorharry always mek play.' He grunted as the memory of the past ran through his mind. 'Lil' boy so high, Harry Lall Boorharry. Always play-play. From morning to night. Good boy, Harry. Mmmm.'

They crossed over the deep ditch on the southern side of the road, walking on the one shaky board that served as a bridge. They found Sukra squatting near the mud-oven behind Jannee's home-stead. Sukra was busy making roti. Her hands were white with flour. She looked up and hailed them with a smile, and Beena smiled back and said: 'Ow! You busy, na, gal? Wheh Boodoo an' Chattee? Sleepin' already?'

'Boodoo gone a-fetch water. Chattee asleep.'

'Chattee like sleep too much. ''E tek after 'e faddah.'

'You hear me like sleep plenty?' said Jannee.

'You like sleep plenty, yes,' Beena laughed. She was self-conscious and still a little uneasy, for though Jannee had spoken to her in his usual way, she did not like the look in his eyes and the way he smiled. It made her feel like a dark night with herself alone on the public road and the 'Who-you?' cries of the goat-suckers making her glance about quickly for danger. It made her feel afraid, as though she were sitting beside a sick person and the jumbie-bird laughed dryly in the bleak gloom outside, showing that death was near.

'Is wheh you-all meet Boorharry?' asked Sukra casually, without looking up from her task of kneading.

''E ride up behin' we,' replied Beena quickly, and began to chant part of a song, for she did not want the talk to return to Boorharry. 'You learn you' new song good, Jannee?'

'Eh? Wha' new song dah?'

'De one you say Bijoolie bin a-learn you.'

'Oh! Eh-heh. Me go sing am fo' all-you.'

'Sing am now lemme hear how 'e go.'

'Na. Me na in mood fo' sing now. Me wan' smoke lil' bit.'

'Me wonder if Boorharry' cow drop,' said Sukra. ''E promise gimme am if 'e turn out bull-calf.'

Kattree laughed. 'You gi' 'e roti an' leh 'e gi' you bull-calf in exchange.'

'You right, gal. Good exchange. Me going keep piece roti fo' 'e, in trut'.'

Beena chanted her song again, walking around restlessly and feigning to be interested in Sukra's roti-making. Now and then she would look quickly at Jannee. Jannee was squatting on the ground near the wall of the mud-house. He was slowly filling his clay-pipe with ganja. Very dark he seemed to Beena in the gathering twilight, like the sound of the wind in a star apple tree. He seemed alone now and she felt alone, too. A queer panic came into her throat so that she sang faster and jerkily and then stopped altogether and sank down suddenly beside Sukra. 'You wan' me help you, gal? Wheh de mutton? It done cook?'

'Long time. Pour out lil' water, hand me. Look how Boodoo spill am down deh. Oh, gawd! Dah boy careless! 'E want proper licks!'

Out of the corner of her eye, as she dipped a tin cup into the bucket of water near by, Beena saw Jannee get up and go into the mud-house. She exclaimed: 'Ow! Dis water got lil'-lil' fish, Sukra! Boodoo mus' be dip am from Big Canal.'

'All-same water. Wha' diff'rence?'

Beena laughed. 'Dem lil' fish mek good meal, na? Cook dem good, gal.'

He was coming out again. He carried an oil-lamp with a clouded glass shade. He rested it on the ground. It nearly toppled over, but he steadied it, shifting it along the earth until he found a level spot where it stood still so that he could light it. He poked at the wick with a little stick, then lit it and lowered the shade with a clicking sound that made her feel hollow in her chest, as though an insect had droned in there and stopped abruptly, leaving behind the tingle of the droning. Anything might happen now. Her heart seemed waiting to stop beating.

'Me na t'ink rain go fall tonight. Wind a-blow lil' bit since dark begin fall.'

He was lighting the pipe now, and puffing...

Ramgolall, who was squatting under the solitary mango tree some twenty yards from the mud-house, began to beat the tom-tom and chant in a low voice, and Kattree who sat beside him, with legs stretched out and Boodoo in her lap, joined him in the chant, patting Boodoo's back in time. Tum-tum-tum, went the tom-tom. Tum-tum – and the sounds went far into the deepening gloom, so that Geoffry Weldon and Baxter Menges, cycling home along the public road, heard them. Baxter tilted his head keenly and said: 'Hear that? Drums. Tadja drums.'

Geoffry gave a sniffing chuckle. 'Tadja drums the deuce! Those aren't any tadja drums, you ass. This isn't tadja season.'

'Well, they're drums anyway. And dashed poetic too. Hear them? Tum-tum. Tum-tum-tum. Something dark-green and macabre about them, you know. Sort of *fantastique*. Like a dance of twilight-ghouls.'

'Oh, you want a dose of salts, Stymphy. Twilight-ghouls. Twilight-ghouls my aunt. Wish we had a few fishes in our bag to show for our half-day's labour. They're going to laugh at us no end when we get home. Fishing from one o'clock to sunset and not even a sherriga to show for our patience.'

'The fish must be on holiday, too,' chuckled Stymphy. 'We had a great day, anyway. A real Corentyne day. Heat and blue sky; mud and water and savannah.'

'Why have you left out the cow dung?'

'And the cow dung, too. Sorry, but hear those drums, Geoff! There's something mysterious in them, you know. Dark and menacing. Where d'you think they're coming from?'

'Somewhere over there – near that mud-house. I like to hear

them at dead of night when I'm in bed. That's when they sound really poetic and impressive.'

'Tomorrow we should go and pay a call on some of these folk, you know. I've never seen the inside of a mud-house. I'd like to capture the atmosphere.'

'I wouldn't. Sure to be bally smelly.'

'Don't get into one of your cynical phases again, for goodness' sake. You know very well I don't mean that kind of atmosphere. When I say "atmosphere" I mean the local colour of the place, the spirit and all that sort of thing.'

'You're not trying to tell me you think the inside of a coolie mud-house would inspire you to write a great poem?'

'And why not? It's simple settings like that which contain the deepest things in this life.'

Geoffry grunted cynically and began to whistle, pedalling harder. 'Front tyre soft as hell,' said Stymphy, pedalling harder, too.

'Mine both want a little pumping.'

Behind them the sound of Ramgolall's tom-tom continued, a low, flat throb in the deepening gloom, a sound that, now and then, got tangled with the cool wind droning past their ears.

13

Jannee's sombre mood got better as the evening grew older. He sang songs and beat the drum that he had borrowed from Bijoolie.

Beena was well pleased to see him in this mood. She felt more at ease now. All the panic left her as though it were blue-grey heat-clouds from the south-east threatening lightning and thunder, but drifting off instead, in slow dignity, to the north-west. She glanced towards the north-west as if really expecting to see the clouds there. Her heart seemed to turn over in her with a kind of trembling joy. She felt happy again in her love for him. She sang now not jerkily, but in a full, steady voice.

And meanwhile Sukra served out the curried mutton and rice and the roti into tin plates that were still greasy from the last meal. She took two discs of roti and folded them over carefully, then wrapped them in a piece of brown paper and put the parcel in her bosom, looking round to see that no one was observing her, for she knew that Jannee would be angry if he knew that she really meant to keep roti for Boorharry as she had promised, in joke, to do. He would strike her hard or kick her if he found out. Sometimes she wished it was Boorharry who was married to her and not Jannee. Jannee was nice, but many things he had not that Boorharry had. Boorharry could ride a bicycle. Jannee could not. Boorharry could read and write English. Jannee could not. And look how many women Boorharry made love to and won. He must be good at making Jove. If she, Sukra, could win him and keep him it would be a great thing for her. Other women would have to respect her and admit that she had done something they could not do… Oh, but it was so stupid of her to go thinking a thing like that. Jannee was her husband, and Boorharry could never have her. Even now she was big with Jannee's child. Boorharry would not want a woman big with child. All the same, she still liked him a great deal and tomorrow when she went to Speyerfeld she would give him the roti and talk to him for a while at the gate of the hospital. It would be nice to hear his jokes. He always made you laugh so much with his antics and shouts and the things he said. And his eyes looked at you and flashed in such a way. It made you feel all warm and trembly inside.

She smiled to herself in the dark. (Her back was to the lamp as she crouched there.) The curry smelt so nice. If only she could keep some for Boorharry. Perhaps he really would give her the calf if it turned out to be a bull-calf.

Behind her the drums were beating fast, prattling loud and long, louder and longer, faster and faster and faster. She felt a little excited.

14

Big Man Weldon sat at one end of the long dining table and Sosee at the other. Big Man wore a heavy brown tweed suit that gave him an even more mighty and sturdy look than when he wore lighter clothing. Sosee wore a bright green silk dress, and her bare arms gleamed and jangled with bracelets while her hands flashed with the jewels of many rings. On her bosom sparkled a necklace of fake emeralds that Big Man had given her in the days when, as a young man, he used to steal her away from her father's home to take her for motorcar drives.

All the children were present, the younger ones and the girls being dressed in their best clothes. Geoffry sat to the right of his father, on one side of the table, while Stymphy sat to the left, on the other side, directly opposite to Geoffry. This was Big Man's arrangement. Dora, who was fifteen, sat next to Stymphy and kept smiling as though well pleased with everything around her, while Belle, her twin sister, sitting next to her, looked sulky. Earlier in the evening there had been a secret argument between Dora and Belle as to which of the two should sit next to Stymphy at dinner tonight, and Dora had had her way by sheer force of will. (Since the arrival of Geoffry and Stymphy a day or two ago, Dora and Belle had decided that Stymphy was a nice boy and worth falling in love with, so they had both fallen in love with him and were now deadly rivals for his favour.)

Elsie sat next to Geoffry, with John next to her. She had always been Geoffry's favourite. She had Big Man's yellow-brown hair, but her blue eyes were her own. Geoffry was fond of stroking her hair and kissing her smooth olive cheek.

Taking his ochra soup, Big Man looked very content – content and proud. Now and then a faint smile would twist his lips as he glanced from side to side. Very solid they all seemed, these children. So alive. Seven of them. Young humans. It was good to know that one was responsible for their existence. It gave one a feeling of power. It made one conscious of the baffling force of life in one and about one. Even a little frightening in a way.

Of a sudden, James, sitting at Sosee's left, made a sucking noise with his soup. Big Man frowned and thundered: 'Jim! *Jim!* Haven't I told you a hundred times before that you must not make a noise when you're drinking soup?'

'I didn' mean to do it, Pa,' said Jim, going red all over.

Elsie and John giggled and Jim scowled and asked them: 'Well, wha' you laughin' at?'

'Phew!' whistled Geoffry, looking pained. '"Well, wha' you

laughin' at?" Heaven paint us red! What sort of English is that, Jim?'

'Oh, you go an' hide you' face,' Jim grumbled. 'What you know 'bout English at all?'

'No, no no,' rebuked Big Man, frowning at Jim. 'Your brother is quite right to correct you. Your English is putrid. You mix too much with those confounded coolie boys around the place. Bad influence. Better see less of them in future.'

Jim sucked his teeth and looked gloomy.

'Geoff, can I come fishing with you and Stymphy tomorrow?' Dora suddenly asked.

'No, we don't want any followers, thanks.'

'But I can show you where to get plenty fish. I know a good pond at Nairnley,' said Dora.

'You don't say you do?'

'You needn't be sarcastic. If I want to come you can't stop me. Stymphy, would you like me to come fishing with you all?'

'Why, certainly. By all means,' said Stymphy, who had not yet found out that he was a young man beloved of the twins. 'Let her come with us, Geoff. She can act as our guide and lead us to the good pond at Nairnley.'

'Lead us into the canal, you mean. No thank you. You just stay at home, miss. A pity that school in the village can't have special vacation sessions for the six of you. I must drop the headteacher a note.'

'Oh, you're a fool. I am coming with you all. As long as Stymphy says I can come I'm coming.'

'Sufficient unto the day is the ochra soup thereof.'

'You must try to be clever, eh?'

'Ow! All-you na row!' Sosee cut in suddenly. 'If de gurl want to go wid you-all tomorrow leh she go, na, Geoffry. Is wha'? You hate gurl-company?'

Geoffry made a sound of impatience and lowered his spoon to his plate with a clatter. '*That* settles it finally now. She's not coming with us. I say she's not coming and she's not coming.'

'You can't stop me from coming!' flared Dora.

'Hey! Hey!' barked Big Man. 'That will do now, Dora. That will do. No wrangling at table, please. If your brother doesn't want you to accompany him on this fishing expedition you can't go, that's all. After all, they're boys. They would want their own company.'

Dora mumbled something and grew silent.

Belle giggled, and Jim, across the table, made a long nose and said: 'Meh-h-h-h!' like a sheep.

After that there fell a silence among them, and only the faint clatter of spoons could be heard – and the wind droning in at the windows and at the doors of the sitting room. Then the wind died to a low hum and the throbbing beat of the Petter engine outside that supplied the house with electric current came to the ear... Something crackled in the sitting room, softly, and David glanced with fear into the room, growing rigid. David was a 'queer' boy. He could see jumbies. He had often seen them. He was born that way, an old black woman once told Sosee. And it was true. Over and over he had seen things. Only a month ago he had seen, in broad daylight, a strange old gentleman sitting in a rocking chair on the back veranda. He had called Dora and pointed, asking her who that gentleman was sitting there, and Dora had frowned and replied that she could see no one sitting there. Only then did David know that the gentleman was not of the earth. He had screamed and turned away and fled to his mother, trembling all over.

The wind fell to nothing, and during the calm one could hear another sound besides the throb of the Petter engine: the faint prattling of far-away drums – the drums of Jannee and Ramgolall. Corentyne drums from over the savannah.

Stymphy tilted his head abruptly, listening. 'Those drums,' he smiled, glancing at Geoffry. 'Hear them again?'

'Still goofy about them, Stymphs?' grinned Geoffry. 'Forget the bally drums.'

'I know where they're coming from,' said Dora.

'You do?' Stymphy looked at her in mild inquiry.

She went a little pink under his gaze, feeling suddenly shy. 'Yes. They're at Jannee's place. They're having a curry-feed there. Jannee and Ramgolall and Beena and Kattree.'

'Oh, but I say! You seem to know one or two things. Who is Jannee? And Ramgolall and – and the others?'

Ramgolall is our grandfather – mother's father, and Kattree and Beena are our aunts.'

'Our half-aunts,' corrected David.

'Oh, well, what does it matter, stupid?'

'There is a difference. Mother is only a half-sister to Beena and Kattree – '

'Ow! All-you stop all dah family talk, na?' said Sosee, uncomfortably. 'We na wan' hear 'bout Beena an' Kattree. Beena an' Kattree not on your level of sociology.'

'"Sociologity"! Holy sherrigas!' Geoffry whistled and looked at the ceiling.

'I'm not a snob, anyway,' Dora replied to her mother. 'If they're my aunts I don't see why I shouldn't talk of them.'

'I talk *to* them,' cut in Elsie. 'Last week I met Beena and Jannee in the village and I spoke to them and they gave me a ride in their donkey-cart.'

'What! Elsie, an' Ah always tellin' you not to have anyt'ing to do wid dem? You go on. De nex' time you talk to dem an' Ah hear 'bout it Ah going flog you good. You wait,' threatened Sosee.

'That would be rather a silly thing to do,' said Geoffry. 'Why should we disown our relatives? I think it's about time we stopped all that ridiculous snobbery. I've met Beena and Kattree once or twice and I think they're pretty good sorts. Not exactly A1 so far as culture and refinement go, I'll admit, but they're friendly and simple – especially Beena. Kattree is a bit quiet and reserved.'

'Oh, they're a common, dirty lot,' said Belle abruptly. 'I certainly won't have anything to do with them.'

'Nobody asked for your opinion,' snapped Dora. 'Your opinion doesn't count.'

'You can't prevent me from giving it if I want to give it. Who are you at all?'

Big Man threw back his head and guffawed. 'See what a happy family I have, my boy?' he said to Stymphy. 'Snapping at each other all the time. All the time.'

'My sisters and brothers behave just the same,' smiled Stymphy. 'They're always rowing over something or the other. They even fight sometimes.'

And then followed another lull in the talk, and in the lull one heard the wind again, droning and then growing quiet, and the beat of the Petter engine, and then once more the animated thudding of the tom-toms from far over the savannah, faint and only barely audible, coming now in soft, padding booms, now flatly and with a little devilish rattle, brought as though on a veering wave through the blue-black night. But the wind came again and blotted out the sound. Hear the droning and humming! Cool trade wind from the north, whirling round the building, curling in at the doors and windows, and round the furniture.

Something crackled in the sitting room. What could it be? A jumbie perhaps. Who knew? A Corentyne ghoul wafted in by the wind from out the samphire shrubs. Or it might be a duppy, one of the tiny, evil men who lived in the deep twilight of the courida bush and who chased you and killed you with poison-arrows if you strayed alone near the seashore after the sun had gone down. Or perhaps it was the old gentleman who haunted the back veranda. He had lived in this house long years ago, and the legend went that he cut his throat with a razor one night and was found the next morning by his servant lying dead in a pool of blood on the back veranda.

The wind began to die down.

15

Ramgolall and Beena and Kattree slept very deeply after the curry-feed. They had eaten well, and, on the whole, enjoyed themselves very much. Jannee had brought them home in his donkey-cart as he always did when the feed was held at his home. Beena had felt happy to sit beside him as they jogged along in the dark. The 'Who-you?' of the goat-suckers had held no fear for her, nor the jumbies and the duppies. Nothing could harm her when Jannee was near.

By eleven o'clock they were all a-bed, and a good thing too, for by midnight clouds had gathered overhead. It rained heavily for over three hours, though when dawn broke all the rain had gone and the east looked sad with the blood of a hurt pink flower. Only a few small rags of clouds, purple or brown in hue, remained floating in the pale blue, and the wind came softly and chillily, but steadily, from the north, betokening a fine day.

'I have a queer sort of premonition,' said Stymphy as he and Geoffry were dressing, 'that something unusual is going to happen today – something sort of exciting, and with a kick in it.'

'I hope the premonition does turn out true,' said Geoffry. 'We can do with a few thrills very well. I won't mind capturing a twelve-foot alligator, or a young labba tiger.'

'Or a twenty-foot boa.' Stymphy began to do battle with an imaginary boa. 'Can't you see us fighting the beast, struggling and twisting, and then squeezing the throat like that…like that…harder and harder until it grows limp and the twitchings get fainter and fainter – '

'Not as easy as all that, I can tell you. Now, if we had a high-powered rifle – a ·450, say – we could put a few juicy chunks of lead into its hide. That would make it squirm with a veng – '

'Oh, but there's a dawn for you, Geoff! It's getting better and better every minute.'

'Jolly lovely, yes. I've been noticing it. Look at that part over there – the part where the pink wisps seem to come out from a sort of honeycomb. Good subject for a painting.'

'Pity Clara isn't here. She'd do a watercolour.'

'And a spiffing good one at that, too.'

Stymphy winked. 'You would say so, of course.'

Geoffry went red and said: 'Oh, rot! Rot!' hastily and in confusion. 'Don't begin all that again. Seen my stud anywhere around, by the way?'

'Your stud? But aren't you wearing open-necked shirt? What's the idea of – ?'

'Why, of course. Spoke without thinking.'

'Don't you miss her a lot, Geoff? Aren't you pining for her?'

'Oh, behave yourself, can't you? Why on earth should I miss her? Why should I pine for her? I'm not as mawkish as all that.'

'Of course, I can excuse you for being soft on her. Harder men have fallen for her.'

'Soft on her the devil's great-aunt! Because I admire her paintings and her music?'

'What about her lovely face and figure? She has a very *seductif* figure, you know. Good hips and mellowy curves and contours and all that.'

'Ugh! I don't go goofy over girls' figures.'

'I believe she's soft on you, too, Geoff. With a little delicate and patient manoeuvring you ought to be able to do things.'

'And who said I haven't done things already? You think I'm a shy young duffer with girls? No fear, my good lad! No fear!'

'Have you ever kissed her?'

'Don't trouble your head about that.' He suddenly began to laugh ironically, all his confusion gone. 'Who knows, my pretty friend? Kissed her? And more perchance! Who knows? Ho, ho! *Who* knows?'

'I believe you're a dark 'un, Geoff.'

'Perchance, *mon ami*! Perchance! Ho, ho, ho! Who knows?' Then abruptly he clicked his tongue and made a wry face, looking very grown-up and manly – and hard. 'Oh, hang it all! You know, Stymphy, I do feel a bit futile now and then. Futile and *distrait*.'

'Futile and *distrait*? Why? How do you mean?'

He shrugged, smiling a twisted, far-away smile. 'Oh, nothing, nothing.' He looked out at the brightening dawn, his face suddenly troubled. He took a deep breath of the chilly air. 'Great to look at, eh? Pity it can't last for ever.'

'It's spiffing. Corentyne beauty. Look at the different tints of green. Those shrubs are really lovely, you know – at any time of the day. A choppy ocean of varied greens. One would hardly think they were growing wild. They look as if they were purposely planted to beautify the savannah.'

'I know,' nodded Geoffry, his eyes narrowed slightly as though in pain. 'Samphire they're called.'

'Samphire, eh? Great name. I must make a note of it in case I want to use it in a poem.'

'It's queer,' Geoffry said slowly and as if speaking to himself, 'but at most times when I look upon scenes like this I get the feeling that I'm locked out. I want to feel deeply about beauty, but something in me always seems to say that it's not for me. That's why I get cynical sometimes and sneer at you for raving over all these things.'

Stymphy frowned at him. 'But how do you mean? You can appreciate beauty all right. I don't see what you're getting at.'

'That's just it. What am I getting at? What do I mean?' He shrugged and made a wry face. 'Oh, forget it. All this groping, groping, groping after things. It's all rot.'

'It isn't rot, and you know it. You've got plenty in you – plenty that only needs a bit of – a bit of – well, a bit of hauling out, if you see what I mean. Look at your music. You're almost a master already – at the violin as well as the piano.'

'A master my eye! Tell that to the marines. I'm shackled, that's what I am. I try to put everything of me into music, but it just refuses to enter it. I wasn't born a poet, I suppose. I've just tried to acquire poetry. You and Clara are the poets. You can submerge yourselves completely in your respective arts. You can live, you can tremble. You've not – you haven't got a brake on your soul. You're not just an animal like me. That's all I am – an animal.' He spoke with a great deal of intensity, and one saw the power in him. It seemed to flow from him in waves, from his steady-gazing eyes. His hands gripped the sill of the window. Stymphy stared at him in some surprise, puzzled. 'Just an animal, Stymphs. I know it only too well – and so does – and so does – oh, hell! I'm worried, Stymphy, I'm worried.'

'Worried? Worried over what?'

'All right. All right. Don't bother. It's nothing. I'm just a bit *distrait*.'

'But what's the mystery all of a sudden – ?'

'Oh, I say! Wait! Listen to that!'

'What's it?'

'Don't you hear it? That fish-horn we heard yesterday morning.'

'Oh! Why, yes. I've just heard it.'

They both fell silent at once and stood at the window listening to the sound. It was the moaning of the conch-shell, the fisherman's horn. It came from far east where the savannah was bare of shrubs and rough and where cattle grazed on the short grass. It came drifting along over the areas covered with the samphire shrubs, moaning quietly, telling a tale of peace and simple folk minding cows, of mud-houses and rice-fields, creketteh hawks and muddy-watered canals, brown and rippled; moaning like a portent, too, as though foretelling the things of the future in the veiled core of its lonely cooing. It made Stymphy shudder a trifle and Geoffry clench the sill of the window harder.

Then abruptly Geoffry relaxed and gave a brief laugh. 'What ridiculous romantic asses we do make of ourselves, Stymphy! A fish-horn. A silly, rotten fish-horn that the fisherman probably doesn't think twice of. And we here weaving a whole heap of magic around it like a pair of goofy old ladies.'

'You're talking rot. There's poetry in it – beauty. It's a great sound. It's nothing to scoff at.'

'No, I suppose not.'

'Oh, don't try to be cynical, Geoff. It's no use. That sound moves you, as it moves me, and you know it. There's depth in it as well as fairy glamour; and life and death, too. It sounded just like a portent – warning and omen-filled. Menacing.'

'To me, too, somehow.' He gave a little twisted smile, but there was nothing cynical in his manner now. 'Strange that it should have left the identical impression on both of us. Perhaps it is an omen. Your premonition must be right. Something out of the ordinary must be going to happen today.'

16

After adding water to the milk, Ramgolall and Beena set out for the public road to await the coming of Joseph and his bus. The morning was fresh and bright with sunlight and white-winged birds, and the sky clear. Wind blew in a steady draught, and far to the west the samphire looked like the crest of an emerald wave.

When they reached the road they found that the sun had not yet dried it into dust. It still looked damp, and here and there a small pool of water could be seen reflecting the sunlight. They rested the can near the grass parapet and then squatted down to wait, Ramgolall sighing loudly in relief. 'Ah-h-h-h! Me a-get ol' nowadays, bettay. Eh-heh. Me go dead soon.'

'Na. You got plenty mo' year live, ol' man,' smiled Beena. 'You na got worry 'bout dead in a hurry.'

'Ah-h-h-h! Me bone dry-up, bettay. Me going fas'. Eh-heh.'

'When you go mek big house, Ramgolall? You na got 'nough money buil' big house yet?'

'Eh-h-h-h! Na, bettay! Na got 'nough money yet. We got to live quiet-quiet fo' de while. Long time come perhaps we buil' big cottage. But not yet. Na money na deh yet.'

'Me wan' buy new dress, Ramgolall.'

'Eh-h-h-h! New dress? Huh! Money na deh, bettay. Me pore man. Wait lil' time Kattree save up money buy new dress. Me na got na money buy new dress, bettay.'

Beena laughed. 'Ow, Ramgolall! You stingy bad! Ent you got plenty money in big canister?'

'Plenty money! Me na got plenty money in big canister, bettay. Only one, two copper. Me pore man. When me get plenty money?'

Beena laughed again. She often teased her father in this way. 'One o' dese days me go t'ief out *all* you' money an' t'row am 'way in Long Canal.'

Ramgolall gave a deep nodding laugh. 'Ow! You wicked gal, bettay. You too wicked. Mmmm.'

A minute or two later a horn sounded from the west and a green bus approached and went by. Somebody in it waved and Beena waved back.

'Sukra in deh,' said Beena. 'She mus' be a-go Speyerfeld.'

'Sukra? Oh! When she baby go ready born?'

'Soon. One mo' mont' an' she get baby. She say she want gurl, but Jannee want annodah boy.'

'T'ree boy! Wha' Jannee want wid t'ree boy? Two boy na 'nough?'

Another horn sounded, and this time it turned out to be the yellow bus called *Clark Gable*. It came droning to a stop, its bonnet gleaming, and Ramgolall and Beena rose at once.

Joseph got out, sulky as usual, and thrust his hand into his pocket to take out the money for yesterday's milk. Ramgolall held up his hand and Joseph dropped the five shillings and sixpence into his palm. Joseph stood waiting while Ramgolall counted the money. Then Ramgolall nodded and looked up. ' 'E right, Joseph.

'E right. Five shillings, sixpence.' And Joseph gave a queer smile and said: 'Me glad 'e right because we done do business now, Ramgolall.' Ramgolall looked foolishly at him and said: 'Eh-h-h? Me na savvee, Joseph. Wha' you mean?'

'Ah say we done do business,' repeated Joseph in a loud voice. 'From today we done. Jairamsingh say 'e don't want na mo' milk from you. You understan'?'

'Eh-h-h-h? But wha' wrong? Jairamsingh na wan' no mo' milk? Why 'e na wan' na mo' milk?'

'Don' ask me dat. Ask Jairam 'eself.' He turned off to re-enter the bus, and at that moment a rather tall black man in the uniform of a policeman came out of the bus and said: 'Awright, Ramgolall, you done do business wid Joseph. Come do lil' business wid me now. Lemme see a sample o' you' milk.' He spoke the last sentence in a voice of great authority and took from a khaki haversack a clear bottle, with a blank label. He was smiling faintly, in a sneering way.

Ramgolall looked at him blankly, then at Joseph and then back again at the policeman. 'Is wha' gone wrong? Eh-h-h-h? Wha' gone wrong?'

'Come, man. Come. You na savee English? I want a sample o' you' milk.' He bent down without further preamble and opened the smaller milk-can which stood at Ramgolall's feet. (The larger can stood farther off near Beena, for she had brought it.) He poured some of the milk into the cover, then from the cover began to pour it into the bottle. Of a sudden, however, Joseph gave a shout. 'Oh, hell! Quick, Sergeant! Stop dah lil' bitch! Look wah' she doing!'

The Sergeant straightened up and twirled.

But he was too late. Beena had flicked off the cover of the larger can and tilted it over with her foot. The Sergeant made a dash at it, but the parapet being on a slant, the can went rolling down into the canal, the milk gushing from it in a rich, white cascade and with a mellow, gurgling sound.

'You sly lil' bitch!' roared the Sergeant, glaring at Beena. 'You know very well de milk got water, so you spill it in de canal!'

'Eh-eh!' said Beena. 'But wha' you talkin'? Who say de milk got water? Me na put na water milk.'

'Oh, shut you' mout'! You're a liar! Ah have a good mind to arres' you for obstructing de Law!'

Beena laughed shrilly and said: 'You mekin' sport. Is-who you t'ink you can frighten? Eh-eh! De milk belong to we. If we wan' to t'row am 'way we can t'row am 'way. You na got na business.'

'I ain' got na business, eh? Wait till Ah sen' dis milk to de Guv-ment Analys'. If 'e fin' you got water in it you going know good! A hundred-dollar fine you got to pay – or gaol for you' tail!'

'Well, na water ain' deh in dah milk, so nabody caan' mek we pay na hundred-dollar fine.'

'Huh!' said the Sergeant. 'You got plenty mout', eh? Because you know was de odder can who' had de water! You're a sly lil' bitch! But one o' dese days Ah going catch you good. You wait an' see.' He corked the bottle and returned into the bus.

'Ah going catch you good one o' dese days!' he repeated, wagging his finger at her as the bus moved off. 'Sly lil' coolie bitch! Wait good.'

Ramgolall, who had been staring stupidly at everybody during the past few minutes, now spoke. 'But, bettay, is wha' wrong? Wha' happen? Me na savvee everyt'ing yet. Why you t'row 'way de milk?'

'Because 'e woulda take sample an' put we in court. We woulda have to pay hundred-dollar fine or go to gaol for five, six mont'.'

'Eh-h-h-h! Look trouble, na! Eh-h-h-h! An' is wha' Joseph say 'bout Jairamsingh na wan' na mo' milk?'

'So 'e say. Jairam fin' out you does put water a-milk, so 'e na want de milk na mo'.'

'Eh-h-h-h! Look trouble, na, bettay! Ha! Me na tell you before? Jairamsingh clever man. 'E does wo'k wid Black Arts. Eh-heh. Me know so long time. Me know. 'E does wo'k wid Black Arts.'

Beena, always practical, set about at once to recover the larger can. She had rolled her skirt in a knot above her knees, and now edged her way cautiously down the parapet. She put her feet, one at a time, into the water, feeling about for foothold. The canal was deep, this being the rain season, and the water, even at the edge, reached her well up to her knees. She stretched out her hand uncertainly towards the floating can, the other hand braced against the parapet to steady herself. Her fingers barely reached the bobbing neck and she drew it towards her and pushed it up the parapet where her father grasped it.

'Milk still deh in it,' she laughed as she scrambled back up the parapet. 'We can have a feast wid am when we get back home.'

'Ow! Bettay, you mek fun, eh? Wha' go happen now? Bad story come. Tomorrow morning Joseph na go bring na money. Me go have to sell milk meself.' Ramgolall groaned and wagged his head. 'An' me ol' man. Ow! Look bad story, eh? Look bad story!'

'Na help for am, Ramgolall. Wha' use grieve!'

'Bad story, bettay. Na mo' money go come in as 'e come in before. Wha' me go do now?'

'Kattree an' me can help you sell am. We can go every mornin' a-Speyerfeld an' – ' She broke off at the sound of a hail, and glanced across the canal.

'Hey, Beena!' came the hail again. The figures of two young men in shorts and open-necked shirts could be seen not far off plodding their way across the savannah in the direction of the road.

'Eh-eh! Is Geoffry,' said Beena. She waved.

'Geoffry? Wha' Geoffry? Who dah?'

'Geoffry, na? Geoffry Weldon. You' grandson.'

'Oh-h-h-h! You mean dah Geoffry? Me na know 'e come back from school. When 'e come?'

'Me na know. 'E mus' be come fo' de holiday season like 'e always come. Easter holiday.'

'Oh-h-h-h!' Ramgolall shaded his eyes to see better the approaching figures. ''E tall boy. 'E grow big since last time me see 'e.'

'Me na see 'e since las' year July holiday. 'E nice boy. 'E always talk to me good.'

They crossed over the canal, taking with them the milk-cans, and in a minute or two Geoffry and Stymphy came striding up, haversacks on backs and fishing tackle under arms. 'I made you out from a distance, Beena,' smiled Geoffry, gripping her hand. 'This is my friend, Stymphy.' She shook hands with Stymphy who smiled and said: 'How do you do?' in his usual half-shy way when meeting anyone for the first time. 'And, Ramgolall, how are *you* keeping? You're getting old, you know.'

'Eh-h-h-h!' said Ramgolall. 'Baaya, you grow big. Me hardly rec'nize you. Tall, tall boy.'

'Yes, one does grow, doesn't one?'

'You come home spen' holiday, na?'

'That's right. The Easter holidays. And I've brought my good friend along with me – Stymphy. We're trying to do a bit of fishing. We left home since six o'clock this morning.'

'You come walking all de way!' said Beena in surprise.

'Good Lord, no! We started off on our bikes. We left them at the Brankers' house, about a mile from here, and came the rest of the way on foot. I was hoping to meet you all, as a matter of fact. Where's Kattree? She didn't come out with you?'

'Na. She a-ketch fish fo' we breakfas'.'

'You don't say! You mean you actually catch fish every day for your breakfast?'

'Eh-heh. Every day. Mullet plenty a-Long Canal now rain a-fall.'

'Ho! That's just the information we're looking for. We're trying to find a good pond or canal with plenty fish. Is this the Long Canal?' he asked her, pointing at the canal that ran north-south, at right angles with the big canal bordering the public road.

Beena nodded. 'Eh-heh. Dis is de Long Canal. 'E go right out to de sea. But you caan' ketch na fish round about here. If you wan' ketch fish you got to go high up near we home. You get plenty deh.'

'Then that's where we're going to camp for the day, lady. If you're going that way, too, we can all go along.'

'Eh-heh. We going home now,' smiled Beena.

All the while Ramgolall had been gazing up at his tall grandson, feeling within him great pride and admiration, and, for the time being, quite forgetful of the trouble that had come upon him only a brief while ago. It was a great thing for him to think that he, Ramgolall, had a grandson like this. A grandson of Ramgolall tall and fair of skin and able to talk like an estate overseer! Ah! Honour, indeed, had come to him now in the ebb of his life. Every cane-cutter could not brag of such honour. The Lord of Life had been good to him. Were he to die tonight he should die feeling that he had not lived in vain. He should die feeling that he had added to the good things of the world. He had seen the flowering and the ripening of his seed and of his seed's seed. He had done what the Lord of Life had sent him to do and his content was great. Let the wind blow chilly now or the sun scorch him. Let the rain beat him. Nothing mattered. He had done his part on the earth. He could sigh now and feel at peace when the twilight of death began to gather about him.

But soon the trouble of the present arose among his thoughts like a dark animal of evil, and the peace and content that had crept over him began to drift away like fair white clouds blown to the south by the hot winds of noon. He remembered the sulky face of Joseph and the taunting smile Joseph had smiled when he had said that Jairamsingh did not want any more milk. An evil black boy, Joseph. And he remembered, too, the tall policeman demanding a sample of his milk, and the sudden shout of Joseph…then the white milk gurgling out and the can rolling into the canal. For a long time to come he would remember this dark picture – this picture that Jairamsingh, with his Black Arts, had caused to be painted on the brightness of this lovely day.

The others kept chattering all the while as the four of them moved along the dam towards Ramgolall's home. Ah! But it was good to hear their young voices talking. It cheered his troubled mind in patches, like the pretty colours of motor-oil floating on the still black water of a punt-canal.

17

They found Kattree sitting by the edge of the canal waiting for fish to bite. She had already caught one, a cuirass, and it lay on the dam looking very fierce with the sharp prong jutting up on its back, its brown, smooth, domed body shining in the sun. It wriggled every now and then or turned a somersault in a vain effort to get back into the water.

Kattree did not get up to greet them, nor did she show any surprise at seeing Geoffry and Stymphy. She sat in her calm, quiet way and smiled at them, smiled a little shyly, especially when Geoffry bent down and playfully pulled her long pigtail. 'Well,

Kattree bettay! How are you getting along? Haven't seen you for quite a little longish while, eh?'

'Me awright. You come spen' holiday again?'

'Yes. The Easter holidays are on. This is my good friend Stymphy. He's a poet and a learned man generally. And he catches fish, too, just by way of general relaxation.'

She smiled. 'You come ketch fish?'

'That's what we were supposed to have been doing for the past day or two, but up to now we haven't caught a half-grown tiger-fish.'

'Is that where you live?' asked Stymphy of Beena, pointing at the mud-house twenty or thirty yards off, and Beena nodded and told him that it was. 'What about taking me inside?' he asked her. 'I've never seen the inside of a mud-house in all my natural,' and Beena replied that there was nothing to see. 'Only a hammock an' de bed me an' Kattree does sleep on – an' Ramgolall got 'e canister an' drum in one corner. Come see, if you want.'

'Coming with us, Geoff?'

'What? To see the inside of the mud-house? No, thank you. I've seen it already. I'm joining Kattree here to see if I can't bag a few mullets and cuirasses.'

So Stymphy alone went with Beena into the mud-house. Ramgolall, who had overheard Stymphy's request, walked slowly behind them, frowning a little, for he felt impatient at being delayed in making the daily visit to his money-bags. Delay was bad, and, besides, he was eager to add these the last five shillings from Jairamsingh to the new bundle of shillings he had started a few mornings ago. He never liked keeping money on his person. Money, he felt, was always safer when it was tied up and stored away in his canister.

Beena rested the milk-can outside the doorway and invited Stymphy to enter. He had to bend to enter, for the door was not more than five and a half feet in height. In spite of the bright sunshine, the inside of the mud-house was dark, for there were no windows. Stymphy could not help wincing at the dank, frowsy smell of coconut oil and earth. When his eyes grew accustomed to the gloom he made out the hammock and the rough wooden bed and the canister and the drum. Two bundles of clothing lay tied up in a corner near the bed, and, though Stymphy did not know it, these bundles contained all the clothes Beena and Kattree possessed.

'But there aren't any windows,' said Stymphy. 'How do you sleep at night? You ought to suffocate.'

'Eh-h-h-h! Wha' de door deh fo'? Plenty air come in t'rough de door,' said Beena. 'We caan' suffocate.'

'I suppose you're inured to it. Is that where you and Kattree sleep every night?'

'Yes.'

'And Ramgolall sleeps in the hammock there?'

'Eh-heh. Dah is where he is sleep.'

'This is awfully officious of me, I know, but you mustn't mind. I'm just interested, that's all.'

'Ask any question you like,' smiled Beena. 'Me na min'? And as though to prove that she did not mind she went on to say: 'Dah is Ramgolall' canister wheh he is keep all 'e money. 'E got plenty money in deh.'

Stymphy looked dismayed. 'You mean he hoards his money in that canister like a – like a miser?'

'Eh-heh. Every day 'e put money in deh fo' long years now. Since me lil' baby so high we know dah canister.'

Stymphy kept staring at her as though she were telling him an unreal and far-fetched tale. 'All these years he's been hoarding money there… Well. And what about thieves? He's never been afraid of thieves?'

'Na. We na got na t'ief-man in dis part o' de country. Everybody live good in dis part. Only big town got t'ief-man.'

Stymphy smiled. 'What a simple faith you've got in the world!' He looked at her for a moment and then asked: 'Are you all quite happy, living here like this?'

'Happy? Eh-h-h-h! Wha' go mek we unhappy?'

'What, indeed!' He grunted. 'I should like living like this for a week or so just to see what it's like. Ought to be good experience.'

He asked her many questions, and made himself at home despite the dank smell. He sat for a moment on the bed 'to try it out', as he put it, and then he went over to Ramgolall's canister and rapped the sides with his knuckles. 'Let's see if we can hear the shekels jingle,' he grinned. 'No. Nothing doing. He must have them tied up in bundles or something.'

'Yes. 'E got dem tie up in bundle,' she smiled. 'Me an' Kattree used to spy on 'e plenty time when 'e open it to put in mo' money.' He grinned and muttered something about Molière's *L'Avare*. 'I heard you had a curry-feed last night. Is that the drum you beat?' She told him that it was. 'We had two drum. Jannee borrow Bijoolie' drum. How you know we had curry-feed las' night?'

He told her that Dora had mentioned it when they were dining. 'They sounded great in the silence of the night, you have no idea – especially heard at such a distance. They moved me a great deal.'

'You like coolie drum? You got coolie blood in you?'

'As a matter of fact, I think I have,' he smiled. 'If I'm not mistaken, I think my grandmother was a Eurasian – half East Indian and half white.'

'Oh! Well, dah is why you like coolie drum,' she laughed. 'One day, by an' by, we going invite you to a curry-feed – you an' Geoffry.'

'That would be great. But you'd have to let me beat the drum, you know.' He laughed and made a move towards the door. 'Let's go and see what's happening to Geoff and Kattree.'

On emerging, they found Ramgolall squatting on the ground outside the doorway. He looked up with a benevolent smile and made an amiable grunting sound, though inwardly he was seething with impatience to be alone with his hoard.

When they had got out of his hearing, Stymphy looked at Beena and said: 'He must have overheard what we were saying about him.'

Beena laughed. 'An' wha' if 'e hear? We na talk nutting bad 'bout 'e.'

They reached the canal just in time to see Geoffry jerk a small cuirass out of the water and jerk it off his hook back into the water. Even Kattree laughed aloud. 'You musn' jerk it so quick!' she said.

'But it would have got away, if I didn't – '

'Oh, you're a greenhorn, Geoff! Shame! Can't even catch a fish when it's on the end of your line and hooked on!'

'You go and sink yourself! Are you any better? You would have lost it just the same.'

'Oh, greenhorn! Greenhorn! Look at Kattree. She's caught two more since Beena and I left – '

'Wrong! I caught one of them!'

'Yes. He ketch one,' smiled Kattree.

'What a wonder! Toenails clap! Which one did he catch? The mullet or the – ?'

'Another bite! Another bite!' Geoffry gave a great swinging heave and Stymphy and Beena ducked, with cries of alarm, while a struggling cuirass barely missed their heads, landing with a dull 'bup!' on the hard ground.

'Ouch! You've spattered half a ton of water down my neck!' Stymphy protested. 'Careful! He's going to jump back in the water! Hold him down! Good! Got him! No, you don't, you little demon you!'

'Mind! That prong on the back will prick you!'

'No fear! I've got the blighter well in hand.'

After this success of Geoffry's, Stymphy joined the fishing and before very long had caught two hassars while Geoffry had caught a mullet.

Beena left them, saying that she had to go and make fire to cook the midday meal.

So engrossed did they become in the fishing that they failed to notice the heavy grey clouds that had been gathering in the sky. It was not until Kattree suddenly exclaimed: 'Eh-eh! Rain coming! Look yonder!' and pointed towards the east that they became aware of the change in the weather.

Looking towards the east and the north-east, they saw a hazy, grey-white curtain of rain approaching swiftly across the savannah. Full of power and menace it seemed. They could hear it in the breezeless silence coming with a hollow, far-off roar – an awing roar that came in waves, rising to a whoop and then falling to a soft swashing as though thousands of busy devils were groaning and hissing for all they were worth behind the thick, misty sheet of drops. The savannah hazed and vanished at the edge as if it were crumbling off into a fog of space beyond the horizon and would never reappear. Flocks of white birds uttered thin, harsh cries of panic and flew waveringly towards the south and west.

'Ha! I can see we're in for it,' said Geoffry, pulling up his line from the water. 'Let's make for the mud-house. I'm in no mood for a drenching.'

'Nor am I,' agreed Stymphy. 'Quick! It's coming fast like blazes. Let's run.'

In less than half a minute they were all huddled together within the frowsy gloom of Ramgolall's home. The rain hissed down in a fierce, slanting shower of drops. It crashed and prattled on the dry-leaf roof, and Stymphy, who kept glancing up, marvelled at the fact that no water leaked through on to them.

'Whoever put this roof together knew what he was about,' he remarked. 'Doesn't it ever leak?' he asked of Kattree who sat on one side of him on the bed.

'No. It caan' leak,' she smiled, looking more calm than ever, and secret-filled, in the half-dark. 'It mek so as to keep water from leak t'rough.'

'Quite an experience this, eh, Stymphs?' grinned Geoffry, who crouched near the door close to the inward-bulging flour-bag curtain. 'We'll have something to tell 'em about when we get back.'

'You mudder na go like hear you bin wid we,' smiled Beena, who sat on the bed, on the other side of Stymphy. 'She na like you-all talk to we.'

'Doesn't matter tuppence to me what mother likes and doesn't like,' said Geoffry with conviction. 'I'm getting rather fed up with mother nowadays, to tell the truth.'

'Oh, I don't know,' said Stymphy. 'Somehow, I like her a lot. In spite of her crudeness, she has something about her that takes you on the spot. She's so absolutely carefree and unaffected, you know. It's sort of refreshing to hear her speak.'

'Oh, yes. She's not a bad sort, on the whole. I like her myself. Her very lack of refinement is attractive. She has a kind of Philistinian bluntness that has always appealed to me. But it's her snobbery I can't stand. It irritates me. And it's so completely ridiculous. It's silly, stupid.'

Ramgolall, who squatted near his canister as if to guard it, kept smiling at them in quiet benevolence and making little grunting, old-man sounds at intervals. Within him, however, he felt troubled. The crash of the rain troubled him and the thought of the future. Even the sight of Geoffry, for some strange reason, had within the past few minutes begun to raise dark phantoms in his mind. It was as though his soul sensed some great coming trouble in which this tall, fair-skinned grandson of his would play a big part. Queer that he should feel so. What trouble could come, and how could his grandson be mingled in it? Hear how harshly the rain prattled on the roof! As if the drops would smash in the dry-leaf. Very spiteful it seemed, as if it wanted to take vengeance on them for something they had done. For all he knew, Jairamsingh, with his Black Arts, might have sent it specially for them. It smashed down on the roof with such fierceness. Listen to it! Swash-swish! Swash-swish! Like teeth tearing and crunching at the dry-leaf. It was frightening. Perhaps it was the teeth of a devil sent by Jairam in the form of rain. Jairam was angry with him for watering the milk. This must be his vengeance. Ah! He could feel evil in the air. A grey spirit might even be lurking somewhere within here hidden in a corner and plotting dark work…

Seeing Stymphy's gaze rest upon him for an instant, he broke into a smile and uttered a faint amiable grunt.

'I'm beginning to feel a bit peckish,' said Geoffry. 'About what time do you think it is now, Kattree?'

'Nearly twelve o'clock,' Kattree replied. 'Sun did nearly over-head when de rain begin fall.'

'We've got some grub in our haversacks. What about joining us in a general spread?'

'Eh-h-h-h! You want we share you breakfas'!' Beena exclaimed.

'And why not? We've brought enough here to feed a battalion. Mother always takes good care to cram our haversacks. Day before yesterday we took back more than half the stuff she put in.'

'De rice did done cook before rain come down,' said Beena. ''E in de corner deh if you want some.'

'Don't bother with rice. Keep it over for your dinner this evening. I'm not very fond of rice, besides. Ramgolall! Come over here and join the party! We're going to have a little tuck in.'

After explaining to him what they meant, they got him to come closer to them. Geoffry and Stymphy opened their haversacks, and soon they were all eating ham sandwiches, cheese and bread, small puddings and Peek Frean's biscuits. There were four bottles of ginger-ale, too, and Geoffry shared one bottle with Kattree – they drank from the bottle – while the others each had a whole bottle. It was a very friendly meal, and Ramgolall smiled many happy smiles, all the dark thoughts of a brief while before fading from his mind. Beena and Stymphy laughed a great deal, making many jokes, and so did Geoffry. Kattree often while eating kept casting long, deep looks at Geoffry, her eyes pregnant with secret things, and Geoffry's eyes, meeting hers, would gleam strongly for a brief moment and then stray off. And throughout it all the rain crashed down in gallons upon the roof, reckless of human life and the dramas of the earth, crashed down as if it would never end until it flattened them all into the mud, as though it were, indeed, a rain of vengeance sent by Jairamsingh.

18

The rain continued to fall heavily for several hours and then it began to thin off to a fine, steady drizzle. The sky curved above them, an unbroken dome of grey. Geoffry and Stymphy returned to the Brankers' for their bicycles by way of the public road, for the savannah had become a great sheet of water, and it would take two or three hours before the water drained off.

By the time they got home they were wet through and through from the drizzle which had thickened a great deal while they were on the way. They found Sosee and the children on the front veranda waiting to greet them.

'Ow! All-you get wet, na?' Sosee broke out, smiling at them. 'Oh, me gaad! But look at dem!' She slapped Geoffry's shoulder. 'Boy! You soakin'! Is where de rain ketch all-you?'

'Oh, we had good shelter. It was only in coming back through the drizzle that we got wet. All in the day's fun. Eh, Stymphy?'

'I should think so,' smiled Stymphy.

'You caught any fish?' asked David.

'You bet we did. I caught a mullet and a cuirass, and Stymphy's got two hassars to his credit.'

'Where are they?' asked Belle, looking shyly at Stymphy as she asked the question. 'Didn't you bring them with you?'

'No, we decided to leave them behind.'

'We left them for Kattree and Beena.'

'Kattree and Beena! You met Kattree and Beena?'

'We spent the greater part of our time with them. We sheltered in their mud-house when the rainstorm broke on us.'

'Is wha' you mus' go deh fo'?' frowned Sosee. 'You mus' learn to choose you' company, Geoffry. You gettin' big now, you know, Beena an' Kattree not de sort o' company – '

'All right! All right!' cut in the rumbling voice of Big Man who had just emerged from the sitting room. 'Don't keep them talking here. They must be wet. They've got to change into dry things without delay. Had a tough day, eh, young men?' he added, smiling at them. 'Caught anything?'

'Oh, yes, we were in luck today,' Stymphy told him. 'We caught several.'

'A letter's come for you, Geoff!' said Dora as Geoffry and Stymphy began to move inside, and Geoffry glanced sharply at her and said: 'Eh? A letter for me? Where is it?'

'Mother put it on the dressing table in your room. It's in a blue envelope and the writing is a girl's. And it smells of perfume.'

Geoffry went a trifle pink and said: 'Oh!'

All the children tittered and Dora and Belle gave significant chuckles. 'You're getting on, boy,' remarked Dora.

'Oh, shut up and go and sink yourself,' said Geoffry, flushing. 'Can't I even get a letter from a girl without all this fuss and ado?'

When he and Stymphy got upstairs, he dashed to the dressing table and snatched up the square blue envelope that stood leant up against a hairbrush. His face looked tense and anxious. He kept turning the letter over in his hands and staring at it. It gave off a faint perfume.

Stymphy frowned and said: 'What's all the drama about? Why, you're behaving as though you were expecting to find your death-warrant in the thing.'

Geoffry gave a dry, hard chuckle. 'Death-warrant isn't so

far from the mark, I can tell you. Hell! Stymphs, you don't know how important this letter is. I'm afraid to open it, that's the truth – scared stiff.' He stopped speaking and moistened his lower lip, staring at the letter still and turning it over and over in his hands.

'Who is it from at all?'

Geoffry made no reply. He put back the letter on the dressing table. 'I can't open this now. When I've changed into dry things…'

'But what's the big idea at all? Is it from Clara?'

He nodded. 'M'm-h'm. Oh, hell! Oh, hell! Oh, hell!' He tore off his wet shirt and flung it at the towel rack.

'But what can she have to tell you that – that gets you all dithered up like this?'

'Oh, don't make it bother you!' He spoke a trifle impatiently. 'It's nothing important, really. Nothing at all. I'm making a molehill out of a – a mountain out of a molehill.' He began to dry his body briskly with a towel, staring the while at the closed windows, his face gone troubled. And Stymphy frowned at him, wondering greatly. Above them on the corrugated iron roof the rain made a steady, trickling noise, dull and monotonous, and through the streaming glass of the closed windows the sky looked pale grey, with not the slightest sign of a break anywhere. The cow-minders were driving the cattle into pen for the night. Dimly their wailing shouts could be heard and the baa-ing of the sheep, the occasional 'maw-w-w!' of a calf and the shrill, piteous 'eh-h-h-h!' of the goats – all pale and remote sounds, like the sky and the hazed horizon and the faint trickling drip-drip of the rain.

They changed without uttering a word, and it was not until they were quite ready to go downstairs that Stymphy said: 'Well, look here, you'd better stay up here and read this fateful letter of dread. I'll go downstairs to the others and give you a chance to ponder in solitude on the vicissitudes of life.'

'Oh, don't make an ass of yourself.'

'That essay of Bacon's on the vicissitudes of things ought to be of some help. "Certain it is, that matter is in a perpetual flux, and never at a stay. The great winding-sheets that bury all things – "'

'Oh, shut up! I don't want to hear any silly Bacon.'

The sudden scamper of footsteps sounded outside the bedroom door, and Dora's voice called: 'Stymphy! Geoff! Lunch is ready. We're waiting for you, as soon as you're ready!'

'I don't feel hungry, thanks!' called back her brother, with a frown.

'Not hungry? But you must be hungry. You haven't eaten anything since – '

'Oh, run off and play with your dolls!'

'Which dolls? I have no dolls! Stymphy, what about you, boy? Aren't you coming down for lunch?'

'Yes, I'm coming now – in two ticks! Why don't you come down and have a bite, Geoff? Don't be an ass.'

'I'm not hungry. Really. You go and tuck in.'

Stymphy shrugged. 'O.K., Sir Roger. Stay and read your letter.' And he left the room.

Dora was standing in the passage waiting for him. She smiled in a half-shy way and said that she had been waiting for him to accompany him downstairs.

'Well, there's a nice girl,' he smiled in a patronizing manner, gripping her arm. 'Let's go down. Geoff isn't coming. Says he isn't hungry.'

'He must be lovesick,' she sniggered, her cheeks flushed a little at the grip of his hand on her arm. 'He must want to read his precious letter alone, I suppose. He can go ahead and eat it for lunch if he wants.'

Stymphy laughed and told her that she was right. But within him he felt no cheer. Within him dark gnomes murmured and made ugly grimaces at his soul. He kept hearing the drip of the rain and the far-off, dreary lowing of a calf. He saw in his mind Geoffry alone up there in his room slowly preparing to open that blue letter, his face troubled and tense. A letter from Clara Macleod. What could be in it to affect him in such a way? 'You don't know how important this letter is. I'm afraid to open it, that's the truth – scared stiff.' Hear the rain. Drip, drip. Drip, drip. When the deuce would it stop at all? So depressing. Windows closed. Sky grey. Large pools of water everywhere you looked outside. It made him think of a dead tree near a pond of still water – black water with blades of grass jutting up sparsely and the grey tree leaning over like a spectre of death; and hear the goats out there making such a plaintive sound.

The sheep, too, poor creatures. Sheep in the rain always seemed so pathetic, somehow…

And Stymphy, brooding in this way, did not know that at that very moment Ramgolall and his daughters were driving home the cows for the night, braving the flooded savannah and the coarse drizzle. Beena and Kattree, their long skirts rolled tightly above their knees, walked slowly after the herd. The water reached halfway up their shins and, at times, nearly up to their knees. Their clothes were soaked from the rain and stuck tightly to their skin so that their bodies were clearly outlined.

Ramgolall, who walked a little way behind them, kept wagging his head and groaning, for in his mind he told himself that this rain, for a certain, had been sent by the Black Magic of Jairamsingh. It would not cease for days to come and the cows would all drown, or die for want of grass to eat. Ah! Jairam was an evil man. He had many devils in his power, devils whom he controlled with the Black Arts he practised.

Beena, who was quite cheerful in spite of everything, looked back once and said with a laugh: 'Ol' man, is wha' wrong wid you? Why you groanin' so? You sick?'

'Ah, bettay!' groaned her father. 'Bad story come. Dis rain wha' fall bad rain. Jairam sen' am.'

'Jairam sen' am? How Jairam could sen' am? Only God can sen' rain, Ramgolall.'

'Huh! God na sen' dis rain, bettay. Jairam sen' dis rain. Jairam wo'k wid Black Arts. He sen' am because me put water a-milk.'

Beena laughed. 'Na, you wrong, Ramgolall. Nowadays is rain-season. Rain a-fall nearly every day. Jairam na sen' dis rain. Dis rain is God' rain.'

But Ramgolall continued to wag his head and groan. There was evil in the air, the evil of Jairamsingh, and nothing would change his mind.

At length, the cows were all safely penned for the night. The calves lowed very drearily, so that Beena felt sorry for them and wished she could take them into the mud-house so that they would not have to sleep all night in the damp. She and Kattree were just preparing to take off their wet clothes when Kattree suddenly exclaimed: 'Eh – eh! Look Sukra coming!'

Beena glanced along the dam and exclaimed, too, in surprise. 'Wha' she doing here in all dis rain?'

'Somet'ing mus' be happen,' said Kattree.

They moved a little way along the dam and met Sukra. She was sobbing, sobbing so that she could not speak at once when they asked her what was the matter. Her clothes, like theirs, were soaking wet and stuck tightly to her skin. Her hair hung loosely down her back and around her shoulders, wet and untidy.

'Is wha' wrong wid you, na, gal?' asked Beena for the third time. 'Is why you cryin' so?'

'Jannee beat me,' she sobbed. ''E beat me, put me out.'

''E beat you? Eh-eh? Wha' 'e beat you fo'?'

''E say 'e na want me back in 'e house.'

'But is why 'e beat you? Wha' happen?'

''E say me want Boorharry. 'E say me na want 'e na more. 'E say me mus' go live wid Boorharry.'

Beena kept staring at her in dismay. 'But is wha' happen? You had quarrel wid 'e? Wha' you quarrel over?'

'Sumatra Pooran tell 'e say she see me wid Boorharry. Dis mornin' when me go a-Speyerfeld buy rice, me tek two piece roti fo' Boorharry from last night curry-feed. Sumatra Pooran see me when me give 'e an' she go back tell Jannee, an' when me reach home hi' while ago Jannee quarrel wid me an' beat me. 'E put me out de house in de rain, an' 'e say 'e na want me back. 'E say me mus' go live wid Boorharry. 'E say is Boorharry me want. Me na want he.' Sukra uttered many sobs between this speech. She was deeply distressed.

'But is wha' mek Sumatra mus' go tell Jannee you tek roti fo' Boorharry? Na she business.'

'How you know is Sumatra tell Jannee?' Kattree asked.

'Jannee say so when 'e quarrel wid me, an' me did see she in Speyerfeld when we stan' up by hospital gate talkin' to Boorharry. She get baby las' year fo' Boorharry, an' she jealous o' every woman she see talk to 'e. She always go 'bout mek mischief fo' somebody.'

'She got dirty tongue,' said Beena angrily. 'If she min' she own business it serve she better. Come inside, tek off you wet clothes, gal. You can stop de night wid we. Tomorrow morning me go talk to Jannee an' try mek t'ing right fo' you.'

They took her into the mud-house and explained to Ramgolall what had happened, and Ramgolall wagged his head sagely and said that there was evil in the air. Beena laughed and told him that everything would soon come right, and there was no evil in the air.

She and Kattree and Sukra took off their wet clothes without further delay. Beena lent Sukra her one clean dress, while she herself remained naked, saying that she was hardened and would not take cold.

'Me accustom' stay naked-skin,' she laughed in reply to Sukra's protests. 'Nutting happen to me. Me na tek col' easy. You a-get baby. You mus' keep warm.'

For a long while they sat crouched up on the wooden bed talking of this trouble that had come between Sukra and her husband. Beena and Sukra did most of the talking, Kattree only now and then putting in a word or two. Beena uttered many angry words against Sumatra Pooran and said that when she met her on the road she would give her a cold look and pass her without a word. 'She's a dang'ous woman,' frowned Beena. 'Me done-done talk to she – from dis day.'

She made an odd, beautiful figure crouching there, brown and naked in the half-gloom, her arms wrapped tightly around her drawn-up knees. Her feet twitched in her anger and her brow was lowered in a frown.

'Never again me talk to she – not in dis worl',' she vowed again, and a short lull followed her words. Sukra stared at the ground, and Kattree looked serene. They could hear the rain, dripping softly, steadily, with a chipping noise, on the dry-leaf roof, a damp, leaky sound that seemed as if it would never cease. Chirip, chip. Chirip, chip. All the time.

Ramgolall, near his canister, groaned quietly, wagging his head.

19

Shortly after six o'clock, when the twilight of the coming night had gathered into a deep burnt-umber hue, the sky had ceased to drip. The grey had split in the west and long veins of pale gold ran in parallel bands across the sky, beginning in the south and ending hazily in the north-west. In the east and in the north and overhead the grey had become transparent and high, and hazily mottled, rigid like frosted grass, with specks of cobweb clinging to it. No wind blew and the air smelt fresh and watery. The sun had already gone down, and the pale gold bands in the west were slowly fading into a drab white colour, the colour of cold sandstone.

A silent peace seemed to have drifted down upon the savannah. Geoffry, looking out of his bedroom window, regarded the samphire, grown dull-green now in the dim light and rather sombre. His gaze went farther off and he saw the ragged fringe of the courida bush on the northern horizon and the mud-houses spotted here and there on the grassy parts of the savannah, all looking grey and misted over. He heard the thin, pitiful crow of a cockerel. It came from some way off, perhaps from the poultry-shed to the leeward of the house, a brief, immature squawk, ending almost as soon as it began and answered by a long, full-throated crow that screwed its way like a spiral of fine wire through the bleak air. Another followed, and another – all thin, far-away wires of sound that, somehow, added to the calm of the early evening. There was something detached about them, yet serene and yearning, like the shepherd's song of thanksgiving after the storm in the Pastoral Symphony. They soothed his soul. The whole scene soothed him – in a cold, forlorn way. The umber twilight and the distant mist, the dull-green of the samphire, the still, damp air and the high stratus mottled with little ragged fragments of cumulus, all contributed to the peace of the evening. All soothed him, all blended with his reflections: calm and sombre, bleak.

He turned his head slightly. In the gloom he could barely make out that letter. It lay on the dressing table, one corner of the square envelope accidentally tilted up against a lacquered toilet box, the box in which he kept his studs and links.

He smiled slowly. She would have liked that box if she could have seen it. There were figures etched on its black, smooth surface: slim, angular Oriental ladies and the flat-topped peak of a distant volcano. She was fond of Oriental art, she once told him. In her bedroom, above the chest of drawers, hung a print of a picture by Whistler: a girl in white holding a fan with an Oriental scene painted on it. Her own work bore no traces of Oriental influence. She called herself a 'simple colourist'. She had modelled her manner after that of the earlier impressionists: Monet and Manet, Renoir. It would be a long time before he forgot those keen talks she and he had had on art. They would spend hours in that drawing room with the brown-varnished walls and old-fashioned furniture, the black, upright Pohlmann piano. They would talk art or play the piano; in the late afternoon, oft-times, with the red sun wavering between the leaves of the big mango tree outside the window and making shifty patches of light on their faces and bodies; or in the evenings, all by themselves in the sitting room (in the whole house for that matter, for her parents trusted him), one blue-shaded electric light burning near the piano, leaving the rest of the room in a pale unreal twilight: 'twilight of a lonely moon' she called it in her quaintly fanciful way.

He smiled again, a little twistedly this time. He was remembering the dark, straight hair cut à la Jeanne d'Arc, smooth and lank, shifty under his hand, and smelling faintly of the same perfume that the letter there smelt of. He could see the pink-white skin growing pinker on the spots where he caressed it. His favourite trick was to press the tips of his fingers firmly in the hollow between her breasts and then take them off suddenly and watch the scarlet imprints glow for a moment and then slowly fade off and merge into the delicate carmine of the breasts. He wondered whether he would ever do that again… Afraid not. All that was over for good. That letter on the dressing table was a symbol of the end. Unless…ha! There was that 'unless', of course.

He grunted and shook his head slowly. No, no, no – emphatically. That could not be now. It must not be. If that happened it would mean the crumbling of all his amber dreams, of his father's dreams, too. This was April. In July he would be sitting for the Guiana Scholarship. His chances of winning it were first-rate. Indeed, there was hardly any doubt that he would win it. He was miles above the others. Stymphy would have been the only serious problem, and he was not sitting for the Guiana this year. He was trying for honours in the Senior Joint Board. He was only seventeen. He would have two chances at the Guiana.

If he, Geoffry, won the Guiana this year, be would leave for London during the latter part of August next year to take up medicine at St Bartholomew's. Everything had been planned to the last detail, for whether he won the Guiana or not he would still go. The question of expense meant nothing to his father.

He couldn't throw up all that just so that he could marry her and save her from the 'disgrace'. Nothing doing! He had his head screwed on too firmly. He never let his heart govern him in such matters. And, of course, he was selfish. He realized that only too well. He had been made that way. He couldn't help it. He did not mind admitting it. Where matters of his own personality were concerned he never attempted to fool himself. He knew just what he was and he admitted it to himself at least, if not to others.

He wanted to do big things – great things. Since he had been eight years old he had wanted to do big things. The simple life would not suit him. Mediocrity would not be good enough for him. He wanted to he a glaring success. He wanted to be famous, to be a renowned figure, to be a household word. Sir Geoffry Weldon, the celebrated surgeon. Or Geoffry Weldon, the distinguished pianist. He wanted to be a world figure. He wanted to be everything…everything, even British Foreign Minister or Prime Minister…everything.

He clenched his hands nervously and began to pace up and down in the dark room. He wore crêpe-soled shoes and they made soft, padding sounds on the floor – commonplace sounds, he thought…commonplace…commonplace. Yes, that was what would happen to him if he married her. It would mean settling down to a commonplace life. He would have to go into some office in Georgetown or he would have to live on the coast here and be a cattle-rancher like his father.

He came to a stop. Talking about his father, he wondered what *he* was going to say to the whole thing. It would come as a great shock to him, he knew. It would worry him. He would be disappointed in him. He had always cherished such great hopes for his son's future. It was terrible letting him down. The two of them had got on so well together so far. Their views agreed on almost everything. From the time he had been a small fellow.

He heard footsteps approaching in the passage. The door opened and Stymphy came in.

'Hullo! In the dark all by yourself?'

'All my myself. Jolly restful the dark can be at times, you know.'

'We've been playing a bit of bridge. Your mother is a good player, you know. I wouldn't have thought so.'

'Oh, yes, she's always been pretty good at bridge – most card games, in fact. The old man, too – and Dora and Belle.'

'Dora and I were partners. We played against your father and mother. We beat them by six hundred and eighty points.'

'Not bad. Dora seems as if she's developed a soft spot for you, by the way. Haven't you noticed it yet?'

'Soft spot for *me*! What on earth are you talking about?'

'Ugh! I can see you blushing in the dark, Stymphs. You don't mean to tell me honestly that you haven't noticed all her attentions. Why, it's as plain as a pikestaff to anyone with half an eye.'

'Oh, rot! She only tries to make me feel at home. I'm sure there isn't anything else in it.'

Geoffry made no reply. He switched on the light.

'Looks as if it's going to turn out fine tonight,' said Stymphy in a self-conscious voice.

'Looks so. I say, Stymphs!'

'Hullo!'

'You can have a read of that if you like.'

'Eh? What? The letter?'

'Mm.'

'Oh! But if you don't mind, of course. I mean, if it's anything very *sub rosa* I shouldn't like – '

'Cut that. Cut that. Read it and don't be an ass. I'm asking you to read it. When you've finished tell me what you think.'

When Stymphy had got halfway down the second page he

uttered a sharp exclamation and glanced up, a blank look on his face. 'But – but is this…? But surely she can't mean this, Geoff.' He spoke in a low, awed voice. 'She says she's *enceinte* – over two months.'

Geoffry made no reply. He stood in a careless attitude at the window gazing out at the dark.

Stymphy read on with parted lips, a look of utter dismay on his face. When he came to the end of the letter he folded it up and replaced it in the envelope. He rested it on the dressing table and looked across at Geoffry. He seemed a little stunned. After a moment, he gave a half-shy, uneasy smile and said: 'But what are you going to do, Geoff?'

Geoffry grunted. 'There's the rub, my dear chap, as our friend Hamlet said. I'm in the soup, Stymphs. I know it. She gave me a hint before I left Georgetown, but she said she wasn't certain. She said she'd write me in a day or two and give me the verdict – and here it is now. And it isn't particularly cheering, is it?'

'But you're taking it lightly. This is serious, Geoff.'

'I know it's serious. Don't judge from my offhand tone. I'm taking it far more seriously than you may think, I can tell you.'

'What's your old man going to say?'

'What indeed? It'll be a nasty shock for him. Though it shouldn't, really. *Tel père, tel fils.*'

'But you'll have to marry her.'

'Nothing doing. I've got all my plans cut out for the future. I'm not going to have them upset all for this little – all for a contemptible little foetus inside her.'

'Contemptible little foetus! You don't think when you say that. A foetus is far, far from contemptible. Mussolini was once a contemptible little foetus. And Hitler.'

'All right. All right. Don't get preachy. I know all about that. But I'm not marrying her, anyway. That's straight. Even if my old man consented I'd refuse. Marriage spoils one's chances, and I've got to get somewhere in this world. No ordinary family-life for me.'

'But what about her? Aren't you going to consider her at all?'

'Consider her the deuce! I didn't tell her to go and get pregnant. She should have prevented it in some way. Worst with

96

these females…' He clicked his tongue impatiently, and, thrusting his hands deep in his pockets, started to pace up and down.

A soft wind had begun to blow. It came from the south – a land-breeze. It touched his cheek gently, and he saw the flimsy pink curtains at the window bulging inward in ghostly billows. It felt very chill and watery, but it was good to breathe it in and feel the freshness of it going deep in your lungs. You could smell the wet grass and the shrubs in it, the savannah and the cattle. Pausing abruptly by the window, he saw that one or two stars had begun to wink hazily through the thin stratus. Regulus of Leo and Castor and Pollux, the twins.

'When are you going to tell your old man?'

'Tomorrow – or perhaps tonight just before going to bed.'

He began to pace again, slowly.

'I think it would be better to tell him tonight and get it over at once.'

'Mm. Sense in that. I think I will. Yes, I will.' He came to a halt. 'You know what? I'm going to give a recital this evening.'

'A recital?'

'Mm. After dinner. A piano recital. I'm just in the mood to play. I'll play those two Chopin ballades – the A flat one and the F. And the Debussy piece you like, *La cathédrale engloutie*. And the Medtner studies, too.'

After he had stood at the window for a while, he gave a slight shudder, feeling the chill in the wind and the chill of fear in his soul. The darkness of the night seemed to him suddenly a thing of dread. The incidents of the future seemed to crouch hidden in the gloom out there like huge monsters waiting to overwhelm him – unknown monsters which made them all the more fearsome. He leant a little way out of the window and looked up at the sky. Regulus had vanished, but Castor and Pollux still winked ruddily.

20

No rain fell during the night. The sheet of stratus cloud grew thinner and thinner, and the stars, one by one, came out, winking mistily at first and then brighter and brighter and more plentifully. By midnight not even a tiny wisp or rag of cloud could be seen anywhere one looked. The sky had a purple tinge, cool and rather sinister, as though it were made of dark-blue glass and there might be belladonna behind it. Even the stars had an evil look, like emeralds and rubies cursed by the high-priest of a temple centuries ago.

By two o'clock the air had grown cuttingly chill. The chill woke Beena who had gone to bed naked. Huddled between Kattree and Sukra – for all three of them slept on the wooden bed – she found herself awake and shivering all over. Her toes and the soles of her feet felt icy cold, her nipples were hard and pointed and her legs and arms felt rough with the gooseflesh. She tried to hide her toes under the hem of Kattree's skirt, but it made little difference. After a while, she had to take from under her head some of the bedding that served as pillow and wrap it round her feet. That helped a little, but the chills continued to run up and down her legs and body, so that she had to keep rubbing her hands along her skin to try to put some warmth into it.

She could not get to sleep again, and gloomy thoughts began to run through her mind. Suppose she took a severe cold and grew ill with fever. She would have to lie for days on the bed here burning and getting thin. And Kattree would buy those brown quinine tablets – the Government quinine sold in the post office at six tablets for a penny – and she would have to swallow one tablet in the morning and one at midday and another in the evening. Perhaps for a whole week, or a fortnight, she would not be able to see the savannah or the sky or help to mind the cows. She would not be able to see Jannee or sit with him in his donkey-cart. This thought gave her a feeling of alarm. It would be terrible not seeing him all that time. She felt a sudden longing to be near him. If only he could come now and spread a warm sheet over her and kiss her cheek and keep patting her body with his hand until she felt asleep, as her mother used to do when she was a child!

She wondered if he felt cold like her. Perhaps he was awake, too, at this very moment and feeling lonely without Sukra. Or maybe he wanted her, Beena, instead. The thought made her shift about uneasily. She wondered how he would receive her when daylight came and she went to plead with him to take Sukra back. He might be angry with her for giving shelter to Sukra. He might beat her and drive her from his house as he had done to Sukra not many hours ago. He might shout after her that he did not want to see her or speak to her again for the rest of their lives.

She shivered all over and squeezed her bent arms tightly across her breast, gripping her shoulders. She almost regretted now giving her dress to Sukra. If she had kept it she would have been warm now and asleep. It would have been Sukra who would be shivering now like this, Sukra whose belly was big with Jannee's child. She felt suddenly jealous of Sukra. The happy nights Sukra must have had lying with Jannee. If only she, Beena, could have one such night. She wouldn't care what happened to her afterwards. She could die even. The duppies could kill her or she could drown in the canal… But it was wrong of her to think these things. Jannee was Sukra's husband, and as long as Sukra lived she, Beena, could never hope to lie at night with Jannee.

She shivered again and was attacked by a sudden fit of dry coughing. The cold was penetrating to her lungs. Maybe she would get lung disease and lie for months coughing and spitting blood as her mother had done five years ago. She would get bony and ugly as the weeks passed, and one day she would cough and cough until blood trickled from her mouth and she would die.

She sat up and looked around in the dark. She must find something to cover her. She would get up and see.

Very quietly, so as not to disturb the others, she got off the bed and groped about in the dark for her dress and cotton panties which she had hung up on a wooden support in the low roof, near Ramgolall's corner. After a moment, her hand touched cloth, and, groping upwards, she found that the panties were still damp, being not properly opened out, while the dress was only partly dry, the areas around the hem and the seams being damp and cold still. If she wore it like this she would take cold.

After she had wracked her mind for a little, the thought came to her that if she made a fire in the mud-furnace outside she could dry the damp parts. The heat of the fire would keep her warm in the meantime.

She did not find any difficulty in lighting the fire, for Kattree had put some dry wood under the bed since yesterday morning and there were also the scraps of paper that had contained the sandwiches and cakes brought by Geoffry and Stymphy. Soon the bright flames were crackling and flaring in the mud-furnace. Her shadow looked large and ugly on the wall of the mud-house. It frightened her a little, but she did not mind, for the warmth made her feel comfortable and happy. Perhaps she would not take cold, after all, and die. She would still be able to go on walking under the sky in the sunlight and sit with Jannee in his cart. It was a cheering thought.

It took her a long time – it must have been over an hour – to get the dress dry enough to be worn. She used up all the wood and paper and eventually had to content herself with holding the damp parts over the glowing embers, for all her fuel had given out.

When, at length, she put on the dress, and sank down once more on the bed between Kattree and Sukra she felt as though she had achieved a mighty task. In less than a minute she was sound asleep.

When they all woke at dawn and she told them of what she had done during the dark hours of the morning they hardly wanted to believe her. 'You shoulda wake me,' said Sukra, after Beena had convinced them. 'Me woulda help you ketch de fire.'

But Beena made light of it and said that it was nothing. 'Me had plenty paper an' wood. Me use all de wood you put under de bed yesterday mornin', Kattree.'

Kattree smiled and said that it did not matter.

Despite the biting chill of the morning, the two of them had their usual morning bathe in the canal, for they always felt greatly refreshed after it. Sukra did not join them owing to her pregnant condition.

By the time they were ready to milk the cows the sky in the east had flared into pink and orange and the stars had faded into pale sparks. Filmy feathers of cirrus formed a rigid trail from north to south, throwing hazed tendrils towards the zenith, while small, smudgy purple clouds, like puffs of cigarette smoke, drifted slowly in a southerly direction. A very faint, damp wind could be felt – a mere drift of air. The savannah looked red-brown and filled with a still, unreal peace. Not a sign of moving life could be seen anywhere and the deep quiet of everything gave one a soothing pain far within.

As Beena began to milk the first cow she felt a throb go through her. In about an hour from now she would be setting out in the sunlight for Jannee's home to plead for Sukra. She felt fearful and yet, in some strange way, happy and excited, eager to be on the way.

21

Shortly after eight o'clock, when the sun was shining brightly and large, puffy white clouds drifted, one after the other, in the trade-wind, Big Man got into the large maroon Vauxhall and, seating himself in front beside Joshua, was driven off east along the public road.

When at breakfast (called 'tea' in Guiana) he had suddenly given orders to the maid to tell Joshua that he would require the car in half an hour, Sosee had stared at him in wonder, and so had the children (save Geoffry), for Big Man very rarely went out in the car so early in the day. No one, however, asked him why he wanted to go out so early in the car or where he was going. They knew better than to question him concerning his actions. Geoffry was the only one who would have risked plying Big Man with such questions, though on this occasion he remained silent, for he had no need to ask anything. He already knew what was taking his father out so early in the car.

Big Man and Geoffry were their ordinary selves at breakfast, and Sosee and the children, hearing the two of them talk and laugh, did not dream for a moment that anything untoward was afoot. Not even the prying Dora, who somehow generally knew everything, had the faintest idea of what Geoffry's letter of yesterday contained or of what had passed between Big Man and Geoffry late last night after the rest of them had gone to bed. Sosee knew that Geoffry and Big Man had talked together for a long while last night in Big Man's room, for she had heard the murmur of their voices, her room being next to Big Man's, but she had fallen asleep, thinking nothing of it, for when Geoffry was home on holiday he and Big Man often talked together about school matters and of Geoffry's plans for the future. She had taken it for granted that it was about such matters they had been talking last night.

When Big Man left in the car, Geoffry and Stymphy were in the yard helping the children to fly their kites. Each one of them had a kite, and, the wind being strong and steady, all six kites were in the air, one or two of them dodging about rather erratically through lack of enough tail.

Big Man smiled a faint, affectionate smile as he regarded the children. He always felt oddly content and proud when he saw them all together like this. Something glowed pleasantly within him. It made him feel important, generous and big. It gave him a sensation as though he were the wielder of solid power, even more so than his money gave him. It made him feel that he had done something momentous for mankind – for the universe as a whole. Owing to him, the human species was the richer by seven active, hopeful young creatures, vital units in the scheme of life. He was their author. He was responsible for their existence. It was a big thing to contemplate – big and significant.

They soon drifted from his view as the car turned out into the road, and within a moment his thoughts had become centred once more on the reason for this early morning excursion. After his talk with Geoffry last night he had sat for a long time in his rocking chair smoking his pipe and reflecting on what the two of them had discussed. A very satisfying talk it had been, in many ways. They had both been calm and sensible and that was what had satisfied him most. It was good to see one's son reflect one's own qualities. It was good to know that he was made of stern stuff and could face up squarely to a crisis, just as one had done at his age. No stammering or shy confusion. No evading of gazes. They had both looked at each other straight in the eyes. Very few people could look at him straight in the eyes for long. But Geoffry had done it. Facing each other last night, they had each felt the power in the other, the magnetic force. They had subconsciously challenged each other and neither had flinched.

'I suppose what I'm going to tell you is going to give you something of a shock, Dad. I daresay you'll be disappointed in me.'

Well, it had been a shock, certainly – that was to say a great surprise. But he had not been disappointed. 'That would be foolish of me, my boy. Disappointed in you for being natural? Nonsense! It is unfortunate that she's got pregnant as a result, but that's no fault of yours. That's Nature again, though, of course, under the present arrangement of civilized conduct it's considered disgraceful. Disgraceful my eye! The damned world wants reorganizing. That's what's wrong. Less talk about morality and religious myth and more simple, practical common sense.'

Yes, a very satisfactory talk. The boy had his head screwed on right. No confounded sentimentality about him. No mushy, romantic tommy-rot. He recognized that to marry the girl now would ruin his future. He cared very deeply for her, he said, but marriage with her at present was out of the question. If she waited, he would marry her in years to come, when he had achieved what he intended to achieve, taking it for granted, of course, that they still felt the same way about each other. That was a rational attitude to take up. There was plain common sense in that. Any other boy, with a lot of foolish, sentimental dreams in his head, might have wanted to throw up his whole future so that he could marry the girl and settle down in a cottage. It was gratifying to note that one's son had no such humbug in his make-up. It made one feel that there was really something in heredity. Like father, like son.

Big Man grunted and settled back comfortably against the leather upholstery, feeling very contented. He looked out at the bright sunshine and liked it. He liked, too, the steady humming of the car and the drone of the wind past his ears. Gazing out over the flat savannah country, he felt no romantic or poetic thrill. He was merely conscious of a complacent triumph. There lay the land that he had conquered. There lay the land from which he had won the wherewithal to be comfortable in a large house and have a woman to satisfy his sexual appetite and breed him children, the wherewithal to procure good food, a comfortable bed, servants, rapid means of transport and, above all, a thorough education for his children. He felt master of all that he saw about him, but in a serene way, not with a throbbing sense of power. In the early days of his success he had felt so. But not now. Now in middle-age a quiet completeness had settled upon him. He viewed life now as though it were the picture in a difficult jigsaw puzzle that he had struggled to fit together and had, at length, succeeded in doing. The whole thing lay before him, complete, void of all mystery, no more a source of worry and perplexity. All that was left for him to do now was to see that the parts continued to hold together and were not scattered by any disturbing wind. That was the only real interest life held for him now: the guarding of his property and his family. He must see to it that the land continued to yield wealth and that this wealth was utilized for the benefit of his family. He must see to it that no intruder came to upset his scheme of things. He must see that his children grew into fine specimens and got what they wanted.

One or two people had chaffingly accused him of being absorbed only in Geoffry's welfare, claiming that Geoffry was the only child about whom he cared anything. That was wrong. If they could have seen into him they would have known better, they would have known that he regarded all his children with an affection that went deep in him. Geoffry was certainly his first and supreme interest, but that was merely because he was the eldest and showed unusually great promise. Had he been a weak-natured nitwit he would have treated him as he treated the younger children – with affectionate indulgence or stern correction. Geoffry had reached an age, and a stage in his life, when his future must be planned with care. His soul had early begun to reveal itself, had early begun to show in what direction its hopes and longings lay. Not so with the others. The others were still mere animals: intelligent animals who had not yet emerged from the oblivion of their immaturity. In this state they did not interest him. He felt towards them a deep parental love and the pride of being their creator, but no interest. They would not begin to absorb his interest until they showed signs of awakening to a responsibility of things, until they showed that they were growing aware of, and interested in, the future that lay before them. Only then would they begin to glow with that green glamour with which, for him, Geoffry glowed.

Joshua gave the electric horn a few sharp toots.

Looking ahead, Big Man saw a slim East Indian girl coming west along the road. As they drew nearer he recognized her as Beena. He gave her a smile and a brief jerk of his hand as the car flashed past her.

Pretty little thing, he thought. If it had been long ago he would have stopped the car and asked her where she was going and tried to get her to meet him at some lonely spot in the evening. For a brief, whirling instant he sensed again the pink and white glamour of the past, but only for a brief instant, for glamour of that sort made his thoughts run at once to Sosee and the thought of her fat, flabby body and her lazy, easy-going habits immediately slew any illusion he might try to harbour. It always irritated him when he thought about Sosee. It was a good thing that he felt so apathetic towards her nowadays that he hardly ever thought of her. In the back of his mind he saw her only as a kind of slave – a healthy female slave whom he had brought into his house to satisfy his sexual needs and to reproduce his kind. Somehow, he never thought of the children as belonging partly to her. He had always thought of them as being wholly his, as though he had taken them from his body as complete seeds and planted them in her as in a fertile soil and then watched them sprout one after the other into the vital creatures that they now were.

He supposed that very soon he would have to marry her: that was to say, go through the legal formalities that would make it possible for his children to have legitimacy. All bunkum and humbug so far as he was concerned, but if it were not done the law could easily make things awkward for his children when he was dead. He had to prevent that. He had to protect them in every way possible. He must not leave the smallest gap through which any intruder might slip and try to oust them.

They were entering Speyerfeld Village. On either hand stood a line of small, low cottages with corrugated iron roofs and shingled walls. One or two mud-houses with trash roofs were interspersed here and there, but they were definitely in the minority. Soon these cottages and mud-houses were replaced by high, tropical wooden buildings painted white or yellow or pink: dwellings some of them and business places some. In many cases there occurred buildings that were combinations of shop and dwelling, the ground-flat serving as the shop and the upper as dwelling. An abundance of groceries, haberdasheries, rum-shops, drug-stores, tailoring establishments and various kinds of little business concerns met the eye, all presenting a very bright and garish appearance. An air of bustle pervaded the High Street (in reality, the public road). People moved here and there, well-dressed or nearly well-dressed; black, East Indian and one or two Chinese and Portuguese. Lorries piled with grey bags of rice or white bags of flour stood stationary before the provision shops while figures loaded or unloaded them and nasal East Indian voices shouted orders in broken English.

Speyerfeld Village could even brag about a cinema, this being a large white building like a box that looked very gay on the northern side of the street with its innumerable coloured posters depicting the faces and bodies of film-stars in expressions or attitudes of terror, devotion, lust or gaiety.

A quarter-mile or so farther up they came upon Speyerfeld Estate (or Plantation Speyerfeld, as it was also called). There was no real dividing mark. One only knew that one was in Speyerfeld Estate because of the sudden appearance of the sugar-factory with its tall brick chimneys on the one hand, and the huge three-storeyed dwelling-house in spacious grounds that was the manager's residence on the other. Farther on came the hospital, a long, red building on tall wooden pillars, and a series of bungalows where certain members of the estate-staff – the deputy-manager, the chemist, the engineer, all white – lived singly or with their families. The overseers, all white, too, but very young and boisterous, had a building to themselves, a red, high, two-storeyed building that was shown as the Overseers' Quarters. (It was here that Jairamsingh, as butler, managed and superintended the Mess.) Big Man, glancing at this building, smiled faintly, remembering the days long ago when he would come here to carouse with the overseers. He had been friendly with them all – indeed, popular – for though known to be a quadroon, he had the look of a pure white and they had accepted him as such. Many were the wild sprees they had had in this building. Many were the pretty East Indian girls they had brought here to be made love to and disputed over. It was through driving here in his old Ford car of an afternoon or evening to take part in these gay sprees that he had come to meet Sosee and eventually claim her for his own woman.

Soon Speyerfeld had been left behind them and once again the scene reverted to open savannah country. Once again the samphire spread out in an ocean of changing greens or gave way to open pasture-land where sheep or cattle grazed leisurely. The red road ribboned out before them into the distance, hazed and quivering with heat far away. Here and there, in areas where drainage was bad, the savannah, owing to the recent heavy rains, had become one great sheet of rippling water. Big Man, glancing out once, saw the swollen body of a cow high and dry on an islet of land. Dozens of carrion crows, black lumps of activity, scrambled over the carcass, tearing and pulling at it in a fierce, hungry panic and with dull, fluttering, squelchy sounds. A sudden stink whiff made him grimace and put his fingers to his nostrils.

At length, after they had covered several miles, a high, three-storeyed pink house, with a tower whose windows flashed in the sunlight like dewdrops, came into view around a bend in the road, and Joshua at once blew his horn and reduced the speed of the car.

The surface of the drive into which they swung was covered with shells that made a crunching noise under the tyres of the car. They drew up before stone steps. A bright brass plate gleamed over the dark-brown door with the word 'Vrjheid' engraved on it in German text.

Joshua alighted and pulled a brass knob and a bell jangled far away in the depth of the building.

A few minutes later an East Indian maid was showing Big Man into the study of Doctor Roy Matthias.

22

Beena had been delayed in setting out for Jannee's home. When the milking was over, it was decided that Kattree should accompany her father to Speyerfeld to help him to sell the milk. Speyerfeld being three miles distant, it was necessary for them to start without delay, for they had no donkey-cart, and Ramgolall would not agree to pay the two pennies that would have taken them by bus. He was too poor, he said, to pay two pennies to go to Speyerfeld. Such things were for the rich man of the land. Hence Beena it was on whom the job of driving the cows into pasture fell. She did not mind, even though she knew that it would mean the delay of another hour or more before she set out for Jannee's home. Delays that could not be avoided never troubled her. What could not be avoided must be bravely borne. That was her way of looking at things.

The sun was high in the sky when, at length, she set out. She wore her clean pink dress – the one she had lent Sukra the day before. (Sukra's own dress was now dry enough for her to wear.) Her hair hung in two long plaits behind. Jannee, perhaps, she reasoned, would not want to beat her and drive her from his home when he saw her two long plaits, for he had once told her that he liked to see her hair done like this.

Her heart beat fast as she crossed the big canal and turned west along the road. For the first time in her life she felt as though something really big lay on her shoulders. She felt as though the power to make things right or wrong in the lives of other people had now been given her. She was a woman now, not a girl. The words she spoke during the next hour or two might make Sukra happy for the rest of her life – or unhappy. Everything depended upon how she spoke to Jannee, upon what she said to him. Even her own happiness, perhaps, depended upon what took place during the next hour or so. Jannee might break friendship with her for good, and that would leave her in misery for the rest of her life. She would have to try to win his patience and do what she could to keep him from flying into one of his angry tempers. She would have to be very careful.

The sudden warning toots of a motorcar's horn ahead made

her move quickly from the middle of the road to the parapet. She watched the car approach, and as it flashed past she made out the strong, pink face of Big Man Weldon, saw him smile and jerk his hand at her. She felt a warm wave of pride and pleasure go through her at his noticing her. It gave her more courage in herself, an added confidence. She was still of some worth, after all, if Big Man Weldon could notice her. That feeling of being a woman came over her again. She felt grown-up, capable.

But as she drew near to Jannee's home and saw Jannee himself sitting before the door smoking and Boodoo and Chattee frolicking about at the edge of the trench, her courage began to fade like water trickling off into a crack in the earth and vanishing. Fear began to creep through her limbs and her body like little black beetles.

'Ay, Jannee!' she hailed, and Jannee seemed to start, for he had had his head bent as if in deep thought. He rose and came forward to meet her as she crossed the wide ditch on the sagging board that served as a bridge. He looked faintly surprised, but pleased.

'You mek me start,' he smiled. 'Me na see you comin'.'

'Like you' mind did stray far,' she laughed.

He nodded, the smile fading from his face, and a frown taking its place. 'Me did t'inking.'

'T'inking? Is wha' you got t'ink so much 'bout?'

He grunted, avoiding to look at her directly. 'Me got plenty t'ink 'bout.' He lowered himself to the ground before the door of the mud-house and told her to sit down, too, speaking in that quiet tone that always frightened her. She sat down opposite to him, feeling all a-tremble within as though lightning had flashed sharply and her soul were awaiting the deafening roar of the thunder. Doom seemed to be in the air.

For an interval neither of them spoke. She sat watching him as he drew at his pipe, his brows dark, his eyes fixed on the ground. He seemed to be looking at a black ant that darted about near his foot.

At length, not able to stand the silence, she said timidly: 'Sukra sleep home wid we last night.'

He said not a word. He did not even shift his gaze.

'She come to we t'rough de rain yesterday.'

Jannee slowly knocked out his pipe and began to refill it, and Beena thought of a black cloud moving silently overhead in calm air.

'She cry plenty. We did sorry fo' she.'

'Wha' she cry fo'?' said Jannee, looking at her abruptly with his deep black eyes. 'Me tell she go live wid Boorharry. Why she na go Boorharry?'

'She na want Boorharry. Wha' mek you t'ink so? You mustn' listen to wha' people tell you.'

'If she na want Boorharry wha' mek she tek two piece roti give 'e yesterday morning?'

She did promise give 'e when 'e shout out beg fo' piece night before last. She na want break she word so she tek two piece nex' morning.'

'She turn sly. She tek am secret give 'e. When she lef' here yesterday mornin' she na got nutting in she hand. She hide de roti in she bosom.'

'Well, she did 'fraid you mighta get vex' if you know she tek roti fo' Boorharry. She na mean nutting mo'. True-true. You must believe.'

Jannee smiled without mirth, in that slow way he had of smiling sometimes and that, to Beena, always seemed to portend some coming danger. He said nothing, and that seemed to add to the danger.

'Sukra good gal, Jannee. You mustn' believe all wha' evil-minded people tell you. Sumatra Pooran got bad mind. She get baby fo' Boorharry an' Boorharry won' marry she, so she jealous o' every woman who she see talkin' to 'e. She talk 'gainst Sukra 'cause she want mek bad between you. She's a bad woman.'

'Sumatra Pooran talk wha' she see wid she own eye. She see Sukra gi' Boorharry two piece roti. She na tell na lie. She see Sukra stan' up talkin' to Boorharry. All da true. She na tell na lie.'

'She's a bad woman. She want mek bad fo' Sukra. Dat's why she tell you all wha' she tell you.'

'Dis na de first time Sukra talk to Boorharry. She always mekin' fun wid 'e. Me tell she over an' over not to talk to 'e, but she na hear.'

'If she talk to 'e once, twice na harm. Only friendly talk. She na mean nutting by it. You mustn' treat she bad, Jannee. She good gal. True-true. She good gal.'

'She say me treat she bad?'

'Na. She na say so. But me ask you treat she good.'

Jannee said nothing, staring moodily at the ground and drawing at his clay-pipe.

'You mus' leh she come back home. She want see you.'

'Me na stop she come back home.'

'Me can tell she come back today?'

'Tell she, na?'

'You going treat she good if she come back?'

'If she promise once for all na talk to Boorharry she can come back. But nex' time me hear she talk to 'e me going kick she out 'pon de road, an' me na want see she at-all, at-all after dat.'

'Na. She won' talk to 'e again. She going promise. Me go now an' tell she.'

'You go so quick? Siddown talk wid me lil' bit.'

She tarried a while longer, therefore, feeling happy at having gained her end so easily and at having put him into a good mood again. For nearly an hour the two of them sat there talking. They talked of the heavy rain of yesterday, and Jannee said that if the rain continued to fall like this there would be a flood in the rice-fields and the young plants would all be killed. If that happened it would mean having to buy fresh seed from the Agricultural Department with which to plant over the fields, and that would mean that the crop would not be ready for reaping until November when there would be danger of rain ruining the ripe grain. (The long dry season lasted from August to November, and if reaping were not done within that time the crops would be lost. November being an uncertain month – it might be dry or rainy – farmers always tried to finish reaping by the end of October.) Last year, said Jannee, Balgobin at Auchlyne, through being ill, had to wait until the middle of November to reap and the rain came and spoiled his whole four-acre crop. Balgobin cried like a child. He had for years attended services on Sunday at the Scottish church at Auchlyne, but after that he stopped going, saying that he did not believe any more in any God of love. He went to the minister and told him that if God had really loved man as the minister had said, He would not have allowed the rain to come and spoil his crop and make him poor. The minister told him about Job, how God had sent Job many troubles even though Job was a righteous man, but Balgobin would not listen, saying that the Bible did not talk truly and that he would not believe in it any more. If God, by a miracle, made his crop come back good again he would believe, but not otherwise.

Then after a while, Beena told Jannee of how Jairamsingh had stopped taking milk from her father and of how the police sergeant had tried to take a sample of the milk so that he could bring a charge against Ramgolall for putting water in the milk, and of how she had upset the larger can and rolled it into the canal. Then she told him of Geoffry and Stymphy, what nice boys they were, and of the happy meal they had had together in the mud-house during the pouring rain. At this point Jannee frowned and interrupted her, saying that he did not like these bakra boys (meaning white boys).

'Deh got too much airs to put on,' he frowned.

'Not dese two,' Beena defended. 'Dese two nice boys. Deh na got na airs put on. Deh talk to we nice. Stymphy mek me tek 'e in de house an' show 'e everyt'ing – de hammock, de bed, de canister, everyt'ing. We laugh an' talk like if we did good-good friends. 'E say 'e got coolie blood in 'e. 'E nice boy.'

'If 'e nice boy why you na marry am?' said Jannee in a sudden temper. His face had turned dark and angry, and Beena stared at him in dismay, wondering what could have gone wrong with him all in a twinkle like this.

'Wha' wrong, Jannee?' she asked quietly. 'You vex' wid me?'

'Na, me na vex',' he growled, and, rising, he turned off and went into the mud-house.

Beena followed him in, feeling ill at heart. 'Jannee, you vex' wid me? Me na say nutting bad.'

'You na say you like de boy? Well, go back an' look fo' 'e. Go talk wid 'e. Na talk wid me.'

He sat down on one of the two wooden beds and stared moodily at the floor, and Beena, regarding him, knew that he was jealous and did not know what to think or to say. She had never thought that he could be jealous on her account. If he were jealous because she had talked to Stymphy it could only mean one thing: that he must have some love for her, as she had for him. She had never thought that such a thing could be. She had thought all along that the love in him had been for Sukra and that for her, Beena, he had only a friendly feeling. It was only in her dreams that she had seen him loving her.

After a long silence, she said quietly: 'Me didn' know you woulda jealous if me talk to 'e.'

He still kept staring darkly at the floor.

'Me won' talk to 'e again if you na want me to.'

'Me na like na bakra boy,' he growled. 'If you want talk wid me you mustn' talk wid na bakra boy. Me na like am.'

'Awright, me promise you. Me na talk to 'e again.'

The frown began to fade from his face. After a moment he got up and told her not to look so serious. He smiled with his white teeth, his black eyes twinkling in that way that always made her heart feel unquiet and excited behind her ribs.

'Lemme tek you back home in de cart,' he said, and she said 'Awright' and accompanied him to his provision farm which lay about a hundred yards off, to the west of the mud-house. It was there that he kept his donkey and cart. He had a shed for the donkey and the bridge of four wide planks spanning the ditch so that the cart could cross over to and from the road.

There were many narrow drains and ditches to jump over on their way to the farm, and every time they reached one he gripped her hand as though to help her. It made her very warm and happy to feel the tight grip of his hand. The sound of his voice, too, as he talked, and his laughter, gave her joy. Everything in her felt a-tremble and singing like a cool morning with dewdrops and mild sunshine and the conch-shells cooing through the blue, foggy air. She almost hoped they would never reach the farm, but would go on forever half-walking, half-running like this through the short grass and jumping trenches, laughing and talking.

23

Along the forty-odd miles of the Corentyne Coast there are no more than five or six very old residences in a state of good preservation. Of these 'Vrjheid' happens to be one. It is a wooden building throughout, its frame being of bullet wood, the wood that is said to be incapable of rotting. Though repaired and re-painted many times by its succession of owners, it has never been materially altered. Judging it on this basis, therefore, 'Vrjheid' may truthfully be said to be over a century old, having been originally built in 1827 by a Dutch planter, Mynheer Vanderhyden, whose tombstone may still be seen in the backyard, an oblong slab of stone sunk now almost to the level of the ground. Legend went that on the ninth day of August, every year at dawn, the jumbie of a negro slave-boy could be seen sitting on the tomb, a large axe in his lap. In life, long ago, he had been ordered by Mynheer Vanderhyden (who had appeared to him in a dream) to guard the tomb, because a large earthenware jar of gold coins had been secretly buried in the grave here along with his master's coffin. A terrible death by fright would befall any person who made himself so daring as to try to unearth the treasure, hence no one ever ventured to go near the spot after dark for fear of meeting the jumbie of the old Dutchman. Only a month or so ago the gardener, newly taken on and not knowing of the legend, stopped near the tomb one afternoon at twilight, meaning to scrape some mud off a shovel against the edge of the stone slab, when, to his alarm and horror, he heard a deep warning grunt close behind his head. He turned round with a gasp, but there was no one there. Greatly frightened, he threw down his shovel and fled to the house, and after that, nothing on earth would make him venture near the tomb when the sun had gone down.

'Not even for two shillings he wouldn't go there alone,' laughed Dr Roy who had been relating the incident to Big Man after a remark by Big Man on the age of the house. 'I offered him two shillings, but he refused point-blank.'

Dr Roy was fond of relating stories connected with 'Vrjheid'. He was proud of 'Vrjheid' which he had purchased six years ago from the widowed mulatto lady who had owned it last.

His study, high up in the tower, was tastefully decorated. On the brown-varnished walls hung two or three watercolours and a Cézanne print. A tall bookcase stood in the north-eastern corner, the upper shelves filled with leather-bound medical books, the lower with works of modern fiction and biography still in their wrappers. Dr Roy was an avid reader, and his taste in literature was high.

Big Man had found him in a Morris chair, clad in a deep purple dressing-gown over his pyjamas, smoking a cigarette and glancing through a copy of the *New Statesman and Nation*.

After expressing his surprise and pleasure at seeing Big Man, he had offered him a chair and cigarettes, and then Big Man had remarked casually on the age of the house and Dr Roy had told him of the legend connected with the tomb and related the incident of the gardener. They both laughed over it and then went on to talk about superstitions, Big Man telling of the old gentleman who was supposed to haunt the back veranda of his own house and of how David had once seen him.

It was not for some while before Big Man broached the matter that had brought him. 'I suppose you must be curious to know what could have dragged me here so early,' he said. 'Well, the trouble is Geoffry has got himself into a bit of a scrape.'

'A bit of a scrape?'

'Yes. There's a girl he's been friendly with in Georgetown, one Miss Macleod, and, to cut a long story short, he's got her in the family way.'

'Oh!' Dr Roy raised his brows and nodded slowly. 'Begun to sow his wild oats, eh?'

'Like his father. Blood will out, Roy. What to do?'

They both laughed over the sally and Dr Roy told a *risqué* story with childbirth as the theme. When they had laughed over this, too, the doctor grew serious. 'How old is this girl?' he asked, and Big Man told him nineteen. 'She's a few months older than Geoffry. Left school last year,' he said.

The doctor looked faintly thoughtful, his grey-green eyes fixed on the bookcase. He rubbed his chin slowly with a nicotine-stained forefinger.

'How long gone? Did he give you any idea?'

'Little over or little under two months, I believe.'

'Plain-sailing. But I don't like doing these jobs, Big Man, to tell the truth. Apart from the illegality, it's against all my principles.'

Big Man grunted. 'I know. It would be against my principles, too, if I were a medical man, but, then, of course, there are occasions when we've all got to do things counter to our strongest principles. The civilized scheme of things under which we live is such that one often has no alternative but to cast precepts to the winds.'

Dr Roy chuckled. 'Talking about that, I've just finished reading Olaf Stapledon's *Last and First Men*. If you want to read about civilizations read that. It covers a period of two thousand million years – '

'Two thousand *million* years! Aw! Behave yourself, man. How the devil can anybody know what's going to happen in the next two thousand million years?'

'Oh, it's all make-believe, of course, but, all the same, you can't help admiring the man's imagination. It's simply staggering. The man makes you feel small. And the supreme beauty of it is that he's so coldly logical and scientific in everything he puts forward. It's no wild romantic fantasy. Even while you shake your head and smile at it you've got to respect the superb intellect of the man. And he's a great poet, too. A particular chapter there towards the end – it's entitled "Cosmology", I think – the thing reads like a piece of music, the movement of a Brahms sonata or something. Oh, it's a wonderful book, man. You should read it. I must lend you.'

But Big Man shook his head. 'Sounds too heavy for me. Geoffry would probably like it. I prefer a good baffling detective story.'

'Well, I've got a Dorothy Sayers here. Not bad, but I was never too keen on these thrillers, even at their best.'

'When are you going to Georgetown?'

'Well, as a matter of fact, I have to take a run down there day after tomorrow. I've been invited to an installation ceremony. Owing to Jemmott's death, you know. He was Worshipful Master for this year.'

'Oh, yes. I read of his death. Who are they going to install as the new Worshipful Master?'

'Flanagan. Wheeler Brothers' man.'

'Flanagan, eh? I didn't know he was a Freemason. Thought he was a Roman Catholic.'

'Flanagan? Oh, no. Church of England. He's an old Mason. One of our best men. But look here, tell your boy to write his girl at once and tell her to call round at Dr Giles's surgery in Camp Street and I'll fix things up for her. Say at eight-thirty Friday morning. Giles doesn't begin the day until nine.'

'Dr Giles's surgery, eh? Camp Street.'

'That's right. Eight-thirty. I'll fix everything up.'

'Good man.'

'And you'd better tell him what to use not to let it happen again. You're sending him away next year, eh?'

'Yes. He's going to have a try at the Guiana this year, but whether he comes out on top or not I'm sending him off. He's very keen on going.'

'Oh, he'll get somewhere – no doubt at all about that. You can see it in his face.'

'Yes, he's got it in him all right. Promising lad. He got exempt from Matriculation in the last exam he passed.'

'Aha. I read of it some time ago. You want him to take up medicine, I hear, eh?'

'Yes. It's his own choice, though, not mine.'

Dr Roy chuckled. 'What would have been your choice, Big Man? Law? Or ranching?'

Big Man shrugged. 'Oh, it didn't matter to me what he took up, that's the truth. I don't believe in choosing for children. So long as they make a success of whatever they put their hands to, that's all I care about.'

'I thought you might have wanted him to succeed you as owner and manager of the estate.'

'In a way, I do, but the boy has ambitions of his own – big ambitions. He wants to conquer the world. You can't conquer the world as a rancher on the Corentyne Coast of British Guiana, you know.'

Dr Roy nodded and smiled a faint, philosophical smile. They both fell silent for a while and the wind came in at the open window and cooled their faces, wind that smelt of the sea and of the savannah, wind the odour of which they had known from boyhood. It wrapped them round with a primeval bond of camaraderie. It brought with it the memory of winds like itself that had hummed with a soothing peace or moaned in the gloom of evening when the duppies and jumbies were abroad. It brought with it the squeak of vicissi duck high in the sky at night, a portent of rain, and childhood reveries in the yearning shade of a coconut glade, besprinkled with sunshine and lulled by the crackle of the fronds overhead.

Big Man of a sudden said: 'Oh, well!' and, rising, said that he must be going, but Dr Roy told him to sit down and smoke another cigarette, so Big Man sat down again and they talked for over an hour.

24

Between Big Man and Geoffry it was decided that Geoffry, instead of writing to his girl, should go in person to Georgetown so that he would be able to take her round to Dr Giles's surgery and introduce her to Dr Roy. It would make things much easier for her this way. The proposal came from Geoffry himself and Big Man readily agreed that it was sound.

Stymphy, from whom no secrets were kept, said that he would get along perfectly until Geoffry returned. 'Don't trouble about me,' he assured Geoffry. 'I'll be as right as rain. The children will see to it that I'm well entertained, you can be sure.'

'Why, of course,' Geoffry nodded. 'I was forgetting Dora. Don't make her seduce you in my absence, Stymphy. It'll spoil your poetry.'

His departure the following morning created a mild sensation among the other children and Sosee. The reason he had given – 'to consult the shipping people on Big Man's behalf concerning the export of cattle to Dutch Guiana' – did not hold water. After he had gone Dora and Sosee openly expressed their scepticism. Sosee said she was sure something else was behind it, and Dora declared confidently that she *knew* that he hadn't gone down on any cattle business. 'Nobody can fool me,' she asserted. 'His going down has something to do with that letter he got day before yesterday. I *know* it's that.'

Big Man looked at her and chuckled. 'You try to know too much that isn't good for you,' he rumbled. 'One of these days you'll get hurt if you don't look out.'

During the course of that day and the two following days Stymphy, who was regarded as being 'in the know', came in for unabated attention. He was offered bribes of all kinds to divulge the true reason for Geoffry's departure for Georgetown. David said that he would show him where to find plenty fish. 'Or I can show you the path that leads out to the sea, if you want.' John was ready to surrender his balata ball and two glass marbles, and Jim said that he would lend him his 'Daisy' air gun 'to go an' shoot birds wid'. But Stymphy shook his head to all these tempting offers. Even when, the situation grown desperate, Belle boldly offered him a kiss and Dora two kisses would he agree to divulge the important information. He breathed very deeply in relief when Geoffry returned on Saturday.

It rained steadily from shortly after eleven on Friday night until about nine o'clock on Saturday morning, but at one o'clock when Geoffry arrived the sun was shining palely in a sky hazed with sheet-like wisps of white cloud.

Everything had gone according to plan, Geoffry confided to Big Man (and later to Stymphy). She had made no fuss about submitting to the operation. 'In fact, she behaved like a regular sport,' he told Stymphy. 'No sloppy tears or anything of the sort as one would have expected from a female. She's a real brick, I can tell you.'

For the rest of that day, however, he was silent and contemplative, and whenever he did laugh his laughter sounded hard and forced. Stymphy could see that something had moved him deeply.

25

A few brief showers of rain fell on Sunday, but for three days after the weather proved fine. The sun shone brightly and in the evening the sky was without a trace of cloud, being so clear, indeed, that the Milky Way was clearly visible.

On Tuesday Geoffry and Stymphy went fishing. They made straight for Ramgolall's mud-house, and, arrived there, found Kattree alone at home. She sat by the edge of the canal washing her dirty dress: beating it with a piece of wood and then squeezing it. The sound of their bicycle bells made her look round, and when she saw them approaching along the dam, trundling their bicycles, she broke into her calm, pleased smile, but did not move or in any way attempt to get up to greet them. She just stopped beating the wet dress and sat upright, waiting for them to come up.

'How's life, Kattree bettay?' Geoffry greeted her, pulling her pigtail. 'Doing a bit of washing?'

'Eh-heh. Me a wash me one dirty dress.'

'Your one dirty dress? Why do you say one? Haven't you got any other dresses?'

'No. Dis de only one me got beside de one me got on now.'

'Eh? But you don't mean that seriously?'

'Yes. Only two dress me got; one me wear, one me keep clean fo' change. Same wid Beena.'

'Well, I'll be blowed! Where's Beena, by the way?'

'She gone – to Speyerfeld wid Ramgolall sell milk.'

'And when are they going to be back?' Stymphy asked.

'Not till dis af'noon late.'

'What a pity, I had hoped to see her, too.'

'You disappoint you na see she, na?'

'Rather. But I'm quite glad to see you, too,' smiled Stymphy. 'Aren't you going to do any fishing today?'

'Na, not today. Today me got salt-fish fo' breakfas'. Beena buy salt-fish in Speyerfeld yesterday.'

'I see. And I suppose Ramgolall and Beena are going to eat their breakfast in Speyerfeld?'

'Eh-heh. Beena cook breakfas' since early dis morning. She tek it in de saucepan.'

'You needn't bother to cook for yourself today,' said Geoffry. 'Stymphy and I are picnicking here until afternoon. You can have breakfast with us.'

They spent a very happy day. Kattree sat between them while they waited for the fish to bite. They talked of many things, of fish, of the weather and of human beings. Kattree told them of how Jannee had beaten Sukra and put her out of his house and of how Beena had made them friends again. Stymphy told of the kite-flying and of the games he and the children had played. Both he and Geoffry, however, took good care not to mention anything of Geoffry's visit to Georgetown or of the trouble concerning Clara Macleod.

Once a fisherman and his wife passed, on their way to the seashore. Their seine was doubled up and slung over a pole. They walked one behind the other, the pole stretched between them and resting on their shoulders. Kattree greeted them cheerfully and they greeted her cheerfully in return. Their names were Poonar and Chuttree, Kattree said. Geoffry and Stymphy also called out to them, and Stymphy, in an impulse, wanted to follow them to the seashore, but Geoffry told him not to be an ass. 'It's over a mile to the sea, and you'd have to walk through mud and courida bush to get to the beach. It won't be worth the game.' After some argument – Stymphy claimed that it would be a great adventure – he decided to take Geoffry's advice and remain where he was.

Poonar and Chuttree soon became tiny specks in the distance and eventually vanished altogether in the courida bush.

By midday Geoffrey and Stymphy had caught between the two of them, nine fishes: four mullets, three hassars, one cuirass and a flat, brown fish that Kattree called a 'flounder'.

They ate sandwiches and pastry and drank ginger-ale in the shade of the mud-house, and a merry meal it was. Geoffry dropped crumbs down Kattree's back and Stymphy tied the end of her pigtail with brown paper. Geoffry bet Stymphy two mullets that he could stand on his head and eat a pâté. Stymphy said that he could not, so Geoffry stood on his head and let Kattree feed him with a pâté. When he had eaten half the pâté he choked and had to desist, and Kattree and Stymphy laughed a great deal as they watched him sit with red face coughing and wiping the tears from his eyes.

After the meal, they did not feel inclined to continue fishing, so they reclined in the shade of the mud-house and talked and made jokes. At length, the heat and their well-filled stomachs caused a lethargy to creep over them. Geoffry said he felt like dozing and within a minute he was sound asleep. Kattree and Stymphy talked on for a while until they, too, fell off to sleep.

A quaint sight they made sprawling there on the bare earth. Stymphy slept flat on his back, his head pillowed on the palm of his hand. Kattree, between them, lay on her right side, her legs doubled up nearly to her chin. Geoffry sprawled loosely, partly on his back, partly on his left side, one of his knees bent upward.

Being the most westerly of the three, it was he whom the creeping line of sunshine first reached. It shone on the tip of his nose and then on his eyelids and cheek, and, with a sigh, he opened his eyes, squinted them, rubbed them, then sat up. In sitting up, his leg grazed Kattree and she, too, opened her eyes and sat up. They yawned almost in unison and then looked at each other with watery eyes and smiled.

'Slept well, Kattree?'

She nodded. 'Eh-heh. Me sleep good. Me sleep 'til me dream. You sleep good, too?'

'Perfectly – until the sun woke me. What time do you think it is now? Look at the sun and tell me.'

' 'E 'bout quarter past two now.'

'We've slept for nearly two hours, then.'

'Eh-heh.'

They sat staring before them for an interval without speaking, and the silence of the white day whooped and hummed like a hot, spectral wing around them. Wind blew very faintly. The sky looked grey-blue from the heat like a September or October sky. Far off the savannah seemed to be a mirage, unreal and trembling, and the air felt like a warm silk scarf wrapped tightly around their faces and threatening in a half-hearted way to stifle them.

Stymphy slept on peacefully, his lips slightly parted.

Abruptly they turned their heads and looked at each other, and for an instant Kattree's eyes gleamed faintly and then looked

122

away. Geoffry smiled and gave a grunt. 'You have deep eyes,' he said.

'Deep eyes?'

'Mm. Full of unquiet secrets.'

'You na like me eyes?'

'Oh, yes. I like them. They rather intrigue me, in fact.'

'Intrigue you? Me na know dah word.'

'Interest. You know? Fascinate, puzzle.'

'Me eyes puzzle you?'

'Yes, in a way.' He smiled at her and let his hand glide along the smooth skin of her arm down to her hand. He stroked her hand lightly with the tips of his fingers and told her that she had rare eyes. 'I've been studying you a bit through your eyes. There's something a little baffling about you, something that attracts me and yet sort of evades me.'

She only kept looking at the ground.

'Savvy what I mean, Kattree bettay?'

He put a finger under her chin and raised her face so that he could look into her eyes. He smiled in that calm way and said quietly: 'If Stymphy weren't here…' and would not finish the sentence. She smiled a trifle and tried to avoid his gaze, saying nothing, but her eyes were filled with gleaming secrets.

Of a sudden he removed his finger from under her chin and grunted, the calm smile still on his face, but a smile now without mirth. 'I'm an unscrupulous sort of cad, when you come to think of it, Kattree. Give Stymphs a prod there for me, won't you? I feel like catching a few more mullets before the day is over.'

Kattree, without a word, did as he bade. She jabbed her forefinger in Stymphy's chest and said: 'Wake up! Wake up, Stymphy!' and Stymphy's eyes opened.

They caught several more fishes during the next two or three hours. The sun was low in the west when Geoffry and Stymphy took their departure. Beena and Ramgolall had not yet returned. Before they left, Kattree asked them when she would see them again, and Geoffry replied: 'Day after tomorrow.'

26

For Ramgolall, life was not going easily. The people of Speyerfeld bought his milk, but they would not pay him more than four cents a pint – in many cases, only three cents – for other milk vendors there were and competition was rife. Moreover, after what had happened he could not venture to add water to the larger can as he had done formerly, and that meant that when he and Beena set out for Speyerfeld in the morning they took with them only two gallons and six or seven pints. The takings of the day hardly came up to more than three shillings and sixpence.

Three shillings and sixpence for twenty-two or twenty-three pints of milk! When hitherto he had got five shillings and sixpence, and that was leaving out the sixpence Joseph had charged to take the can to Speyerfeld. It was terrible, thought Ramgolall as he and Beena returned home in the fading light. Bad fortune had, indeed, come to him. Look at the effort that it took him to walk the three miles to Speyerfeld and then go from house to house selling the milk. His days for such effort were past. He could not go on much longer with it. When he woke in the mornings now his joints felt stiff and sore, and a weary, lazy feeling enveloped his whole body so that he did not want to get out of the hammock. It was only the thought of the few shillings at the end of the day that gave him the will to get up and stir himself.

This morning he had spoken of the stiffness of his joints and the weary feeling in his body, and Beena had suggested that she and Kattree should take the milk to Speyerfeld and sell it, but he had shaken his head and said that he could not leave it all to them. People might rob or cheat them, seeing that they were only girls. 'Plenty evil in dis worl', bettay,' he had said, groaning and wagging his head. 'Plenty, plenty evil. You lil' girl yet, bettay. Ha! You na know how people bad. Huh.' Beena and Kattree had argued that they were big enough to care themselves and see that no one robbed or cheated them, but their father would not heed. He held out that they were too young to be trusted to sell the milk. People would cheat and rob them. There was too much evil in the world.

When they got home, Kattree told them of the day she had

spent with Geoffry and Stymphy, of all the fun they had had together, but Ramgolall was too tired to give heed and Beena listened in a queer, half-interested way that was unlike her. She even gave a brief, half-sneering laugh once and said: 'Dat's right, gal. All-you have you' fun.' Her manner puzzled Kattree a lot.

'Me ask dem when deh comin' back an' deh say deh comin' day after tomorrow.'

'Leh dem try,' said Beena. 'Me got to go a-Speyerfeld help Ramgolall sell milk. Me won' be here.'

'Is why you talk so?' frowned Kattree.

'How you mean?'

'You talk as if you na got na interest in dem na more. Is wha' gone wrong?'

'Nutting na wrong,' said Beena, turning away a little impatiently. 'You drive home dem cow awready, na?' she asked as though to cover up her impatience.

'Eh-heh. Long time,' said Kattree. 'You na see dem in de pen deh yonder?'

'Eh-heh. Me only ask to mek sure.' She began to chant a song in a quick, self-conscious voice, and Kattree looked at her, feeling profoundly puzzled.

Around them the twilight had grown deep and pale shadows lay on the ground, for a half-moon, bulging a trifle on the growing side, hovered in the sky, nearly overhead.

Glancing at the moon, Kattree remarked: 'Sunday come a-full moon. Curry-feed got to hold home here.'

'Full moon Monday,' said Beena. ' 'E gone a day ahead like 'e does do sometimes.'

'You fin' out in Speyerfeld?'

'Eh-heh. Me ask Jaigan an' 'e look at 'e almanack an' say full moon Monday. Jannee say is Monday, too. Me bin a-talk to 'e 'bout de curry-feed yest'day. 'E say 'e go try borrow a sitar from Bijoolie or Moonsammy. 'E going try play it.'

Kattree said: 'Oh!' and after a brief pause she suddenly came out with: 'Me bin t'ink we coulda invite Geoffry an' Stymphy come to de curry-feed.'

'Eh? Geoffry an' Stymphy! Invite dem! Eh-heh! How we can do dah?'

'An' why not? Wha' mek we caan' invite dem?'

'Na, we caan' invite dem,' said Beena. 'Jannee an' Sukra might na like it. We got t'ink 'bout dem, too.'

'We can ask dem, see wha' deh say.'

'Awright, but me na t'ink deh go like it. Curry-feed is fo' coolie like we. Geoffry an' Stymphy na coolie. Dem is bakra boy.'

Kattree was silent. For the rest of that evening she said nothing to Beena, nor did Beena say anything to her.

27

Two days later Geoffry and Stymphy came again to the home of Ramgolall. As on the previous occasion, they found only Kattree at home, Beena and her father having gone to Speyerfeld to sell the milk. On this day there was rain. The morning broke fine, but at about ten o'clock a sudden shower drove them into the mud-house. It only lasted for ten minutes or so, however, when the sun came out once more and they were able to continue fishing. But hardly an hour after another shower made them hurry into shelter again. So it continued throughout the day – brief shower, a spell of sunshine, brief shower, sunshine…

Despite this fickle weather, they still enjoyed themselves. Kattree brought out her fishing-rod, and, between the three of them, they caught fourteen fishes by afternoon. Kattree shared their sandwiches and other eatables and many jokes passed between them and much laughter.

When the time to leave came Geoffry said to Kattree: 'We may not see you again, Kattree, so perhaps we'd better make this goodbye.'

Kattree looked dismayed and said: 'Holiday over so quick? When you going back to Georgetown?'

'Sunday coming. School opens on Monday.'

'Why so quick? Holiday short dis time.'

'We've had three weeks, my dear girl. Isn't that enough? Holidays started since Maundy Thursday. We arrived here on the Saturday after Easter.'

'Why you didn' come as soon as holiday start?'

'Stymphy and I had to take part in the Athletic Sports in Georgetown on Easter Monday, and after that we spent a few days with Stymphy's cousins at Plaisance.'

'Where Plaisance?'

'On the East Coast, Demerara. It's a village. Have you never been that way?'

'Na. Me na bin nawhere. Me never even been to New Amsterdam.'

'What! Never even been to New Amsterdam Then you've never seen a steamer or a train in your life?'

'No. Me see aeroplane pass over an' over, but me only see steamer an' train in picture. Same wid Beena. We never travel furder dan where donkey-cart can tek we.'

'But couldn't you take bus and go to New Amsterdam for a day?' said Stymphy. 'Why, you could go in the morning and come back in the afternoon.'

'Eh-h-h-h! Wheh we go get money from? Ramgolall na like spend money. 'E hardly want buy food to eat an' clothes for wear. 'E save up all 'e money in a canister in deh. 'E na like spend.'

'I see,' said Geoffry, and his face took on a sudden thoughtful look. 'A miser, eh? His face does give one that impression, now I come to think of it.' Abruptly he went on: 'Anyway, when I come back here on the Summer vac. I'll take you and Beena places. I'll have got my driving certif. by then. You'd come with me to New Amsterdam for a drive, wouldn't you?'

'Yes. Sure t'ing. Me never drive in car yet.'

'Well, well! Pretty low state of affairs, Kattree. I'll certainly have to do something about it.'

'You say you going back to Georgetown Sunday come?'

'That's right. And we want to spend tomorrow and Saturday higher up the Coast – at Number Sixty-three Village. The place where you get good sea-bathing.'

'Eh-heh. Me hear 'bout it. Me won' see all-you again, den? Not till August month?'

'Not until August. But you'll only see me. Stymphy will be off to Trinidad to spend a month or two with an uncle of his. He's got relatives all over the bally globe.'

'Oh! Well, me go look out to see you in August.'

'Good girl. But look here,' he added abruptly, 'if you take a walk out to the road tomorrow morning, say at about half past eight, you'll see us when we're passing on our way up to Sixty-three.'

'Awright. Me go wait by de roadside.'

'Good. Don't forget to be there. Tell Beena and Ramgolall goodbye for us when they come back from Speyerfeld. Tell them to keep well until I come back in August.'

'Awright. Me go tell dem.'

28

In Speyerfeld, meanwhile, Ramgolall and Beena had not had an ordinary day. Two untoward incidents had befallen them.

At about eleven o'clock, when they were sheltering from the rain, under the awning of a draper's store, the tall figures of two policemen suddenly came striding across the street towards them. One was their old friend, the Sergeant, and, recognizing him, Ramgolall, who had been crouching on the pavement, scrambled up quickly, a look of fear on his face.

'Uh-huh!' said the Sergeant. 'Tekin' shelter from de rain, eh, Ramgolall?'

'Eh-heh,' said Ramgolall. 'Me a-shelter from rain.'

'Wedder behave bad today. How business going nowadays, Ramgolall?'

'Business? Business na good. Time bad.'

'Time bad, eh? How you' milk going? Still putting water in to mek am plenty? Eh?'

'Eh-h-h! Ow me gaad! Me put water milk! Ow! Me na put na water milk. Never na time. Me swear to Gaad!'

The Sergeant chuckled deeply. 'You never put na water in you' milk, na? Huh! Awright, Ramgolall. But all de same, lemme tek a sample so as to mek sure.' He looked grimly at Beena. 'You ain' got canal now, you know, so you needn' try to overturn de can.'

Beena laughed. 'Me na got na cause overturn na can. Tek sample if you want, na? Me na stop you.'

128

'Hey! You talk confident. Like you' milk awright today. You na bodder put in water, eh?'

Beena sucked her teeth 'Me na know. Tek sample an' fin' out fo' you'self.'

'You got hot tongue,' grinned the other policeman, who was a constable. (A khaki haversack, bulging with what looked like bottles, was slung over his shoulder.) 'If you talk too much we lock you up in prison.'

Beena sucked her teeth again and tossed her head. 'You must t'ink me stupid, na?'

The Sergeant proceeded to take a sample from each can, he and the constable chuckling the while and making jokes.

When they had gone, Beena and Ramgolall ate their luncheon (called 'breakfast' in Guiana) and then, the rain having held up, they started off again on their tedious round from house to house.

At about three o'clock, when Ramgolall's small can was empty and Beena's large can was half-filled, they happened to be passing the gateway of the hospital in Speyerfeld Estate. Suddenly there was a loud hail: 'Hup, hup, holoy!' and Harry Lall Boorharry, in his white dhoti, came bounding out of the gateway towards them. 'Hup, hup, holoy! Beena-teena-weena! Beena bettay and Ramgolall selling milk! Hup, hoy!' He tapped Ramgolall playfully on his white head and gave Beena a pat on her head-cloth, there being no pigtail to pull, for Beena had coiled her hair in a pile on her head as she often did.

'Boorharry, is why you so stupid, na?'

'Hoy! Me stupid. Beena bettay? Harry Lall Boorharry stupid? Na, na, na, bettay, Harry Lall na stupid. Harry Lall de cleverest man on de whole Corentyne! Better dan estate-manager self!'

'Who mek you so clever, Harry Lall?'

'Who? Me mek meself clever. Ha! Harry Lall got big book at home. He can read and learn plenty great sciences. You must come home one day lemme show you me big books, bettay.'

'Wha'! *Me* come home to you!'

'Why not? Me treat you good, bettay. Me give you nice t'ing eat and drink. Milk-cake, sugar-baby, biscuit, mango, lemonade! All kind o' nice t'ings!'

'Na, me na want none, t'ank you.'

'Ow! Harry Lall going cry just now.' He made his face into a grimace and feigned a sniff. 'Ramgolall, you hear how Beena bettay treat me? Me offer she nice t'ing eat and drink and she say she na want none.'

'Eh-h-h-h. She bad girl,' smiled Ramgolall. 'She bad lil' bettay. Me beat she when me go home.'

'Beat she? Na! Me beg fo' she, Ramgolall! Me beg fo' she! Na beat Beena bettay. When one or two months pass me going come to you and ask you to lemme marry Beena bettay. You hear dat, Beena? Harry Lall come and make you wife. You going tek Harry Lall?'

'Na,' laughed Beena. 'Me na want you. Look fo' odder gurl. Plenty odder gurl in Speyerfeld.'

'Na, na, na, na! Me na want na odder gurl! You more pretty dan all de odder gurl in de worl'. Me going come soon marry you. Me come softly at night like so…' He went down on all-fours and began to creep along the ground. 'Me creep softly in you' house, wrap you up in a cloak and run off wid you! Me put you quick in aeroplane and fly off wid you to annoder country like how de men in de film-picture do it. Ha! You wait good, bettay. Soon me come carry you off.'

Beena laughed. 'You idle big man, Boorharry. Lef' we 'lone leh we go 'bout we business.'

'Awright! Go on you' way. But me warn you! Me come soon to mek you me wife! If you see Sukra, tell she me got bull-calf fo' she.'

'You got bull-calf fo' she? Wha' bull-calf?'

'Hoy! Wha' bull-calf? Me promise she long time ago if me cow drop bull-calf me will give she de bull-calf. Well, tell she me cow drop Sunday gone an' it turn out bull-calf so it belong to she. She must come an' see it soon.'

'Me na able tell she nutting. Jannee na like she talk to you. 'E beat she last time she talk to you. You mustn' encourage she anymore to talk to you, Boorharry – fo' she own sake, me ask you.'

'Why me mustn' talk to she? Jannee stupid boy. Jannee-pannee-chimpanzee! When me see 'e again me go tease 'e good. 'E too stupid.'

'You mustn' tease 'e. 'E got bad temper.'

'What me care if he got bad temper? Harry Lall Boorharry not afraid of anybody in dis world! Hup, hup, holoy!' He pushed out his chest and beat it with his fist. 'Hup, hup, holoy! Harry Lall can fight any man and beat him! Let Jannee come. Harry Lall Boorharry twist Jannee round his little toe! Hup, hup, holoy! Jannee-pannee-chimpanzee!'

That evening, when she and Ramgolall were walking slowly homeward in the deep twilight, Beena felt a dim trouble stirring within her. Boorharry's boasting words kept running through her mind, words that portended no good, lightly as Boorharry had uttered them. Looking ahead along the straight road, she seemed to see the future, and in it there flitted dark shadows, dark like the twilight. The 'Who-you?' of a goat-sucker sounded a little way behind them and it made her shiver in dread. It seemed like an omen of evil.

Ramgolall groaned in fatigue and that too made her shiver a little. She wished they had reached home already. Perhaps a duppy was on their track, a duppy with a face like Boorharry's... 'Let Jannee come. Harry Lall Boorharry twist Jannee round his little toe! Hup, hup, holoy...!'

'Who-you?' went the goat-sucker again.

The moon had begun to make pale shadows.

29

That night a strong wind blew from the north. It moaned and shrieked around the great angular bulk of Big Man's house, while it made a deep droning roar as it whirled by Ramgolall's low abode.

Kept awake by thoughts for over an hour, Kattree lay in the dark and heard it, and it made her turn often and look about her in the black gloom. Geoffry, eight miles away, kept awake, too, by thoughts, heard the moan and shriek of the long gusts and fidgeted in a troubled manner, frowning about him now and then at the furniture in the room, the outlines of which he could make out clearly in the reflected moonlight. Once he got out of bed and went over to the window. He took a few deep breaths of the cool air, then hung out of the window for a while looking at the scene. In the sky he saw hurrying rags of cloud, pale green, some of them, in the light of the moon, and others jet-black with rain.

A wild-looking sky, he thought, as though the gods were on the spree and the jumbies and duppies were fleeing over the savannah with moans and shrieks of terror.

A cloud would blot out the moon and then a great gloom would spread over the scene like a frown, only to vanish in a moment when the magic green light once more revealed the whole flat panorama as though in a glow of immobile lighting.

Shortly after midnight rain fell in a sudden squalling burst, prattled sharply on the roof and hissed in at the windows, borne on a whooping gust of wind. It lasted for about five minutes, then died off in as abrupt a manner as it had begun, leaving the wind to howl and whistle alone through the night which had grown black now, for the moon had gone down and thick dark clouds moved swiftly towards the south, dropping rain fitfully as they went. The squeak of vicissi duck sounded bleakly overhead, calling rain.

About an hour before dawn the wind died down to a soft, cool drift of air that could hardly be felt against the cheek, the sky was without a cloud and the stars gleamed clearly in millions, so clearly, indeed, that the tiny ones in between the bright ones looked like clusters of dust. The spree of the gods was over, and the jumbies and duppies had gone to rest. Not a sound could be heard anywhere. The night seemed waiting for the dawn to happen.

30

Geoffry and Stymphy left in the car for Number Sixty-three Village at a quarter past seven – more than an hour earlier than they had planned. Geoffry it was who was responsible for this early start. He wanted to catch the morning tide, he explained to the others, and this being a fairly good reason, no one thought of questioning it. Only to Stymphy did he confide the real reason.

Joshua expressed surprise when Geoffry made him stop the

car near the bridge that spanned the canal to the dam that led to Ramgolall's home. 'Is wha' you going do here, Mas' Geoffry?' he asked.

'I'm going to pay a brief call at the residence of my grandfather,' Geoffry told him, with a grin. 'I'll be back in a few minutes, Josh. Don't get the wind up – and you needn't mention this to the others when you get back.'

'No, chief. You can trus' me,' grinned Joshua.

Geoffry alighted, crossed the canal and set out along the dam in the bright, slanting sunshine. The distance to the mud-house was only a little over two hundred yards, and, being in shorts, he covered the first hundred yards at a sprint, running with the light grace of a practised athlete.

Kattree saw him coming, and, unlike her habit, advanced a little way along the dam to meet him.

'You come early,' she said in surprise. 'You say you woulda come half pas' eight. Na half pas' eight yet.'

'I know,' he smiled. 'I came an hour early on purpose. If I'd come at half past eight I would have found you waiting by the road and that would have meant talking to you before Stymphy and Joshua. I wanted to see you alone.'

She said: 'Oh!' quietly, smiling faintly.

'Where're Beena and Ramgolall?'

'Deh gone a-Speyerfeld since half pas' six time. Me did just done tek tea when me see you runnin' comin'.'

'You had, eh? And I suppose you'll soon be getting ready to catch fish for breakfast?'

'Eh-heh. Jus' now me go start fishin'.'

'Wish I could join you. Ought to be pretty lonely for you all by yourself here the whole day.'

'Me accustom' to am. Me na mind.'

'I see. Well, look here, when I was in bed last night I thought of something. By the way, how did you like the high wind?'

'Me na like it at all. It frighten me lil' bit. Me stay awake long time hearin' it. All kind o' t'ing pass t'rough me mind in de dark.'

'Like myself. Quite a good many thoughts passed through my mind before I eventually dropped off to sleep. The gods were on the binge last night, Kattree.'

'De gods? Wha' gods?'

'The gods of Life and Fate. But look here, I mustn't stop here talking rot. Stymphy and Joshua are waiting for me out there in the car. I promised them I wouldn't be long.' She saw him take from his hip-pocket what looked like a greenish slip of paper. 'I brought this for you,' he said, proffering it. 'You must buy a few nice dresses for yourself and Beena.'

She took it in dismay, staring from it to his face. 'You gimme dis?'

'Yes. Buy nice dresses with it for yourself and Beena. You must have nice dresses to wear when I take you to New Amsterdam in August, you know.'

'Oh! T'ank you.' She spoke in a bated voice, looking in awe at the bank-note in her hand. 'But dis is a five-dollar note. Plenty money.'

'Oh, it isn't such a lot when you come to think of it, I can tell you. Wait till you start spending it, then you'll know.'

'How much silver in five dollars?'

'Silver? Oh! Well, if you change that into loose cash you'll get twenty shillings and ten pennies.'

'Twenty shilling, ten penny! Dah is a lot!'

'Not at all.' He began to fidget a trifle in discomfiture. 'You go ahead and buy nice things for yourself and Beena. Don't make anyone rob you, though. See that you get correct change.'

'But you good to gi' we all dis money.'

'Oh, don't mention it. It's nothing at all. Well, look here, Kattree, stay well until August, see? I've got to go now. Can't keep them waiting any longer. Shake hands and call it a day.'

'Awright. Stay well. An' t'ank you plenty, plenty.'

'Forget it. Cheero! Watch me do a two-twenty yards sprint back to the car.' He broke into a swift run, his arms swinging high and his long legs leaping lightly over the hard, clayey soil.

She stood looking after him, a faint smile around her lips, her eyes a-gleam with a cool, deep fire. She watched him until he reached the car, saw him wave and waved back. The car, shining in the sun, moved off, gathered speed and soon became a tiny dark speck in the distance.

She lived through that day with an air of dreaming. At every

134

odd moment she would take the bank-note from one of the two small pockets in the front of her skirt, spread it out and look at it in awe, turning it over and over and crackling it, for it was new and crisp.

She had often seen a five-dollar note, but had never handled one in her life, let alone owned one. Twenty shillings and ten pennies! She could hardly believe it. It was as though a miracle had happened and Geoffry the magician who had performed it. Thinking of Geoffry, she grew aware of something stirring deep in her, something deep and alive and full of power, like the wind last night. It was a feeling that frightened her a little by its strength. It made her mind go into a kind of pained whirl, so that she seemed to hear the moaning of wind, with thunder, and the roar of flood-water, all making a dreadful chaos in her soul. For the past day or two she had tried to smother the feeling, but without avail. Instead, it had grown and grown, like the deep-wavering drone of an aeroplane when it was coming from far away to pass overhead. It would fool her for a moment that it was dying away, then it would come again in a sudden deeper roar, deeper and deeper as though it would overwhelm her. Why such a feeling should come to her she did not know. She had not wanted to feel so, did not want to feel so, for it troubled her too much – troubled her far inside. Yet she could do nothing to stop it, try as she would.

That evening when she had driven the cows into pen for the night, she set out to meet Beena and Ramgolall, for she was eager to tell them of the miracle that had happened and to show them the five-dollar note.

They were very surprised when they met her on the road. 'Eh-eh, bettay! How you come here?' exclaimed Ramgolall. 'Is wha' happen, gal?' said Beena, staring at her a little anxiously in the pale moonlight.

'Plenty happen,' smiled Kattree. 'Plenty good t'ing. Look wha' Geoffry bring fo' we dis mornin'.' She took the five-dollar note from her pocket and held it out. Beena took it in her free hand. She said: 'Eh-eh! Dis is a five-dollar note!'

'Wha' dah?' said Ramgolall. 'Five-dollar note?'

'Eh-heh. Look,' said Beena, holding it out to him. 'It wort' plenty money.'

'Twenty shilling, ten penny it wort',' Kattree nodded. 'So Geoffry say. 'E give it to you an' me. 'E say we mus' buy nice dress to wear.'

'So 'e say? When 'e come?'

' 'E come dis mornin' early. 'Bout half pas' seven time. 'E come in de car. De car stop on de road an' 'e run come on de dam an' meet me, an' after we talk lil' bit 'e tek out dis note an' gimme. 'E say we mus' buy nice dress wid it.'

'Eh-h-h! Bettay, dis money big money.'

'Twenty shilling, ten penny.'

'Twenty shilling, ten penny! You mus' keep am safe, bettay. Better lemme put am in canister fo' by-an'-by.'

'Na,' said Kattree, taking the note from him. 'We got to buy dress wid am – nice dress to wear.'

'Nice dress to wear? Ow, bettay! You mustn' waste money so. Time come, you go need am. Lemme put am away safe fo' you in canister.'

'Na. We need am now. We want new dress. Geoffry say when 'e come back in August mont' 'e go tek me an' Beena in car to New Amsterdam, an' we must got new dress wear.'

' 'E go tek you in car, bettay? Eh-h-h! Careful, bettay. Me na like dah. Car na good. Same t'ing Sosee do long time pas'. Geoffry fadder tek Sosee drive out in car. Plenty trouble come wid car-drive, bettay. Ha! Plenty, plenty trouble.'

'Wha' trouble can come, Ramgolall?'

'Ha! Me ol' man, bettay. Me know. Geoffry got fair skin an' plenty money. 'E tek you drive in car, 'e gi' you nice t'ing, den you get baby an' 'e na want see you na more. Ha!'

'You talk stupid now, Ramgolall. How me get baby 'cause me go wid 'e fo' drive? Beena go come wid we, too.'

'Me?' said Beena, who had been silent for a while. 'Me na go fo' na drive wid Geoffry.'

'Why? You na want see New Amsterdam?'

'Na. Me preffer stay here. An' me na want na money from Geoffry. Geoffry is bakra boy. Me is coolie gal. Jannee talk right.'

'Jannee? Wha' Jannee got do wid dis?'

'Jannee advise me na got nutting do wid na bakra boy, an' 'e talk right. Geoffry got white skin. Me got dark skin.'

'You listen too much to wha' Jannee say.'

''E talk right.'

'You ungrateful. Look how nice Geoffry treat we when 'e come here. 'E share 'e breakfas' wid we. 'E talk to we nice. 'E mek sport, an' now 'e gi' we money to buy dress. You ungrateful bad.'

'Awright. Me na care if me ungrateful.'

'Like Jannee turn you' head.'

''E turn me head like how Geoffry turn you' head.'

'Ow, bettay! A-you na quarrel. Na quarrel.'

But Beena and Kattree continued to bicker, saying many bitter, spiteful things. Kattree wanted to know who Jannee was that he should have any say in their affairs. What right had Beena to listen to what Jannee advised her to do? Was Jannee God? Then Beena, in a great passion, said yes, that Jannee was her god and that whatever he said she would go by, and she did not care what anyone thought. Kattree, speaking in her calm voice still said that now she knew why Jannee had beaten Sukra the other day and put her out. Boorharry was only an excuse. Jannee wanted to put away Sukra and take Beena to live with him. Beena shrieked at her that she was a liar and that she had a nasty, evil mind. 'Me never, never talk to you again!' she vowed, and she began to sob all of a sudden, so that Ramgolall, who had in vain tried to stop them from quarrelling, spoke soothing words to her. 'Na cry, bettay. Na cry. Ow! Quarrel na good. A-you mustn' quarrel. Quarrel bring bad.'

Beena's body, however, continued to shake with sobs. The moon, bulging largely now on the growing side, shone brightly upon them as they slowly walked homeward, for the twilight had thickened into deep gloom and the shadows were black. From far away came the lonely 'toot-toot-toot' of an owl, and once a goat-sucker, lying flat on the road a little way ahead, said: 'Who-you?' and flew off in swift silence. But Beena, sobbing, had no ears nor eyes for these things, and Kattree bettay looked calm but not serene. Her lips were tightly drawn in, and her eyes held a gleam tranquil like the moonlight but as cold.

Ramgolall still uttered soothing words. 'Na cry, Beena bettay. Na cry. A-you mek frien' again. Na cry.'

'Toot-toot-toot,' went the owl much farther away now.

31

Days went by, and then a week and then two weeks, three weeks, four, and throughout all this time not a jest passed between Beena and Kattree, not a single word. The rain fell, the sun shone and sometimes the dawn was grey, sometimes pink. The rice-fields began to look green, and farmers said that this year's crop would turn out fair after all. The cane-fields, too, were looking fresh, and many folk were hoping for a big grinding season with high wages. Sukra's baby was born. It proved to be a boy, and Jannee registered it at the Speyerfeld Village Office under the names of Bharat Ragoonandan. He was very proud at having three sons, and nine days after the birth of the new son he gave a big curry-feed to which he invited all his friends, including Bijoolie and his wife, Nanwa, and Bijoolie's brother Moonsammy and his wife, Heedai, and Jaigan, who kept a provision and grocery shop in Speyerfeld. But Kattree and Beena, throughout all these events, continued to be cold to each other. Kattree would not go to Jannee's curry-feed, saying to her father (in Beena's hearing) that she did not want any of Jannee's curry and roti. 'Me na go dead if me na eat Jannee' food. You go 'long, eat you' bellyful.'

A few days later she went to Speyerfeld with her five-dollar note and bought cloth. She bought cotton cloth and silky cloth in different colours and took it all to the Chinese lady who sewed for her and Beena whenever they had dresses to be made. She had bought enough cloth to make four dresses, two out of cotton and two out of the silky cloth – rayon-silk, the Chinese lady called it. The two silk ones were done in the latest style and made her look like a lady when she tried them on. After paying the dressmaker, she found that she had two shillings and three pennies left, so she bought herself a pair of rubber-soled canvas shoes for two shillings – the first pair of shoes she had owned in her life.

She brought everything home in a large wooden hat-box that the dressmaker gave her. She put the box on her head – handling it so gingerly that it might have been made of glass – and walked the three miles back home. The following morning she took out the dresses and showed them to her father in the early morning light, trying on the silk ones to let him see what a lady she looked like in them.

Beena, meanwhile, feigning to be greatly bored, walked off, humming a tune casually to herself.

Early in June Ramgolall fell ill. He woke up one morning and complained of feeling weak and 'trembly-trembly'. When he got out of his hammock and attempted to go about the usual tasks of the day he broke out in a cold sweat and collapsed near the cow-pen. Kattree and Beena, greatly alarmed and thinking that he was going to die, lifted him back into the mud-house. A little later he was groaning arid shivering with ague in his hammock, and Kattree and Beena, the coldness between them forgotten, set about to do what they could for him. They gave him hot milk and covered his thin body with their rice-bag bedding. This, however, proved of little avail, for by mid-morning he was burning with fever, and Beena had to take a bus and go to Speyerfeld where she bought seven Government quinine tablets for a penny. They made him swallow one of the tablets (five grains) with water, and towards sunset the fever broke and left him in a cold, unhealthy sweat. He groaned a great deal.

Beena asked him if she should hoist the sick-flag (this being a rag of cloth tied to the top of a bamboo pole that, in times of sickness, had to be set up by the side of the road so that the Government medico of the district should know that there was someone ill and drop in when on his daily round).

Ramgolall groaned and shook his head. 'Na, bettay. Na!' he gasped weakly. 'No hoist sick-flag. Me too pore. Na able pay doctor.'

'But you sick, ol' man. You prefer dead radder dan pay doctor iii' money to get better?'

'Ow, bettay! Me pore man, me tell you. Na able pay doctor. Bide lil' time, bettay. Me tek quinine.'

'Quinine alone na get you better. You want doctor's medicine. Doctor mus' sound you, see wha' wrong, den 'e write paper, an' dispenser mek up medicine.'

Ramgolall groaned and shook his head. 'Me na got na money pay doctor, bettay. True-true. Ow! Me pore man.'

'Canister full o' money,' put in Kattree. 'Lemme tek out two, t'ree shilling, Ramgolall. Better to spend two, t'ree shilling an' get better dan die an' lef' all you' money.'

'Na, bettay. Me na go dead. Me tek quinine t'ree time every day. Me get better soon.'

It took him nearly a month to get better. They fed him regularly on plenty of milk and made him swallow a quinine tablet three times a day. Had it not been for the milk he must surely have died, for his illness had resulted from sheer lack of nourishment. His daily journey to Speyerfeld and the tedious round from house to house had taxed his body severely, and the poor food he had eaten had not been able to restore the energy he had expended. It was from debility that he had collapsed. The milk built him up slowly and the quinine kept at bay the malarial parasites that threatened to weaken his blood and bring on the ague and fever.

The four weeks of his illness proved a very unhappy time for Beena and Kattree. It rained nearly every day, in brief, heavy showers or in steady, coarse drizzles that lasted for hours. The sky was always grey, and when the sun did manage to shine it shone palely through a hazy layer of cloud. The savannah was often flooded and the cows suffered greatly. Two of them got stuck fast in the bed of a shallow pond and could not be pulled out. They had to be left there to die. Added to all this Ramgolall did not make an easy patient to care for. The hardest task was to keep him clean, for where dirt of any nature was concerned he had never been very particular. Often they would come in and find him lying in his own filth in perfect comfort, neither the stench nor his soiled condition troubling him in the slightest degree. Before the first week was out they had to condemn his hammock and throw it away and make a bed of straw for him near his canister. He insisted on being near his canister, and many times they would find him pressed close against its side, one of his thin arms thrown over the top and struggling feebly to keep clutched over the lid.

They had to take it in turns to go to Speyerfeld every other day to sell a gallon or two of milk, for he refused to take a penny from the canister. On their return (at about three o'clock) he demanded the greater part of the takings, and, in spite of his weak condition, would sit up, open the canister and carefully add the coins to his hoard. The effort cost him many groans, and when it was over he would sink back on to the straw greatly fatigued and almost fainting. And they dared not try to give him any aid. When Kattree, one afternoon, seeing him in difficulty, put out her hand to lift the lid for him, he uttered a wailing cry and threw both his arms over the top as though he thought her a robber come to rifle his hoard. 'Na-a-a-a! Na-a-a-a! Lef' am 'lone, bettay! Lef' am 'lone!' he wailed. 'Me go manage meself. Me go manage.' And for nearly five minutes he leant against the canister panting heavily and sweating, his arms still stretched out over the cold metal, his gaunt face pressed against the edge of the lid. Kattree had stared at him in fear, thinking he would die.

By dint of careful spending, they were able to buy, out of the few cents he allowed them for food, three rice-bags and a flour-bag. These were needed as bedding for him as well as for themselves, for he had befouled the old bedding so badly that they had had to throw it away.

One day, during the second week of his illness, Beena went into a drug store in Speyerfeld and spoke to the dispenser about her father's illness, relating how Ramgolall had collapsed near the cow-pen and telling of the ague and fever and of his weak state and cold sweating. The dispenser, a short black gentleman, kept smiling and nodding in a casual way all the time as though the whole thing had been clear to him even before she began to speak. 'Mm-h'm. I know what's wrong,' he said, with a little wave of his hand. 'General debility. He must be an anaemic, too. What he wants to pick him up is a good quinine and iron tonic.' He showed her a bottle of a patent tonic and told her that that would get her father better in no time. The price was thirty-six cents (one and sixpence).

Beena considered the day's takings which had come up in all to fifty-one cents (two shillings, one and ha'penny), and after some debate with herself, she decided to buy the tonic.

When she took it home and told Ramgolall, he set up a great wail. 'Ow, bettay! You t'row 'way me money! Me na want na tonic! Ow! Ow me gaad! De man rob you! Ow! Ow, bettay! Me good money gone!'

'But de tonic is to get you better, ol' man,' said Beena. 'Is wha' wrong wid you? You want dead radder dan buy somet'ing mek you better?'

'Ow, bettay! Me na want na tonic. Me na drink am. Tek am back, get back de money. Tek am back.'

'Me refuse tek am back!' said Beena angrily. 'Me buy somet'ing do you good an' dis de way you behave? Ow! You bad ol' man. You ungrateful.'

For the rest of that afternoon and throughout the whole night, Ramgolall wailed and cried, actually shedding tears. He beat his fists and his head against the side of the canister. 'Ow! Ow! Me bettay t'row 'way me money! Na money na deh today put in canister! Ow!'

There was no sleep for any of them that night. Beena coaxed him or threatened him, but it was of no avail. He continued to wail and bemoan his loss. It was not until towards dawn that, from sheer exhaustion, he grew quiet and fell asleep.

It was during the third week of his illness that Jannee and Boorharry had a row.

Beena was in Speyerfeld selling milk. At about two o'clock in the afternoon, when her can was nearly empty, she saw Jannee approaching in his cart, going east. His cart was laden with yams, pumpkins, cucumbers and lettuce, and he told her that he was on his way to the Overseers' Quarters where Jairamsingh would buy his load of vegetables. He would give her a lift home on his way back.

She sold the last pint of milk at the bungalow of Mr Bender, the factory-engineer, and then stood waiting at the side of the road for Jannee.

Soon she saw him coming in his empty cart, and her heart beat happily at the thought of being with him on the three mile drive back home.

They were jogging along at an easy pace and Jannee was telling her how, with some money he had saved up, he intended to buy a few head of cattle, when, without warning, a loud hail of 'Hup, hup, holoy!' made them glance quickly towards the entrance of the estate-hospital. A frown at once darkened Jannee's face.

Boorharry came bounding towards them, moving in a series of little hops, in the manner of a galloping horse. 'Hup, hup, holoy!

Beena-teena-weena! Jannee-pannee-chimpanzee! Boorharry tek ride wid Beena and Monkey-man Jannee!' He jumped lightly into the cart from behind, and Jannee, drawing rein, glared at him coldly and said in a quiet voice: 'Boorharry, get out me donkey-cart!'

'Drive on, man! Drive on! I'm Lord Boorharry of Speyerfeld. You're my chauffeur. Ho, ho! Drive on, dog! Take me to my stately mansion.'

'Boorharry, get out me donkey-cart.'

'Is why you so foolish, Boorharry?' said Beena, trying to sound serious and amused both at once. 'Get out de cart an' go 'bout you' own business.'

'Ho, ho! Me get out de cart? No! Dis is my motorcar. I'm Lord Boorharry of Speyerfeld! Jannee is my chauffeur. Ho, ho! Drive on, dog! Do you hear me? I'll stop your wages if you don't drive on. I'm in a hurry. Hup, hup!'

'Boorharry, me warn you fo' de last time. Get out me donkey-cart.'

'Warn me? Me your great master? Have a care, my fine servant. I will have thee thrown into the dungeon of yon castle where the rats will nibble at thine foul-smelling toes! Ho, ho!'

A little group of urchins and one or two grown-up people had begun to gather round the spot, attracted by Boorharry's ringing voice. They all tittered in amusement at this taunting speech of Boorharry's.

Jannee got out of the cart, and, walking round to the back, gave Boorharry a chuck and ordered him out of his cart in an angry voice, his eyes blazing.

'Hoy! You chuck Boorharry, Jannee? Your big lord and master? Hoy!' And jumping agilely out of the cart, Boorharry seized Jannee in a swift, scientific hold, gripping him at the back by his shoulder and thigh and whisking him off his feet at one jerk. 'Hup, hoy! Hup, hoy!' bawled Boorharry and walked round and round the cart, the small struggling body of Jannee held aloft like a bundle. The urchins shouted with merriment while Beena stared in fear and dismay, her lips a little apart.

At length, Boorharry planked down his burden in the middle of the cart and capered off a little way, doing a comical dance.

Jannee, scrambling out of the cart, rushed at him. But Boorharry, shouting 'Hup, hup!' dodged him like lightning, made a darting grab at his ankle and sent him sprawling forward.

The urchins yelled, while Boorharry did another comical dance, shouting: 'Hup, hup, holoy! Jannee-pannee-chimpanzee! Hup, hup! Hup, hoy!'

When Jannee got to his feet he made no attempt to rush at Boorharry again. He just glared at him, panting a little in his fury, and then wagged his finger at him and said in a quiet, cold tone: 'Awright, Boorharry. Today is you' day. Me day come soon.'

'Ay! Shut you' mout', Jannee! Jannee-pannee-chimpanzee! Hup, hoy!' cried Boorharry, and did his comical dance again. 'Monkey-face Jannee! Boom, boom!' And, with that, he went bounding off back into the hospital compound, shouting: 'Hup, holoy! Hup, holoy!'

When Jannee brushed the dust off his trousers the urchins jeered at him, and when he and Beena resumed their journey the boys followed the cart shouting: 'Jannee-pannee-chimpanzee! Monkey-face Jannee! Hup, holoy! Hup, hup, holoy!'

32

Soon Ramgolall was well enough to drive the cows into pasture. With milk added to his former diet of rice and salt-fish, or rice and plantain, he gathered strength rapidly. He still refused to drink the tonic that Beena had bought for him (in the hope, no doubt, that Beena might take it back and retrieve the money spent on it), so, eventually, Beena and Kattree decided that they would drink it instead in order that it might not be wasted.

The rain began to hold off a little and lightning flashed at night. For two days there would be bright sunshine and blue skies, and then for a whole day grey skies and rain with intermittent thunder, then blue skies again. Some mornings thick blue mist would veil the landscape. On fine evenings there would be vivid lightning in the distance, but no thunder. The heat was growing more and more intense. One evening in the middle of July a violent thunderstorm broke. The lightning sounded like the cracking of a giant whip and wriggled in the sky like the crooked fingers of a hundred madmen, while the thunder made them think that ten million motorcars and buckets were colliding all together or being tumbled one over another up in the sky. The storm lasted half the night, and the following morning they found that a coconut palm, not a quarter of a mile away and only ten yards from a fisherman's mud-house, had been struck by the lightning and cut in half. Luckily for Manoo, the fisherman, the severed half had fallen away from the mud-house, thus doing no damage.

Manoo came over to tell them about it and they went with him to look at the fallen tree. 'Me hear a big loud noise,' he explained to them. 'Ply! An' den like de whole sky did fallin' 'pon me. Somet'ing hit de side o' de house – bup! – an' when me go out an' look me find dis nut.' He pointed to a green coconut lying on the ground before the small stairway that led up to his abode (for his was one of the mud-houses that were raised a few feet off the ground on wooden blocks).

Ramgolall uttered many groans and told them of the terrible thunderstorms of the past, of how one night the lightning split open the roof of a labourer's cottage and of how another time a thunderstorm had caught him and the other cane-cutters far aback during the day and of how the lightning had scorched the left arm of a black woman called Mary, leaving the arm paralysed for the rest of her life.

'Ha! Bad, bad storm me see in long-time day, baaya,' he groaned. 'Bad, bad t'under-lightning. Do plenty damage.'

Beena went to Jannee and Sukra to tell them of Manoo's coconut palm. She found Sukra sitting before the door suckling Bharat Ragoonandan and Jannee a little way off chopping firewood. Sukra gave her a hearty welcome, but Jannee was quiet and pensive. For the past two or three weeks (since the day of his row with Boorharry) he had been like this: silent and glum and always staring before him as though deep in thought, a queer glint in his eyes. When Beena told them of how the lightning had cut Manoo's coconut palm in half, Jannee grunted and muttered: 'Shoulda Boorharry 'e cut in half.'

'Aw! Why you na f'get Boorharry?' said Beena. 'You mustn' go on t'inkin' 'bout Boorharry. Fo'get 'e.'

He gave a deep grunt, smiling in that queer, faint way that always made her feel that danger was near. 'Fo'get 'e, eh? Wait good, see if me go fo'get 'e. Wait good.'

Returning home, Beena thought dark things, despite the bright sunshine and the patchy blue sky. It troubled her deeply to see Jannee in this mood. She and Sukra had tried their best during the past two or three weeks to put him into a good mood and make him forget Boorharry, but to no avail. On the other hand, he seemed to get worse and worse as the days went by. He had not taken the donkey-cart to Speyerfeld once since the day when he and Boorharry had come up against each other. Sukra had had to go for him, driving the cart and taking the vegetables and fire-wood that he sold in the village or to Jairamsingh. 'If me go a-Speyerfeld an' dah man trouble me again, bad go happen,' he had said in a low voice.

During the past two or three days he had taken to going off alone on foot to Speyerfeld after dark had fallen, and when Sukra asked him what he was going to Speyerfeld for he told her not to bother him and that if she tried to follow him he would beat her. Sukra was very worried. She had told Beena about it and Beena had tried to make light of it, telling her not to be worried over it, but to herself Beena felt afraid. Every time she thought of Jannee leaving his home after dark and walking to Speyerfeld something circled coldly around her heart. The nights were so dark now. The moon did not rise until after midnight. She wished it were full moon. If only she could order the moon to be full every evening and the sky to be clear. She hated dark nights, especially these dark nights in which the lightning kept flickering in the distance and the air kept so still, as though it were waiting for something to happen.

That evening, after eating, she stood on the dam in the dark and looked for a long time towards the south, wondering whether Jannee had left home yet to set out on his lonely walk to Speyerfeld. If she were not so afraid she would have walked out to the road and waited by the bridge to see him go past. Look how the lightning flickered over there in the south-east! So silent and yet so bright and alive... She wondered if he had anything in his hand – a stick or a cutlass. Oh, but it was stupid of her to think that.

Sukra had said nothing about his taking a stick or a cutlass with him.

The white lights of a car appeared in the east, and she looked eagerly to see if she could make out anyone on the road in the bright wavering beams, but the distance was too great as she had known even before she looked. The car went past and its red rear-light gleamed like an evil eye moving towards the west.

The sound of a tom-tom suddenly came drifting through the dark, and from the direction whence it came she knew that it must be Moonsammy, who lived with his wife, Heedai, at Nairnley, not very far from Jannee and Sukra. Moonsammy, like his brother Bijoolie who worked on Big Man Weldon's ranch, was a good player of the sitar and serangee. He must be having a feed tonight to celebrate the ninth day after the death of Heedai's sister. Heedai's sister had died last week at Kildonan.

Look at the lightning again! She wondered if he had hidden the stick or the cutlass down his trousers. He might have done that. Every night he might have been doing that so that Sukra should not know he was going out with any evil intent. She had heard that Boorharry often rode along the road on his bicycle round about this time on the way to some one of his many women. There again! That was the brightest flash she had seen for the evening. It had nearly made her start. She hoped it would stop soon. It looked so full of danger as though it were a warning signal that told of some terrible bloody deed that was about to be done in the dark out there on the road. There it went again. Flicker, flicker!

Kattree, too, was watching the lightning – she sat by the fireplace – but her thoughts were not dark like Beena's. They were bright and hopeful like the one or two stars that twinkled in the clear patches of the sky, for Kattree was thinking of the white days of August soon to come when she would wear her new cotton dresses and sit by the canal with Geoffry. They would talk and catch fish, and at midday he would share his breakfast with her, and then they might lie down in the shade of the mud-house and sleep. When they awoke he might talk nicely to her and put his finger under her chin, stroke her arm, and after that, the two of them being alone, he might kiss her. Flicker, flicker! went the lightning. A crooked wire of red darted out of the cloud. A good thing it was so far away. He might kiss her and even do more. She would not stop him. She would like it. It would not matter to her what happened after. She was not afraid of having a baby. As long as it was his she would like it.

Very faintly from the south came the deep boom-boom of thunder, a low, troubled muttering that died off almost as soon as it had begun.

Then on some days she would wear her silk dresses and her shoes, and he would take her for drives in the large dark-red car. They would go to the beach at Number Sixty-three Village where they would both take off their clothes and swim in the sea, or, on other days, to New Amsterdam. A town it was called. It had many roads, she had heard, and long lines of buildings close to each other like the buildings in Speyerfeld, and at night the roads were lit with bright lights called electric lights. He would drive her through the roads and show her all the buildings and perhaps now and then he would take her at night so that she could see the electric lights. She would see the big river, too, the Berbice River, and the steamers and sailing ships she had heard of. It would be the best time she had spent in all her life.

Flicker, flicker, went the lightning all the time. Far away, twenty or thirty miles south, somewhere over the jungle perhaps, the thunder was roaring like a hundred angry bulls and the rain was hissing down in spiteful torrents. But that was far away. Here on the coast all was calm and safe, though the air did feel rather still and electric as if there might be some big, vague thing waiting to happen.

From the west came the prattle of Moonsammy's tom-tom. Overhead the stars kept winking. Queer, she thought, how they winked and winked no matter what happened to anybody.

33

The following day broke fair, but the dawn was streaked with blood and Ramgolall predicted rain before noon, though Kattree said that she thought it would be a fine day.

Ramgolall announced that he would go today to Speyerfeld to

148

help sell the milk. He felt quite strong again, he said, and it was time he began to make the daily journey. Kattree and Beena told him that he had better let them continue to sell the milk for him as they had been doing during the past few weeks. 'You get ol' now, Ramgolall,' said Beena. 'You mus' rest you' bones.' But he insisted, saying that he was strong enough to do it. 'Me go drink plenty milk keep strong, bettay. Na fear. Me got good strengt' lef' in me. Me awright.'

He and Beena, accordingly, went off to Speyerfeld as before, leaving Kattree behind to take care of the home.

That morning when the sun was high in a sky of trailing cirri and Kattree was catching fish for the midday meal, a hail came from south along the dam, and, turning her head, she saw the short figure of a man in a light grey suit and felt hat coming towards her. A little surprised and puzzled to know who he could be, she withdrew her hook and rose to meet him.

'Eh-eh! You mean is you, Kattree bettay?' he exclaimed as he came up. He smiled at her with large white teeth. 'Hey! You grow big girl, Kattree. I hardly know you. Where Beena and Ramgolall?'

'Deh gone a-Speyerfeld,' she told him, staring at him in wonder, though in her mind far back she felt as though she knew him. 'Who you?' she asked.

He laughed. 'You don't recognize me, Kattree?'

She smiled, shaking her head slowly in half-doubt. 'You' face look like me know you, but me na sure.'

'Tek a good look at me an' see if you don' recognize me.'

She smiled, regarding him a little shyly, then of a sudden she frowned and broke out: 'Oh, wait! You is Baijan?'

'Only now you mek me out? Yes, me is Baijan – you' half-brudder.' He gripped her hands and squeezed them. 'You grow big girl, Kattree. When I leave you here you was a lil' girl so high.'

'Me remember you' face now,' she smiled. 'You bin live in Essequibo all dis time, na?'

'Eh-heh. I got a rice-mill deh and odder property. I buy annoder rice-mill on de Corentyne here – at Sixty-eight Village – so I come to see after t'ings. I just drop in to see you-all on de way up. De car waitin' out dere now.'

'You come in car?'

'Eh-heh. Look it out deh on de road. I hire it in New Amster-dam. I been in New Amsterdam since day before yesterday lookin' after de passing of transports an' so on, you know.'

Kattree looked at him with awe.

'You surprised to see me, na?' he laughed.

'Yes. You is de las' person me expect to see dis mornin'.'

'I know. I been away a long time now – years and years. I used to keep a lil' grocery shop in Speyerfeld. You say Ramgolall and Beena gone to Speyerfeld? Wha' deh doing in Speyerfeld?'

'Deh sellin' milk.'

'Deh sellin' milk? Oh! Well, look, come wid me in de car an' lemme tek you to Sixty-eight Village. We can pick up Ramgolall an' Beena when we passing t'rough Speyerfeld.'

'Eh-eh! But me caan' come sudden so. Me fishin' fo' breakfas'.'

'Fishin'? Don' mind fishin' now. You going tek breakfast wid me. I arrange to get breakfast at Sixty-eight. Ramjit an' 'e family preparing breakfast fo' me. I gettin' married to Ramjit' daughter nex' mont'.'

'You gettin' married?'

'Eh-heh. I going marry an' settle down at Sixty-eight Village. I selling all me property in Essequibo.'

'Oh! An' who is Ramjit?'

'Ramjit? He belong Essequibo, but de early part o' dis year he retire from business an' come wid 'e family to live on de Corentyne here. It more healthy here dan in Essequibo, you know. Ramjit got plenty money. In Essequibo 'e did own four rice-mills an' a small sugar estate. 'E got t'ousands an' t'ousands o' dollars. Rich man. 'E youngest son going to Queen's College in Georgetown.'

'Queen's College? Dah is wheh Geoffry is go.'

'Geoffry? Oh! You mean Sosee' eldest son? Oh, yes. Eh-heh. Paul say 'e meet 'im. Paul in a lower form, though. 'E only fourteen years ol'.'

'Oh! Well, lemme go change me dress. Me caan' go in dis dress. It too dirty.'

He waited for her while she changed into her blue silk dress and canvas shoes and when she emerged again he exclaimed: 'Hey!' and said that she looked nice, though he did stare at her at first in a rather queer way, she thought. 'You look like a great lady now, Kattree. Where you get silk dress from?'

'Geoffry gimme five-dollar note when 'e come on Easter holiday. 'E say me an' Beena mus' buy nice dress, but Beena get vex, an' say she na want none o' de money, so me buy cloth an' mek four dress fo' meself – an' me buy dis pair o' shoes, too.'

'Oh, I see. You look real nice, man. Like great lady.'

When they had got into the car – a negro chauffeur drove it – and it began to glide forward, Baijan lit a cigarette which he took from a silver case. She watched in awe as he clicked the case shut again and put it back in the inner pocket from which he had taken it. He leant back in the car like a rich man, and, sitting beside him, she felt as if she were really a great, rich lady. It was queer, she thought, how things worked out. Here she was driving in a car for the first time in her life, with Baijan her half-brother beside her, when she had fully expected it to be Geoffry with whom she would first drive in a car. During the past two or three weeks, even up to last night, when she had dreamt of herself driving in a car it had always been Geoffry whom she had seen in her mind sitting beside her; but now here, without any warning at all, she was sitting in this big dark-blue car, and it was not Geoffry beside her but Baijan. If anyone had told her when she got up this morning that this would have happened she would have laughed at them and said that it could not happen.

On the way to Speyerfeld Baijan asked her many questions. He wanted to know how Ramgolall was getting on, how many head of cattle he had now and how much money he had. When Kattree told him how Ramgolall hoarded his money in a canister he said 'What! You mean he is still keep 'e money in dah canister!' and he laughed, but in a moment grew concerned and said that Ramgolall should have put his money in the Post Office Savings Bank, that it was not safe to keep money in a canister. 'Any day somebody could go in deh and rob 'e of every bit.'

'Na. We na got na t'ief-man hereabouts,' she smiled. 'People live good in dis part.'

But Baijan shook his head and said that it was unsafe to keep money like that. And, besides, if Ramgolall had put his money in the Post Office he would have been getting three per cent interest per annum. He would have had more money than he had now. Did she know how much he had stored away in his canister? She told him that she could not say how much exactly. 'But he got plenty hundred shilling tie up in bundle. Shilling-piece, two-shilling piece, copper money. Plenty, plenty.'

'Eh-h-h! You mean Ramgolall still such a miser? I t'ought 'e did stop all dat in 'e ol' age. You mean to say 'e don' give you an' Beena no money to spend?'

'Only enough to buy rice an' salt-fish an' one, two plantain. 'E didn' even want drink 'e own milk. Only since 'e get sick bad 'e start drink milk. An' years ago a doctor once tell 'e say dat 'e heart not too strong.'

'Ow! But dah is bad. 'E gettin' ol' now. What's de use o' hoarding away all 'e money like dat?'

'Same t'ing me an' Beena tell 'e. Last mont' 'e get sick bad, but 'e won' leh we hoist sick-flag. 'E say 'e na got money pay doctor. 'E too pore.'

In Speyerfeld Village they met Ramgolall and Beena on the point of entering the gateway of a small pink cottage. When the car slowed down and Baijan hailed out to them they turned and stared at him in surprise and without recognition. When he got out of the car and explained who he was, their dismay and pleasure were great. For quite a while Ramgolall could say nothing but 'Eh-h-h!'

'You t'ink you wouldn't ha' never see me again in all you' life, eh, Ramgolall?' laughed Baijan, patting Ramgolall on his shoulder.

'Eh-h-h! Boy, me can hardly believe me eye! Baijan! Eh-h-h! Baijan!' He looked at him with wide eyes. 'Eh-h-h!'

'Ol' man, you lookin' meagre,' said Baijan. 'An' why you don' wear clothes? You shouldn' walk about naked so. You mus' buy cloth an' mek dhoti and shirt.'

'Ow, baaya! Wha' me go do? You' faddah pore man. 'E caan' afford buy clothes. Na money na deh buy clothes. Me pore man, Baijan.'

'Aw! Behave you'self, ol' man,' laughed Baijan. 'You na got big canister wid plenty money save up all dese years?'

'Eh-h-h! Me got plenty money save-up? Na-a-a-a! Me only

got one, two copper put aside fo' by-an'-by. Ow! Me pore man, Baijan. True. Na got na money buy clothes.'

Baijan laughed. 'Awright, ol' man. Awright. I going buy clothes fo' you. Come inside de car.'

'Come in de car? Ow, baaya! Na. Me busy now. Me a-sell milk mek one, two copper.'

'Fo'get de milk, Ramgolall. How much money you going get fo' de milk you got here?'

'You mean how much money fo' *all* de milk in both de cans?'

'Eh-heh. How much fo' all?'

'Some day me get two shilling, some day me get t'ree shilling. Me na get plenty money fo' milk nowaday. Me pore, pore – '

'Awright. Well, don' worry to sell milk today. I going give you two dollars instead.'

'Two dollar? Eh-h-h! How much shilling in two dollar?'

'Eight shilling, four penny in two dollars.'

'Eh-h-h! An' you gimme all dah?'

'Yes, if you come in de car wid me. I want to take you-all to Sixty-eight Village to see a rich man – big rice man name' Ramjit. I gettin' married to 'e daughter nex' mont'.'

'You gettin' married?'

'Yes. To rich man' daughter. I buy a big rice-mill at Sixty-eight Village an' I sellin' all my odder property in Essequibo. I going settle down on de Coast here after I get married.'

'Ow! Dah good, baaya. Dah good. Me glad you come back Corentyne. Dah good.'

'Me glad you glad,' smiled Baijan. 'Come in de car. Gimme you' milk-cans. Lemme help you, ol' man.'

Baijan made the car stop at one of the shops farther up the road. He took Ramgolall into the shop and bought him three shirts, one of which he made him put on at once. It was a bright-pink shirt and fitted loosely over Ramgolall's thin body, giving him a very odd look indeed. Beena and Kattree laughed a great deal when they saw him come out of the shop. ''E look like dem red curri-curri bird,' said Beena, and Baijan frowned at her in mock rebuke and said: 'Bad girl. You mustn' say dat. Ramgolall look good. *Now* 'e look like a respectable gentleman. Great ol' man.'

Ramgolall, meanwhile, gave his deep grunting laugh, his

whole body quivering shakily. He looked pleased but not too comfortable. It was a great many years since he had worn any clothing. 'Ah-h-h! All-you laugh at me, na, bettay? Ah-h-h! Baijan good boy. Buy me one, two shirt. Good boy. God go bless you, baaya. Ah-h-h-h!'

Everybody stared curiously at them, and the sight of Ramgolall in a pink shirt caused many smiles.

When the car was moving off, Kattree saw Sumatra Pooran, one of Boorharry's women, looking at them with wondering eyes from the other side of the road. Suddenly she turned and whispered something to her mother who was with her, and from the look on her face and the way she nodded and pointed it seemed as though she had recognized Baijan.

34

The sun shone very weakly. The cirri had fallen, had turned into cirro-stratus and stretched now across the sky in one great mottled sheet through which the sun looked like a blob of cotton-wool soaked in castor-oil. No blue could be seen anywhere and the air was still and hot.

As the car hummed east along the red road, however, none of them took heed of the weather. There were too many things to be talked about with Baijan. Ramgolall's eyes shone brightly when Baijan told him of his growing wealth. Baijan said he had over five thousand dollars in property and nearly two thousand dollars in the bank, and if this year's rice crop proved fair he would be worth nearly ten thousand dollars, for he had some big deals pending. In October he hoped to export five thousand bags of rice to Guadeloupe, and, in November, about three thousand to Trinidad. Besides the rice-mill at Number Sixty-eight Village, he had bought a fair-sized cottage in the same village where he and his bride would live. He was to be married with Christian rites, not with Hindu. He had turned Christian. In February, year before the last he had got baptized under the names Charles Christopher, in the Anglican Church, and in July of the same year he had been confirmed. Ramjit and his family were Christians, too. 'It carry more influence in business when you is a Christian,' Baijan explained. 'Ramjit was a big church-man in Essequibo. Since he was young he join de Church. Deh mek 'im churchwarden. He talk wid estate-manager an' 'e shake hands over an' over wid de Lord Bishop of Guiana. I see it wid me own eyes. One Easter Sunday he put a twenty-dollar note in de collection-plate. *Twenty* dollars! Rich man, I tell you. 'E got t'ousands an' t'ousands o' dollars.'

All Ramjit's children, Baijan said, had been baptized in the English Church and given English names. The daughter Baijan was going to marry was named Elizabeth and she could read and write English like any great white lady. She had plenty books and novels by big authors in England and she could play the piano. She had played at a concert in Essequibo given in aid of the Church Organ Fund and everybody had clapped loudly and called for an encore. She was an educated lady. She had great talents. 'Once she even write a long story in a exercise-book an' send it away to a magazine in America called *True Romance*. She subscribe to all kind o' high-class magazines. *True Romance*, *True Story*, *True Confession*, *Love Mirror*. Oh, she got big, big education, man.'

'How much money she going get when she marry?' asked Ramgolall.

'Oh, don' fear 'bout dat,' Baijan assured him. 'Ramjit going settle five t'ousand 'pon she when she marry me, an' 'e want to buy a property fo' me at Seventy-four Village. 'E like me a lot. De whole family like me. Ramjit will do anyt'ing in dis world fo' me. An' Liza is 'e only daughter, so 'e caan' do enough fo' she. Oh, man, no fear about dat at all. Plenty money in dis marriage. Plenty, plenty. You know how much men envy me? Huh! Too much, too much men would be glad to be in my place.' Baijan lit a cigarette and leant back. 'Too much, too much men,' he repeated, blowing out a long cloud of smoke.

When they were passing Dr Roy's big house, he looked out and said: 'I hear Dr Matthias buy over ol' Mrs Clyde' house, eh? Good place, you know. One o' dese days I got to own a house like dat. Big house wid a tower and plenty bedrooms and servants, an' a piano fo' Liza to play.'

'Wha' is a piano?' asked Beena.

'A piano? You never see a piano? It's a sort o' box-like t'ing wid notes. You can siddown at it an' play music. You going see one when you get to Ramjit' house at Sixty-eight. 'E got a big brown one. I going mek Liz play a piece fo' you on it.'

'Rain drizzlin',' said Kattree.

'Ha! Me na tell all-you rain go fall before midday, bettay?' said Ramgolall. 'When sky look red at daybreak rain mus' fall during daytime. Eh-heh.'

Baijan stretched across Beena and turned a handle, and a section of glass rose up slowly until the whole open square beside Beena was closed. To Beena it seemed almost like magic the way everything worked in this car. When she pondered on it it frightened her a little. At moments she felt as though she were trapped in the belly of some terrible iron animal and that any minute the animal might get angry and out of control and vomit them all into the canal, or into the road by itself. She wondered what Jannee would say when she told him of this trip. He might be angry and jealous, though he ought not to be, for Baijan was her half-brother, and he was not young like Stymphy and Geoffry. He must be double her age. In Jannee's present mood, however, anything might anger him. It was such a pity he had fallen into that dark mood. If only he would forget Boorharry and stop going for those lonely walks to Speyerfeld when night fell! She had felt greatly relieved this morning when she had seen Boorharry alive and well cycling along the road in Speyerfeld. She had almost dreaded that she would have seen him lying a corpse on the road and a crowd of people around him... Ugh! But that would have been horrible. Let her stop thinking such things.

The rain came down suddenly and heavily. She saw the chauffeur stretch up his hand and touch something, and at once there came a faint whirring sound, and a thin, straight piece of metal began to wag about before the glass in the front part of the car. Her lips opened in wonder.

'Wha' is dah t'ing for?' Kattree asked Baijan, and Baijan said that it was the windscreen-wiper. 'It wipe away de water so de driver can see ahead clear widout any trouble. Ramjit's car got two windscreen-wipers. 'E got a great car. You should see it, man, oh

God! Seven-seater. When you siddown in it you feel like you in heaven.'

The rain came down in a thick torrent of coarse drops. Around them the whole scene had grown hazed. The windscreen and side windows looked blotchy with the pattering drops as though the glass were melting. The tyres made a continuous swish-swash on the streaming road. Beena felt as if at any moment the wheels would skid round and send the whole car plunging into the canal. She kept gripping her knees and peering out at the white curtain of drops.

35

The rain was still pouring when they reached Number Sixty-eight Village, but in the north-east a patch of pale blue, like the blue of a duck's egg, had appeared, and Kattree said that in another ten or fifteen minutes the rain would stop. Beena said she thought it would go on for the rest of the day.

'Dat's de place,' Baijan said to the chauffeur, pointing. De two-storey house wid de red roof.'

When the car came to a stop, Baijan told them not to get out until he had brought them umbrellas and overcoats. Kattree was glad of this, for she had been fearing that her new silk dress would get wet. It would be too bad if she got it spoiled the very first time she wore it. She wanted to have it looking nice so that Geoffry would like it when he saw it next month. Had she thought that the rain would have fallen like this she would have worn one of the cotton ones instead.

Baijan returned shortly with two black umbrellas and two raincoats. 'Ladies first,' he said. 'Come on, Kattree and Beena. All-you two mus' come out first. I going come back fo' you jus' now, Ramgolall. Wait lil' bit.'

When they had fumbled their way into the raincoats, Kattree and Beena alighted, and Baijan, opening the umbrellas for them, hurried them over a wide bridge with wooden rails and up a long stairway into a railed-in portico from the roof of which dangled small baskets with ornamental ferns. Both halves of the double door were open and an elderly East Indian gentleman and a short, plump girl of about twenty-five stood waiting to greet them. 'Come inside. Come inside,' said the gentleman. He gave them a kind smile, and as they entered the gallery he and Baijan helped them to take off the raincoats. 'Kattree, Beena, allow me to introduce you to Mr George Ramjit,' said Baijan in a very stiff sort of tone, and Mr Ramjit shook hands with them in a friendly, easy way, saying to Baijan: 'You got nice sisters, boy. Why you didn' bring dem to Essequibo to see me? Come inside, girls. Come in de drawing room an' make you'selves at home.'

'Dis is Liza who I been tellin' you about,' smiled Baijan, indicating the plump girl. She was very plain-looking and had a silly, fixed smile. 'Liza, you mus' play somet'ing fo' dem on de piano. Deh never hear piano yet.'

While he hurried off again to take umbrella and overcoat down to the car for Ramgolall, Liza, still with her silly, fixed smile took Beena and Kattree into the sitting room. It was a fairly large room and the floor was stained deep brown and shone brightly. It was crowded with chairs and tables and thick rugs, and Kattree and Beena looked round them with awe, feeling a little bewildered. It was the first time they had entered a sitting room like this. They felt almost afraid to walk on this dark, shining floor lest they spoil it. Already Beena's bare feet had left faint toe-prints. They carefully avoided walking on the rugs, though Liza, in her high-heeled shoes, walked over them without a single downward glance.

'Dis is de piano,' she smiled, taking them over to what appeared to them to be a large, queer-looking thing made of brown wood in the south-eastern corner. 'And over dere,' she went on, pointing to a radio-set, 'is a radio. I going tune-in fo' you jus' now. You can hear music from London an' New York – all part o' de world.'

'Eh-heh. We know radio,' smiled Beena. 'Almost all dem big store in Speyerfeld got radio. Every day deh play music wid it.'

'Well! Fancy knowing a radio and not a piano! Dat's queer,' laughed Liza. She seated herself before the piano and opened it. Kattree and Beena stared with wide eyes at the keyboard. 'Wha' is all dem black an' white t'ing?' asked Beena.

'Dese are de notes,' Liza explained. She struck a note, and

Beena and Kattree smiled and exclaimed: 'Eh-h-h!' Liza struck a chord, then several chords and said: 'Dat's how you play it, you see? But wait! All-you don' stand up. Siddown. You mus' make you'selves comfortable.'

When they had seated themselves, she played a piece for them. She called it a classical piece and said it was named *Hearts and Flowers*.

In the middle of the piece Ramgolall came in with Baijan and Mr Ramjit. He kept smiling in a shy, uncomfortable way and looking all about him, and Liza stopped playing to shake his hand. 'Dis is your future daughter-in-law, Ramgolall,' Baijan said in introducing her. 'Miss Elizabeth Irene Ramjit.' Liza smiled widely and said: 'I'm pleased to meet you,' giving a slight bow of her head as she shook hands. Ramgolall smiled, too, made his groaning sound and replied: 'Me please meet you, too, bettay. Eh-h-h.'

'Go on playin' de piano, Liza,' said Baijan. 'Where mudder an' Joseph? Lemme go an' call dem.' He went into the dining room and they heard him calling out: 'Mudder! Joseph! Where all-you gone to? Come downstairs an' meet Ramgolall an' Beena an' Kattree!' And a nasal voice from upstairs replied: 'Me comin' down jus' now, Charlie boy! Joseph in de bath! He comin' down jus' now, too!'

'All-you hurry up!'

Mr Ramjit called: 'Charlie boy, make you'self useful in deh an' bring out some biscuits an' soft drinks fo' Beena an' Kattree an' de ol' man! Keep deh mout' occupy till breakfast time!'

'Awright! Good! I comin' in a minute! Where you got de biscuits? In de sideboard press?'

'Yes! We keep everyt'ing in de same place as we keep am in Essequibo! Nutting change up!'

Liza, meanwhile, played Tobani's *Hearts and Flowers*, making many mistakes, though Kattree and Beena did not know this. They thought it wonderful that she could play this brown wooden thing called a piano and make such pleasing, though queer, music. It was the same sort of music they often heard the radios and gramophones in Speyerfeld shops playing. They called it among themselves 'English music', but did not like it. They only liked 'coolie' music because they were used to coolie music

159

and could understand it. When Liza turned, however, with her smile and asked them: 'How you like dat?' they both broke into smiles and said that it was nice.

'I going play you annoder one,' smiled Liza. 'It nicer dan *Hearts and Flowers*. Charlie like it. It call' *Backerollee*, from de *Tales of Hoffman*.'

Beena and Kattree and Ramgolall did not enjoy their visit. It lasted over three hours, and they felt awkward and out of place all the time. Ramgolall's shirt kept him hot and Kattree's shoes squeezed her toes and made them burn. Moreover, every now and then Kattree would find Joseph Ramjit's gaze on her. Joseph was a year or two younger than Liza and rather handsome. He kept staring at her in a queer, furtive way when no one else was looking, a half-smile around his lips, his eyes gleaming, and after a while she began to realize that he was attracted by her figure. (Save for her cotton panties, she wore no underclothes.) It made her feel so shy that she could fain have hidden herself behind the piano or asked Baijan for one of the raincoats so that she could wear it until it was time to leave.

When they were all seated around the dining table, Beena felt keenly aware of her dirty, everyday dress. She regretted now not having bought a new dress out of the five-dollar note Geoffry had given to Kattree and herself.

The cutlery and crockery proved very baffling, for they were accustomed to eating with their hands out of saucepans. These knives and forks and spoons seemed odd implements with which to convey food to their mouths. They were grateful to Mr Ramjit when he said: 'All-you don' worry wid knife an' fork. Eat wid you' hands. Mek you'self at home.'

Mrs Ramjit, who was short and very fat and not unlike her daughter, kept asking them if they had had enough to eat and helping them to more curried chicken and rice. Like her husband, she seemed a very kind person. She did everything she could to make them feel at ease.

It was a great relief when they got into the car again with Baijan and drove off west on the return trip. The rain had stopped over two hours ago and the sun shone now in a blue sky arrayed with small ragged white clouds and here and there a wisp of cirrus.

When they reached Benab (Number Sixty-three Village), Baijan made the chauffeur turn the car north into the narrow, uneven lane that led to the beach. It was a wide, yellow beach separated by sand-dunes from the vegetated area inland. The tide was coming in strongly. The wind droned and the grey waves with their white crests crashed and roared endlessly on the yellow sand. They got out of the car and walked about on the beach, breathing deeply of the fresh wind. Beena picked up shells.

'If we had bathing-suits we coulda go in de sea and have a lil' swim,' said Baijan. 'I going bring you-all here again soon one o' dese days. Nice place, dis.'

In Speyerfeld Baijan bought silk and cotton cloth for Beena – enough to make her three dresses, one of silk and two of cotton – and canvas shoes like Kattree's. He offered to buy shoes for his father, too, but Ramgolall demurred, saying that he had never worn shoes in his life and that they would hurt his feet. Baijan laughed and gave him the two dollars he had promised him earlier that day, and Ramgolall promptly asked one of the shop-assistants to change the note for eight shillings and four pennies.

Before they left Speyerfeld, Baijan made arrangements with a butcher and a grocer to supply his father and sisters with anything they wanted. 'Give dem anyt'ing deh want,' he said to the grocer with a wide sweep of his arm, 'an' charge it to me. I'm opening an account wid you from now. I'll pay you at de end of every mont', an' if you doubt my financial stability, go an' ask Mr George Ramjit of Sixty-eight Village an' he will tell you about me.'

'Oh, no, no, it's awright, Mr Baijan,' said the grocer hastily. (He was Jaigan, whom Kattree and Beena knew well and from whom they had always bought their foodstuffs.) 'Me hear 'bout you. Me know you' credit good. It's quite awright, sir. Don' worry at all. I'm pleased to do business wid you.'

The butcher was equally willing to open an account with Baijan. Like the grocer, he was an East Indian. 'I hear 'bout you, Mr Baijan,' he smiled. 'Everybody in de village bin talkin' 'bout you today. One or two people recognize you when you stop in de car dis mornin'. I'm very glad to know you. I know your fadder an' sisters for many years.'

Ramgolall and Beena and Kattree felt very proud at hearing

Baijan spoken to in this way. In the street people stared at them all the time and murmured to each other, as though Baijan might be some great and famous man just arrived from England or America.

At parting, he gave Kattree and Beena a dollar each and told them to buy nice things for themselves. He said he was going back now to Essequibo to wind up his business affairs, but would come back in three or four weeks' time. 'An' when I come,' he said to Beena and Kattree, 'I going give you-all money to buy special dress to wear at me wedding. You got to look like grand ladies. Everybody mus' admire you. It going be a great wedding, you know. People from all over de colony – Essequibo, Demerara, Berbice coming to it. Champagne going flow like water. Ramjit don' do anyt'ing half-way, you know.'

As the three of them stood looking after the car, watching it grow smaller and smaller in the west, Ramgolall groaned and nodded his head, smiling. 'Baijan great boy,' he said, and he spoke in a pensive, far-away voice as though he might be standing here alone. 'Eh-heh. Baijan great boy. Me na disappoint' in 'e. 'E great boy. 'E bring me honour in de worl' – like Sosee bring me long time ago. 'E great boy. Me proud call 'e me son. Eh-heh.' He made his groaning sound again and kept nodding his head slowly over and over. Glancing at him, Kattree saw that his eyes looked wet in the corners.

36

During the four days following Baijan's advent the weather held fine. The sun shone hotly and the sky was alive with clouds like cobweb that came sprawling hurriedly from the north and melted into the nothing of the blue overhead. A cooling wind blew steadily over the savannah and helped to lessen the burning heat. The rice-fields that for three months past had lain like bright-green rugs to the south of the public road, far aback, had taken on a dull green hue and were beginning to look ragged and beaten, for the young grains bowed the stalks down with the weight of their gathering starch. No more did the wind pass over these fields like a buoyant, playful tide that ruffled the tops of the slim, waving plants and set into motion the changing tints of green. All that was over, as though youth had passed and the cares of maturity were beginning to burden the fields. The grains were filling out. Soon the green would fade altogether and the pale yellow of age set in. Lower and lower the stalks would bend and deeper and deeper grow the yellow. The white sun would dry up the water so that only a wet brown slime remained to tell of the freshening torrents of earlier months. The air would stink as though the fumes of decay had preceded death. And then one morning early the mild sunlight would pierce the shroud of blue mist and gleam on grey crescents of steel and the chatter of triumphant voices would float over the field and frighten away the last lurking jumbie of the night before, for the reapers would be at hand: brown men with unrelenting grins.

The evenings, too, were fine, the sky being without a cloud, and the stars glowing like a million mirrored candle-flies. Lightning flashed often in the empty dome, futile dry-weather lightning thin as a veil that fitted into life, twinkled and was gone. Ramgolall beat the tom-tom and Kattree and Beena sang, for the coming of Baijan had gladdened their spirits. They ate good food now: curried meat and potatoes and bread and cheese, peas and rice and, in the morning, an egg or two. They had lard and butter with which to fry the fishes Kattree caught. They bought a new frying-pan, for the old one had a hole, and new saucepans. On the second evening after Baijan's coming they ate so heartily that Ramgolall had a bad dream and woke up with a scream in the middle of the night. Kattree and Beena woke, too, startled out of their sleep by his scream. They asked him what was wrong and he told them that he had dreamt that Jairamsingh and a whole band of devils and duppies had crowded into the mud-house and begun to prod him with the handles of frying-pans. They had tried to pour melted butter and lard, hot from the frying pan, down his throat and that was what had made him scream out. Kattree and Beena laughed at him and he, too, laughed in his groaning way, and soon they were all deep in sleep again while the wind outside continued to hum serenely about the smooth mud walls like a friendly murmuring veil that wanted to wrap itself around their abode so as to keep out all the flitting evil of the black midnight.

On the fourth evening after the coming of Baijan there was no drum beating or singing of songs. Instead, the three of them, having had a hearty meal and feeling lazy, sat before the door of the mud-house and talked of trifling things or kept silent and let thoughts pattern the dark with faces and incidents: light mirages of the mind that glittered with dewdrop fancies or wreathed like a fog of twilight shapes troubling to the soul. The futile lightning flickered often in the starry sky and wind came very faintly from the north, filled with the rank smell of fish and iodine.

'Tomorrow night new moon,' said Kattree, breaking a long silence. 'Curry-feed got to hold at Jannee' house.'

'Me talk to Sukra 'bout it in Speyerfeld dis mornin',' said Beena, 'but she say Jannee' mood get so bad dese las' few days she na know if 'e go want have curry-feed.'

'You mean 'e still vex' wid Boorharry?'

'Boorharry did really treat 'e bad dah day in Speyerfeld. 'E mek all dem lil' boy laugh at Jannee.'

'Jaigan tell me all 'bout it. 'E say Boorharry only bin a-mek fun. Jannee got too much quick temper – dah wha' wrong wid 'e. An' 'e like hold bad mind fo' people too long. 'E shouldn't hold bad mind fo' people so long. Na good. It show 'e got bad nature.'

Beena said nothing, for, though it hurt her to hear ill spoken of Jannee, she knew that there was truth in what Kattree said. During the silence that followed she kept staring at the black savannah, and out there on that night-gloomed background her thoughts painted pictures of umber hue. Ugly mirages these were in which she saw the lonely figure of Jannee trudging stealthily along the dark road, vengeful and threatening... crouched now by the parapet waiting, waiting like a duppy, fidgeting...and then after a while, the white-clad form of Boorharry pedalling, unaware, along the road, easily and with a faint creak of metal. The tinkle of a bell came from the canal behind Jannee. On pedalled Boorharry. Lightning glowed and she saw the grey gleam of a cutlass. Then dark cloaked the scene. When the lightning glowed again she saw something sprawled white and still on the parapet and Jannee running in a panic homeward.

Half-sitting, half-lying, crouched up beside her, Kattree saw brighter pictures. Hers was a golden mirage trembling in the white heat of an August day. Cotton-wool clouds drifted in a blue sky and the wind droned steadily, making the grey sea crash and roar on the yellow beach of Sixty-three Village. She and Geoffry, laughing and naked, hurled themselves at the oncoming waves and the water gurgled and foamed around them as they emerged... Wearing her pink silk dress, she sat beside him in the big maroon car, and the car hummed swiftly along the red road, throwing up a cloud of dust behind. Nearer and nearer New Amsterdam. Feel how the rushing wind made her hair tremble...! He sat with her by the canal and they talked while they waited for fish to bite... At midday they ate cakes and slices of bread with ham between, and drank sweet drinks out of short bottles. He made many jokes and dropped crumbs down her back and stood on his head and let her feed him with a cake... When they had slept and awakened he spoke to her in a quiet voice, his eyes looking into hers. He stroked her arm and kissed her and caressed her body everywhere. The day was without wind and the savannah a-tremble in the heat far away, and she felt very happy lying with him in the cool shadow of the mud-house... Every day he would come – every day for a whole month. They would fish together one day, go driving another day – to New Amsterdam, or to Sixty-three where they would bathe in the roaring sea or lie on the beach naked and laugh and caress each other and be very happy. And when he had gone back to school, perhaps her belly would begin to swell with child and she would look as Sukra had looked some months ago. Ramgolall would regard her with dismay and gloom and wag his head, but she would not mind. She would be happy to have a child of her own. She would take great care of it and show it to Geoffry when he came to spend holidays on the Coast. It would be the best moment in her life when she showed him her baby.

As for Ramgolall, his mirage had been brief and mixed. He had seen himself jostled by a great crowd of strange people, then, somehow, the scene had changed and he had found himself crouching by his canister adding the daily two shillings to his hoard. He began to count the shillings, shillings and pennies and sixpences… Shillings tinkled all around him, and then he went off into a doze, his head sunk on his chest.

'Every night 'e tek walk go a-Speyerfeld,' said Beena, breaking the silence again. 'Every night fo' more dan a week now. Sukra talk to 'e, but no use. Every night, soon as dark fall, 'e lef' home.'

'But why 'e tek walk alone after dark?'

Beena made no reply, but she fidgeted. The faint wind of a sudden felt very chilly on her bare arms. She shivered slightly.

'Me hear 'e stop going a-Speyerfeld since de quarrel 'e had wid Boorharry,' said Kattree. 'Is true?'

'Eh-heh. 'E stop going. Sukra does tek de cart to Speyerfeld. 'E say if 'e meet Boorharry in Speyerfeld an' Boorharry trouble 'e again bad go happen, so 'e prefer stay home.'

'But why 'e tek walk a-Speyerfeld after dark?'

'Me na know,' said Beena in a quiet voice. She felt Kattree's eyes on her in the dark, those deep secret-filled eyes. She felt as though Kattree were seeing into her mind, seeing Jannee with a cutlass and the still white figure of Boorharry. She must not let Kattree know her fears. Kattree did not like Jannee. She was forever ready to speak ill of him. If she learnt that Jannee was planning to kill Boorharry she might go and tell Jaigan and Jaigan might go and tell the police and then Jannee would be in trouble. Nobody in Speyerfeld liked him. Everybody liked Boorharry – even the children. She herself liked him in a way. She would be sorry if Jannee killed him. Every morning, for the past week, she had awakened with one great dread in her – the dread that she would see someone, perhaps Manoo or Poonar, come running quickly along the mud-dam. 'Boorharry dead, Beena!' Manoo gasped. 'Deh fin' 'e lying dead by de roadside! 'E cut up and bleeding!' Any morning now she expected something like that to happen. The first thing she did on waking was to stand and look towards the public road to see if people were running towards Speyerfeld or if anyone were coming in a hurry along the dam.

Ramgolall rose and said in a sleepy voice that it was time they went to bed.

'Me na sleepy yet,' said Beena. 'You go in.'

'Me can sleep now,' said Kattree. 'Me feelin' tired.'

She and Ramgolall went in to bed, but Beena continued to sit

166

where she was, staring out at the savannah and thinking dark thoughts. The wind made her shiver. Strange fears wound themselves like crooked bony fingers around her heart. She felt afraid to go to bed, for sleep would bring her near to morning, and, somehow, she felt that tomorrow morning would be the black morning. For the past eight or nine nights she had told herself before going to bed that the following morning would be the black morning, and yet the morning always broke without anything being wrong. Perhaps tomorrow morning it would be the same. She would wake, emerge and look anxiously towards the south, but there would be no one hurrying along the road towards Speyerfeld or no one coming breathlessly to say that Boorharry was dead. And later in the day, when she went with Ramgolall to Speyerfeld to sell the milk, she would see Boorharry alive and cheerful as always and her fears would all melt in the sunlight. Every morning it was the same. But one morning soon it would not be the same. Of that she felt certain. And perhaps tomorrow morning would be that morning – the black morning.

37

Long after Beena had gone to bed, a squalling shower of rain broke upon the savannah. Lightning flashed in glowing sheets from a pile of black clouds in the east and thunder rolled in deep rumbling booms between long intervals. The rain hissed down very fiercely, and whooping gusts of wind seemed to make circles on the savannah, whisking round and round the mud-houses, rustling in the plumes of coconut palms and hurling raindrops wildly everywhere. Within half an hour, however, it had all passed off, the black clouds drifting rapidly to the west and stars appearing again. Lightning continued to flash, though, and now and then a low, half-hearted grumble of thunder would come from the west.

When dawn broke the sky was clear overhead, and at all points save in the east where a solid band of cloud stretched like a rampart low down along the horizon and turned from grey to purple in slow dignity as the sun rose behind it. A thin blue mist veiled the landscape so that the courida bush in the north looked like a filmy land far away in a dream. From Nairnley, in the west, came the cooing of a conch-shell, low and soft like wool, as though muffled by the mist. Vicissi ducks squeaked high overhead, calling back the rain of the night before. They could be seen as tiny black dots in the pale sky, flying in a V-like squadron of bombing planes.

Beena, the first to emerge, stood for over a minute near the canal looking southward to see if there were any people hurrying along the road towards Speyerfeld or along the dam towards her. But like yester morning and the mornings before, everything seemed normal. Dimly through the mist, she could make out a donkey-cart jogging slowly towards Nairnley. It was the only moving thing on the road.

She breathed deeply in relief, and pulling off her dress, shivered a little and then plunged into the canal to have her usual morning bathe. The water was chilly, but she liked it. No one was hurrying along the road. Nothing had happened. That was why the water felt so nice in spite of its chill. If there had been signs that anything had happened it would have felt very cold. She would have shivered and her teeth would have chattered. Fishes would have nipped at her toes. But nothing had happened so her relief was great. Everything seemed good now. Nothing could be unpleasant. The chilly water was delightful and refreshing.

Seeing Kattree standing naked by the edge of the canal as though chary of jumping in, she trod water and called: 'Jump in, na, gal? Water nice dis mornin'!'

'Mornin' feel col'!' called back Kattree, squeezing her small breasts together and shivering. 'Me 'fraid to jump in!' But even as she spoke she arched her body forward and plunged in. Beena chortled and the two of them swam about, ducked, turned somersaults and made a great splashing noise.

The sun cut a cleft in the purple band of cloud and threw a red beam of light on their wet brown bodies. The water sparkled like beads of amber as it splashed up into the air around their whirling limbs, and the little ripples and wavelets retreated about them like glittering amulets and bangles. Beena trod water and blinked at the east. She liked to see the sunrise. Two fans of gold and two of pink were sprayed out above the thick purple wall of cloud. The mist was breaking up in thin swirls like sheets of ghostly tissue-paper. In the north it glowed pale opal in the sunlight, seeming like an aura above the courida fringe, but in the south and the west it still looked blue and quiet.

Ramgolall hailed out from the cow-pen, telling them to hurry up and come out of the water. Every morning it was the same, every morning he had to tell them to hurry up and come out, for, once in the water, they were never eager to leave it.

When they were drying their skins with old rice-bags, Kattree, who stood facing south, gave a little grunt and said in a casual voice: 'Plenty people out dis morning. Me wonder if anyt'ing happen.'

Beena stopped drying her skin and looked southward. A sudden shiver passed down her arms and legs, and her heart gave a queer thump inside her chest. There were people on the road, people moving in a line of grey dots against the blue mist in the south. The air felt chilly – very chilly. She shivered again. People moving like grey dots along the road, moving east towards Speyerfeld. The air felt icy now. Her limp wet hair had of a sudden become snakes that dangled about her neck and shoulders and down her back. They might hiss and bite her at any moment. Two donkey-carts – no, there were three. Two were going east, one west. A thin scarf, made, it seemed to her, of morning air and jumbie ice, wrapped itself about her legs and twined its way up and around her body so that her skin grew prickly and her nipples hard and pointed. She clenched her hands tightly and quivered all over. She heard Kattree grunt and say: 'Is wha' wrong wid you? Why you stop dry you' skin?'

'Nutting,' she answered quietly, and began to dry her skin again, though her eyes kept staring southward. Abruptly, she threw down the rice-bag, and, taking up her dress, pulled it on over her half-dried body.

'Me a-go see wha' happen,' she said, and began to run south along the dam.

'You na go help milk de cow dis mornin'?' called Kattree after her.

'When me come back!'

She kept running and walking, running and walking. When

she walked it was like a jerky half-trot. Her hair tickled her neck and she could feel water creeping in tiny streams down her temples and cheeks and down the hollow of her back and the hollow between her breasts. It seemed like blood trickling from wounds and gave her an empty, panicky feeling inside.

This was the black morning. She knew it. It had tried to fool her when she had first got up and looked south. There had been no people then. But now the people were there. Moving dots hurrying east, just as she had imagined she would see them on this morning – the black morning.

Under her as she ran over it, the bridge made a dull thud that sickened her. Coffin-boards it sounded like.

Now that she had reached it, the road did not seem to have so many people on it. Two black boys in shirt-tails were the first persons she met. They were trotting eastward and must have come from far, for they were blowing hard. 'Wha' happen, baaya?' she asked.

'Overseer dead,' gasped one.

'Wha overseer? Wha' 'e name?'

'Me na know. Me only hear dem say a man get kill near Speyerfeld. Somebody say is overseer.'

The boys went past, panting in regular rhythm all the time. She looked west and saw a cart coming. She ran to meet it. Moonsammy and his wife Heedai were in it.

'Moonsammy, wha' happen a-Speyerfeld?'

'You na hear, bettay? Boorharry dead. Manoo fin' 'e 'pon roadside, dis morning four o' clock time.'

Yes, she had known it. This was the black morning. 'How 'e dead? Wha' happen?'

'Me na know, bettay. Me only hear 'e dead wid blood all over 'e head. Perhaps car knock 'e down las' night.'

'Come inside cart wid we,' invited Heedai. 'We a-go Speyerfeld side now see wha' wrong.'

Beena shook her head. 'Na. Me na like see dead people. Wheh Sukra? You see Sukra an' Jannee?'

'Eh-heh. Deh deh home. We pass dem jus' now.'

'Awright, t'ank you. Me want see dem lil' bit.'

She broke into a run along the road, feeling sick and scared. A car's horn sounded ahead, and she veered towards the southern parapet, stumbling for no reason at all. When it rushed past her she saw that it was a long blue car. She had a glimpse of uniformed figures. One figure was in khaki and seemed to be a white man, but she could not be certain. Everything appeared, somehow, unreal. Even the mild sunlight looked a queer coppery colour. She felt trembly and guilty, as though it were she who had killed Boorharry last night. She was running now so as to get as far away as she could from the huddled form lying on the parapet yonder there up the road. She was running to get away from the police, but she was sure they would catch her.

When she reached Jannee's home she was blowing hard. She found Sukra standing on the one plank that served as bridge, as if waiting for her. Her face looked pale and frightened. She said, 'Oh, gaad, Beena! Me glad you come, gal,' speaking in a hushed voice. 'Wheh Jannee?' asked Beena, speaking in a hushed voice, too. Sukra glanced towards the mud-house. ''E in deh,' she said. 'You hear wha' happen?' asked Beena. 'Eh-heh,' Sukra nodded. 'Boorharry dead. Oh, gaad, Beena! Ow! Me hear 'e cut up bad.'

'You bin up de road to see?'

'Na. Jannee na lemme go. 'E na come home till late las' night – after rain an' t'under-lightning stop. 'E go straight to de farm, den 'e come home naked-skin, an' when me ask 'e wha' wrong 'e hit me a cuff an' tell me to shut me mout' an' mind me own business. Oh, gaad! Me frighten-frighten so much me na sleep whole night.'

''E tek cutlass when 'e go fo' walk las' night?'

'Me na know. 'E lef' home an' go to de farm. Me keep watch an' see 'e pass back going a-Speyerfeld way, but me couldn' see if 'e had anyt'ing in 'e hand. It did too dark.'

They were silent for a short while. Beena cast fearful glances towards the mud-house. 'Wheh Boodoo an' Chattee?' she asked suddenly in a low voice. 'Deh still asleep. Baby asleep, too,' Sukra told her. 'Jannee asleep, too?' Beena asked. Sukra shook her head. 'Na. 'E 'wake. 'E siddown 'pon de bed an' smoke clay-pipe till morning break. 'E come out jus' now an' look up de road. Moonsammy an' Heedai pass an' tell 'e mornin' an' 'e say mornin' an' go back inside de house.'

After another silence, Sukra said: 'Motorcar pass jus' now wid police inspector from New Amsterdam.' Beena nodded and said that she had seen the car – a long blue car. The Inspector was a white man, Sukra said, and he was clever at finding out things, she had heard. Beena gave a shiver.

After they had stood talking for a while, they saw a donkey-cart come jogging slowly along the road from Speyerfeld way. In it they made out Bijoolie and his wife, Nanwa. 'Ay, gal!' Bijoolie hailed. He brought the cart to a stop and Beena and Sukra went out on the road to them.

'Wha' happenin' yonder, Bijoolie?' Sukra asked.

Police from New Amsterdam come in big car,' Bijoolie replied. 'Deh tek photograph o' Boorharry.'

'Photograph? Wha' deh tek photograph fo'?'

'Me na know, gal. Me see Inspector wid camera, an' 'e put am to stan' up an' tek photograph o' Boorharry, but me na know why.'

'You see Boorharry close up?' asked Beena.

'Eh-heh. Close up. Police stan' up on guard an' deh won' let nabody come more close dan t'ree yards. If you see blood! Oh, gaad! Plenty blood deh. 'E spatter all over de roadside.'

'Boorharry cut up bad-bad?'

'Bad-bad. 'E head cover wid blood. All 'e beard got blood. Even de bicycle – all good blood.'

' 'E bin ridin' bicycle?' asked Sukra.

'Yes,' said Bijoolie, nodding. 'Me hear dem say 'e did jus' lef' Sumatra Pooran' house midnight time after t'under-lightning stop, an' 'e did ridin' home back when de person attack 'e an' cut 'e up.'

'You hear if deh fin' out who de person was?'

'Me hear all kind o' wild talk. Some say Sumatra Pooran sheself do it. Some say Dookie' wife. Some say you' husband do it because 'e had quarrel wid Boorharry two-t'ree week ago.'

Beena and Sukra stared at him in silence. Beena felt as though the cold bill of a bird – an owl perhaps or a goat-sucker – were squeezing her heart slowly so that soon the blood would all be drained out of it.

'All kind o' wild talk about going about,' said Bijoolie. He glanced at the mud-house. 'Wheh Jannee? Me na see 'e fo' de mornin'.'

''E inside,' said Sukra. ''E smoke 'e pipe.'

'Oh-h-h!' said Bijoolie, and to Beena his voice sounded a little queer.

They were all silent for a brief interval, and then Nanwa looked east along the road and said: 'Car a-come.'

Beena looked – and then Sukra and Bijoolie.

''E look like police-car,' said Sukra.

'Na. Me t'ink is maninger' car,' said Bijoolie.

It turned out to be the blue car. It slowed down and drew up by the side of the road, the gleaming nickel of the headlamps coming to a stop within about a foot of the back of Bijoolie's cart. The white Inspector of Police, in khaki tunic and shorts, and two men, one in police uniform and one in an ordinary grey suit, came out of the car. The uniformed man was a negro, the plain-clothes man an East Indian.

'This where Jannee lives?' the Inspector asked, and he looked from Bijoolie and Nanwa to Beena and Sukra in quick, alert glances of his blue eyes. Beena liked him at once, somehow, even though she knew what he had come about. He had a cheerful sort of face and his eyes twinkled as if at any moment he might break into a laugh and tell them a good joke.

'Yes,' Sukra replied to him in a faint voice. 'Jannee live here.'

'Which of you is his wife?'

'Me 'e wife,' said Sukra.

'Your name Sukra?'

'Yes.'

'And where's Jannee? Not at home?'

'Yes. 'E deh inside de house.'

'Don't mean to tell me he hasn't got out of bed yet?' He broke into a faint smile and lit a cigarette which he took from a silver case – a case like the one Baijan had. He flicked the match far off into the ditch with a neat fillip that Beena liked.

'Na, 'e awake,' said Sukra. She seemed very scared and kept rubbing the palms of her hands together slowly. Her face looked pale. ''E inside de house.'

'Let's go and pull him out,' said the Inspector in a joking voice,

173

and he and the two men began to move across the plank-bridge. Beena and Sukra followed. Bijoolie and Nanwa sat on in their cart and stared after them.

'What's your name?' the East Indian policeman in plain-clothes asked Beena.

Beena told him and he grunted and said: 'You're a friend of Sukra and Jannee?'

'Yes,' said Beena.

'Nice bettay,' smiled the Inspector. 'Better keep your eye off her, Jeenarine.' He blew out a long cloud of smoke, and pausing at the open door of the mud-house, pushed his head inside and said: 'Jannee!'

Peering past him, Beena saw Jannee lying on one of the two wooden beds. He seemed to be sound asleep. On the other bed lay Boodoo and Chattee and Bharat – all asleep.

The Inspector chuckled and looked round at Sukra. 'I thought you said he was awake. You've got a lazy husband, Sukra. Jannee! Wake up!'

Jannee started violently and scrambled to a sitting position. He looked at them in alarm. 'Wha' wrong? Who you?'

'Lazy fellow,' smiled the Inspector. 'We've come to pay you a call, Jannee. You shouldn't be asleep now. Didn't you sleep well last night?'

'Who you? Wha' wrong? You want to see me?'

'That's what we want, Jannee – to see you and have a little chat with you. You don't mind, do you?'

Jannee got up slowly and came to the door. Boodoo and Chattee were awake now. They sat crouched up, staring in wonder at the little crowd outside the door. Bharat Ragoonandan slept on snugly amidst his rag-bedding. Jannee hitched up his trousers – clean khaki trousers. 'You want talk to me?' he said, his deep black eyes staring open, but still reddish with sleep.

'Yes. Tell us why you didn't sleep well last night,' said the Inspector.

'Me sleep awright las' night. Who say me na sleep good?' He cast a furtive look at Sukra.

'You did? But you've overslept this morning.'

Jannee said nothing. His face began to take on a baffled, sulky look.

'What time do you get out of bed every morning?' the Inspector asked him.

'Me na got na partic'lar time get up,' he replied, frowning heavily.

'You didn't go out last night?'

'Las' night? Na. Wha' me got business go out las' night? Las' night me bin in bed.'

'The whole night, Jannee? You didn't go out at all?'

'Na. Me na go out at all. Me bin home all night.'

'And you've just awakened, eh? When I came here and called you a minute ago you awoke from a whole-night sleep?'

'But why you ask me all dis?'

'You haven't heard what's happened, Jannee?'

'Wha' happen? Me na know nutting. How you mean if me na know wha' happen? *Wha'* happen?'

'You haven't heard Boorharry is dead?'

'Boorharry? Boorharry dead? When 'e dead?'

'Last night. Cut up all over the head and neck. Bad story, Jannee. Bad story. Jeenarine, better go ahead and make a little search,' added the Inspector in a lowered voice.

'Correct, chief,' nodded Jeenarine, and he pushed his way past Jannee into the mud-house.

Bharat awoke and began to struggle and make coughing sounds.

'Wha' you want in me house?' demanded Jannee angrily, glaring at Jeenarine.

'Don't mind dat,' Jeenarine said in a curt voice.

'No need to get riled, Jannee,' the Inspector smiled. 'We're looking for something and we want to make sure it's not in your house.' He turned to Sukra. 'Sukra, you'd better go in and look after the baby. It's crying.'

Sukra went in and took up Bharat. She left the house again by way of the back door.

Wha' deh in me house you can want to search fo'?' Jannee grumbled. 'Me na got nutting you can want.'

'Wha' about a cutlass, Jannee? Haven't you got a cutlass?' The

175

Inspector flicked away his cigarette-end in the same neat way he had flicked away the match. Beena smiled faintly in admiration. He was a really nice man. She liked him. A pity he was here to arrest Jannee for killing Boorharry. She would have liked him even more if he had not come here to do that.

Jannee hesitated, frowned and said yes, he had a cutlass. 'An' wha' if me got cutlass?' he added in his sharp, angry way. 'Why you want know if me got cutlass?'

The Inspector chuckled and lit another cigarette. This time he did not flick away the match, but kept waving it before him until it went out. 'Let's have a look at your cutlass, Jannee.'

'Me na got it now,' snapped Jannee, fidgeting.

'Why? What's happened to it?'

'Me loss am las' week time.'

'You lost it last week time? That's unfortunate. Where did you lose it? Tell us.'

'It not in de house here, chief,' said Jeenarine. 'I search everywhere possible.'

'Not there, eh? Well, come, Jannee, tell us. Where did you lose it? How you managed to lose it?'

'Me loss am aback in rice-fiel',' mumbled Jannee.

'Aback in the rice-field? But this is not rice-cutting season. How you managed to lose it in the rice-field?'

'Me loss am deh. Na you' business how me loss am.'

'Ent you got a farm, Jannee?' This question came from the uniformed policeman who stood behind the Inspector. Jannee flashed a glance at him and said: 'Yes, me got a farm. Wha' 'bout it?'

'You don't use cutlass in your farm?'

'Where's this farm?' asked the Inspector.

Jannee kept silent, looking glum and hitching up his trousers. The Inspector repeated his question, calling Jannee's name. 'Tell us, Jannee. Come on. We've got to find out some time.'

'It deh over deh,' said Jannee, jerking his chin towards the west and hitching up his trousers.

'Oh, that, eh? Where the plaintain trees are growing yonder?' As he spoke, the Inspector backed a few paces, craning his head and looking west. 'There seems to be some sort of bridge there, if I'm not mistaken. We'd better take a walk. Let's go and have a look, Jannee. Come with us and see that we don't steal any of your plaintains.'

'But me na got na cutlass on me farm,' said Jannee. 'Wha' me mus' go deh fo'? You na got na right come here trouble me. Me na do nutting 'gainst de law.'

'Never mind, Jannee. Come with us. We'll all go and have a look over your farm.'

A moment later they were walking along the road towards the farm. Beena followed. She felt calm inside now, calm and dull – not tense and full of dread any more. Everything had happened as she had foreseen it on those many nights when she had stood looking at the silent lightning in the south. Boorharry was dead. Jannee had killed him. The suspense was over. The panic in her had simmered down. She only waited now to see the police take away Jannee. She was going to miss him because her love for him was still great despite the terrible thing he had done. That was why she felt so calm and dull. Every day after this would be dull for her as though it were a grey day of rain. She would look at the blue skies of August and they would not make her spirits bright. She would not take deep breaths of the cool wind and feel that to be alive was good. Weeks ago she had imagined all this. The thought of it came to her now as no shock. She had known it would have happened this way. She had known that Jannee would have done this cruel deed and she had known that she would have felt dull like this.

They walked over the bridge. They were on the farm now, standing near the shed. The cart lay at a slant, its grey shafts resting on a heap of half-dried grass. It looked sad, somehow, as if it knew that she and Jannee would never sit in it again and drive to Speyerfeld. The donkey, too, seemed to her to look sad. It was tethered to one of the corner posts of the shed and munched gloomily at the hay, not even bothering to raise its head to look at them.

Jeenarine bent down and hauled a garment from under the hay. It was Jannee's trousers. It looked damp – damp with the rain of last night, and there were many daubs of blood on it. Jeenarine bent again and hauled out a shirt. The shirt had only one daub of

177

blood. The Inspector hauled out the cutlass and that had plenty of blood on it – dried blood that looked dark-red – dark-red like the colour of Big Man's car, thought Beena, and the dullness in her seemed to grow cold like wet clay-mud.

38

Beena spent the whole of that day with Sukra. Sukra cried a great deal, and though Beena tried not to cry, many times throughout the day she found tears running down her cheeks. Boodoo and Chattee wailed in sympathy.

When the car with Jannee and the police officers drove off, Beena watched it grow smaller and smaller in the west, and her eyes were tearless as though the spot in her where the tears should have come from had grown empty and dry like a trench in the middle of October. She felt almost ashamed of herself that she could not cry. It seemed queer that in this moment when she knew Jannee was going away never to come back she should be unable to cry. It looked just as if she had no more love in her for him, and yet she knew for certain that she still had plenty.

It was only later in the morning when she and Sukra began to call to mind and discuss incidents of the past in which he and the two of them had taken a part that she felt tears welling from her eyes. She could see Jannee taken away by the police and feel dull and empty without shedding a tear, but to recall those burning days in the rice-fields with the screech of the creketteh hawks overhead or those nights when the moon was new or full and the drums of the curry-feed were prattling merrily through the cool air, mingling with their voices and the strong smell of curried mutton – to recall those things was to make hot bubbling water come alive in her – water that gushed up to her eyes with a scalding pain.

At about five o'clock when she got up to go, Sukra began to sob and implore her to stay the night, but Beena said that Ramgolall would be vexed with her if she did not go home now and drive the cattle into pen for the night.

'Well, come back after you drive in de cows,' Sukra begged her.

'Me na want lef' alone tonight. True-true, Beena. Me frighten stay here alone tonight wid dem lil' pic'nee.'

'Ramgolall na go want me sleep away from home. 'E mus' be mornin' widdout help wid de milkin'. An' me shoulda go a-Speyerfeld wid 'e to sell de milk. Kattree musta had to go instead.'

But Sukra still implored her to try to come back after she had driven the cows into pen, so she told her that she would ask her father and see whether he would agree.

On her way home, Beena met David and Dora. They were cycling west along the road and hailed out: 'Hello, Beena!' and then dismounted to talk to her.

'I haven't seen you for an age,' Dora smiled. 'How are you and Kattree getting on nowadays?'

'We awright,' Beena told her, smiling. 'Is wha' you doin' dis side so far from home?'

'We came to have a look at the spot where the murder was committed,' David put in. 'Did you hear any screams last night, Beena?'

'Na,' said Beena, shaking her head and smiling faintly. 'Me didn't hear nutting 'bout de story till me wake up an' finish bathe dis mornin'.'

'How did the body look like?' Dora asked. 'Is it true his head was cut clean off?'

'Me didn' go to see de body.'

'You didn't go! What! And you live so near? I would have gone first thing – like a shot.'

'So would I,' said David. 'It was a great chance. I've never seen a murdered man in my life.'

'Did you see Jannee arrested?' Dora asked.

'Yes, me bin a-Jannee' house from early dis mornin' – soon as me done bathe.'

'You were? Oh, yes, you're a good friend of theirs, aren't you? You saw when the police found the cutlass and the blood-stained clothes?'

'Eh-heh. Me see.'

'Oooh! I would have given anything to see them. You're lucky.'

'How did Jannee look? Did he look guilty?'

'Na, 'e na look guilty.'

'You were very fond of him, weren't you, Beena?' Dora asked, looking at Beena very keenly as she put the question.

'Eh-eh! Why you ask dat?' said Beena. She avoided Dora's gaze and began to fidget in discomfort.

'Well, you were always with him, you know. Whenever I met you in Nairnley you were driving with him in his donkey-cart. And I hear you were always in Speyerfeld with him. I thought perhaps the two of you must be in love or something.'

'Na, you mustn' t'ink so,' said Beena, lowering her head and fidgeting.

Dora gave a knowing smile. 'I believe you have a soft spot for him, Beena. You can't fool me. There's nothing to be ashamed of in it. I think it's jolly romantic, though it's tough on you being in love with him now he's turned out to be a murderer. Did you cry a lot when they took him away?'

'Na,' said Beena, shaking her head, but there were tears in her eyes even as she spoke. She tried to blink them away, but it was of no avail. They ran down her cheek.

Dora at once became soothing. She patted her and said: 'Don't cry, Beena. I understand how you feel. The best thing is not to think about it too much. If you think about it too much it'll prey on your mind and make you miserable. Poor dear. I'm sorry I asked you so many questions. I was just curious to know how things stood with you and Jannee, you know. Don't cry.'

'You're sure to see Boorharry's jumbie soon along the road here,' said David. 'I won't come here in the night if you paid me a million dollars.'

'Oh, don't try to frighten the girl,' Dora frowned. 'Don't listen to him, Beena child. You won't see any jumbies. That's all stupidness. There aren't any such things as jumbies.'

'But you forget I've seen?' said David. 'What about the old man who haunts the back veranda at home? I saw him twice.'

'That's all silly imagination. I don't believe you saw anything. You must stay well, Beena. We've got to get home before dark or we could have walked back with you as far as your bridge. You must try and keep cheerful, see? Don't worry too much.'

'Awright,' smiled Beena, and as she continued her way home-ward she did feel somewhat cheered. The mild sunlight and

Dora's soothing words seemed to mingle together and form a kind of orange-coloured cloud inside her chest so that the grey spot left in her soul by Jannee's evil deed took on a brighter look. If only this orange cloud could have remained in her like this for good! It was such a pity, she thought, that these soothing fanciful things could not go on forever giving her soul delight with their magic instead of fading off into the air and leaving her to feel dull again like muddy water in the canal.

A car's horn sounded up the road and she remembered this morning, how she had run in a panic along the road here and how the blue car with the police had rushed past her. Just like a dead dream it seemed to her now. Look at her at this moment, how calm she felt and how calmly she was walking. It was queer that only this morning she could have felt as she had and acted in such a wild and panicky way. Now it seemed so stupid. She felt a sudden sinking in her. Perhaps everything in life was stupid: she herself and her love for Jannee, and the sunlight and the sky – the savannah. All were stupid things that only gave you one kind of mood now, another kind of mood another time and then you found that the mood was not real – oh, she didn't know how to put it, but everything was stupid and she wished she were not alive. Perhaps it would be a good thing if she threw herself in front of this car coming now and got killed. When the car had rushed past her she felt a queer ache of fear go through her chest. She thought she could see herself lying dead on the road, her head crushed open.

She shivered and looked about her with a wry face. The wind of a sudden grew cold and the red sunshine looked like the reflection of some evil fire. The jumbie of Boorharry was walking behind her, she felt certain. Any moment now and she would feel his hand tap her head and hear his ringing hail: 'Hup, hup, holoy! Hup, hup, holoy!'

She broke into a trot and went on trotting all the way home.

39

Ramgolall did not object to her sleeping the night with Sukra, but he said that she must return home early in the morning to help milk the cows and to go with him to Speyerfeld to sell the milk. He was much upset over the death of Boorharry and the arrest of Jannee. He groaned a great deal and wagged his head. He spoke of the evil in the world and told them of a murder that had happened years ago when he was a young man. The dead body of an overseer had been found lying in a trench aback in the cane-fields, and the doctor had said that death had been caused by shots from a gun. A day or two later the police arrested one of the house-boys in the Overseers' Quarters for the murder. There was a long court-martial. A great lawyer defended the house-boy and many witnesses were called by the police, but in the end the house-boy got off.

On her way back to Sukra, after driving the cows into pen for the night, Beena pondered deeply on what her father had said. If a house-boy had shot an overseer with a gun and had got off, why could not Jannee who had killed Boorharry with a cutlass get off, too? A cutlass was no worse than a gun. A gun was even more terrible because it made a loud deafening noise and spat out fire and smoke and iron bullets that bored holes through and through your body. She would much prefer to be killed with a cutlass than with a gun. Perhaps if a good lawyer told this to the court-people they might let Jannee off.

As she looked around her at the deep twilight, a soothing hope began to cut itself around her heart as though the soft wind that was blowing from the north had entered her chest through a little slit that had just opened under her breasts. It was a nice feeling. It brought back her old longing to live and be happy under a blue sky and walk in bright sunlight. She must tell Sukra about it. It might make her feel nice, too.

Long after they had eaten their evening meal, she and Sukra sat talking over this hope that had come with the wind to soothe Beena's heart. Sukra said that Jannee had forty-two dollars saved up in the Post Office. He had intended to buy a few head of cattle with it, but now that he was in trouble with the police perhaps the best thing would be for her to draw out the money and offer it to a good lawyer to defend him in court. The lawyer might be able to get him off in the same way that that other lawyer years ago had got off the house-boy. Beena said that it might be better if Sukra waited a little before withdrawing the money from the Post Office. Tomorrow when she, Beena, was in Speyerfeld she would go to Jaigan and ask his advice on the matter. Jaigan was educated and knew plenty of things about business affairs and law matters. He would be able to tell them what to do.

They talked for many hours and did not turn in to bed until a squalling shower of rain, with thunder and lightning, broke suddenly upon the savannah. The rain hissed down just as fiercely as it had done the night before and the wind whooped around the house in great driving circles. The lightning was bright, but the thunder boomed in a brief, moody way as though annoyed with the wind for making such a loud droning and whooping. In a short while it was all over. Only the wind lingered on. It hummed faintly, whined loudly for a moment and then died down again to a low, steady hum, whined of a sudden, died down, on and off like that all the time.

It kept Beena awake for a long while. Every time she felt herself going off into a doze it would whine out loudly and wake her so that soon she began to grow afraid, thinking that it must be the jumbie of Boorharry hissing at her because she was lying on Jannee's bed. She tried to allay her fears by telling herself that Boorharry was only hissing at her in fun, for she could not imagine him, even as a jumbie, being anything but playful. At the thought of all his lively pranks, she felt tears coming to her eyes and her nose getting sniffly. Poor Boorharry. He had been such a merry fellow, always with a joke for everybody. It was very sad that he had had to meet such a bloody death. Speyerfeld would never be the same without him.

Thunder barked briefly far away, in the west, and after that she knew nothing more until dawn.

40

The time was shortly after half past three when Beena entered Jaigan's shop. There were only three customers at the counter: a black girl, a black young man, and Toola, the wife of Dookie the lorry-man. (Toola was well known as one of Boorharry's women. She and Dookie lived apart.) The black girl was taking up her basket to leave, but the black young man and Toola lingered on, the black young man lighting a cigarette and leaning his elbow on the counter. They were talking about the murder. When Beena entered she heard the black young man saying as he lit his cigarette: 'Dem one, two clothes? Na, man! No court could hang 'e 'pon dah evidence.'

'But what 'bout de cutlass an' de blood on it?' Jaigan said. 'Dah is conclusive evidence.'

'An' Jaundoo see 'e walking on de road de night before coming dis way,' said Toola. 'All dah evidence going work 'gainst 'e.'

'Ay, Beena girl! How you do?' Jaigan greeted with his wide smile, and Toola and the black man turned to glance at her.

'Me awright,' Beena replied. 'How business going today?'

'So-so. Me na see you yesterday. Wha' happen to you?'

'Me couldn' come. Me bin a-keep Sukra company.'

'Oh! Yes, me hear you bin deh yesterday when de police arrest Jannee. You see de cutlass an' de blood-stained clothes?'

'Eh-heh. Me see dem.' She could feel their three pairs of eyes looking at her with interest, staring at her as though she held many dark secrets that they would be glad to find out.

'De newspaper got de whole story in big headlines,' Jaigan said, and he took up a newspaper from the shelf behind him, spread it out on the counter and ran his finger along the words printed across the top of the front page in large black letters. Knowing that she could not read, he read them aloud to her. '"Shocking Murder on Corentyne Coast." "Body of Hospital Gate-Porter Found Hacked to Death." "Young East Indian Farmer Arrested on Murder Charge."'

Beena said 'Oh-h-h!' in a faint voice. These words in the newspaper sounded terrible. They frightened her. The hope that she had felt curling so soothingly around her heart last night and all today began to shrink up slowly and coil itself like a poor shivering snake far back in some lonely corner inside her. The sunshine and blue sky she had seen in her mind began to look coated over with a grey pall as though someone were painting smoke on her joy. She wondered if it would be of any use asking Jaigan about the lawyer to defend Jannee.

In a timid voice she said: 'You don't t'ink Jannee stand a chance o' gettin' off, den?'

'Gettin' off?' Jaigan made a sceptical sound. 'Poor chance, gal. Not wid dat evidence deh got against 'e. Dat cutlass an' de blood-stained clothes is damning evidence – '

'But wha' 'bout motive?' the black young man cut in. 'Wha' motive Jannee had fo' kill Boorharry? In all dese cases you got to establish motive, an' de police ain' establish na motive yet.' He suddenly took up the newspaper. 'Look. Look wha' de paper say: "It appears that Jannee and Boorharry were on terms of enmity for some time past. A violent quarrel, it is alleged, took place between them about a month ago outside the hospital gate and Jannee was humiliated by Boorharry before a small crowd of spectators. Jannee, it is alleged, used threatening words and since that occasion has not been seen again in Speyerfeld." Now, wha' kin' o' motive is dah?' said the black young man, looking at them. 'Any lawyer can smash dat motive to pieces. If Boorharry did carryin' on wid Jannee' wife, *dat* woulda been a good motive fo' Jannee to kill 'e. But jus' a stupid row about a mont' ago? Man, tek it from me, no British court will convict a man on dat evidence. *Me* say so! Eh-heh.'

Jaigan gave a slow smile. 'George boy, you young in dese matters,' he said. 'You in you' early twenties. Me forty-two nex' mont'. Me see plenty 'bout dis world – plenty, plenty. Too much men I see get hang on less evidence dan wha' deh got 'gainst Jannee. Of course, me don't tell you dat if 'e could afford to get a good lawyer 'e mightn' put up a good fight. But even de best lawyer couldn' get 'e off. Evidence, man! Evidence too black against 'e. How 'e going account fo' having human blood on 'e cutlass an' on 'e clothes? How? He didn' have no wounds on his own body. He didn' meet wid no accident. An' 'e clothes was damp, proving dat 'e was out in de rain de night before. An' den *why* 'e hide de clothes an' de cutlass under de hay on de farm? How 'e going answer all dem questions satisfactory? Eh? Tell me how.'

George chuckled. 'Jaigan, man look,' he said. 'You know wha' wrong wid you? You ain' know de principles o' law yet – '

'Me na know de principles o' law yet?'

'Na. If you did know de principles o' law you woulda know dis: When a judge summing up 'e does tell de jury dat if deh got *any* reasonable doubt in deh minds concernin' de evidence given in de case, deh will by duty bound have to acquit de prisoner. No matter *how* conclusive de evidence against a man might look, if de lawyer who defendin' 'e can put *any* reasonable doubt in de minds o' de jury, de jury can bring in a verdict of "not guilty". You see? Dah is wha' you ain' know yet. Eh-heh.'

'Awright, George. Awright. Me done argue. Me done. In October come all o' we going see who right an' who wrong. Beena gal, come lemme attend to you. Wha' you want today? Rice, butter, potatoes, peas, lard?'

'Eh-h-h-h! You t'ink me want buy out you' whole shop?' Beena laughed. 'Me only want half pint rice an' a pound o' potatoes.'

George and Toola took their departure while Jaigan was weighing the potatoes, and no sooner had they passed through the door when Beena said to Jaigan: 'Me did want to talk to you private, Jaigan, but since me hear wha' you say jus' now me na know if it wort' while any more.'

'You want talk to me? Well, go on. Na mind wha' me say jus' now. You talk wha' you want.'

'Me want ask you 'bout Jannee. You na t'ink 'e can get off if Sukra pay a good lawyer to defend 'e?'

He shook his head slowly. 'Jannee stand poor chance, Beena bettay. Hear wha' me say. 'E might stand a chance if Sukra could afford to get a really good lawyer to defend 'e. But she won' get de money to pay good lawyer.'

'Jannee got forty-two dollars in de Post Office.'

'Forty-two dollars! Wha' is forty-two dollars? An' in any case, de Crown got to provide a lawyer to defend 'e. Whenever a man charged wid murder can't afford to hire a counsel, de Crown got to provide counsel, an' de Crown pay ten pounds for his services.'

'Ten pounds?'

'Yes. Ten pounds sterling. Forty-eight dollars. Dat's de minimum – de smallest amount you can offer a lawyer to defend a murderer, an' only one o' dese poor struggling barristers will accept dat. De big lawyers don't tek less dan five hundred dollars.'

'Five hundred dollar!'

'No less dan dat. An' you got to go to Georgetown to get de really good lawyers. J. A. Luckloo, K.C., G. J. De Freitas, K.C., Van B. Stafford, E. G. Woolford, K.C. Dem is de big lawyers. But you can't go an' offer any a' dem forty-two dollars to tek on a murder case. Deh laugh at you an' chase you away, man.'

She stared at him in dismay, feeling very tiny and foolish, as though she might be a mole-cricket listening to the roar of rain around her. After an interval she said: 'Den you mean, is no use worry to get lawyer at all?'

He shook his head. 'Na. No use. Tell Sukra to save she money. Na t'row it away. Forty-two dollars caan' do nutting at all, an', as I tell you awready, de Crown must provide a lawyer to defend 'e.'

'Wha' is de Crown?'

'De Crown? De Guv'ment. De British Guv'ment.'

'Oh.' She nodded slowly and watched him as he wrapped up the potatoes. Then she looked up and asked him: 'How much shilling in five hundred dollar?'

'How much shillings in five hundred dollar? Mm. Lemme see.' He put his head at a slant and wrinkled his brows. 'A hundred dollars got four hundred and sixteen shillings and sixteen cents. Five hundred dollars got over two t'ousand an' eighty shillings.'

'Eh-h-h-h! Two t'ousand an' eighty shilling!'

Jaigan smiled. 'Man, dah is like nutting to some rich men. Tek Ramjit, an' even you' half-brudder Baijan. Five hundred dollar is like pocket-money to dem. Ramjit an' Baijan accustomed to deal in t'ousands o' dollars. Five t'ousand, ten t'ousand. Dat's why me tell you over an' over not to frighten to tek wha' you want in de shop here. During dese past six days you know how much wort' in food all-you tek from me? Includin' wha' you tekin' today, it come up to t'ree dollars an' seventy-one cents. Dat mean, in a mont' you na going buy more dan twelve or thirteen dollars wort' in groceries. When Baijan hear 'e going laugh. Twelve dollars is like a drop o' water to 'e. Just de suit 'e had on de day 'e come here cost 'e at least fifteen dollars. One suit! Fifteen dollars. 'E shoes t'ree dollars. 'E shirt two dollars. So dat mean de clothes 'e had on cost twenty dollars. Just de clothes 'e had on! Rich man, you see? Credit sound. An' nex' mont' 'e gettin' married to Ramjit' daughter. Man, Baijan is a great boy.'

As Beena walked slowly homeward, the sun seemed to glare at her. It looked like a big spiteful eye hovering up there in the cloudless sky, and it burnt her skin as though it wanted to be cruel on purpose. It seemed angry with her as though it had heard something bad spoken against her – something spoken, perhaps, by Sumatra Pooran. Or it might be that it knew that she and it would no more be good friends. It was glaring at her now and burning her skin to show her that it could only be friendly with people who were happy and able to enjoy its bright light. People who were dull like rain and without hope as she was it shone on with spite.

She heard a tiny bubbling splash in the canal, but it came as though from very far away and did not seem meant for her to hear.

41

During the days that followed, time, for Beena, seemed to pass like the slow dripping of water, a bleak trickle that went on dimly somewhere in the back of her thoughts. But, for Kattree, the hours bubbled in a green pond full of ripples. The sunshine glittered on everything like laughing gold, and one morning when it rained steadily from a blank grey sky, the rain chuckled at her in fun as much as to tell her that this was a farewell falling and that the blue and white days of August were at hand. Even the lightning at night and the moody thunder brought an exciting message for her from the waves on the sea-beach and from the duppies in the courida bush. The chill dawns murmured with a shivering rapture that breathed like a hidden thing in the blue mist as though it were a nice surprise only waiting for the hours to reveal it to her. The cooing of the conch-shells ran through her heart like thin spills of perfumed water and made her blood frolic with a panicky kind of delight. The growing crescent of the moon leered in the west, and every evening its glow seemed to tell her a new sly tale – a wicked tale but a lovely one. The whole of Nature seemed to her to be filled with magic ripplings and gurgles, shifting shadows of trees and shafts of jumbie light, the chirrup of happy frogs and the cheep of crickets.

All the talk about the murder of Boorharry and Jannee's arrest, Beena's silent and gloomy moods, troubled her not at all. They were like dark happenings in a far-off country. She had nothing to do with them.

One morning, during the last week of the month, she knew that August had already come, for not only was the sky a clear blue with white cobweb rags and the wind steady and dry, but she heard a hail and saw Geoffry trotting along the dam towards her. He wore shorts like that morning in the last days of April when he had come to bid her goodbye and give her the five-dollar note. As then, too, the dark-red car stood on the public road waiting, and she knew that in a few minutes she would be sitting in it beside him, wearing her blue silk dress and feeling the wind rushing past her cheeks as she had felt it in all those dreams she had dreamt during the past few months.

'Kattree bettay!' he greeted in his cheerful way as he came up. 'How has the world been wagging with you since Easter? Top-notch, I'll warrant. Eh?'

'Me keep good,' she smiled. 'You come before August. Me glad an' surprise.'

'You're glad and surprised? Good girl. Exams are over, you know, so there was no sense in waiting until August to trek home. I've come to take you for a day's outing. Sixty-three beach calls in loud roars, Kattree. Go in and put on your nice dress. You've had nice dresses made, haven't you?'

'Eh-heh. Me get four new dresses an' a pair a' shoes wid de five-dollar you gimme. Two cotton one, two silk one.'

'Two cotton ones and two silk ones *and* a pair of shoes! You're a financial genius. I couldn't have done all that with a fiver.' He looked around abruptly. 'Beena and Ramgolall are in Speyerfeld, I suppose? Selling milk as usual.'

'Yes. Deh lef' 'bout a hour ago. Me go in now an' change me dress quick. Me na keep you wait long.' She could not prevent her voice from trembling in her excitement. Her hands trembled a little, too, as she changed into the blue silk dress. She felt a pain in her from joy. All of a sudden he had come to take her driving to Sixty-three beach. She had not expected him until next week. She nearly squealed in her delight. Today – in a few minutes! No more days to wait – not even hours. Only a few minutes. This time she could not help it. She gave a squeal.

When she appeared from the mud-house she saw him skipping about on the mud-dam in regular movements of his arms and legs. He stopped at once when he saw her coming towards him. 'Doing a few jerks to keep the blood going,' he smiled, and then his brows went up and his lips parted a little as he looked at her. He smiled a queer, twisted smile and said in a lowered and surprised voice: 'But I say, Kattree...' and then stopped short, staring at her.

'You na like me dress?' she smiled.

'Eh? Well, of course. I do like it, but – but...well, look here, don't you wear any underclothes?'

'Underclothes? Oh! Na, only pants.'

'Oh, I see.' His cheeks grew a little pink and he gave a brief laugh and said quickly: 'It's all right. Don't bother. I don't suppose it matters, really. Let's go.'

She walked along the dam with him to the car, and as they drew near she saw with dismay that the back of the car was filled with his sisters and brothers.

'Eh-eh! You' sister an' brudder in de car?' she exclaimed, glancing up at him. 'Deh going wid we?'

'Yes. The whole bunch of them. I promised to give them a treat on this the first day of my official chauffeurship. I told Dora to bring an extra bathing-suit to lend you. I hope she remembered. She has two pairs, and the two of you are about the same size.'

She said 'Oh!' faintly, and her eyes lost some of their excited sparkle. This was not how she had dreamt things. In all those pictures she had built up she had not included his sisters and brothers. Something had gone wrong. The dream was not coming true as she had dreamt it.

She could feel all their six pairs of eyes fixed on her as she and Geoffry crossed the bridge. She heard a giggle from one of the girls – and then several muffled giggles.

'Well, here's our guest,' said Geoffry, with a wave of his hand towards her as the two of them reached the car, and a chorus of 'Hello's!' and 'Hello, Kattree's!' at once broke out. 'I've got a bather here for you, Kattree,' said Dora, and Geoffry said: 'You remembered to bring it, eh? I forgot to remind you before we left the house. Get in, Kattree. You've got to sit in front with me. It's worse than a sardine tin in the back there.'

'I can sit in front if you like, Geoff,' offered David.

'I don't like,' Geoffry replied.

'Who made your dress, Kattree?' Dora asked.

'Miss Chan Ching in Speyerfeld,' Kattree smiled.

'Oh! Yes, I've heard of her. It looks nice.'

Belle gave a muffled giggle, her hand to her mouth.

'Who made your undies, Kattree?' Jim asked.

'Hi, Jim! What the devil do you mean by asking that?' Geoffry frowned. 'Don't bother to answer that question, Kattree. Any more examples of sarcasm like that from you, Jim, and I'll turn right back home and leave you there. Today is a school-day, you know, don't forget. If I take you home you'll be packed off to school.'

Jim was unable to reply, for his face was buried in Belle's lap in order to muffle his giggles. Dora was frowning at him. 'He's a little fool. Don't worry with him. He's never satisfied unless he's misbehaving.'

Geoffry still frowning angrily, engaged the gears, and the car began to glide forward. Sitting beside him, Kattree felt shy and uneasy. She knew that Jim was laughing at her for some reason that she could not understand, and it made her feel awkward and out-of-place. She wondered what it could be that made him laugh. 'Who made your undies?' he had asked. What was 'undies'? She had never heard the word before. She fidgeted, telling herself that the dream was certainly not turning out as she had imagined it. She hoped that when Geoffry came again to take her driving he would not bring with him his sisters and brothers. That would spoil everything.

'This is the spot where Boorharry was murdered!' David shouted of a sudden, pointing to the parapet, and Geoffry said: 'Oh, yes?' in an interested voice and glanced out at the spot. 'I hear you've been having some excitement around here, Kattree. Did you see the corpse?'

'Na. Me didn' got time to come. Me had to milk de cows. It happen early in de morning.'

'Yes, I read about it in the newspapers. Pretty horrible. And Boorharry was such a nice fellow. I can remember him in the days when I was a small chap. Always hopping around the place shouting "hup, hup, holoy!" He used to work on our ranch before he became gate-porter to Speyerfeld, you know.'

'Yes. Me hear so,' smiled Kattree.

'The coroner's inquest is to take place tomorrow,' said Dora.

'I'd give anything to be able to go,' said David.

'You've got a morbid mentality,' Geoffry told him.

When they had passed Speyerfeld, Geoffry made the car go very fast, so fast that Kattree's hair flew wildly behind her head and the air sounded like crackling thunder in her ears. She gripped the seat tightly, liking it all and yet fearful. She had never thought a car could go so fast. She heard John shout behind her shoulder: 'We're touching fifty-five!'

Soon, however, they came upon a bad stretch of road and Geoffrey had to reduce the speed a great deal. He handled the car with confidence as though he were an old and expert driver. The wind had tousled his hair, and the dark, loose locks kept waving about and falling over his forehead. It looked very nice, thought Kattree. She liked, too, the flapping of his open shirt-collar against his pink neck and the set look of his eyes as he gazed ahead at the road.

A big blue car, coming from the opposite way, rushed past them with a deep humming swish, and Kattree had a flashing glimpse of Mr and Mrs Ramjit inside it. 'Eh-eh! Dah is de Ramjit' car!' she exclaimed. 'Mr an' Mrs Ramjit inside.'

'Oh, was that they?' said Geoffry.

'Eh-heh. Me jus' mek out deh face when we pass de car. Baijan tek me an' Beena to deh house at Sixty-eight Village couple week back.'

'Baijan? Oh, yes, of course. Your half-brother and my uncle, incidentally. He's going to marry one Miss Elizabeth Ramjit, eh? Dad received an invitation yesterday from the Ramjits asking the whole family to the wedding. Dora's been asked to be a brides-maid or something. Baijan wrote mother.'

'It's been fixed for the twenty-seventh of next month,' Dora put in. 'You and Beena and Ramgolall will be going, won't you?'

'Yes. Baijan say when 'e come back in two-t'ree week time 'e going buy nice wedding-dress fo' me an' Beena. 'E say Paul Ramjit going to Queen's College, too,' she said to Geoffry. ''E say Paul know you well.'

He nodded, making a wry face. 'I know him, too, disgusting little toad. He's in the Lower Fourth. Famous for cribbing and playing mean tricks.'

''E's a bad boy?'

'A very bad boy. As a prefect, it has often been my duty to put him in detention. He likes me even as little as I like him. His brother Joseph was a much better fellow. He left Queen's last year.'

'Oh, Joseph used to go to Queen's College, too?'

'Yes. He left last year. He wasn't very brilliant at class-work, but he was a pretty good inside-right – a footballer, you know – and he's a jolly fine fast bowler. He was a good sport generally. Never indulged in all the mean petty tricks Paul is noted for. Hey! Hey! What's all the noise behind there about?'

'Elsie was sitting on my bather,' said John.

'And he had his foot on mine,' said Elsie.

'I hadn't! My foot was on the lunch-basket!'

'It wasn't, John! Look, Geoff! He's left a footmark on it!'

'All right. All right. No need to make so much noise over that. You've got to go in the water, haven't you? You're not going to a party in your bathers.'

'He hit me on my head, Geoff!'

'And she hit me first on my knee!'

'All right! All *right*! It isn't too late for me to turn back, you know. School is always there waiting for you.'

The wrangling soon died down, and before many minutes had elapsed they were at Sixty-three Village. Geoffry swung the car into the narrow lane that led to the beach, and the children began to squeal and giggle as the car bumped up and down on the uneven ground. Kattree's head nearly touched the top of the car once. Geoffry frowned and said that it was a beastly shame that the Government couldn't make a decent road out to the sea.

When they emerged, at length, on to the smooth beach, they found that the sea was rather far out, but coming in strongly. The wind was blowing in a steady hum.

There was no bathing-hut, so they had to undress on the open beach, boys on one side of the car and girls on the other. Kattree felt very queer in the pink bathing-suit Dora lent her. She had never worn a bathing-suit in her life. It made her feel confined and awkward. Dora said of a sudden: 'Two people are in the water already. I wonder who they are.' Kattree looked seaward and saw two heads bobbing about in the grey water.

'Come along, everybody!' bawled Geoffry. 'Out we go!' And he set out at a run towards the waves, David and John, and then Jim, following him, Jim yelling at the top of his voice out of sheer good spirits.

'All O.K., Kattree?' said Dora. 'How does it fit? Not too tight for you, is it?'

'Na, it awright,' smiled Kattree. 'It fit good.'

When they were in the water they heard Geoffry shout: 'Hi, Joseph! What are you doing here?'

'Hallo, Geoffry!'

Kattree brushed the water from her eyes and made out the faces of Joseph and Liza Ramjit. A few minutes later Joseph was introducing his sister to Geoffry, and then Geoffry proceeded to introduce his sisters and brothers to Joseph and Liza. 'You've met Kattree already, haven't you?' said Geoffry, and Joseph said: 'Oh, yes,' smiling, and Liza, who had been smiling widely all the time said: 'Oh, yes, we meet Kattree.'

Joseph explained that his parents had gone to Speyerfeld to do some shopping and to pay a visit and would be passing back in about an hour's time to take himself and Liza home. 'We just decided to come to Sixty-three as papa and mama were coming this way in the car,' he ended. 'You're on a whole-day picnic, eh?'

'Whole-day. I've made my dear brothers and sisters play truant from school so that I could have their company for the day.'

'I heard you took the Guiana. How did you get through?'

'Oh, swimmingly. The maths papers were a bit stiffish, but I think I've done pretty O.K. in them.'

They spent a very merry day in the water and on the beach. In the water they played a game of 'scramble', as Jim called it, with a tennis ball, and it gave them an exciting time. In the middle of it the Ramjit car arrived and Joseph and Liza had to leave. After luncheon they ran races and played cricket (both John and Jim had brought bats). The lunch-basket served as wicket. When they grew tired of this, Geoffry took them for a drive along the beach. He drove very fast, and more than once the speedometer registered sixty miles. But throughout it all Kattree was not happy. She felt awkward and out-of-place. Geoffry hardly took any notice of her. He treated her as he treated Dora or any of the others, and she began to wonder if this meant that he did not find any more interest in her. It was queer. It made her feel as though all her dreams of the past few months had been in vain. Once she found herself almost wanting to cry.

On the way back home, however, her hopes began to rise again, for he insisted on having her sit in front with him. Belle had wanted to sit in front, but he said no, that he wanted Kattree. 'Kattree is our guest of honour,' he said. 'I'm not going to have her squeezed to a jelly in the back there with you all.'

Long before they reached Speyerfeld the sun had gone down, and ahead of them the west flared with curling tongues of gamboge and daubs of chrome-yellow. Blue-black anvils of cloud hovered rigidly in sharp silhouette and sinister alligators of dark brown gaped and clawed after some unseen prey down below in the far-off fringe of treetops. Kattree felt as if they were driving towards a midnight jumbie land where cold frogs would hop around them croaking and screeching, and long black snakes lay coiled around slimy rocks waiting to swallow them. She was glad that Geoffry was near her. He looked very strong and safe. He would never let anything harm her.

The twilight was very deep when he stopped the car to put her out, but the half moon overhead had begun to coat the scene with its pale green glimmer. Before driving off he told her that he was going to do a bit of fishing tomorrow and that she must look out for him. This made her so happy that as she walked along the dam on her way to the mud-house the savannah seemed to ripple and sparkle in the pale moonlight like joyful silver water. And when a goat-sucker said: 'Who-you?' it sounded tinkly as though a friendly duppy had rung a bell made of moonlight and wildflower scent.

42

She put on the new pink cotton dress and sat by the canal and fished while she waited for him to come. As he sank down beside her to join her fishing he said: 'Well, now that we're alone, Kattree, you can fire ahead and tell me all that's been happening to you since April. Afraid I won't have much to tell you, though. All that happened to me was books and lessons, books and lessons – and then the Exam. Pretty gruelling it was, I can tell you, but I'm satisfied with what I've done. Is this one of the new dresses?'

'Eh-heh. Dis is de first time me wear it.'

'It smells newish. But wait. Didn't Beena have any dresses made, too, out of the fiver?'

'Na. She get vex' an' say she na want na money from you.' She went on to tell him about her row with Beena and the many weeks during which the two of them had not been on speaking terms. She told him, too, of Ramgolall's illness in the middle of the rain-season, of the miserable time she and Beena had had caring him and his fear lest anyone stole the money in his canister. At this point Geoffry's float grew agitated and sank, and for the next few moments everything was forgotten save the silvery mullet that struggled at the end of his line.

'Pretty big fellow, you know. Pretty big fellow. Two pounds at least, or I'm a Dutchman.'

'What! Dah na weight two-pound! Not even one.'

'Come, come, Kattree. Come, come. Don't you try to discredit my catch, miss. That's a whopping good mullet. I bet you anything you don't catch one as big for the day.'

'Awright. Wait good an' we going see.'

By midday, however, she had only caught two small fishes which she called hourih, while he had caught two hassars and a cuirass. Once, towards ten o'clock, he pointed to the south and said: 'Looks as though it's coming to rain.'

She looked southward and saw that the sky far away was grey and hazed. A solid wall of cloud stretched low along the horizon. 'Rain a-fall aback in cane-fiel',' she said. 'It mightn' come dis side. Wind blowing from de nort'.' As the morning advanced, she proved to be right. The haze grew fainter and fainter and the grey wall moved around to the south-west and melted into the distance. Geoffry kept watching it all the time as he talked to her. Once he remarked: 'That thing fascinates me, somehow. It's like a Turner picture seen enacted in the real.'

'Wha's is a Turner picture?' she asked.

'Eh? Oh! A painter. Turner was the name of a great English painter who lived about a hundred years ago. He painted pictures of landscapes and seascapes. Nobody has ever been able to paint a sky like Turner.' He kept staring at the south. 'A great deal of power in that, you know. Look at those greyish fan-like columns of rain slanting downwards. You can just imagine how the whole thing is slashing down on the bending canes. Seems queer that the sky over us should be clear and blue and the sun shining.'

'We might get t'under-lightning tonight.'

'Yes, we're in the storm-period now, aren't we?'

'Eh-heh. But in September an' October t'under-lightning more bad. Lightning flash dang'ous. Cut down coconut-tree an' kill sheep an' cattle.' She told him about Manoo's coconut palm, and he grunted and said that some people got all the excitement in life.

When they were eating ham sandwiches at midday in the shadow of the mud-house, she noticed that he had grown a little quiet as if his thoughts were far away. She asked him what was wrong, why he was so quiet, and he grunted and said: 'Oh, I'm getting old and sober. I was nineteen on the sixth of last month, you know. Next year this time be twenty. When is your birthday, by the way?'

'Me na know,' she smiled, shaking her head.

'You don't know! But how do you mean? Don't you know how old you are?'

'Yes. Me know me sixteen or seventeen, but me na know fo' sure wha' day me born on or wha' exact year.'

'Doesn't Ramgolall know? You've never asked him?'

'Yes, me ask 'e, but 'e na know. 'E na even know 'e own age fo' certain,' she smiled.

'Well, well. What a terrible state of affairs.' He looked at her for a while, a faint smile on his face, and then he said abruptly: 'But I wonder what it must be like living as you all do.' He was silent a moment, looking reflective, then he made a wry face. 'Ugh. Sometimes I get very sick of myself for being so ambitious. I often wish I'd been born without any of these strong inclinations for power and fame and all the rest of it. I sometimes think of myself living in perfect content with somebody like yourself in a mud-house and not reading a book or a newspaper or listening to any music. Just fishing and minding cows – walking in the sunlight or the rain or in the moonlight or under the stars. It ought to be great. I suppose most people will say I'm romantic, and I daresay I am. But I don't care. Your sort of life is the sort of life I want deep in me, but, of course, my ambitions and artistic longings upset everything. If I tried to live the simple life, before a fortnight was out I'd be wanting to play the piano, and then that would lead on to books and art, and then I'd get restless and dissatisfied with things. I'd begin to dream of the cultured world beyond all this savannah and water, of London and symphony concerts, I'd hear horns and oboes and fiddles and drums – the drums and all the wild noise in the finale of Beethoven's Seventh. I'd just go mad unless I could satisfy my hunger for music. I've made dad buy a radio-set, you know. This evening at eight-fifteen the B.B.C. Orchestra is on the air. They're going to play Arnold Bax and De Falk and Villa Lobos – the Brazilian chap. He's great. Yesterday I heard Rimsky-Korsakov's *Scheherazade*. You see, I couldn't do without all that. I'd starve. I'd pine away and go out of my mind.'

She had watched him throughout this speech with intent eyes, her lips parted a little. It had all sounded a bit queer his talking like this. He had seemed to her as though he had not been speaking to her herself, but to her jumbie sitting beside her like a pale yellow shadow. She did not understand half of what he had said, but the other half was very clear, so clear that it made her feel troubled far within her, even as the sound of howling wind at midnight troubled her.

He sat now frowning at the wall of the mud-house behind her back and squeezing his thumb slowly. Abruptly he scowled – scowled at her jumbie – and told it: 'Ugh! The trouble with me is that I haven't yet made it clear to my soul what I do want out of life. I'm still groping about in a roomful of rainbows.'

He gave himself a little shake and rose. 'Up we get, Kattree Kat! Let's go back to our fishing and see how many more we can hook by four o'clock. When the weather gets very dry, you must let's follow this dam out to the sea – just for the adventure, see?' He was talking to her herself now, not to her jumbie. She felt relieved and happy, as though her hands and feet had been bound and the cords had just been cut. 'You haven't caught your two-pound mullet yet, you know, Kattree. Looks as if I'm going to win the bet.'

'Na. De day na over yet,' she laughed. 'Me still got time to catch it.'

At about two o'clock, however, when the day had grown hot and trembling, he said that he was tired of fishing, and that they should do something else. 'Make a suggestion, Kattree. Come on. How shall we kill time until five o'clock? Let me see if you can think up an original idea.'

'Me caan' t'ink wha' to do,' she said, smiling. Within her she was remembering her dream of the two of them sleeping in the shadow of the mud-house and then waking and talking quietly and then his making love to her. She added: 'Only t'ing me can t'ink of is to go to sleep like we do dah day when you an' Stymphy come here.'

'Oh! Yes, I remember. But I don't feel like sleeping now. I want to do things – move about and look for new and unusual things. What about taking a walk along the dam as far as the courida bushes? We can take a peep at the duppies and then come back.'

'Awright, if you want to go.'

So they set out north along the dam. But they had hardly covered a hundred yards when Manoo, who was coming south, said, 'Eh-h-h-h! Kattree bettay, you going yonder side? Mosquito full a-crooda bush. Me nearly dead while back. No go dah side, bettay. True-true. Mosquito go kill you.'

'That means right about turn, then,' said Geoffry, and a minute or two later they were back at the mud-house. Geoffry lowered himself to the ground and said that that was that. Kattree asked him what next they were going to do, and he said: 'Well, it looks to me as if it's your turn to put forward something, don't you think? My idea has proved an abortion. You go ahead now and think up something else.'

'Only t'ing me can say left to do is to bathe in de canal.'

'Bathe in the canal!' He sat forward and looked up at her with raised brows. 'But, my dear girl, has it struck you that we lack bathing costumes? Or am I to assume that you don't care a damn whether we flaunt our persons in the nude or not?'

She laughed. 'Me na understand dah big talk.'

'Sorry, sorry. What I mean is, you don't mind if we bathe without clothes or not?'

'Na, me na care,' she said, but she turned away her face as she said it and stood there swaying her body slightly from side to side. There was a brief interval of silence while he stared up at her, his lips twisted in a faint ironical smile. She stopped swaying abruptly, glanced at him furtively and said: 'You care?' and he shook his head slowly. A sudden gust of warm wind made a lock of his hair tremble above his forehead. His eyes were not staring directly at her now, she thought. They were staring at her jumbie standing beside her, a pale yellow shadow. He chuckled of a sudden. He and her jumbie were enjoying a secret joke now. She envied her jumbie. 'One day,' she heard him telling it, 'I'm going to commit suicide, Kattree, and people will wonder why.' After another silence he gave himself a little shake, made a wry face as though he had seen something ugly and got up at a jerk. 'All right, come along, Kattree. We'll bathe. It's a good idea. You've got more imagination than I have.'

This had not been in her dreams. She had not seen herself

bathing in the canal with him. But it was nice. She was certain now that when they came out of the water he would make love to her. He was bound to, unless her jumbie came in the way again and he began to talk to it. That would spoil things. She wished she were her jumbie.

They swam and splashed about and made a great deal of noise. He shouted and made all kinds of queer sounds like a boy. 'Suppose anyone were to happen along and see us, Kattree!' he said once, and she replied: 'Na! Hardly anybody ever come dis way! Only one or two fisher-people, an' we get good chance to see dem comin' from far up de dam!' He laughed jerkily and said: 'That's done it!' and she wondered what he meant by that. He gave a loud whoop and dived, and she dived, too, and when they came up they were near to each other. He said to her, 'Let's climb up on the bank,' and she said, 'Awright'. And when they had climbed up on the bank it turned out just as she had thought. He made love to her, dripping wet as they were and lying on the short, tickly grass that felt hot from the sunshine. She had not dreamt of hot grass tickling her wet skin like this and water trickling from his forehead into her eyes. But it was all nice. She liked it so. She liked everything as it was at this moment, even the sun that dazzled her eyes – dazzled her eyes until she closed them tightly, more tightly and more tightly until, at length, everything became too dreamy and nice even to be thought of any more.

43

August came with its white heat and sudden wild showers in the late afternoon. On many mornings a thick brume, ethereal like white fungus, covered the savannah so that nothing could be seen for fifty yards around and the blue of the sky seemed stranded in the midst of some vague brown waste. On these mornings the sun did not appear until seven o'clock, and then it seemed shadowy and covering. Wads of shifting mist like dirty wool kept giving it the look of a sun seen through smoked glass and long skirts of fog writhed, phantom-like, all over the landscape. By eight o'clock the mist had melted and in the clear yellow sunshine the savannah became revealed as a damask tablecloth that glimmered in filmy patches of moisture. Here and there long-legged scarlet ibises (called curri-curries) stood dotted on the delicate surface, looking like fragments of cirrus left over from a vivid dawn-sky, while not far from them a flock of white cranes made restless flights from spot to spot, uttering harsh cries – cries that seemed moist, somehow, and fresh, as though filled with dew.

Nearly every day Geoffry came. The clearing of the mist was the signal for his coming. Today he would fish with her and they would bathe in the canal and make love in the hot sun, and tomorrow he would take her in the car to the beach at Sixty-three Village where they would splash in the grey waves, run races on the beach and go to sleep together in the back of the car. One day he took her to New Amsterdam, and for the first time in her life she saw wide streets and long rows of high buildings and electric standards. They went across the broad river-estuary in the small ferry-steamer, and at the train-terminus, on the western bank, she saw the train depart for Georgetown: her first sight of a train. But what she considered the most wonderful moment of the whole day came when he took her to the top of the Town Hall tower and she looked down upon the town eighty feet below. She had never thought any building could reach so high in the air. From the ground it had not looked so high. She gripped his arm and asked him if it was safe to stay up here, if the tower might not topple over in the wind and go crashing down to the street with them. Not even in her sleeping dreams had she seen anything to equal this marvel. She would never forget it.

During these days of her happiness Ramgolall was very worried. One evening in the early part of the months when she related to him and Beena what a nice day she and Geoffry had spent together at Sixty-three, he wagged his head and groaned as he had wagged his head and groaned several evenings before when she had told him of the pleasant day she had spent.

'Me na like dah, bettay,' he had said. 'Me na like dah at-all, at-all. Nice time bring bad story. Eh-heh. Me warn you again-again, bettay. Nice time bring bad story.'

'Wha' kin' bad story?' she had frowned. 'Wha' go happen if me go fo' drive wid 'e once, twice?'

'Ha! Time pass, you get baby, Kattree bettay, an' me pore man. Ma na got money keep baby.'

'Awright. Na worry 'bout dah. Me can work in cane-fiel' an' get money. Or Baijan can gimme money.'

That evening, sitting before the door of the mud-house, Ramgolall thought dark thoughts, as for over a week of evenings now he had been doing. He recalled the troublous days of long ago when he was a cane-cutter at Speyerfeld and Big Man Weldon came in the evening in his car to take Sosee driving. Now it was Big Man's son who came. He came in the day and took Kattree for drives in the big red car. No good could come of this, felt Ramgolall. Geoffry would not want to do as his father had done. He would not want to take Kattree for his woman and live with her in a big house. Geoffry wanted to go to England to become a great lawyer or doctor. When he went away he would not think of Kattree. He would not send money to keep Kattree's baby, and that would mean that he Ramgolall, poor man as he was, would have to provide for the baby. That would be hard on him. She would not be able to work in the cane-fields, for who would care for the baby when she was away? She had spoken without thinking when she had said that she would work in the cane-fields. And as for Baijan, Baijan would be married in a few weeks' time. How could she count on him to give her money to care for her baby? He might even be angry with her for having the baby and might stop allowing them to take food on his account at Jaigan's grocery and Balgobin's butchery. Ah! What troubles there were in the world! Everywhere one turned there was a dark cloud. An evil world. His own grandson of whom he was so proud coming to bring trouble into his life. It was a hurtful thing – more hurtful than it had been with Sosee and Big Man long ago, for Big Man had been a stranger. With Kattree and Geoffry it was different, for Geoffry was his grandson. His own blood ran in his veins. It was a bitter thing to think that one's own grandson, a tall, fair-skinned boy of whom one was proud, should come and get one's daughter with child and cause one to have to spend extra money to care for the child. It was a dark and grievous thing. It took much money to care for a baby. They would have to buy clothes for it and when it got ill, as it certainly would, the doctor would have to be called. Fifty cents would have to be paid to him for every call, and then many shillings would have to be spent for medicine from the dispenser in Speyerfeld. It would mean that he Ramgolall, poor, poor man as he was, would have to delve into his savings and take out money to meet all those expenses. Ah! What a black thing, indeed, to think on! His hard-earned shillings going one by one to buy medicine and clothes, to pay the doctor's fees. Two shillings and a penny to the doctor every time he called, three shillings to the dispenser every time a new bottle of medicine was made up!

Ramgolall wagged his head and groaned, and in the dark there, unseen by his daughters, he wiped the corners of his eyes, for they had grown wet with grief at the thought that in time soon to come he would have to open his bundles and spend the money he had so carefully saved. He turned his head and looked behind him into the gloom of the mud-house, looked in the direction where he knew his canister of money stood. To him at that moment it seemed as though his whole life lay stored away in that canister: his youth, the immigrant ship that had brought him from Calcutta – the canister had contained all the valuables he had possessed at that time – the five years of his indentured labour on the estate and the many years of voluntary labour that had followed. In it lay stored away all the troubles and pleasures that life had brought him: kicks and angry words from the overseers, his first marriage – the drums and the feasting and the gifts of money and jewellery – the labourers in riot and the shooting by the police, Pagwah festivals, the death of his first wife and that dark day when his eldest son had got killed in a dray-cart accident, his second marriage, Sosee getting of age and Big Man coming to take her out, and the birth of Kattree and Beena, Baijan and his provision shop; all those things, and more, lay hidden in the gloom within his faithful canister. They were mingled with the many tarnished shillings and florins and pennies carefully saved throughout all the years gone by. Each shilling could tell its own tale of joy or of trouble, each penny. And to think that soon he might have to open the bundles and spend those shillings and pennies! Ah! It was a black, bitter thought.

Sitting not far from him, Beena, too, was thinking sombre

thoughts. She remembered the moonlight of two nights ago when the moon was full. Sukra had come and they had held the curry-feed. She and Sukra had not wanted to hold it, but Kattree and Ramgolall had insisted, arguing that Jannee was not dead so there was no reason why they should not enjoy themselves. Ramgolall had beaten the tom-tom with great spirit in order, thought Beena, to drown the fears within him concerning Geoffry and Kattree, and Kattree had sung in a lively voice, happy at her love-making with Geoffry. Beena and Sukra had sung, too, but not with any spirit. For the two of them no curry-feed could hold any delight if Jannee were not there to share it with them.

Beena looked up at the sky and saw that there were many stars out and not a cloud anywhere. The stars, she thought, were winking very coldly as though they did not mind one jot whether she were sad or not. Every night they looked the same – blue and cold. It did not matter to them that Jannee was sleeping now in a damp prison-cell and that next Tuesday he would be taken before the Magistrate. Jaigan had read in the newspaper that on Tuesday next the Preliminary Inquiry, as he called it, would begin. After all the evidence had been heard, the Magistrate would 'throw Jannee off for Supreme Court'. Supreme Court would begin in October and would be held in New Amsterdam. This would be the big trial, Jaigan had told her. If the jury found Jannee guilty, the Judge would put on a black cap and pass sentence of death, and then Jannee would be taken to the big gaol at Georgetown, and one morning a week or so later, on the stroke of nine o'clock, he would be hanged on the gallows.

Hanged on the gallows. For the past two days those four words had been going through her mind. They made her shiver. Such cruel words, and frightening. Hanged on the gallows. They had nearly made her go wild yesterday. She believed they were evil words – words of Black Art, for it was through thinking them so often that the new plan in her mind had come to life. When on her way home with Ramgolall yesterday afternoon, the plan had of a sudden sprung into her mind – a plan to save Jannee, a dreadful, frightening plan. So horrible it was that she was sure some evil thing had put it into her mind. Hanged on the gallows. Those were evil words. Since Jaigan had spoken them to her she had repeated them so often in her mind that yesterday evening in the twilight some devil of Black Arts had heard them and been attracted to her. Walking slowly home on the road with her father, she had been attacked by this devil. It had crouched on her shoulder and whispered the evil plan into her thoughts, the plan whereby she could save Jannee from being hanged on the gallows. It was so terrible and wicked a thing that whenever it writhed its way into her thoughts, as at every odd moment today it had been doing, she tried to push it off into some deep hole in her mind where it would be forgotten for ever. But she knew that she would not forget it. She would do it. Everything was set in her mind and the time was drawing near. She knew just what she had to do. She would be very much afraid. Her limbs would tremble and a cold sweat would break out on her skin. But she would do it, all the same. The thought of saving Jannee from being hanged on the gallows would help her to do it.

Sitting there in the dark, she gave a shudder. Looking towards the east, she saw that the sky had begun to grow pale. One or two tiny black clouds hovered like wicked duppy-devils waiting for the red moon to come up.

44

On the day after the next, Beena, on awakening in the morning, said that she was not feeling well and asked Kattree if she would go to Speyerfeld with Ramgolall to help in selling the milk. Kattree, in dismay, said that Geoffry was coming to take her to Sixty-three. Beena said that Ramgolall, then, would have to go alone to Speyerfeld because she was feeling too ill to go with him. Her head was hurting and her stomach felt sick.

She would not get out of bed, but lay doubled up, a hand pressed to her stomach.

Ramgolall told Kattree that she would have to go with him to Speyerfeld, but Kattree said that she was not able to go. Geoffry would be vexed if he came to take her to Sixty-three and found that she had gone to sell milk. Ramgolall was greatly grieved at her refusal, and said that she was a bad girl and that Geoffry was spoiling her. Kattree said that she did not mind if she was a bad girl. Let her stay bad and let Geoffry spoil her. She did not care. She spoke angrily and walked out of the mud-house into the misty morning, leaving her father to groan and wag his head and speak of the trouble that Geoffry was bringing on them all.

Later in the morning, when she was sitting in the car beside Geoffry, she related to him what had happened, and he chuckled and said: 'Oh, yes, I daresay he must think me an awful villain.' He chuckled again. 'In a manner of speaking, I am a nasty kind of villain. The blasted roué type, if you know what I mean. Ugh!' He made a wry face. 'Life can be a beastly sort of thing sometimes, you know.' He was talking to her jumbie now. She knew it. 'There are so many things one would like to root oneself away from but just can't. Where sex is concerned especially. I can't help myself when it comes to sex. I'm like a piece of wood moving towards the centre of a whirlpool. For instance, I could have spent the whole of today at the piano and really enjoyed myself, but when I woke this morning the image of your nude body beside me alone on the beach at Sixty-three predominated above every other thought. If I'd wanted, of course, by an effort of will, I could easily have put you out of my mind and spent the day at the piano, but what would have been the sense in that? I'd have had to come to you tomorrow or the next day. Sort of inevitable. Or even if I did succeed in keeping away from you entirely for the next four or five weeks that I'm here, when I go back to Georgetown there'd be more of the same thing awaiting me. It's just inevitable, you see. Every girl I meet sooner or later "falls for me" as the phrase goes, and there you are. Another sex affair materializes. It's sort of monotonous. In a way, the thought of sex irritates me. It seems so petty and contemptible. And yet it attracts me such a terrific lot that I can't do without it. That's what makes me want to commit suicide sometimes, you see.'

She made no reply, for she had hardly understood anything he had said. She never understood him when he spoke to her jumbie. She never tried to understand him. As soon as she realized that he was speaking to her jumbie she would just be silent and listen to the sound of his voice until he stopped speaking. She had got used to him now, and it did not worry her when he forgot her herself and made a long speech to her jumbie instead. She put it down as one of his habits and accepted it as such. It even amused her a little.

He kept staring ahead at the road and then abruptly glanced at her and said to her herself: 'You're looking nice this morning, Kattree. I think pink becomes you even more than blue.'

'You prefer me in pink dan blue?'

'Yes, I think I do. Though I'm not saying you don't look all right in blue. I believe any colour would suit you.'

They spent a very happy time on the beach and in the sea. He did not even speak to her jumbie once. He spoke to her herself all the time, even when they came out of the water and got into the back of the car.

At about one o'clock, however, they had to leave, for the tide had reached its dead nap and thousands of sand-flies attacked them. To have remained would have been torture.

When he brought the car to a stop at the side of the road, he said: 'If Beena hadn't been at home I could have come and bathed with you in the canal. It's hardly two o'clock.'

'Na mind. Come tomorrow,' she smiled. 'She might be better tomorrow. She na serious sick. Only she head an' she belly hurt she.'

'Good. You can look out for me, then. I'll bring my fishing tackle and we can catch a few mullets.'

When Kattree entered the mud-house she found to her surprise that it was empty. This was odd. Had not Beena said that she was ill and could not go out today?

After a moment's thought, however, she told herself that Beena must have felt better and gone to Sukra. She put the matter out of her mind and let her thoughts return to Geoffry and the happy hours she had just spent with him at Sixty-three. She looked down at her pink dress and remembered what he had said in the car when they were on their way up. He preferred her in pink than blue. She let her hand glide lightly down along the smooth, shiny cloth. The feel of it was nice, nice like some coloured magic. She could imagine his hand stroking her body through the thin silkiness. That, too, always seemed like some

208

coloured magic, but dreamy as well and too nice to be imagined as it really was. She frowned of a sudden, feeling sorry that she had not known before of Beena's absence. He could have come, after all, and bathed with her in the canal and they could have made love again.

She took off the dress and put it away carefully in the hat-box where she kept it and the other dresses, and then, having nothing to do, she went outside and plunged into the canal. She swam and splashed about for nearly half an hour, making believe that Geoffry was bathing with her. She laughed and talked to him, imagined she heard him reply and talked to him again, saw him dive and dived, too. Then she came out of the water and lay on her back in the shadow of the mud-house and told herself that he was there making love to her. She let her thoughts paint blue and gold images in the trembling heat-haze far away on the savannah. Grey shadows of the future tried to swirl amidst the pretty images, but she wafted them off with a green magic-smile. In the middle of it all thin jumbie-music piped her to sleep.

When she awoke it was to find that the sun was low in the west and that ranks of solid blue-grey clouds had formed overhead in a menacing array. The air was still and the savannah looked odd and unreal with the red sun shining on it and heavy thunder-clouds hovering above. The whole scene had a weird look. It seemed to grin like a skull.

After looking at it for a short while, she got up and put on her old blue cotton dress, then made her way north-east over the savannah to drive the cows into pen for the night. As she went, the wind without any warning began to blow strongly and with biting chill from the south-east, and the whole array of clouds started off on a furious but orderly rush towards the north-west. Rain came down abruptly in savage giant drops far apart, lasted for about two minutes and then stopped. But the wind continued. A loud bay of thunder broke from the clouds and died away. The wind felt warm and chilly by turns. It would die down abruptly, leaving a dead, dreadful calm, then come again in a strong startling gust. The hurrying clouds looked yellow at their ragged bases, reflecting the sunlight, and this made them seem weirder than ever, evil and devilish. She felt very helpless under them and was glad when, at length, the cows were all safely in pen. She sat by the edge of the canal and watched the drama for a while, then got up and went into the mud-house. She lay on the wooden bed in the half-gloom and thought of Geoffry, then her father came in and spoilt her thoughts. He asked for Beena and she told him that she had come home and found her not there. 'She mus' be feel better an' go to Sukra,' she added.

He groaned and wagged his head and handed her two pennies. 'One shilling, two penny. Dah all de money me get today. Ah-h-h! If you did come wid me, bettay, me woulda had t'ree shilling put in canister now. But now me only got one shilling. *One* shilling.'

She sucked her teeth, but made no reply.

He kept groaning all the time as though in pain. Going over to the canister, he opened it and crouched before it, wagging his head at the dirty bundles. He opened the bundle on top, gazed at the shillings in it, smiled, groaned, wagged his head and then dropped the solitary shilling into it. 'Seventy-seven,' he said in a deep mutter, gave a groan, wagged his head and began to tie up the bundle again.

When he had locked the canister and put the key back underneath it, he rose, muttering gloomily: 'One shilling. One shilling. Ah-h-h-h!'

Kattree was cooking the evening meal when Beena returned. Beena went straight into the mud-house, a whitish bundle under her arm. When she came out, Kattree asked her casually where she had been to, expecting to hear her reply that she had come from Sukra. But Beena said: 'Me bin to town.'

Kattree stared at her. 'You bin to town?'

'Eh-heh,' said Beena, avoiding to meet her eyes directly.

'New Amsterdam town?'

'Eh-heh,' said Beena briefly and began to pull off her dress. Kattree noticed that it was one of the new cotton dresses Baijan had given her. On her feet, Kattree saw, too, were the canvas shoes Baijan had bought for her.

'Wha' you bin to town fo'?' asked Kattree.

'Me bin to do lil' business,' Beena replied, and quite naked now, moved off towards the canal before Kattree could ask her any more questions. Kattree looked at the bubbling saucepan of rice and felt sadly puzzled. Beena going to town 'to do lil' business'. What could she mean by that? What business could she have to do in town? It was very queer. Why had she not said this morning that she was going to town? She could not have been feeling ill in truth. She must have been pretending. It was strange that she should have done that. She was not in the habit of doing deceptive things, and she was not secretive. What could have come over her like this all of a sudden? An idea came to her abruptly. Perhaps she had gone to town to visit Jannee in prison. Yes, that must be it. She had gone to the prison and asked them to let her see Jannee. It was stupid of her to be in love with Jannee. To begin with, he was Sukra's husband and would not be able to make love to her, unless he did it on the sly. Perhaps they had been secret lovers before he was arrested. But no, that could not have been or by now her belly would have been big with child. In any case, it was stupid of them being in love and not able to lie together and be happy as Geoffry and herself did every day. And besides, he was a murderer. He had killed a man. He was evil, and Beena should hate him now instead of loving him.

She saw Beena emerge from the canal and come towards the mud-house. Ramgolall, who was squatting near the door, saw her, too, and said in some surprise: 'Eh-eh, bettay? You tek late bath. Tek care you ketch col'.'

She gave a jerky laugh. 'Na. Me na ketch col'.'

She came near to where Kattree sat by the fireplace and took up a rice-bag that lay on the ground. A drop of water from her hair fell on Kattree's foot and the sudden chill made Kattree shiver, but it was a shiver that, somehow, seemed not to have been caused by the chill only but by some secret fear that had crawled over her skin at Beena's approach.

The twilight had grown deep now. The wind had died down to a hum. The northern and western parts of the sky were clear, but overhead and in the south and east long rows of small grey clouds like sheep could be seen hovering high up in a still, peaceful array. Low above the southern horizon it was very dark. A blue-grey monster squatted there, with one long claw stretched upwards towards where the orange tongues of sunset had a while ago flared, as though it were trying to feel its way into the pale yellow light that the sun had left in the west. Very deathly it looked, thought Kattree, though, in a way, rather pitiful, as if it were asking people not to think too badly of it because it looked so ugly.

She glanced up at Beena who stood a little way off drying her skin. So slim and tall she seemed in the dull afterglow of sundown and in the flickering glimmer from the fire. She might be a jumbie, thought Kattree. She stood there so silently drying her skin and looking so dim in the fading light. The flames in the fireplace made spectral images tremble shiftily on her smooth skin. The dark points of her breasts seemed like eyes of mystery that kept quivering jerkily as she moved her arms about, and her black, long hair might be the legs of some weird spider that lived on the crown of her head enrooted in her brain.

A wave of warning went through Kattree. Something bad, she felt sure, was going to happen before long.

45

The days continued to be made of pink and gold for Kattree. Shadows were brown or dreaming mauve, and wizard-bells tinkled in the splash of water. Candle-flies sparkled in the dark at nights like the playful blue eyes of jumbie-mullets swimming in the wind and the dark that flowed over her in cool waves of wine. The night hummed about her body and lifted her on a cloud of perfumed magic higher and higher towards the stars in the August sky so that soon everything changed into a muddled dream of nice nothings and when she opened her eyes again it was morning and mist, and Geoffry coming soon to make love to her lips and limbs.

Meanwhile, however, the drab things of life continued, too, and Beena and Ramgolall and other people who were not living in a coloured dream of love-making, noted them. For instance, when Jannee was brought before the Magistrate in New Amsterdam, he was represented by a lawyer from Georgetown named Mr Burlock. Everybody in Speyerfeld was puzzled to know how

Sukra could have found enough money to hire such a lawyer. Jaigan said to Beena: 'Is where you' frien' Sukra get money from to hire such a good lawyer, Beena?' and Beena replied: 'Me na know. She na tell me. You say 'e's a good lawyer? You really t'ink 'e can talk good an' defend Jannee?'

'Oh, yes,' said Jaigan. 'He's a good lawyer. He's not de best deh got in Georgetown, but 'e good. Me read 'bout 'e in de newspapers before. Sukra na tell you how she manage to arrange to brief such a good man?'

'Na,' said Beena, her eyes growing shifty. She fidgeted a little. 'She na tell me nutting at all. Gimme two ounce butter an' a poun' o' sugar.'

'Dah is funny,' Jaigan frowned, moving off to serve her. 'A man like Mr Burlock will want at least two hundred dollars to tek on de case.'

Beena made no comment. She stood there at the counter looking slowly all around the shop, her face a blank.

About an hour later that same afternoon Sukra came into the shop to buy rice, and Jaigan at once broke into a smile and greeted her. 'Hey, Sukra gal!' he greeted. 'Me na see you dis past two-t'ree days. Wha' happen to you?'

'Me bin a-wo'k on de farm,' smiled Sukra. 'Only me alone deh now, you know. Me got to hustle mek a livin'.'

'Me notice you get a good lawyer to defend Jannee.'

'A good lawyer? Wha' good lawyer?'

'Mr Burlock, na? De Georgetown lawyer. You talk as if you na know.'

'But me na know nutting 'bout na lawyer,' said Sukra, a blank look on her face. 'Georgetown lawyer?'

'Eh-eh! But you na brief 'e? How you na know?'

'But me na know wha' you talk 'bout. True-true.'

'You na know Mr Burlock defendin' Jannee?'

'Mr Burlock? Na. Who name so?'

Jaigan laughed. 'Well, man, dis t'ing funny. You Jannee' wife an' you na know nutting 'bout de lawyer who defendin' 'e? You didn't make arrangements wid no lawyer to defend Jannee?'

'Na,' said Sukra, shaking her head. 'Fuss time me hear 'e get lawyer to defend 'e. Me na got enough money pay good lawyer.'

Jaigan stared at her, and for a moment there was silence. Then Jaigan said: 'Eh-eh! But if you na arrange wid 'e who arrange wid 'e?'

'Me na know,' said Sukra. 'Unless Jannee 'eself mek arrangement. But we na know how 'e woulda get money to pay de lawyer.'

Jaigan smiled. 'Dis t'ing look mysterious, gal. Eh-eh! How Jannee in prison would be able to make arrangements wid Mr Burlock in Georgetown? An', as you say, where 'e woulda get de money to pay Burlock? Before Burlock tek on de case 'e woulda want some money in advance as a retaining fee. Who pay de retaining fee?'

More than one person in Speyerfeld wondered how a poor man like Jannee had been able to brief such a good lawyer as Mr Burlock, but nobody could solve the riddle so the matter remained a mystery.

Beena came every day to Jaigan to ask for news, and when the Magistrate's inquiry was over (it only lasted three days), Jaigan told her that Jannee had been thrown off for Supreme Court in October and that Mr Burlock had decided to reserve his defence. 'Dat's de usual procedure,' Jaigan went on to explain. 'A murder case can't be tried in de Magistrate's court. It got to go to de higher court. A judge got to preside.'

Beena said: 'Oh-h-h!' only understanding half of what he had said. The two of them were alone in the shop. After a pause, during which she gave a quick glance towards the door, she asked him: 'You know if Mr Burlock in New Amsterdam still?'

'Me can't tell dat,' said Jaigan. 'Me na know.' He frowned of a sudden, and, looking at her in a rather sly way, smiled and said: 'You been askin' me some funny-funny question dis past week or two, Beena. Is wha' wrong? Last week time you ask me how much lawyers in New Amsterdam an' wha' is deh name, an' den you ask me how people does change silver money into notes an' where you got to go to change it, an' now you ask me if me know if Mr Burlock still in New Amsterdam. Funny, you know. Me been t'inking over de matter in me mind. All dese past few days me been t'inking it over.'

Beena stared at him, and her face had gone a queer greyish

colour. 'How you mean, Jaigan?' she said, and her voice quavered a little. 'Me only ask you because – because me want get lil' knowledge 'bout de worl'. Dah is all.'

Jaigan smiled slowly, looking sly still. He wagged his finger at her. 'Tek care, Beena bettay. Tek care. You look like you clever gal. Eh, bettay?'

'Wha' you mean? Me na know wha' you talk.'

'You sure? Who arrange fo' Mr Burlock to defend Jannee? Na you, bettay? Who pay de retaining fee? Na you, bettay?'

'Me? Eh-eh! How me can pay lawyer defend Jannee? Me na got na money. Where me go get money from?'

'Wha' 'bout Ramgolall' canister? Suppose you tek a few hundred shillings from Ramgolall' canister an' put dem in de flour-bag wha' you buy from me early last week. An' suppose you tek it to New Amsterdam an' get it change into notes at de bank as how me tell you can get silver money change. An' den suppose you go to a solicitor an' tell 'e you want to get a big lawyer from Georgetown to defend Jannee. Den 'e ask you if you got money to pay de lawyer, an' you show 'e de notes wha' you get in exchange fo' de silver money. You tell 'e you is a frien' o' Jannee an' you want to get a good lawyer from George-town to defend Jannee, so 'e agree you hand over de money – an' everyt'ing fix' up. Eh, Beena bettay? Na so you do am?'

Beena kept staring at him with wide, scared eyes as though he were some dreadful demon. Her face was grey. At length, she broke out: 'Is who tell you all dah, Jaigan? How you know all dah?'

Jaigan smiled – not sly now, but kindly. 'Na get frighten, bettay. Me na tryin' to frighten you. Nobody na tell me dis. Me find it out fo' meself. Me been t'inking it over in me mind. Me remember all dem questions you bin ask me dis past two-t'ree week an' me put two an' two togedder.'

'Oh, gawd! Jaigan, you na tell nabody?' Her hand was trembling as she put it up to her face.

'Na! Ow, bettay! Why me go tell anybody? Me na so tell-tale. Me keep am secret. Me na tell a soul. But is how much you pay de solicitor?'

'A hundred dollar,' she said in a faint voice, and glanced round quickly towards the door.

215

'Which solicitor you go to?'

'Mr Wickham. De same one you tell me 'bout.'

'Oh! Yes. He's an honest man. Good t'ing you go to 'e. Any o' de odders mighta rob you. How much more money you go to pay 'e?'

'Six hundred an' twenty-five shilling.'

'Six hundred an' twenty-five shillings?' He put his head at a slant and frowned. 'Dah is how much dollars? A hundred an' fifty dollars, eh? But you got all dah money to pay 'e?'

'Eh-heh. Ramgolall' canister had inside fourteen hundred an' seventy-six shilling in silver money. Me didn' trouble de copper coin. Me only reckon out de silver coin. Me carry fourteen hundred shilling to town in de flour-bag an' change it into twenty-dollar an' five-dollar notes. Me lef' de seventy-six shilling behind because if me did tek dah, too, Ramgolall woulda find out, because dah was de new bundle wha' 'e savin' up in now.' She spoke in quick breathless bursts, and her hands trembled all the while. Her face still looked greyish. 'Me pay out a hundred dollar to Mr Wickham,' she went on, after taking a quick backward glance at the door, 'an' me got de rest o' de notes hide away in de flour-bag in de roof o' we house. When October come me got to go back to town on de day before de trial and pay de hundred an' fifty dollar balance to Mr Wickham – '

'But wait! Suppose Ramgolall find out dat you tek 'e money? 'E will mek a noise – '

'Na, 'e na go find out. 'E don' open de bundles once 'e tie dem up. Me put pebbles an' dry dirt in de bundles in place o' de silver money so 'e won' notice nutting wrong. An' me put all de bundles wid de copper money on top, so if 'e hand hit against any o' dem by accident 'e will know money inside. Me had to do it, Jaigan. Only way to save Jannee from get hang on de gallows. An' Ramgolall only got de money hoard-up in 'e canister an' no use to nobody – '

'Wait! Quiet! Somebody comin'.'

A Portuguese young man came in and bought three packs of cigarettes. When he had gone, Jaigan smiled at Beena and said: 'You got clever head, Beena bettay. You plan dis t'ing good. Me meself couldn' ha' do am better.'

'Ow, Jaigan, but me beg you! Na talk tell a soul. Na even tell Kattree or Sukra. Promise me.'

'Me promise. Na fear, bettay. Me hear plenty secret in me time an' me keep am all to meself. Me won' tell a soul. You can depend 'pon me.'

Returning home in the late afternoon with her father, Beena felt, somehow, greatly relieved in mind. Telling her black secret to Jaigan made her feel better, though why this should be so she could not tell. The gathering twilight soothed her. Far inside her she still felt wicked and guilty, but it did not worry her so much now. It was just as though telling Jaigan about her terrible deed had caused some of the wicked and guilty feelings to melt and leave her body. She hoped she would go on feeling like this.

'Who-you?' cried a goat-sucker a little way off and it sounded like a kind voice trying to soothe her soul.

46

August was soon gone, and with it went the remnants of the rain. The brief, wild showers in the afternoon stopped, the mist in the mornings became thinner – some mornings there was none at all – and the savannah began to grow parched and bare of grass, trenches and ponds dried up, cattle grew thinner for want of good food, and the rice-fields from pale yellow had turned deep yellow. Everyone talked about rice and the grinding season about to begin on the sugar estates. Already there was a shortage of rice. Last year's yield had been good, but much had been exported, with the result that the home supply was low. The price soared every day. The week before last it had been three dollars and seventy-five cents per bag, last week four dollars, four fifty. This week four eighty, five twenty-five. Up, up went the price, and the rice dealers were happy. But this year's crop would soon send the price tumbling down to three dollars or even two seventy-five, and then the poor small farmers would grumble and say how the price of rice had gone to nothing and that life was hard for them.

In the middle of August Baijan arrived. He brought silk cloth bearing flowered designs and had wedding-dresses made for Kattree and Beena. He bought vests and silk panties and brassières for them in Speyerfeld, and hats trimmed with ribbon and pink flowers. He bought for them, too, high-heeled shoes of shining black leather, but Kattree and Beena overbalanced and nearly fell down when they tried to walk in them so he had to buy flat-heeled shoes, instead.

At the wedding they looked like great ladies, but felt very hot and tight, for they were not accustomed to wearing vests and brassières and leather shoes. Ramgolall, too, kept wriggling and fidgeting in the light-grey suit which Baijan had had made for him. During the ceremony he took off his collar and tie and stuffed them into his coat pocket, and the people in the pews behind him gave muffled sniggers. He did not mind, however. He preferred to be laughed at than to be choked to death.

The ceremony took place at four in the afternoon at the Anglican church of St Joseph's at Plantation Port Mourant lower down the Coast, and the church was packed. Big Man Weldon was there with Sosee and Geoffry and Belle. Geoffry had brought to church a tall, pretty girl in a dark-green dress. Dora was a bridesmaid and looked very lovely. Her lips were bright red, like the lips of most of the other lady-guests, and Kattree and Beena wondered greatly at this, for they were not familiar with lipstick. There were many things that seemed strange to them: the hymn-singing and the sound of the organ and the white gauntlets worn by the ladies. It puzzled them, too, to know how these ladies could walk in shoes with such high, slim heels. And why did the parson wear those queer robes and speak in such a droning voice? They could not understand a word he said.

Later on at Mr Ramjit's house, at Sixty-eight Village, they felt lost amidst the great crowd of guests. A yellow bubbly drink (which they afterwards heard was named champagne) was served round to everybody in queer glasses with thin stems, and then the whole crowd gathered around the table where the tall white wedding cake stood. To Kattree and Beena it seemed incredible that such a structure could be a cake: something good to eat. It looked to them like some sort of mound made out of earthenware or white enamel.

The toasts bored them. They could not understand why every now and then there should be a burst of laughter. These speeches sounded dull and in no way amusing. Baijan's speech, for instance, contained words that they had never thought could exist. 'On this most auspicious occasion, ladies and gentlemen,' he said, 'I find myself overwhelmed with emotions of great felicitation. On behalf of my spouse and myself I should like to ponder for a moment on the profound and important state of matrimony upon which we have this day embarked...' What did that mean? And yet everybody clapped when he had finished. Listening to Mr Ramjit was much more amusing. Mr Ramjit, unlike Baijan, did not speak in a stiff voice. He began his speech by saying: 'Well, ladies an' gentlemen, I'm afraid I had a lot o' drinks dis mornin', so if I say anyt'ing in dis speech wha' seem out o' order, well, all-you must call me to order.' This created a big laugh.

When the speeches were at last over, the cake was cut. The parson made a queer sign with his hand and said: '*In nomine patris et filii et spiritus sancti,*' and that did not even sound like English. Baijan held Liza's hand and the two of them cut the cake together. Then Baijan kissed Liza, and Joseph, who was the best man, kissed Dora and there was a great shriek of laughter from the ladies, while Dora's face turned very pink.

Of a sudden, music blared forth, and with parted lips Kattree and Beena saw a black young man seated at the piano and playing it for all he was worth, while on either side of him two other black young men were engaged with other instruments. One played a thing that resembled a sitar. It made thrumming noises. The other played a long curved brass thing with little knobs. It made long wailing sounds and as the young man played it he kept swaying his head and body from side to side.

Couples began to dance. Kattree saw Geoffry dancing with the tall, pretty girl in dark green and she felt a little jealous. When the dance was over, however, he came over to where she and Beena sat eating black cake with white icing, in the north-eastern corner of the drawing room. He asked her how she was enjoying herself and sat for a long time talking to her and Beena. He said that he was fond of dancing. Dora soon joined them and after admiring their dresses, asked them many questions. Was this the first wedding they had attended? How did they like this and how did they like that? She told them that she and Belle were going to Georgetown in September to attend Bishop's High School. She was hugely pleased and excited over this and said that it would be great living in Georgetown. Meanwhile, in the pantry (which had been converted into a bar) Mr Ramjit and several other gentlemen were entertaining themselves and Ramgolall with rum. Though Ramgolall had not drunk rum since he was a young man, he had not forgotten the taste. He drank tot after tot and grew very merry. From amidst the uproar of voices in the pantry his voice would often emerge in a long wail of song.

At the eastern end of the gallery Big Man Weldon, Dr Roy Matthias and three white young men (evidently overseers from some sugar estate) sat at a table drinking whisky and talking and laughing. Dr Roy told many *risqué* anecdotes. All of them looked flush in the face. A blue cloud of cigarette smoke enveloped them.

Ramgolall and his daughters did not get home until after ten o'clock that night. Ramgolall was sick in the car. Beena and Kattree had to support him between them as they walked along the mud-dam. It was a good thing that there was the light from a half-moon to aid them. They were both a little fearful, because years ago the doctor had told him that his heart was not too good and that he should not drink or smoke.

He did not awaken until seven o'clock the following morning and even then was too ill to get up. No milk was sold that day.

And so August faded and September came. The grinding season on the sugar estates began. Strange people from everywhere, Negroes and East Indians, flocked into Speyerfeld. Black smoke once again began to streak the sky from the tops of the huge brick chimneys, and in the south the indigo of night was stained red with the glow of a burning cane-field. All day and all night, like some relentless monster of Fate, the factory worked. Rug-a-rug, rug-a-rug, rug-a-rug. In the early hours of the evening, at midnight, in the deep stillness of the morning hours, through the sepia peace of dawn, the sound went on. The red sunshine whitened into noon and waned into orange and still it went on. Rug-a-rug, rug-a-rug, rug-a-rug: a leisured sound, cold and detached, uncaring, like the sky or the savannah or the stars at night. An overseer was burning in bed with malaria, the wife of the deputy-manager was drinking herself to death, Mr Ralph, the junior pan-boiler, would be married day after tomorrow. But the huge pistons and rollers did not care. The rhythm remained unchanged, night and day.

Meanwhile, the savannah grew drier and drier and the grass more and more stunted and sparse. Only the hardy samphire laughed at the glaring sun. The level of ponds and canals had lowered and in the rice-fields only a brown slime remained. Reaping time had come. Tomorrow or the day after curved knives would begin to slash down the yellow stalks, and oxen would trample on the stacks and separate the paddy from the straw.

Geoffry returned to school at the end of the first week in the month. The penultimate day of his holiday was spent on the beach at Sixty-three with Kattree and his brothers and sisters and the last day with Kattree alone at the mud-house. They fished and bathed in the canal and made love in the shade of the mud-house. She told him that the last few weeks had been the nicest time she had had in all her life and that she would miss him a great deal when he was gone. This made him grow silent and talk to her jumbie. He told it: 'In many ways, you know, I despise myself horribly for having had this affair with you. It's beastly when you come to look at it. I'm not in love with you yourself – only with your body. I told you that on the second day we were together, if you remember, and you said that you were quite satisfied with my loving only your body. Ugh, but I'm sick of loving bodies, Kattree. It leaves me unsatisfied and depressed. It's monotonous and tiresome. Of late I've begun to wonder whether my sex experiences at such an early age haven't atrophied the spiritual part of me. Stymphy and Clara think not. They tell me it's just that I'm groping after some ill-defined ideal and that my soul hasn't fully awakened yet. They're of the opinion that I don't know what I want in life but that I'll discover it one day soon and then I'll have peace of mind. They may be right and they may be wrong. The real truth of the matter may be that I'm just one of those awful bores who suffer from such a strong dose of narcissism that they can't think or

221

talk about anybody but themselves. In other words, I may be nothing more than a great conceited ass.'

Before he left, he gave her two five-dollar notes and told her to buy nice things for herself. She thanked him and asked him if she would see him again at Christmas. He frowned faintly and said that perhaps she would and perhaps not, but as she watched him mount his bicycle and ride off towards where the red sun was glowing mildly between dark layers of cloud, something seemed to tell her that for a certainty she would not see him again. August had come with its coloured dreams, and now August was gone.

47

The rice harvest began during the second week in September and by the end of the month was in full swing all along the Coast. Ramgolall and Beena and Kattree spent two whole days helping Sukra to reap Jannee's fields. At the end of the second day, when the happy task was over and the stacks stood all ready for the oxen to thresh them, a curry-feed was held at Jannee's home, and a very pleasant evening it proved for them all. Sukra and Beena, who were living now in the strong hope that Mr Burlock would get Jannee off in October, sang with spirit. Sukra beat Jannee's drum and Moonsammy, who was there, too, with his wife Heedai, played his sitar. (Moonsammy had helped in the rice-cutting while Heedai had stayed at the mud-house to take care of Bharat Ragoonandan in Sukra's absence.)

Two days after the cutting of Jannee's rice, Kattree awoke in the morning and was sick. Beena saw her being sick and said in dismay: 'Oh, gawd, Kattree! You get baby. Same way Sukra used to get sick in mornin' when she did gettin' baby.'

'Awright, me know me gettin' baby,' said Kattree. 'Me na mind. Me want get it.'

'Ramgolall warn you not to mek baby wid Geoffry. Baby bring big expense, an' Ramgolall na like spend money.'

'Na worry 'bout dah. Geoffry gimme ten-dollar.'

'Geoffry gi' you ten-dollar?'

'Yes. 'E gimme ten-dollar. Me go save am up till me baby come, den me na got to ask Ramgolall fo' na money.'

Beena stared at her for a moment, then said: 'You lucky 'e gi' you ten-dollar. Ten-dollar is plenty money. More dan forty shilling. 'E know you going get baby?'

Kattree nodded slowly, her eyes on the ground. 'Me tell 'e one day me feel me going get baby.'

'An' wha' 'e say?' asked Beena, looking at her with great interest.

' 'E frown an' den 'e smile an' ask me if me really want get baby. Me tell 'e yes, an' 'e say me mus' go ahead an' get it if me really want a baby. 'E say it will gimme somet'ing to occupy me time. But 'e mek me promise dat me won' show de baby to 'e mudder or fadder or tell dem nutting 'bout it.'

Beena laughed. 'Sosee' face will turn black, if she know you gettin' baby fo' she son.'

'She know 'e bin frien'ly wid me in August. 'E say she quarrel wid 'e every day, but 'e na care.'

One morning, a few days later, Ramgolall saw her being sick and knew that she was with child. He at once set up a wail and told her that he had warned her that this would happen. When, however, she told him of the ten dollars Geoffry had given her he stopped wailing and said that that was good and that perhaps Geoffry would give her more money when he came at Christmas. ' 'E good boy,' said Ramgolall, groaning and smiling. 'Ten-dollar big money. 'E might gi' you more, bettay. You must talk to 'e nice when 'e come Christmas time!'

But Kattree frowned and said: 'Money na count fo' everyt'ing, Ramgolall. Me na want na more money from 'e. Ma na frien'ly wid 'e 'cause me want money from 'e.'

Often during the day she would lie on her back in the shade of the mud-house and think of the baby in her, wondering how it would look when it was born. Perhaps it would be fair-skinned like Geoffry, and perhaps it might have his face. It would be good to watch it slowly growing into a tall boy like Geoffry. She felt certain it would be a boy. She would get clothes made for him and send him to school every day so that when he was grown-up he would be able to read and write and talk well like his father.

Lying there staring up at the hot sky, she would feel a little excited of a sudden, seeing the future as a happy mirage tinted with many greens and pinks and the dark-brown hair of her son trembling in the wind.

48

As the dry season progressed, the price of milk rose. By the last week in September the price had reached six cents per pint. Ramgolall was happy, for now the day's takings amounted to over five shillings, and, some days, six.

One afternoon Beena got a great scare.

She and her father had just returned from Speyerfeld, and as Ramgolall was crouching before his canister adding the day's takings to his hoard, Kattree laughingly said: 'Ramgolall, wha' de use o' savin' up money like dah every day? You na even know how much you got. Why you na count over all you' money see how much you got in all?'

Ramgolall gave a low groaning chuckle. 'One day soon me go count am over, bettay,' he said. 'One day soon when me get plenty time spare.'

Beena stood near the door, her heart beating in great jolts.

'When you count am over you should carry am put am in Post Office like how Baijan say you mus' do,' Kattree said. 'It safer keep money in Post Office dan in canister. An' you get interest 'pon am after long time pass.'

'Na, me na like Post Office,' Ramgolall replied, shaking his head. He gave a groaning sigh. 'Ah-h-h! Me wo'k hard fo' dis money, bettay, hard, hard. Me like keep am near me all de time. Me like know all wha' me wo'k fo' safe in canister in me own house. If me put am in Post Office it deh far from me like if 'e na belong to me.' He gave another groaning sigh and locked the canister, and it was not until he had tucked away the key under it and risen to his feet that Beena felt at ease again.

The trial of Jannee was due to begin next week. It was 'the first case on the calendar', Jaigan had told her, and he had said that if he were she he would go to New Amsterdam at the end of this week and see Mr Wickham, the solicitor, in order to find out if Mr Burlock was still willing to go on with the case. She had better take the money along with her, too, so as to make Mr Wickham see that she really had the money to pay Mr Burlock. 'De sight o' de money will impress 'e, you see,' said Jaigan. 'Ha! De sight o' money can work wonder in dis worl', gal. Big wonder.'

On Saturday morning, therefore, she told Kattree to go to Speyerfeld with Ramgolall because she had 'a lil' business to do in town'. Kattree, assuming that she wanted to go to town to visit Jannee in prison, made no demur, and so Beena went to town and saw Mr Wickham, who told her that everything was all right about the case. Mr Burlock was going ahead with it. She did not tell him she had brought any money until he asked her if she wished to 'settle up now in regard to Mr Burlock's fee', and then she said yes and produced a wad of notes from her bosom. She handed it to him and he counted the notes and said with a smile that it was correct.

49

The Berbice Criminal Assizes (or, as many people called it, the Supreme Court) opened on Tuesday of the following week, and as Jaigan had told Beena, Jannee's case was the first on the calendar. Beena went to town for the trial. She took an early bus and arrived in New Amsterdam at a few minutes before eight. The bus-driver pointed out to her the high, square building with its flat Dutch roof and said that that was Colony House where Supreme Court was held. It was situated in a small promenade garden, a very neat, pretty garden with slim palms of all varieties that kept swaying and rustling in the wind and shell-covered walks that crunched under her shoes. There were green swards, too, and a pond of still water that reflected the sky and the trees.

Looking around her, she could see nothing that suggested murder or hanging on the gallows. She had thought of the courthouse as a grim, gloomy place set in bare, grey grounds and surrounded by high palings. But this white building standing here in this pretty garden had a friendly look. It almost seemed to smile at her and tell her that life was good to live, that she was welcome here and could go ahead and enjoy the sunshine on the green swards and the smell of the flowers, the cries of the kiskadees and the cheeps of the blue sakies. There was nothing here at all connected with robbery and killing and prisons and hanging.

Jaigan had told her that court would not begin until nine o'clock, so she decided to take a walk in the garden. After going all around it, she sat for a long time on a green bench in the shade of a low palm with broad, fan-shaped leaves. She inhaled the fragrance of the flowers and let the breeze cool her cheeks. Then she glanced at the sun and at the shadows and knew that the time must be half past eight, so she rose and made her way towards the white building. There were many doors and windows, but by asking a tall negro gentleman in navy-blue she was able to find her way to the stairs that led up to the courtroom. They were long stairs and kept going round and round as she ascended them.

The courtroom awed her. There were hard benches and railed-in enclosures. At the southern end stood the white statue of a lady blindfolded and holding a pair of scales, something like the pair Jaigan had in his shop, and at the northern end stood a high chair like King George's throne which she had once seen in a picture. Behind this chair a lion and a queer animal like a horse with a horn were painted on the wall. One or two people were already present, sitting on the benches talking in low voices, and two policemen stood near the door telling jokes to each other and uttering low, deep chuckles.

She seated herself on the first bench behind the central railed-in enclosure, and as she looked about her a cold fear began to uncoil itself within her. This room, she felt, certainly had the look as though it might be connected with murder and hanging on the gallows. That white statue frightened her a little. It seemed as if it were a jumbie that had turned to stone during the night. And the high chair with the fierce lion and the horned horse behind it and all these benches, she did not like them. They seemed cold and cruel.

Her fear grew as the courtroom filled. The tramp of feet

sounded all the time on the stairs. Gentlemen in navy-blue came in one by one and sat on special benches within the large railed-in section. She asked a black young man sitting beside her who these gentlemen were and he whispered: 'Dem is de jurymen.' A little later she saw Mr Wickham enter with a swarthy gentleman wearing a black gown and a queer curly thing on his head. 'Dah is Mr Burlock, de Georgetown lawyer,' the black young man told her. 'He defendin' Jannee.' Then a tall, slim Portuguese gentleman, also in a black gown and curly headwear, came in, and the black young man said: 'Dah is de Prosecutin' Counsel, Mr Manoel Vimeiro, K.C. He going talk 'gainst Jannee.'

Of a sudden, there came a heavy tramp of footsteps in regular time, and her heart gave a jolt as she saw Jannee being led in between two big policemen. He was made to stand inside the central railed-in enclosure in front of her while the policemen stood at attention near by. 'Dah is Jannee,' the black young man told her. 'De accused,' and she nodded and said: 'Eh-heh. Me know.'

She heard a gentleman prattling something at a window in a loud voice:

'...all manner of persons having business in this court draw near! Oyez, oyez, oyez! God save the King and this honourable court!'

Mr Wickham and Mr Burlock were sitting now at a long table with plenty of papers before them. Mr Burlock got up of a sudden and began to speak in a muttering voice to Jannee, his head close to Jannee's. Jannee nodded once, then shook his head, then nodded again. Mr Burlock nodded, too, once or twice and smiled. She did not like his smile, somehow. It seemed sly as though he were plotting an evil deed. He had a face like a devil's.

'De judge going come in any minute now,' said the black young man. 'When 'e come in everybody got to stan' up.'

He had hardly spoken when a loud voice called sternly: 'His honour the Judge!' and with a swishing rustle of clothes and a scramble of feet everybody rose. It was all very queer and frightening, thought Beena. She began to feel gloomy, for, from what she could see, Jannee seemed to be already caught in some terrible trap from which he could never escape. All these railings and policemen and black-gowned men and the Judge up there in his red gown and long curly headwear. How could he get away from all these? He was trapped. Loud, stern voices would shout at him, policemen would tramp on the floor and then he would be taken away and hanged on the gallows.

She understood very little of what happened. She heard names being called out and men in navy-blue taking seats on two raised benches on the western side of the room. There were twelve in all, and each had to kiss a black book while an East Indian gentleman droned some words in a low voice.

She heard papers being rustled and the Portuguese gentleman in the black gown reading out something in which the names of Boorharry and Jannee were mentioned, then Jannee was asked a question and he said: 'Not guilty.'

She heard a gentleman, whom she recognized as the Government doctor of Speyerfeld district, telling the Portuguese gentleman something about 'the occipital bone...the cervical vertebra...jugular vein', and other things that meant nothing to her.

Other people were questioned, policemen and the Inspector whom she liked, and once she heard Mr Burlock saying to Jaundoo who lived in a mud-house not far from Manoo: 'Jaundoo, you said you saw Jannee going towards Speyerfeld on the evening of the twenty-first of July, isn't that so?'

Jaundoo said: 'Yes,' nodding.

'Was there any moonlight that evening?'

'Na. Na moonlight dah night. It was dark night.'

'It was a dark night. I see. And you and Jannee passed each other on the road?'

'Yes.'

'But mind you, it was dark, Jaundoo. How did you know it was Jannee who passed you?'

'Me mek out 'e shape.'

'Oh, you made out his shape? I see. And did you make out his face?'

'Not too good. But me know was he.'

'I see. You didn't make out his face too good, but you knew it was he. Did you greet him?'

'Me na greet 'e. Me na know 'e to talk to.'

'Did he greet you?'

'Na. 'E na greet me.'

'Did you see anything in his hand?'

'Me na know fo' certain. 'E mighta had – '

'Oh, no, no, no. You can't say what he might have had. Did you or did you not see anything in his hand?'

Jaundoo gave a hesitant smile, then shook his head nervously and said: 'Na, me na see nutting in 'e hand dat me can remember.'

'That's all, Jaundoo.' Mr Burlock sat down, and a murmuring sound rippled over the court.

'Silence in court!' a stern voice bawled, and Beena started, feeling as though it were she alone at whom the voice was directed. She felt afraid to breathe.

At eleven o'clock the court was adjourned until one. She spent the interval in the garden. She ate her breakfast (luncheon) sitting on a green bench in the shade of a tamarind tree. She had brought it in a saucepan tied around with cloth.

The afternoon session ended at four o'clock and by five o'clock she was back home.

Ramgolall and Kattree had already returned from Speyerfeld, for milk was in great demand nowadays and the two cans were generally empty as early as two o'clock. She told them of all she had seen and heard at court, and they listened with much interest and asked her many questions. When she had changed her dress and taken off her shoes, she went to Sukra and told her everything, too. She stayed with Sukra until it was dark and ate with her. 'Me hear people say deh t'ink 'e going get off fo' certain,' she told Sukra once. 'Deh say Mr Burlock messing up de Prosecution. 'E mekin' all dem witness say wrong t'ing.'

50

The trial lasted four days and Beena went to town every day. At the end of the third day she told them that the case for the Defence was now closed and that tomorrow Mr Burlock would address the jury. She had heard that everything would be decided on the following day and it would be known for certain if Jannee was to be hanged or to be set free. Both Kattree and Sukra showed great excitement at this, and, after some talk, the two of them decided that they would go to town with Beena the next day so that they could all three be together to hear the verdict.

Ramgolall, at first, objected to both Kattree and Beena going, wanting to know who was going to take the second can of milk to Speyerfeld; but when he saw that they were determined to go and that all his groaning would not stop them, he gave in and resigned himself to things. As for Sukra, she arranged with Heedai to come and take care of Bharat Ragoonandan in her absence.

On the fourth day of the trial, therefore, Beena and Kattree and Sukra found themselves in the courtroom listening to Mr Burlock's address to the jury, while, in Speyerfeld, Ramgolall went from house to house selling his milk as he had done on any other day, for money, he reasoned, had to be earned. Shillings had to be added to the hoard in his canister. Whether Jannee lived or died mattered not to him. That was Jannee's affair. If Jannee had done wrong he must suffer. He, Ramgolall, had naught to do with it. Thinking thus, he went about the day's business as usual.

By twelve o'clock his can was empty and when he counted the day's takings he found that they only amounted to two shillings. He groaned and wagged his head. See that? Only two shillings. If Beena or Kattree had come with him and brought the big can, he would have taken five or six shillings. Ah! Life was hard on him, indeed, hard and bitter. Even his daughter deserted him nowadays. They did not care how much money he earned. They cared nothing about his canister of money. They only wanted to spend what he earned and indulge in delights. Delights were made for the rich. Poor people should not seek after delights. Poor people should work hard and save their money so that in time to come perhaps good things might turn up. Ah! If only he could make Beena and Kattree see the wisdom of this!

He groaned again and wagged his head.

When he reached home the sun was still high overhead and the time was not even one o'clock. After adding the two shillings to the new bundle he had started last week, making the total twenty-seven up to today, he smiled in a reflective way and wagged his head faintly. It was good, he thought, to look upon all these bundles and know that they contained hundreds and hundreds of shillings and florin pieces and pennies, money earned through years and years of hard toil. He could never think of putting this money in the Post Office as Baijan had suggested. He wanted it all near to him so that he could see it and touch it at will and know that it really belonged to him.

He put out his hand and stroked the topmost bundles, and a quiver of happiness went through him. He lifted one and felt the weight of it. Solid money. Feel how heavy it was. Solid, solid money. Ah! What a nice thing, money! It was the only thing that mattered to him in this bitter world. He dreamt of it at night. Often in his sleep he would find himself sitting amidst a heap of shillings and florins and filling rice-bag after rice-bag with them. No sight was better than the glitter of shillings and florins, no sound more joyful than the tinkle of coins: pennies, shillings, sixpences, threepenny-bits. Nothing made him more happy than when in selling milk the pennies and threepenny-bits and the sixpences began to pile up in the small rag he kept tucked away in his loincloth. Hands handing him pennies, threepenny-bits, sixpences. Money coming in. More money coming in. And then the counting up at the end of the day and changing of the coppers and small coins into shillings. Clink, clink, clink! Hear how the shop-man dropped the shillings one after the other on the counter. And, in the old days, Joseph dropping the shillings into the palm of his hand. One, two, three, four, five – and a sixpence. Happy moment. It was good to recall these things. The past had still given him one or two joys, hard and bitter as it had been. Now in his old age he could still crouch here and throw his mind back upon a pleasing incident here and there.

Looking around him at the empty mud-house, a joyful thought suddenly thrilled its way through him. He was alone here today. Kattree and Beena would not be back until evening. He had many hours before him during which he could be alone with his money. Such a chance seldom occurred. Now was the time for him to have the joyful revel he had dreamt of having some day. He would open the bundles and count over all the shillings and florins, all the pennies and cents.

His head almost grew dizzy at the thought. Think of it! All his florins and shillings and pennies tinkling and glittering between his fingers! It was a long time since he had been able to give himself that delight. He had always promised himself the treat, but it had always got shelved, somehow. The presence of Kattree or Beena or both of them had always hindered him. When he counted over his money he wanted to be alone. No other eyes must see his sacred coins. The sight of them were for his eyes alone, the sound of them for his ears alone.

Ah! But this would be a memorable day. He would look back on it and see it as a large yellow jewel sparkling with many happy lights. For more than a year he would hear the chink of coins and see the glitter of them around him. He would sit surrounded by all the open bundles and it would be as if his night-dreams had come to real life. He would pile them all together in one big heap and sit on the heap. It would be the happiest moment in all his life. He would never forget it.

Trembling with nervous delight at the coming joy, he rose and went to the door, looked to right and left in order to make certain that no thief was lurking near by or no prying person who might want to share with him the joy of seeing and hearing his money. He went outside and walked round and round the mud-house. Then, quite satisfied that he was alone, he went inside again and carefully drew the flour-bag curtain across the door.

51

Mr Burlock's address lasted until shortly after a quarter past ten. It was a good speech. It moved the jury and it moved the general public. Yet it contained no sentiment. It contained no mention of Jannee's wife and children and of the horrible fate that might befall them if Jannee were hanged. It was a speech of cold facts, cold, cunning logic. At one point Mr Burlock said: 'You have seen, gentlemen, of what stuff the evidence of the Crown's witnesses is made. We have one man, Jaundoo, telling us that he saw the accused going towards Speyerfeld on the evening of the twenty-first of July. It was a dark night. He could only make out the shape of the accused. He could not make out his face "too good". He saw nothing in his hand. Is this the sort of evidence, gentlemen, upon which the Crown hopes to send a man to his death?'

Later on in the speech he said: 'And the question of motive. A vital question. But has the Crown established any motive? A paltry row, just a casual chance incident one afternoon nearly a month previous to the crime. Is this, gentlemen, a strong enough motive to drive one human to hack to death another human in the brutal manner Boorharry was hacked to death? Is it feasible that because of a mere chance quarrel a month ago Jannee would leave his home in the early evening and lie in ambush for several hours, through a thunderstorm, so that he should hack Boorharry to death? From your own experience of the motives that govern men's actions, gentlemen, you must know that this thing does not ring natural. Had Boorharry interfered with Jannee's wife, *then* we could have envisaged Jannee plotting murder. Had Boorharry robbed Jannee of a large sum of money or burnt down his home or destroyed his rice-fields, *then* we could have envisaged Jannee plotting to take the life of Boorharry. Had Jannee, at the time of this quarrel, snatched up his cutlass and hacked Boorharry to death we would have said that *that* was something within our experience of human motives and actions.

'How do we know, gentlemen, that Boorharry did not have a rival in his love-affair with Sumatra Pooran? From the witness Sumatra Pooran we have learnt that Boorharry had many love-affairs. He must have had many rivals, many enemies. It is natural. What is to have prevented one of these from getting such a formidable rival out of the way and putting the blame on Jannee, knowing Jannee to have had a row with Boorharry?

'Think of it, gentlemen, consider it a moment. Put yourselves in the place of one of these rivals of Boorharry's. There is a woman whose affections you have been attempting for weeks and months to capture. But this attractive rake, Boorharry, persistently baulks you. There comes a time when you can stand it no

233

more. Boorharry must be got rid of at all costs. You sit down and ponder the matter. If you waylay Boorharry one night and hack him to death, the blame might be put on that fellow Jannee who openly had a quarrel with Boorharry in Speyerfeld not long ago. And suppose you dropped in at Jannee's farm and took Jannee's cutlass to do the job with and when the deed was done took it back and hid it carelessly under the hay so that the suspicious police would find it?

'You carry out your plan, and the gods conspire to assist you. You find when you go for Jannee's cutlass that a pair of Jannee's trousers and a shirt, also his, are spread out on the cart drying. Good! So when you return with the blood-stained cutlass you daub it against the clothes so as to leave incriminating stains. Then you hide clothes and cutlass under the hay and take your departure. The perfect crime! So simple and yet so cast-iron…'

When Mr Burlock sat down, a murmuring sound rippled over the court so that the stern voice had to bark out: 'Silence in court!'

The Prosecuting Counsel's address lasted until ten minutes to eleven. It was calm and logical, but its logic lacked the cunning that Mr Burlock's had possessed. It depended too much on 'the facts of the case' and these facts had already been coloured in Jannee's favour by Mr Burlock. 'The business of a Prosecuting Counsel is to get at the truth of a matter, not, as many people fancy, to prejudice the minds of the jury against the accused.' It was in this scrupulous spirit that Mr Vimeiro proceeded to 'state the facts of the case'. He indulged in no sarcasm, in no high-flown rhetoric nor tricks of language. He was leisured, soft and dignified, and everything he said was to the point.

When he sat down, no murmuring sound rippled over the court.

The session was adjourned until one o'clock.

During the interval everyone was certain that Jannee would be acquitted. How could he fail to get off after such a speech by Mr Burlock? Mr Burlock was a clever lawyer. Look how neatly he had twisted the facts! The verdict was a foregone conclusion. Mr Burlock had messed up the Prosecution.

These and similar comments Beena and Kattree and Sukra heard during the interval, and Beena and Sukra felt a great joy bubbling up in them. Their hopes were coming true. Jannee would get off. Tonight he would be back with them. They would sing and beat the drum and eat curried mutton and roti. They would tell him of the black days of despair and then of the days of hope, they would tell him of the rice-cutting and of how they had missed him. Beena saw herself sitting with him in the donkey-cart on the way to Speyerfeld. Once more the sunshine would make her feel that life was good to live. The sun would not glare at her and burn her. Everything, the sky and the canal, the savannah and the cows, would seem bright and tinged with joy.

It was in this hopeful mood that they returned into the courtroom at one o'clock to hear the Judge's summing-up.

The Judge spoke very quietly and kept glancing at his notes. He related briefly all 'the evidence submitted by the Crown'. He made no comments, but he said in closing: 'If this evidence seems to you, gentlemen, to point to the guilt of the accused then, of course, it is your duty to bring in a verdict in accordance with your findings. If, on the other hand, you entertain any doubt whatever, it is your duty to give the prisoner the benefit of your doubt.'

The jury, dark men in navy-blue, left the courtroom, walking one behind the other. They went through a door at the southern end of the courtroom. A black gentleman, the marshal, locked the door and then stood before it as though on guard.

The Judge left the court, and at once a buzz of murmuring broke out. No stern voice called for silence.

''E done get off,' said a black man on the bench behind Sukra and Kattree and Beena. 'No jury could convict 'e after dat. Burlock mess up de Crown' case.'

'Oh, yes. 'E mus' get off,' agreed an East Indian man. 'De Crown has fail' to establish a case.'

Half an hour had hardly elapsed when the Judge returned and the dark men in navy-blue were walking one behind the other towards the two long benches on the western side of the building.

In spite of their firm belief that everything would be all right and that Jannee would be set free, Beena felt as though her heart were not beating inside her. And her fingers were cold at the tips.

The whole room had grown very silent.

A chair scraped of a sudden.

The Clerk of the Court was standing. He stood just beneath the Judge's raised seat. The jurymen, too, were standing. Their faces seemed so blank. They would not even smile to show that Jannee was free, or frown to show that he was to die.

'Gentlemen of the jury, have you arrived at a verdict?' asked the Clerk.

The juryman at the end of the first bench said: 'Yes.'

'Is that verdict unanimous?'

'Yes.'

'How say you? Is the prisoner at the bar guilty or not guilty?'

'Not guilty.'

52

All three of them kissed Jannee. Kattree found that she was as excited and overjoyed as Beena and Sukra. Beena cried in her joy and Jannee cried in relief. He said he had not thought he would have got off. He had given up all hope when he was arrested that morning in July. It was only when Mr Burlock and Mr Wickham visited him in prison and told him that a friend had paid them to defend him that he had begun to feel any hope. He said that Mr Wickham and Mr Burlock would not tell him the name of the friend who had paid them.

'Deh say de frien' na want 'e name known,' he told them.

'Me na know who de frien' is meself,' said Sukra. 'Everybody puzzle. Beena an' me t'ink every way, we na able fin' out who de person could be.'

'Na mind who de person is,' laughed Beena. 'You get off. Dah is all dat matter.'

'Tonight we got to hold curry-feed,' said Sukra. 'You can borrow Bijoolie' drum, Jannee.'

'Na. 'E mus' play de sitar,' said Kattree. 'Borrow Moonsammy' sitar, Jannee. Me like hear you play de sitar.'

People stared at them, and comments of all kinds were being exchanged. 'Man, it's a shame,' they heard a well-dressed negro young man saying: 'Dat man shoulda get hang!' Another said: 'De police at fault. Deh ain' get up de case properly. Plenty more witnesses shoulda been called.' A black woman said: 'Me glad 'e get off. Me hear Boorharry was a bad man. 'E did frien'ly wid everybody' wife. 'E interfere wid every woman in de distric'. Dat kin' o' man mus' meet a bad end.'

But comments did not matter to them. Jannee was free. That was all they cared about. The sun was shining, the sky was grey-blue and speckled with white clouds moving south in the trade wind. Jannee was with them. He would sing and play the sitar this evening. They would beat the drum and eat curried mutton and roti. Only that mattered. The comments of the crowd were like the tiny bits of black cane-trash floating in the air even at the moment, brought from the burning cane-fields miles and miles away. One alighted on Beena's head-cloth and Kattree blew it off with a laugh.

When they were in the bus on their way back home, Beena, unable to restrain her joy, began to sing, and Kattree and Sukra joined in. Jannee joined in, too, and all the way up the four of them sang songs. Kattree beat her fist against the seat as though it were a drum and Sukra jingled the three silver bracelets around her wrists. The other passengers smiled and chuckled and stared at them, but they did not mind. Let people look at them. Let people laugh. They could even make faces. Jannee was free. Jannee would not be hanged on the gallows. All the panicky fears and the hoping and uncertainty were now no more. The sun was shining in the west and the bus droned and droned as it hurried eastward. Watch the heat trembling there yonder over the grey-green savannah, their savannah. Smell the rankness of fish and cow-dung in the air, the smell of the Corentyne Coast, their Corentyne Coast. And look at the canal, lowered in level from the drought, but rippled in the breeze and smiling its same old muddy smile.

Feel the breeze on their faces and hear how it crackled past their ears. Corentyne breeze coming from the north-east, coming from the grey sea, wafting whispers of mystery from the lonely beach where only fishermen ventured and where at night the rank waves alone roared without fear at the duppies and jumbies in the courida fringe, where in the bleak twilight of a rainy afternoon the quacking cry of an egret, borne on the watery air, came with a soothing gloom to the ears of the fishermen and the duck-shooters wading their way homeward.

They were at Little Benjamin now. There stood Big Man Weldon's high two-storeyed house and the low outhouses around it. Look at the sheep and cattle dotted all over the savannah far into the distance: the wealth of Big Man Weldon. There yonder stood Bijoolie's lonely mud-house. A donkey near by was eating green grass from a heap on the ground, and Bijoolie was hammering at something on the cart which lay at a slant, resting on its shafts... A few black pigs were sniffing about.

Now they were at Nairnley. Kattree hailed out to Moon-sammy, who was just crossing the trench to his mud-house. 'Jannee get off!' They saw him wave his arm and break into a smile. He stood staring after the bus.

Now they were almost at Jannee's home. Yes, there it was yonder up the road. Look! That was Boodoo by the side of the road. The bus began to slow down. The busman knew where Jannee lived. They had no need to call out to him to tell him where to stop.

The brakes made a screeching noise as the bus came to a stop. Heedai and Boodoo and Chattee were coming out to meet them. Beena and Sukra alighted first and then Jannee and Kattree. 'Kattree an' me can walk de rest o' de way home,' said Beena. 'Heedai gal, we got to hold curry-feed tonight. Go home an' tell Moonsammy. An' send tell Bijoolie.'

'We mus' go home change we dress,' said Kattree, 'den we can go to Speyerfeld buy mutton an' chicken.'

'Lemme get de donkey-cart carry all-you,' said Jannee. 'You keep me donkey good, Sukra?'

'Eh-heh. Donkey keep strong. Me give 'e nice green grass every day. 'E miss you, Jannee. 'E going glad to see you.'

A few minutes later Jannee and Beena and Kattree were jogging along the road in the donkey-cart, talking and laughing. Beena sat beside Jannee, facing frontwards, while Kattree sat in the back with her legs dangling over the edge.

The setting sun shone redly on them, mild now and not hot as earlier in the day. The wind touched their cheeks with a coolness that told them that evening was near. Within an hour twilight would be gathering and cows would be plodding slowly into pen for the night, the owls would begin to toot far away and the goat-suckers to cry: 'Who-you?' lying on their breasts flat on the ground.

Jannee said he would wait for them by the roadside while they went to the mud-house and changed into their home-dresses.

'Count five hundred, an' by den we reach back,' said Beena, and she and Kattree hurried off along the dam towards the mud-house.

'Ramgolall mus' be come back long time,' said Kattree. ''E mus' be gone to drive in de cows.'

''E got to come beat drum tonight. 'E going surprise' when we tell 'e we got curry-feed on tonight.'

Nearing the mud-house, they saw the the flour-bag curtain had been drawn across the doorway. Kattree noticed this first and said: 'Wha' happen mek 'e draw curtain 'cross de door?'

''E mus' be inside,' said Beena. 'Me wonder if 'e feel sick.'

A feeling of faint anxiety, a dim fear, began to mingle with the joy in them as they approached the door of the mud-house. They heard the thuds of their footsteps on the hard earth and the faint rustle of their dresses, and somehow these sounds seemed part of the dim fear forming in their minds. The cool wind seemed of a sudden to have become a little chilly so that they wanted to shiver. A frog whistled, and it sounded like a warning.

Beena drew aside the flour-bag curtain and the two of them went inside.

Beena said: 'Oh, gawd!' in a sudden bated voice, and the two of them stood there looking down at Ramgolall who lay on his back on the smooth plastered floor. He lay very still, one thin leg bent upward. His eyes stared glassily at nothing and his mouth gaped a trifle. Near him his old canister lay still, too. It lay on its side wide open and empty. Rags of cloth, pebbles and copper coins were scattered all over the floor, shillings, too, and lumps of dried mud.

'Ramgolall. Wha' wrong wid you? Wha' happen?' Kattree bent down and shook him, but the feel of him was cold and stiff. 'Oh, gawd! Beena, Ramgolall dead.'

But Beena was staring at the pebbles and the lumps of dried mud and listening to all the queer buzzing noises that were going on in her head. She heard a singing and then a groaning and then more singing. Thoughts of people and things seemed to be running in hot trickles of blood through her brain... Jannee and Boorharry... Jaigan talking and Kattree smiling... hanged on the gallows... Everything was going yellow and green... Pebbles and copper coins and shillings...

'Beena, you hear? 'E dead. Ramgolall dead. 'E won't talk. 'E cold.'

Beena turned and went out into the fresh air again. The breeze felt very cool on her cheeks. It cleared her head at once. The sunshine looked redder and milder, she thought. The sky was without a wisp of cloud and looked deep blue, not grey-blue with heat like earlier today. Everything seemed the same as it had always been from the time she could remember herself. The savannah was still grey-green, and far to the north the horizon showed as a jagged line, jagged and dark-green with the courida fringe. Rags of cloth and copper coins, shillings and pebbles and lumps of dried earth, all lay scattered on the floor in there behind her. Ramgolall was dead, cold and stiff and staring glassily at nothing. But not a single thing in the landscape out here seemed to have changed in sympathy. The savannah still had its look of calm peace. The air still smelt rank with fish and cow-dung, and the breeze still brought with it the strong refreshing odour of seaweed and Corentyne mud.

The sunshine was fading. Jannee was waiting with his donkey-cart by the roadside for herself and Kattree. He was free now. He would live on. He would not be hanged on the gallows. But Ramgolall was dead. There would be no curry-feed tonight for herself and Kattree. She had better go and drive the cows into pen for the night. A frog squeaked somewhere behind the mud-house. She looked all about her. No, nothing had changed at all. Surely the savannah must know that Ramgolall was dead and that there were pebbles and pieces of dried mud lying scattered on the floor in the mud-house. It looked so untroubled, so flat and at peace as though nothing at all had happened. And the sky, too, and the wind, the sunshine – all untroubled, the same as they had been

240

yesterday and all the days before: the sky blue, the wind cool, the sun red because it was low in the west.

Ramgolall was dead, but the whole Corentyne remained just the same.

The frog behind the mud-house squeaked again. Yes, she had better go at once and drive the cows into pen for the night. It was getting late.

THE END

GLOSSARY

[Assistance is gratefully acknowledged to Mr Michael Gilkes]

baaya – boy

beti – daughter

creketteh – small, round freshwater snail

cuirass – variety of freshwater catfish; brown, spined, scaleless

curri-curri bird – scarlet ibis

dholl – spiced East Indian dish of thick split-pea broth and seasonings

dhoti – loincloth worn by Hindu men

goat-sucker – bird, more commonly called nightjar

hassar – freshwater catfish with oblong, armoured scales; grey to
    black in colour

hourih – slimy brown-grey freshwater fish; catfish family

jumbie-bird – large black bird like raven; also in Guyana called 'witch-
    bird'

kiskadee – bird; variety of Tyrant Flycatcher

koker – stone floodgate used in Guyana

labba tiger – small brown-coated leopard – so-called because it preys
    on the labba-dog (bush-pig)

sakie – also called *tanager*, small fruit-eating bird

serangee – small (about 2 ft.) East Indian stringed instrument played
    with bow

sherriga – small, reddish *sea*-crab: Mittelholzer apparently uses the
    term for *freshwater* crab

tadja drums – drums originating in Hindu religious ceremonies

vicissi – marsh duck

ABOUT THE AUTHOR

Edgar Mittelholzer was born in New Amsterdam in what was still British Guiana in 1909. He began writing in 1929 and despite constant rejection letters persisted with his writing. In 1937 he self-published a collection of skits, *Creole Chips*, and sold it from door to door. By 1938 he had completed *Corentyne Thunder*, though it was not published until 1941 because of the intervention of the war. In 1941 he left Guyana for Trinidad where he served in the Trinidad Royal Volunteer Naval Reserve. In 1948 he left for England with the manuscript of *A Morning at the Office*, set in Trinidad, which was published in 1950. Between 1951 and 1965 he published a further twenty-one novels and two works of non-fiction, including his autobiographical *A Swarthy Boy*. Apart from three years in Barbados, he lived for the rest of his life in England. His first marriage ended in 1959 and he remarried in 1960. He died by his own hand in 1965, a suicide by fire predicted in several of his novels.

Edgar Mittelholzer was the first Caribbean author to establish himself as a professional writer.

CARIBBEAN MODERN CLASSICS

Jan R. Carew
Black Midas
Introduction: Kwame Dawes
ISBN: 9781845230951; pp. 272; 23 May 2009; £8.99

This is the bawdy, Eldoradean epic of the legendary 'Ocean Shark' who makes and loses fortunes as a pork-knocker in the gold and diamond fields of Guyana, discovering that there are sharks with far sharper teeth in the city. *Black Midas* was first published in 1958.

Jan R. Carew
The Wild Coast
Introduction: Jeremy Poynting
ISBN: 9781845231101; pp. 240; 23 May 2009; £8.99

First published in 1958, this is the coming-of-age story of a sickly city child, sent away to the remote Berbice village of Tarlogie. Here he must find himself, make sense of Guyana's diverse cultural inheritances and come to terms with a wild nature disturbingly red in tooth and claw.

Neville Dawes
The Last Enchantment
Introduction: Kwame Dawes
ISBN: 9781845231170; pp. 332; 27 April 2009; £9.99

This penetrating and often satirical exploration of the search for self in a world divided by colour and class is set in the context of the radical hopes of Jamaican nationalist politics in the early 1950s. First published in 1960, the novel asks many pertinent questions about the Jamaica of today.

Wilson Harris
Heartland
Introduction: David Dabydeen
ISBN: 9781845230968; pp. 104; 23 May 2009; £7.99

First published in 1964, this visionary narrative tracks one man's psychic disintegration in the aloneness of the forests of the Guyanese interior, making a powerful ecological statement about man's place in the 'invisible chain of being', in which nature is a no less active presence.

Edgar Mittelholzer
Corentyne Thunder
Introduction: Juanita Cox
ISBN: 9781845231118; pp. 242; 27 April 2009; £8.99

This pioneering work of West Indian fiction, first published in 1941, is not merely an acute portrayal of the rural Indo-Guyanese world, but a work of literary ambition that creates a symphonic relationship between its characters and the vast openness of the Corentyne coast.

Andrew Salkey
Escape to an Autumn Pavement
Introduction: Thomas Glave
ISBN: 9781845230982; pp. 220; 23 May 2009; £8.99

This brave and remarkable novel, set in London at the end of the 1950s, and published in 1960, catches its 'brown' Jamaican narrator on the cusp between black and white, between exiled Jamaican and an incipent black Londoner, and between heterosexual and homosexual desires.

Denis Williams
Other Leopards
Introduction: Victor Ramraj
ISBN: 9781845230678; pp. 216; 23 May 2009; £8.99

Lionel Froad is a Guyanese working on an archeological survey in the mythical Jokhara in the horn of Africa. There he hopes to rediscover the self he calls 'Lobo', his alter ego from 'ancestral times', which he thinks slumbers behind his cultivated mask. First published in 1963, this is one of the most important Caribbean novels of the past fifty years.

Denis Williams
The Third Temptation
Introduction: Victor Ramraj
ISBN: 9781845231163; pp. 108; 23 May 2009; £7.99

A young man is killed in a traffic accident at a Welsh seaside resort. Around this incident, Williams, drawing inspiration from the *Nouveau Roman*, creates a reality that is both rich and problematic. Whilst he brings to the novel a Caribbean eye, Williams makes an important statement about refusing any restrictive boundaries for Caribbean fiction. The novel was first published in 1968.

Roger Mais
The Hills Were Joyful Together
Introduction: tba
ISBN: 9781845231002; pp. 272; October 2009; £8.99

Unflinchingly realistic in its portrayal of the wretched lives of Kingston's urban poor, this is a novel of prophetic rage. First published in 1953, it is both a work of tragic vision and a major contribution to the evolution of an autonomous Caribbean literary aesthetic.

Edgar Mittelholzer
A Morning at the Office
Introduction: Raymond Ramcharitar
ISBN: 978184523; pp. 208; October 2009; £8.99

First published in 1950, this is one of the Caribbean's foundational novels in its bold attempt to portray a whole society in miniature. A genial satire on human follies and the pretensions of colour and class, this novel brings several ingenious touches to its mode of narration.

Edgar Mittelholzer
Shadows Move Among Them
Introduction: tba
ISBN: 9781845230913; pp. 320; December 2009; £9.99

In part a satire on the Eldoradean dream, in part an exploration of the possibilities of escape from the discontents of civilisation, Mittelholzer's 1951 novel of the Reverend Harmston's attempt to set up a utopian commune dedicated to 'Hard work, frank love and wholesome play' has some eerie 'pre-echoes' of the fate of Jonestown in 1979.

Edgar Mittelholzer
The Life and Death of Sylvia
Introduction: Juanita Cox
ISBN: 9781845231200; pp. 318; December 2009, £9.99

In 1930s' Georgetown, a young woman on her own is vulnerable prey, and when Sylvia Russell finds she cannot square her struggle for economic survival and her integrity, she hurtles towards a wilfully early death. Mittelholzer's novel of 1953 is a richly inward portrayal of a woman who finds inner salvation through the act of writing.

Elma Napier
A Flying Fish Whispered
Introduction: Evelyn O'Callaghan
ISBN: 9781845231026; pp. 248; February 2010; £8.99

With one of the most delightfully feisty women characters in Caribbean
fiction and prose that sings, Elma Napier's 1938 Dominican novel is a
major rediscovery, not least for its imaginative exploration of different
kinds of Caribbeans, in particular the polarity between plot and plantation that Napier sees in a distinctly gendered way.

Orlando Patterson
The Children of Sisyphus
Introduction: Geoffrey Philp
ISBN: 9781845230944; pp. 288; November 2009; £9.99

This is a brutally poetic book that brings to the characters who live on
Kingston's 'dungle' an intensity that invests them with tragic depth. In
Patterson's existentialist novel, first published in 1964, dignity comes
with a stoic awareness of the absurdity of life and the shedding of false
illusions, whether of salvation or of a mythical African return.

V.S. Reid
New Day
Introduction: tba
ISBN: 9781845230906, pp. 360; November 2009, £9.99

First published in 1949, this historical novel focuses on defining
moments of Jamaica's nationhood, from the Morant Bay rebellion of
1865, to the dawn of self-government in 1944. *New Day* pioneers the
creation of a distinctively Jamaican literary language of narration.

Garth St. Omer
A Room on the Hill
Introduction: John Robert Lee
ISBN: 9781845230937; pp. 210; September 2009; £8.99

A friend's suicide and his profound alienation in a St Lucia still
slumbering in colonial mimicry and the straitjacket of a reactionary
Catholic church drive John Lestrade into a state of internal exile. First
published in 1968, St. Omer's meticulously crafted novel is a pioneering exploration of the inner Caribbean man.

All Peepal Tree titles are available from the website
www.peepaltreepress.com
with a money back guarantee, secure credit card ordering
and fast delivery throughout the world at cost or less.

Peepal Tree Press is the home of challenging and inspiring literature
from the Caribbean and Black Britain. Visit www.peepaltreepress.com
to read sample poems and reviews, discover new authors, established
names and access a wealth of information.

Contact us at:
Peepal Tree Press, 17 King's Avenue, Leeds LS6 1QS, UK
Tel: +44 (0) 113 2451703 E-mail: contact@peepaltreepress.com